Half the World

Leissa Shahrak

atmosphere press

PART I

Esfahan nesf-e jahan
Esfahan is half the world.

- Old Persian saying -

PRAISE FOR
HALF THE WORLD

"Set in pre-revolution Iran, *Half the World* manifests exquisite historical and cultural detail as author Leissa Shahrak deftly immerses newlyweds Angela and Doug Weston in a world of underlying conflict and intrigue. With masterful pacing Shahrak explores the world of cultural and political upheaval through the strain of undisclosed secrets that undermine their personal relationship, and the evolving revolutionary cataclysm that engulfs them. Shahrak builds the tension from these inner and outer world conflicts from the first paragraph to the spellbinding conclusion. This is indeed a good read."
    – **Francis Flavin, author of *The Muse in a Time of Madness***

"Using elegant language and touching wistfulness, Shahrak perfectly demonstrates how any society—even a city as majestic as Esfahan—can be threatened by ignorance, betrayal, resentment, and misplaced blame. Reading *Half the World*, I was constantly finding myself reflecting on the people and places I love most—how important it is to protect and support them always. I have argued that Iranians have long provided humanity with some of the most beautiful, most captivating stories, and Shahrak's *Half the World* is further proof of this."
    – **Jacob Reina, author of *Purity of the Sky***

"Inspired by her poignant experiences in Iran, Leissa Shahrak explores Persian culture through the eyes of Angela and Doug, two Americans who are awed by the marvels of mosques and minarets but are also mystified by unexpected cultural challenges. While Angela, a gifted teacher, goes to great lengths to help Hossein Rahimi, her most difficult student, his conflicted relationship with her is full of surprises. Shahrak's evocative prose turns poetic when she describes the streets of Esfahan, vibrant shades of blue, the shifting play of light on the mosque, and the aroma of mimosa. Behind the beauty

is the real smell of fear near the SAVAK building, headquarters of the secret police. In the arched niche of the bridge, squats a blind man with his beggar's bowl, a *leitmotif* of imminent danger. In the months leading up to the 1979 Revolution that ousted the Shah, Angela and Doug must cope with the past they are not willing to confront until moments of crisis test them both."
— Karin Ciholas, author of *The Lighthouse* and *The Bronze Door*

"Set in pre-revolution Iran, this mesmerizing tale masterfully captures the complexities of a volatile era and the heartbreaking consequences of good intentions gone awry. Told through the perspectives of compassionate American teacher Angela Weston, her war-scarred husband, and a troubled young Iranian man, it weaves a rich tapestry of human struggle and resilience."
— Lya Badgley, author of *The Worth of a Ruby*
and *The Foreigner's Confession*

CHAPTER ONE

Could they survive here?

The landscape stretched out below the plane, impressing Angela Weston with its endlessness. Iran's central plateau—flat, barren, hostile. For most forms of life, a death warrant.

In the seat beside her, Angela's husband dozed, tired from the long international flight. Air from an overhead vent ruffled his hair. He breathed through parted lips, his snores deadened by the groaning of the engines.

Five *qanats* in a row freckled the desert's face. For centuries, *qanats* had conveyed water from the base of mountains to cities and fields. Now, though, many of these underground aqueducts had gone dry. Others, however, still brought water and, thus, survival to communities. Amazing in 1977, Angela thought. Even so, dried-up *qanats* could occasionally menace survival. Her guidebook warned that a false step near a *qanat's* mouth could get you killed. The shaft's edges could crumble and send you tumbling to the bottom. If you survived the fall, you could die of thirst before someone hauled you out.

The plane banked as it prepared for landing in Esfahan. Angela shook Doug's shoulder. He blinked and leaned toward the window. "All I see is haze. It must be dust." He squinted as if grains of dirt had already irritated his eyes.

"The books say it seldom rains here," Angela said. A cloudless sky extended over the plateau. The plane's shadow traced a wrinkle on the brown earth below. She strained for a glimpse of Esfahan. The name itself fascinated her, and she whispered it. "Esfaahaaan. Esfaahaaan." She and Doug were newlyweds fifteen months ago when Doug began working on architectural plans for future expansions of Esfahan's first technical university. She had never heard of the city before.

The pilot turned on the seat belt sign, and the hostess said, first in Persian, then in English, that they were making their approach.

"Did you get any of that? The Persian?" Doug asked Angela.

"The gist of it. But I've been studying only a few months." Her Persian grammar book and tapes awaited her in the plane's hold, tucked away in the smallest of their suitcases. She had never dreamed she would spend two years in a foreign country before she turned thirty. An oil-rich, carpet-strewn, bone-dry country. Two years to practice speaking Persian. Persia and Persian evoked the exotic—spices, nightingales, roses.

She would adjust well, she told herself.

She would be accepted.

The plane touched down, and Doug's fingers crushed hers. "Here goes." He pretended to raise a toast with his free hand. "Cheers."

Angela squeezed his arm and landed a kiss on his cheek. They had looked forward to this adventure away from the pressures of family and friends. It would give them time to enjoy each other before they had children.

The aircraft taxied to a stop near a stucco building. A two-man ground crew rolled stairs to the plane's door. A few minutes later, Angela stepped outside onto the landing. Hot wind slapped her face. She staggered, gasping. Dirt coated her lips and stung her eyes. Blinding light reflected off the runway. She dug through her tote bag for her sunglasses. Doug's hand pressed against her back and guided her down the staircase.

A few pieces of checked baggage stood on the melting tarmac beside the plane. Angela gripped her bag's handle, already warm from the sun. Her mouth parched from the dry heat, she carried her suitcase past soldiers with rifles aimed toward the runway. How did they survive this heat in heavy boots and belts, without sunglasses?

Inside, the terminal reeked of sweat and onions. Angela steadied herself. A crowd milled around her. Women chattered; men shouted; children howled. Some women wore the latest fashions, accessorized by gold jewelry and leather heels. Others swept past in chadors, veils that reached to the floor but had no snaps or buttons to keep them in place. Old women in heavy, black *chadors* clutched their veils under their chins, with only their lined foreheads and hooded eyes visible. Young women wore sheer, pastel *chadors*, with their dark bangs and full cheeks exposed. Men squeezed through any space they could find. Children slipped through what seemed like no space at all.

On the wall reigned life-sized pictures of the Shah, the Empress, and the Crown Prince, all in full regalia.

A Casablanca fan suspended from the ceiling turned lazily.

As Angela maneuvered her suitcase through the crowd, the handle slipped from her damp palm. The suitcase toppled over and fell into a gaggle of *chadoris* squatting on the floor, at their feet bulging totes, stuffed plastic sacks, cloth-wrapped bundles. The women cackled and pushed her bag upright. She had only been in Esfahan ten minutes, and she had already embarrassed herself. Apologizing, she retrieved her bag and elbowed her way through a group of young men. Their shirts opened halfway down their chests. Embedded in swirls of black chest hair, gold medallions with shiny Arabic letters: Allah.

Several feet behind her, Doug towered above the passengers who were pressing toward the door to the runway. A swatch of blond hair escaped his khaki safari hat as he squirmed through the crowd, jostling passengers in his way. His height, fair skin, and blue eyes made him conspicuous among the smaller, darker

Iranians. Everyone stared at him. At least the dark hair and olive skin she had inherited from her Sicilian ancestors attracted less attention. She waited for Doug at the exit to the street, eager to escape the chaos in the terminal.

"Gotcha."

Angela jumped in alarm. Doug had caught up with her and pinched her backside. He pulled his hand back, and she smoothed the full legs of her khakis.

"I've taken great care to dress modestly." She tugged down the hem of her knit top.

"You look great to me." He squeezed the bridge of her nose as one might tweak a child's.

Angela slid her bag through the door to the street, wondering which, the pinch or the tweak, Iranians would find more offensive in public. Orientation material provided by Doug's company warned that women in Western dress might experience goosing in Iran. No doubt a Western exaggeration. One or two women in miniskirts or low-cut blouses had probably attracted advances. Now, every American woman who came here was jumpy, afraid some sexually deprived male would caress her bottom. Nonsense. Nonetheless, Angela positioned herself close to the terminal to prevent a wayward hand from accessing her backside.

At the curb, Doug summoned a blue-and-white taxi. A short man with stubble on his cheeks and chin and slightly crossed eyes heaved their suitcases into the taxi's trunk, grunting and growling. "He's not particularly happy about making a fare," Doug said.

"Are you sure he's willing to go to our hotel?" Angela asked. The guidebook offered instructions for hailing cabs in Iran: Stand in the street and yell the name of your destination as the taxi drives by.

"I forgot the name of the hotel."

"*Salam aleikum, agha. Hotel Shah Abbas,*" Angela said.

"*Aleikum salam.*" The taxi driver pressed his hand to his heart and inclined his head. He opened the car door for her and repeated, "*Befarmayid, khanoum,*" several times while motioning for her to get in. She settled in the back seat, proud she had communicated with the driver. All she had to do was make a slight effort to be accepted here. Doug had worked on the university's blueprints at a frantic pace in the weeks before their departure. He would depend on her to gain cross-cultural savvy.

Another passenger with a hooked nose climbed into the back, requiring Doug to slide to the middle, his feet on the hump, his knees up to his chin. Angela wished the man had gotten in on her side. She could have ridden in the middle with greater comfort than Doug. But the man probably considered it improper to sit next to a woman outside of his family. Two more men with high cheekbones scrambled into the front. The air inside became stale in the stifling heat, although the driver had rolled down all four windows. How would New Yorkers or Californians react to a taxi with no meter, no air-conditioning, and no one-fare limit?

The taxi lurched forward, backfiring puffs of smoke as it shot down the street. The sudden motion threw Angela and Doug against the seat back. Here they were in Iran at last, squashed together, hair wild in the rush of dry air, while a cross-eyed taxi driver catapulted them into their future along the banks of a trickle of water that only here would be called a river. Exhilarated by the speed, Angela tilted her head back, squeezed Doug's thigh, and exploded in laughter. Her hair flew into both their mouths. Her eyes filled with dust. Tears ran down her cheeks. She ran her tongue over her lips. Salt mixed with the taste of dirt. The other passengers and the driver, their faces hardened against sunlight and wind, stared ahead as if the two Americans did not exist.

Minutes later, the taxi screeched to a stop. Cars jammed the lanes. Glare bounced off hoods and windshields. No one yielded the right-of-way. Drivers honked. Howled. Yelled. Barked. Inched forward.

An orange car on the left veered within inches of the taxi's front bumper. Doug flinched. "Another near-miss."

His broad shoulders squashed Angela against the door. Unable to reach the tissues in her purse, she wiped her eyes on her sleeve. Doug crumpled his safari hat against his knees. His hair grazed the taxi's roof.

The cabbie shifted gears and gunned the engine. The tires on one side leapt onto the curb. With the car tilted, the driver whipped around several stalled vehicles.

"My mother would have been making the sign of the cross," Angela said once all four tires settled back on the roadway.

The taxi joined a line of cars crossing a stone bridge.

"I love the way you see the riverbed through arches on both sides. And there's even a beggar. Everything except St. Catherine. Remember?" Doug said.

"I don't believe much in serendipity, but maybe this is a good omen." How could she forget? As a senior in college, she had been admiring *St. Catherine of Siena and the Beggar* when they had first met at the Cleveland Museum of Art. The blond man beside her had introduced himself and pointed out details of the work's architectural elements.

"Fascinating," Angela had said. "And here I was focusing on the beggar."

They had finished the afternoon in the museum café, discussing everything from art and architecture to Doug's interest in jazz and Angela's regard for Wordsworth. Doug was on his way to Detroit, he had said, where he had just taken a job. The following year, despite the distance, the relationship had thrived.

Ahead, an elderly man in black pajama pants squatted in one of the bridge's arched niches, his wares—three or four cigarettes, a plastic ewer, a deck of playing cards, a few pieces of chewing gum—spread on a cloth in front of him. The man clutched a brass beggar's bowl and pleaded in a singsong voice. His pupils seemed to be missing. His eyes, too deep in their sockets, were white and blank as hard-boiled eggs. As the taxi edged past him, the passenger with the hooked nose tossed alms out the window into the man's bowl. The coins clanged against the brass, and the blind man raised his arm. "*Shokr-e Khoda. Shokr-e Khoda.*" Thanks be to God.

On the bridge's north side, Angela surveyed hole-in-the-wall shops. Antique stores with astrolabes and ceramic tiles. Fabric and sweet shops. A large grocery with *Kashmir Super* written across the front in the Latin alphabet. Cucumbers and apricots rotted on a stand in the sun. Newspapers fluttered in a kiosk. A carrot-colored mixture spun inside a blender.

"Juice on the spot," Doug said. "You couldn't pay me to drink any. A sure way to pick up dysentery or hepatitis." Angela pursed her parched lips. At this point, she would drink anything.

Hordes of men paraded the sidewalks. A few women hobbled along with shopping bags loaded with limes and greens, onions and cantaloupes. Several hunched over as the wind threatened to slip veils off their heads. Others held their *chador's* edge in place with their teeth. A gust caught a beige *chador* and sent it billowing, its owner scrambling after it. Seconds later, the runaway veil blew across the faces of two men and momentarily masked them as they strolled, holding hands, carrying nothing.

Ahead, men in military fatigues crowded in front of movie houses, one of which advertised a kung fu film. The other displayed a steamy poster—scarlet lips, eyes dusky with kohl. Abundant cleavage.

"Strange," Doug whispered, rolling his eyes.

Angela nodded and turned away, her senses overloaded.

It started when the cabbie let the three male passengers out near a yellow-brick building with decorative tile on its façade but no name. The taxi driver glanced at the building and then kept an eye on the rearview mirror as if he were assessing their reactions.

Angela stiffened. The facilitator in Doug's company's orientation had mentioned that nameless buildings might house SAVAK, the Shah's dreaded secret police. The adjacent roundabout featured a statue of the Shah in its center. The taxi circled the statue and turned north.

"Khiaban-e Chahar Bagh." The driver was apparently playing tour guide. Dirty water oozed through open ditches cluttered with decayed greens, melon rinds, and cigarette stubs on both sides of the main north-south artery, which the cabbie had just called the Street of the Four Gardens. The stench brought Angela's breakfast into her throat, and she swallowed hard. Some shopkeepers had lowered their latticework grills for the hottest part of the day. Others napped on mats or carpets at their shops' entrances. The taxi wove its way north—due north, Doug told her—through the city's center.

The exhaustion of long-distance travel swept over her like a cloudy trail of jet fuel and added to the unease the unnamed building had initiated. She cared little about international politics, but the regime's human rights violations distressed her. Her stomach churned, and she shuddered, overcome by nausea and terror of what she imagined inside that yellow-brick SAVAK building: instruments of torture, odors of burning flesh and involuntary defecation, bloodied bodies, and shrill screams, all concealed from the public. And, anonymity for such a prominent building must contribute to the fear, paranoia, and rumors essential to a tyrant's grip on power.

In Iran, she and Doug might not have the luxury of ignoring the ramifications of megalomaniacal politics.

*　*　*　*　*　*

Hossein Rahimi would have to hike across the city to reach the room his uncle had found for him to share in Esfahan.

Esfahan. Not where he wanted to live for the next four years.

How would he manage to survive here?

Hossein lumbered off the minibus on Esfahan's northern side and headed south, a battered prayer rug rolled under one arm. Out of the rug's end protruded the round belly of a *tar*. The cylinder of carpet protected the *tar*'s neck. Its three strings twanged as they brushed against Hossein's side. In his other hand, he hung onto a bundle wrapped in orange cloth. As he shuffled by the other passengers, he lobbed the bundle over his shoulder.

Sweat trickled down his forehead. It seeped under his glasses and stung his eyes. He would take his time in this heat. He wandered into an alleyway and angled off under the main bazaar's covered archways toward the city's central thoroughfare, Khiaban-e Chahar Bagh. Once out of the sun, Hossein shifted his load and wiped the sweat from his temples with his coat sleeve. A whiff of mud reached him from the path ahead. There, a *bazaari* showered the dust in front of his yarn shop with water from a plastic ewer. The shopkeeper poured the water as if he were measuring each drop while he traced interlacing circles and spirals in the dirt.

"*Salam, agha,*" Hossein said. "I don't want to disturb your design." The pattern was *ghashang*, pretty—beautiful even. Hossein dipped his hand into his coat pocket. His pack of colored pens, a gift from his family for going to the university, had remained safe during his journey. The *bazaari* beckoned for Hossein to pass. "No, *agha*. Take your time. Today, I have all the time in the world, and Esfahan is only *nesf-e jahan*," Hossein said. He smiled at his own cleverness.

The *bazaari* laughed. "*Esfahan nesf-e jahan e.* Esfahan is half the world," he said. "We have half the world's beauty in this city." The man swept his arms in a semicircle, and a few precious drops from his pitcher landed on Hossein's cheek.

The water cooled the air besides keeping down the dust, and Hossein relished the time he spent under the bazaar's brick arches. He emerged into the square adjacent to the bazaar, the Meidan-e Shah. There, the sudden exposure to the sun sent him reeling despite the tinted glasses his father had labored so hard to buy him in Tehran. Hossein missed the years in Tehran before the family had moved to his mother's native village of Khafr nine months ago. He still had several cousins eking out a living in Tehran, earning just enough money to settle in corrugated-tin shanties on the outskirts. Someday, they would move farther into the city, they believed, where they would earn enough to live in an apartment and buy boom boxes, refrigerators, and cars. Hossein scoffed at such dreams. His family's fate testified to the government's repression. If his father had not escaped this government's suspicion, how would those cousins survive?

No one was safe in this country.

The blue-domed mosque towered into a bluer heaven at the far end of the Meidan-e Shah. On one side, sunlight drew a shimmering veil over the dome's blue tiles. On the other side, softer light exposed the dome's rich azure. The mosque filled Hossein with awe. If he had to study here in Esfahan, at least he would have the chance to worship in this mosque, the Masjed-e Shah, the Shah's Mosque, as it was called. He could copy the mosque's floral designs and praise Allah within its walls and under its dome. A shah should commission works such as this in praise of the Divine, as Shah Abbas had centuries ago. A shah should submit himself to Allah's will, not torture and kill those who refuse to submit themselves to the shah's will.

Hossein, thirsty and exhausted, tore himself away and trudged down a side street. He turned south and plodded down the city's widest street, Khiaban-e Chahar Bagh. His feet burned, and he toyed with spending the few rials he had on a taxi to Ahmad's place south of the river. He lowered his bundle to the sidewalk next to a juice stand and fingered the coins in his pocket.

He needed to calculate exactly how much he could offer a taxi driver.

—

The number of the few coins in his hand stayed the same, no matter how many times he counted them. Hossein settled on offering fifteen rials for the trip across the bridge to the southern part of town. Shouldering his bundle, he plodded toward the street to hail a cab. A woman with a child buried in the folds of her *chador* nudged him out of her way as she headed for a juice stand. There, she bargained with the vendor for a drink at five rials less than the price he demanded.

"Let her have it, *agha*," Hossein said. Esfahanis had a reputation for being tightfisted. Hossein's father had preached the law of the desert to him: Always give a person something to drink, even your worst enemy. The vendor stuck with his asking price. Hossein pulled out the change in his pocket and handed it to the woman. "It's enough for some carrot juice," he said, placing his hand on top of the child's head.

His own mouth dry as a riverbed in high summer, Hossein trekked south again, past movie house queues, shops closed for the noontime break, a yellow-brick building with no name. He pushed on along the riverbank where the Zayandeh Rood glittered through dense reeds, and then he crossed an arched bridge with a blind vendor stationed at one end—walking south, always south, away from the city's center.

An hour later, feeling spent and out of sorts, he found Ahmad's building. He would have to exercise the expected formalities, the proper *ta'arof*, when he introduced himself to Ahmad. Only then could he accept something to drink. He limped up the stairs and knocked. No answer.

He had arrived at Ahmad's door with blisters on his heels from the pair of tennis shoes one of his cousins had outgrown.

CHAPTER TWO

Opulence. More opulence in the Shah Abbas Hotel lobby than King Midas could have dreamt of. Niched ceilings, luxurious carpets, vibrant frescoes of falconers and harem girls. Its brilliance blinded Doug; its excess annoyed him. And Mahmud annoyed him, too. Mahmud kept extolling the place. He explained that the government—Mahmud's euphemism for the Shah—had commissioned this hotel and its furnishings and interior decoration, all fashioned by the most renowned Iranian artisans. As an architect, Doug had always capitalized on each design element he used. Simplicity reigned in his work, not overstatement.

Mahmud turned his attention to the tin-washed copper tray balanced on wooden legs in front of them. It depicted courtiers paying homage to Dariush, Mahmud said. He went on and on about the Achaemenid Dynasty that ruled the Persian Empire from Persepolis some 2,500 years ago.

Doug slouched in his chair and jiggled his leg. He could not change the subject for fear of being rude. Minimal chit-chat, he could stand. Wasting time, he could not tolerate. This was supposed to be a business meeting, not a monologue on a hotel's décor. Mahmud was supposed to be his translator at the construction site, not a professor of Iranian history. Doug crossed his legs, and his knee brushed against the tray, nearly jarring it off the stand, rattling the tea service. Mahmud paused to rescue a gold-rimmed tea glass. At last. Silence.

Doug studied Mahmud as he sipped his tea. Mahmud must be a member of the Iranian upper class. His skin was pale, not battered brown from exposure to the sun. He had a faint but virile five-o'clock shadow. His gold watch band drooped like a bracelet around his wrist. His Adam's apple protruded above the collar of his ivory shirt and the knot of his silk tie. He must have selected his clothing to affect wealth and power. His attire did complement the setting.

Doug's impatience increased as he noticed that the glittering hands of Mahmud's watch already pointed to eight o'clock. Finally, Mahmud divulged what Doug wanted to know: the next morning, a minibus would take Doug to the site, where he would brief Mahmud on the plans. Two days later, construction workers would arrive.

"How far away is the site?" Doug asked.

"Fifteen kilometers north of the city." Mahmud spoke English with a slight British accent. He had been educated in Geneva, he said. "But I am from Tehran. I fly to Tehran every weekend to see my family. Your wife is here with you?"

"Of course. She wants to find a job teaching English. She taught in an American community college for two years." Angela had gone to apply for a position at the University of Esfahan that afternoon.

"They hire foreign teachers at the Iran-America Society on Abbas Abad Street." Mahmud flashed a smile that seemed staged.

Something about Mahmud made Doug apprehensive. The feeling was visceral, a combination of fear and hatred. He had just met Mahmud. What could have produced this reaction? Mahmud's long nose? His hair? The scar burrowing its way through his right eyebrow? Yesterday, in the airport terminal, the slow rotation of a Casablanca fan had produced bands of light and shadow as Doug struggled to reach Angela in the crowd. And this identical sense of danger he now experienced had cropped up in him then. Here in the hotel, an intricately tooled pendant hung from the ceiling. From under this shade, a bulb projected a play of light and shadow over Mahmud's face.

"How long have you been married? Do you have children?" Mahmud asked.

"A little over a year. No children." Mahmud apparently wasted no time when he wanted to find out personal information.

The white scar in Mahmud's eyebrow shot up. He inclined the top of his head toward his shoulder and stuck out his lower lip. His eyes drifted in the opposite direction.

Doug clenched his fists. Tian's head used to tilt in that same awkward position. Tian's lip protruded in that same pout. Tian's eyes held that same dark disdain. Tian had betrayed him.

"A year is enough time to get a son. I have three. In four years only."

Doug tried to shake off the memory of Tian. Mahmud expected a reply. "Congratulations." What else could he say? He considered direct comments on a subject as personal as having children rude. According to Angela, Iranian manners—she called it *ta'arof*—differed from the American definition of polite behavior. *Ta'arof* prescribed certain formalities. Behaviors and expressions often repeated over and over. It sounded tedious to him. "Why don't you want to live in Esfahan?" he asked. Was something so inherently wrong with Esfahan that Iranians did not want to live here? Was Mahmud a short-timer who would abandon him in the next week or two? His own Persian was next to nothing—*salam* and *Khoda hafez*, hello and goodbye. *Agha* and *khanoum* to address men and women, respectively. *Merci*, thank you, because he knew a little French. But what was the word for please?

Another tilt of Mahmud's head. Another shift of his eyes. Stippled light swirled over Mahmud's face and neck as he leaned over the tray again. "Esfahanis are tight." Mahmud lowered his voice. "Everyone in Iran knows that. And my family is in Tehran."

"They could move here." Doug wished he had not sounded so argumentative.

"No place here is as nice as Tehran. There is nothing to do here. No good restaurants. No family to visit. My wife couldn't survive here without her mother. All the people are *bazaaris*—petty merchants. They want only to make money in their little shops in the bazaar." Mahmud moved closer as if he were sharing classified information. "Most women here wear *chadors*."

Doug pulled back in his chair. "Your wife doesn't?" Would Mahmud consider his question impertinent?

Mahmud lifted his chin and clicked his tongue against the roof of his mouth.

Doug frowned at the insolent gesture.

Mahmud laughed. "We do this when we mean no." He repeated the chin-lifting and tongue-clicking.

In spite of the demonstration, Doug had no idea how to interpret this no. Did it signify an ordinary no? Or did it mean no, hell no? But he tried the gesture to promote good will, inciting more laughter from Mahmud.

Mahmud rose to leave and pointed toward the center of the hotel. "You must eat in the garden. They have a *donbak* player." He bent over and played an invisible bongo drum on his thigh. When he shook Doug's hand, he held it for goodbye after goodbye after goodbye, and Doug caught a heavy, sweet scent. Jasmine? Tian again. Mahmud continued to hold Doug's hand as they strolled to the hotel's main entrance, where he still held it for what seemed like another 2,500 years of Iranian history. He released it only when he exited the hotel.

Doug sank into a velvet chair. A waiter approached in a brocade coat and old-fashioned jodhpurs, period clothing from Shah Abbas's time, according to Mahmud. Doug waved the man off. No more strong tea. He would be up all night. The waiter bowed his head and retreated. The comic, curled feather in his turban bobbed and quivered.

Doug tapped the arm of his chair, not up to a bongo-drum dinner tonight. The pressure of Mahmud's hand lingered on his. Was Mahmud gay? Mahmud had three sons, yet he had raised his scarred eyebrow when Doug confessed he had no children. Easy to miss some essential cultural clue. Angela had a gay friend who taught in Shiraz for a couple of years. He described the Middle East as a paradise for homosexuals. Mahmud's inclinations made no difference to Doug as long as Mahmud, well, kept his hands to himself. Doug could not allow an international incident that would get him fired and, worse yet, prevent him from collecting the bonus promised upon completion of two years here. That bonus would help finance his own architectural firm. He had answered enough to others during his military service. In Esfahan, he would be the only American on the project. He would travel to Tehran quarterly to report the project's progress and troubleshoot any issues, coordinating with a senior partner from the consulting firm.

He stayed a few minutes longer while hotel guests, mostly Americans and other foreigners, meandered around the lobby, eyes agog. He had graduated and had just earned his certification as an architect when his lottery number won him a stint in Vietnam. Upon his return to the States, he had taken his first job in Cleveland with a diverse firm that guaranteed projects aligned with his training and interests—public buildings and urban spaces. However, his dissatisfaction with the firm, particularly with his co-workers, had mushroomed. He had difficulty trusting anyone else's input and had earned the reputation of a loner best left to one-man projects—a single-family powder room, a residential deck, a make-over basement. It had been devastating. After he had joined the Detroit firm, he eventually was appointed lead on a small project involving an inter-city community center. There, Angela had taught him to brainstorm ideas with his colleagues and community leaders. Here, he trusted Angela to help him navigate interpersonal and cultural landmines. Even if it meant putting up with someone he held in suspicion.

On the winding staircase to the second floor, the old tension mounted until, over his temple, a familiar headache throbbed. Earlier, the stink of rotting vegetables had brought Vietnam back to him, and Mahmud did remind him of Tian. He had avoided telling Angela about Tian and what Tian had done. He would keep his feelings of discomfort and distrust from her now. Dredging up the past would serve no good purpose.

That war was over.

At the door of room 212, Doug took the key out of his pocket. He clicked his tongue against the roof of his mouth three times while jerking his chin upward.

*   *   *   *   *   *

A piercing ring clanged through Esfahan University's Faculty of Foreign Languages the following Saturday morning. Alarmed, Angela dropped her eraser. White powder settled onto the shoes of a male student in the first row. As the class filed out the door, Angela rehearsed each student's name out loud. Most expressed surprise that she had memorized their names and faces during the first class of the fall semester.

Two girls, Mitra and Shireen, stopped at her podium. Stylish, tight knit tops. Blue jeans. No scarves or *chadors*. Parvin joined them. Conservative black *chador*. Wimple pulled around dimpled cheeks. Not one strand of hair strayed into view. If Parvin had a cross hanging from her neck, she would pass for a nun.

Mitra hesitated as if to gather courage, then complimented Angela on her green eyes. "Are you Lebanese?" she asked.

"My family came from Italy." Now, she herself was surprised. After having her Italian ancestry ridiculed during her childhood, Angela rarely acknowledged it. "I don't know how my green eyes—we call them hazel in English—turned up." The girls looked perplexed. "I mean, I don't know how I got green eyes," she explained. "Most people in my family have brown eyes. Like yours except rounder." Both Mitra and Shireen had almond-shaped eyes. Parvin's eyes were barely visible behind her glasses.

"How long have you been in Iran?" Shireen asked.

"A few days. Hardly time to get over jet lag." Angela stifled a yawn.

"I heard you are from London," another girl said. Short. Bad complexion. A scarf low on her forehead.

"Would you prefer an American teacher or an English teacher?" Shireen asked the girl.

"It doesn't matter where I come from, does it?" Angela interrupted the conversation to relieve the girl of the embarrassment of replying to the loaded question.

"I know you're American," Mitra said. "You open your mouth wide and talk out of the back of your throat."

"English people talk like this," Parvin said with a British accent. The girls giggled. Despite Parvin's difference in dress, she seemed accepted by the others, as did the girl with the scarf.

Angela remained noncommittal about her nationality, determined neither ethnicity nor citizenship would color her relationships. In her school years, her parents had lectured her on taking pride in her Italian heritage, but she had agonized over her schoolmates' jeers about her unmistakable "Guinea" looks.

Babbling in Persian, the girls hurried to their next class. Angela picked up the eraser and turned to the window nearest the podium, puzzling over the incongruity between Parvin's black veil and wimple and her outgoing personality. How sheltered Parvin must be. Cloistered by a conservative family, Angela suspected. But even the most conscientious parents sometimes failed to shelter young girls.

Angela raised the window and gazed outside at the mimosas. The front of the room was overheated and stale with the potent odor of youth, like the smell of sweaty bodies fresh from the softball field on that warm spring day in her childhood. Five boys, all older than she—fourteen, fifteen. Four of them pressing her against a wall in the back of a vacant lot. One clamping his hand over her mouth. Her "Guinea" breasts had been bigger than the other sixth-graders', they had said, and they held her down to have a look, ripped the white buttons off her white school uniform blouse. "Do little Guinea girls like you already have dark hair down there?" Another boy had reached under her plaid skirt, shoved his hand inside the crotch of her panties. Probing fingers. Stabbing pain. She had bitten down hard on the fingers over her mouth. When that boy had jerked his hand away and cursed, she had screamed enough to send four of them running. But not the beefy, rosy-cheeked leader. He had jabbed harder inside her, then wagged a bloody finger at her. "If you tell anyone, I'll tell everyone—even your parents. I'll tell them you wanted it, you greasy little Dago."

She never told.

She had been squeezing the eraser against her without realizing it, and now she released her grip and brushed chalk dust off her navy blouse. Pointless reliving this now. Parvin would be all right. So would Mitra. And Shireen. And the acne-skinned girl, whose scarf descended over her eyebrows and whose name Angela had forgotten.

Something rattled, and Angela turned away from the window. In the last row, a male student shuffled papers. She recalled that he had slouched into her class late. Bushy eyebrows slanted in a V above his nose. One of his lips curled over an incisor. Spittle foamed from a corner of his mouth. He must be one of the village students the government brought to the university on scholarship. The other students seemed more relaxed and confident. Better dressed. Likely better educated. Would his university classmates taunt or tease or downright bully him? If so, she had to protect him.

"Hossein Rahimi, I believe." Angela smiled at him. For some reason, she imagined him dressed as a *mullah*, camel-colored robes slipping off his lop-sided frame, a white turban topping off his oversized head.

"I am Agha-ye Rahimi." With proper Islamic modesty, he lowered his eyes when he answered.

Angela hid the gold bracelets she had bought in the Blond Bazaar under her sleeve, aware of the gesture's futility. Earlier, the bracelets had clattered against the chalkboard as she wrote her name and the page numbers for tomorrow's reading assignment. "Are you from Esfahan, Agha-ye Rahimi?"

"I am from village near Natanz." He struggled to force loose pages into a notebook.

"Your family is there, then?"

A breeze from the open window at the back of the classroom ruffled several sheets of paper. They slipped over the edge of his notebook and slid to the floor, a flock of sheep plunging blindly over a cliff. He groped for the errant beasts under the radiator. She envisioned his mother huddled over a charcoal brazier in a mud-brick house, stirring thin, lemony soup. Mr. Rahimi must feel out of place here. She would help him adjust, but his attire would likely serve as a detriment to his acceptance by other students. Grimy white shirt open at the collar. Frayed cuffs. Double-breasted, pin-striped black coat. Two buttons missing. Matching pants—too short. Dirty tennis shoes—too big. His head was shaved. His face was not.

"Your family must be proud that you attend the university," she said when he rose with dusty papers wadded in his fist.

He threw his hand up as if he were brushing away flies. "They do not understand. They cannot even read Koran." He scowled, still averting his gaze from her face, the traditional attempt to avoid temptation.

"You have family?" he said.

She found his accusatory tone strange, but she followed with a short description of Doug. "I'm happy to have you in my class your first semester."

"I do not want be English esstudent."

His bluntness shocked her. He had adopted a strained look during class. He must have had trouble catching the English. But when she had enunciated her policy on cheating, Mr. Rahimi drew himself up straighter and glowered at her. She made an effort to keep her expression unaltered, although she cringed in response to his open defiance. Cheating was the last thing she had expected to become a point of contention.

Mr. Rahimi flopped back down as if he had no intention of going to another class. "I want be engineer. But my exam bad.

No good enough. I must English." His frown engraved the V of his eyebrows deeper into his forehead. "I know only essmall English. I hate English."

According to an American teacher named Vicky, the English Department got leftovers, students with the poorest scores on the entrance exam. "It's an uphill battle you'll never win," Vicky had said. "No one wants to study English. They all want to make money and have prestige. A professional degree with letters behind their names. They don't care about the profession itself. Medicine and engineering don't interest them. Just money and status."

Angela, put off by the stereotyping, had related the conversation to Doug. Mahmud also complained about having to be an English translator rather than a doctor, Doug had told her.

She twisted the cap on her pen, her cheeks growing warm. She could understand why a villager like Mr. Rahimi might not want to teach English to rich children in Tehran. Many of these children had fathers who held posts in the Shah's government. But English would get Mr. Rahimi nowhere in a village. The course content required for the advanced class of freshmen would overwhelm him. Offering to tutor him in her office would set him apart from his peers and smack of favoritism. It would also humiliate him. She needed more time to determine how best to help him. He needed more time to feel at ease in her class.

Mr. Rahimi slammed his notebook shut. Out of it stuck wrinkled sheets of paper soiled with dirt and cobwebs. On the notebook's top were inscriptions written in Arabic. Floral borders in colored ink surrounded the words, likely verses from the Koran. Mr. Rahimi, on his feet now, cast a last disparaging look around the empty classroom.

As he brushed past her and bolted through the open door, he growled the word "*Sheitan*" twice, leaving her to gasp and speculate on just what or who he considered to be Satan.

CHAPTER THREE

The rhythms played on the *donbak* invigorated Doug.

Fingers tapped. Palms banged. Knuckles beat. Thumbs thumped. Drumbeats rapped the evening air, knocked on hotel room doors, punctuated dinner conversations, and pounded down the sinking sun. The blurred movements of the *donbak* player's hands beckoned. Without fail, he hit the right place on the drum, drew out the right tone in the right rhythm.

The drum fell silent, and Doug asked Angela to tell him about teaching her first class at the university. He had proposed the garden dinner to celebrate Angela's new position.

Angela recapped her experience, describing the students, their facility for English, and the girls' openness and curiosity. As she was telling him about Parvin's wimple and black *chador*, her voice trailed off.

"What else?" Doug asked. Angela's features were drawn, and she bit her lower lip. He had seen that look before, usually when Angela was omitting something important.

"A student said the Persian word for Satan as he left the classroom." Angela twisted shreds of her napkin around her forefinger. "I'm not sure if he meant me or something else."

Doug bristled. "If the students don't treat you well, you can always resign. Mahmud said they always want American teachers at the Iran-America Society." How could anyone consider Angela a devil?

"I don't want to teach in an institution sponsored by the U.S. Information Agency. Too much like propaganda."

"They're supposed to spread goodwill." Doug finished a piece of grilled chicken on saffron rice. "Why do they always undercook chicken? It's raw next to the bone." He dabbed his mouth with his napkin.

"I'd rather teach at the university. The faculty employs Pakistani and Indian and British English teachers. Iranians, as well. I don't feel like my Americanism is accentuated there." She pushed away her plate.

"It doesn't have to be accentuated. It's part of who you are."

"It's what I am, not who I am." The last notes of a hoopoe's twilight song floated through the hush in their conversation. "I'm not parochial like Sofia."

"Rest assured that you're not anything like your mother." He found it odd that Angela always used her mother's first name.

He reached across the table and stroked her hand, then withdrew his. Muslims considered a public display of affection inappropriate. The Shah Abbas Hotel, however, was hardly a mecca of religious propriety. They had relaxed with a drink in the bar before dinner.

"Anything else of note happen today?" He studied her face in the fading light. She seemed a bit uneasy tonight, more than a student's offhand remark merited.

She shook her head and told him that the clerk had enlightened her about the hotel's architecture. It resembled a *caravanserai*, he had said. In the past, camel caravans had stopped in such locations for shelter and water to ease their journey over the Dasht-e-Kavir, Iran's Great Salt Desert.

Doug signaled to the waiter, as enthralled by Angela's recounting of the clerk's explanation as much as he had been put off by Mahmud's historical accounts. The two floors of the Shah Abbas Hotel surrounded the extensive garden where they sat. Rooms set into arched niches faced it on all sides. In the center, a single-spouted fountain splashed in a reflecting pool, creating the illusion of a desert oasis. A rose-scented breeze drifted over the pool. Softened with moisture, it refreshed the air and ruffled the napkin on Angela's lap.

The Esfahani night swallowed Angela's features, leaving nothing visible but the outline of her head. A waiter materialized at last and lit a votive candle on the table. He clamped a stippled brass cover over the candle. "Dessert?" he said, handing them menus.

"They have *crème caramel*," Doug said. The dots of light flickering across Angela's face gave her skin a golden glow that he found alluring.

"Francophile. I'll take the *baghlava*."

"*Nist, madame*." The waiter smiled as if he had just promised her the *baghlava* of all *baghlavas*. "*Nist*. Finished." He extended his hands palms down at waist level and sliced the air with a scissor-like gesture.

"How about chocolate ice cream?"

"*Nist*." The waiter mustered up a crooked grin.

"Melon and pineapple sorbet? A fruit cup? A coffee sundae?" The *nist*-and-smile scenario repeated itself each time Angela ordered. "What do you have tonight?" she said.

The waiter took her menu. "*Crème caramel*," he said, his smile broader than a camel's back.

"Make that *dota crème caramels*." Angela held up two fingers.

After the waiter left, Doug groaned. "No desserts in the desert? We could starve to death here. And why didn't he say they were out of everything but the *crème caramel*?"

"He didn't want to disappoint me, I suppose. And if I hadn't ordered all the other items, he wouldn't have to admit he had only *crème caramel*."

The *crème caramel* arrived, flavored with rosewater. It tasted like hand lotion, and Doug gave up after one bite, hoping that Angela was not as disappointed in the celebration meal as he was. He relayed Mahmud's offer to help them rent a house or apartment.

Before Angela had time to respond, a hefty man with a military flattop weaved toward them and called out. "You're Americans, aren't you?" He extended his hand to Doug and introduced himself as Guy Baxter. "Why don't you join my wife and me for a drink?" Guy turned to Angela and, tugging her arm, pulled her out of her chair. "My wife, Maryanne, would love to meet you."

Doug stationed himself next to Angela. A strong whiff of alcohol mingled with the breeze, confirming what he already knew. His mind raced through a list of excuses—his early departure tomorrow for work, jet lag, Angela's need to prepare for the next day's classes—but Guy's onslaught continued, and he stumbled into the table. Glasses and plates clattered. Waiters clustered near the hotel entrance ceased their chatter. The *maître d'* whispered in the head waiter's ear, and he hurried to the Westons' table.

Doug grabbed Guy's arm to guide him back to his own table. "We can come just for a few minutes."

At the Baxters' table, Doug managed to forego any further drink orders, and the couples engaged in routine small talk: Where were they from? Why were they here? How long did they plan to stay? Typical observations: the magnificent hotel, the terrible heat, the enormous roses.

"Persian roses are famous," Angela said. "In the thirteenth century, Sa'adi wrote a book of poems titled *The Rose Garden*." Silence fell over the table as her words thudded against its surface.

Guy complained about his job training Iranian helicopter pilots until his wife, Maryanne, took over. "The res' of the place's not like this." Maryanne's words sputtered out between sips of vodka lime. "Hell cooking here. You can't buy local chickens. They leave the heads and feet on."

Doug feared "Iran According to the Baxters" would increase Angela's anxiety about whatever it was that he had not yet fully ascertained.

"You have to shop at the Indian super. Not at those awful

open-air shops with flies and rotten vegetables. You don't dare eat the melons." Maryanne downed another gulp of vodka. "They inject them with contaminated water to make them bigger so they can charge you more. Eat one, and you'll be down with dysentery in no time." Other wives of men employed by Bell Helicopter had given Maryanne the scoop on Iranian flour before she left the States. "It's heavy and coarse," she said. "Not at all like ours. You can't bake with it." A sip. A sigh. Maryanne's eyes drooped as if she would fall asleep in the middle of her next sentence. Enter Guy to her rescue.

"Maryanne sent a year's supply of flour from the States as part of the luggage allowance the company gave me. Good ol' American flour." They lived a few kilometers outside of town, Guy said. "You can live there, too." His voice boomed across the patio and garden. "The complex is for foreigners only. The houses are pretty decent— wall-to-wall carpets, electric kitchens, AC." He made a magician's flourish with his hand. "And *Western* bathrooms."

"T'ank be to Allah," Maryanne shouted.

"Do all foreigners in Esfahan live there?" Doug lowered his voice in the hope Guy and Maryanne would do the same. They did not.

"No one wants to live in town." Guy spoke with authority. "You have to step over those smelly sewers. *Jubs*, they call them. Iranians blow snot out of their noses on the street. The kids pester you. 'Hello, meessus. Goodbye, meester.' They follow you around and breathe germs on you."

"Touch your hair if it's blond like mine." Maryanne waved a finger at Doug.

Guy beamed at Angela and patted her arm as if he were her chief confidant, kitchen god, and guardian angel rolled into one. His pawing of Angela irritated Doug, and he could see it made her uncomfortable. "You'd like it much more out where we are."

Doug was pretty sure Angela would not.

*   *   *   *   *   *

It would be hard to leave the Shah Abbas Hotel and its silk draperies and rose-scented sheets. Outside, the garden slumbered, heavy with silence. A haven of coolness and tranquility. Angela closed the wooden shutters. Moonlight filtered through them, spreading geometric patterns over the dark room.

"I'd like to find a house with a courtyard garden." She understood now why Iranians treasured gardens as sanctuaries against noise and dust.

"We should consider all our options. The rent for a two-bedroom where the Baxters live is well within our means," Doug said. "Living in a community with other ex-pats has its appeal. We'd have a built-in social life. People who speak English and have already figured out day-to-day survival." Doug squirmed under the sheets as if he were drowning in patterned waves of moonlight.

Doug's words surprised her. "Surely you don't want to associate with people as crude and arrogant as Guy and Maryanne. Those remarks Guy made about his company's contract with Iran—disgusting."

"The American government is getting a deal," Guy had said. "George there in Tehran—that's what we call the . . ." He had mouthed the word Shah. "George thinks he's safer with more troops in his military—American-trained soldiers. But George won't allow the American military to train most of his forces in our country. It would look bad. We're all ex-military. Vietnam vets." Doug had grimaced when Guy mentioned Vietnam vets. Had Doug known men like Guy in his military unit? Guy had blurted out his opinion of Iranian trainees—hopeless, inept, ignorant. "They've never even driven a car." A rhetorical pause. "They're a bunch of whiners. They want to go home to their families every weekend. So, we practice cutting the engine, right? We want to make them execute an autorotation landing. In case of emergency, you know. They let go of the cyclic and collective. Take their feet off the pedals. Forget everything we tried to teach them in ground school. '*Inshallah*,' they say. God willing, they'll die." Another pause. "They stare at the instructor pilot and freeze. By this time, he's yelling at them. Asking them if they want to crash." A longer pause. "And then the instructor ends up taking the controls to save his own life." Guy had let out a scornful laugh. "*Inshallah*. They'll have so many ruined 'copters after we leave there won't be a pilot left standing." He raised his glass in a toast. "God willing."

"Guy's so prejudiced," Angela said. "You don't want us to have neighbors like the Baxters, do you?" She unwrapped a piece of nougat the hotel maid had left on the nightstand and handed it to Doug, who propped himself up on the pillows.

"They don't have to be our best friends. Besides, I'm sure not all ex-pats are like them. We aren't."

"But their compound is for Americans. How can I meet Iranians?"

"You said you'd meet Iranians if you taught at the university." Doug flung back the sheet and threw his legs over the edge of the bed. He turned on the lamp and eyed the nougat with skepticism.

"I also want to live in the city on an ordinary street with ordinary Iranians. Not in a secluded community on the city's outskirts."

"Just consider the advantages. That's all. They have a minibus with a driver to take you into town. He knows where foreigners shop. That Indian super—you saw it—what was it called?"

"If I want to go to the Indian super, I can take a taxi."

"Be rational. You saw how those guys drive."

"Then I'll walk. I don't want to isolate myself with a bunch of rednecks." She wanted to scream. "In ten months, Maryanne's never gone inside a mosque or to the bazaar. Obviously, she's too busy baking." Angela took off her robe and threw it on a chair. "And going to the Indian super."

"You can take the minibus to the airport, too."

"We just got here. Why would I go to the airport?" Her nightgown slipped off one shoulder, and she pulled it back into place. Doug had never been so unreasonable, so off-target.

"I'm just asking you to think about it. You would be safer out there when I'm at work."

His words stunned her. So this was it. "Safe from what? Taxis? Rotten food? *Jubs*?" She adopted a calmer tone. "I intend to eat the melons. Cutting heads and feet off chickens does not upset my equilibrium. I can jump over *jubs*. I have no problem picking over apricots and pomegranates and dill."

"I want you to be safe, Angela. That's all." He slouched as if deflated from expending so much energy arguing with her.

"We will be safe in a traditional city house with a private garden. Forget the isolated modern compound with backyard barbeques. Can you see me measuring American flour for oatmeal cookies with Maryanne while you trade war stories with Guy?"

"To be honest, no. I didn't like them either." Doug bit into the nougat. His jaw worked back and forth and sideways, and she could tell the candy had stuck to his teeth. He chewed until his eyes watered. "Rosewater again." He wrinkled his nose, the rims of his eyes pink.

She had been too harsh. Doug had to get up early the next morning. She crossed the room to the bed and rubbed him on the back. He caught her hand and kissed her palm. "Would you agree to look in the city?" she asked. "You said Mahmud offered to help us."

At the mention of Mahmud, his jaw flexed, but all he said was, "If he can find us a safe place."

Later, Doug slept in her embrace. She lay still, perplexed about Doug's apparent need to protect her now that they were in Iran. She remembered stories of his watching over his younger sister, Kim, after their mother died. For years, they walked together to school. After school, they were latch-key children. Doug fixed peanut butter and jelly sandwiches and doled out vanilla wafers. Later, during high school, he had counseled Kim and identified boys unworthy of her trust and girls undeserving of her friendship.

Angela's arm tingled, and she shifted it from underneath Doug. If only she had had an older brother like Doug who would have protected her from older boys. The incident in the empty lot haunted her yet another time. Did being in a foreign country somehow bring out her and Doug's pasts, their greatest vulnerabilities?

Surely not.

Iran was an amazing country.

CHAPTER FOUR

He threw his book of short stories against the wall, then retrieved it from the folds of Ahmad's green-flowered blanket. The blow had crumpled several pages, and they protruded at odd angles like broken bones. Hossein creased the damaged pages in the opposite direction to restore them to their original positions, without success. He slammed the book shut.

Why had he listened to Ahmad? He had only known Ahmad a few days. The night Hossein arrived, he had slept curled up on his prayer rug, his arms around his *tar*, until Ahmad came home. That night, he had been too drowsy to notice Ahmad's features, much less to size him up.

The following morning, Hossein had estimated his designated corner to be one-third of the room at the most. And he was to pay half the rent. It did not add up, but he decided against bargaining. Arguing over money could put him at risk. Who knew if, irritated, Ahmad might report trumped-up accusations against him to SAVAK? Hossein would have to be cagy to discover Ahmad's political convictions before he showed his colors to his new roommate. He would protect himself until he figured out if Ahmad had dangerous affiliations.

Hossein spread his mat on the floor along with the cushion he had just purchased in the bazaar, the gold quilt his mother had given him, and a flimsy sheet.

"Take the bottom two drawers of that chest." The voice coming from the dim room's darkest area startled Hossein.

"One is enough." Hossein opened a drawer and laid a prayer stone, some turquoise prayer beads, and his Koran in one corner. In the other, he folded three sets of underwear, an extra shirt, and three pairs of dark socks. He shoved several blank notebooks under the clothes and slid the plastic container with his colored pens on its side as a barrier between the religious and secular objects. "Done," he announced to Ahmad, now sitting cross-legged on his pallet. Little light seeped through the fancy blinds the landlord had installed over the room's only window. Hossein preferred knowing exactly what the person with him in the room looked like. Although Ahmad came from Khafr, he had left the village when Hossein's family still lived in Tehran.

Ahmad flipped on an electric fan on the floor in the room's center and adjusted it. It rotated on its stand, and gusts of air blew on each of them in turn.

"A fan, *baba*?" Hossein said. No one in his family spent money on personal comfort. According to Hossein's uncle, Ahmad had recently quit his job as a gardener in a luxury hotel across the river. He must have done well there.

"I saved three months to buy it." Ahmad tossed him a cucumber. "Eat. Feel the air on your face. Pretend we are in a cool garden with flowing water." Ahmad's hand shot out to take an apple, and light shining through a bent slat in the blinds illuminated the lower part of his face, revealing his lascivious smile. "Flowing water and women. Beautiful women. *Houris* in paradise." Ahmad smacked his lips.

Hossein bit into the cucumber. This variety found only in Esfahan tasted sweet and subtle. But he needed more than a cucumber to satisfy his churning stomach, and this room needed more than a fan to resemble a lush garden. Any garden. Especially the Garden of Eden or the eternal paradise promised to the faithful. He had seen little evidence that Ahmad held his faith in high regard. The only prayer rug in the room was the one Hossein had carried rolled under his arm on his trek from the bus station.

Ahmad handed a saltshaker to Hossein. "When do your classes start?"

"Don't know." Hossein sprinkled salt on the cucumber's exposed flesh. "I wanted to get into the Engineering or Medical Faculties, but my entrance exam wasn't good enough." The cucumber he bit into tasted less bitter than his own words. He wanted to be an engineer more than a doctor, even though doctors made more money—and he needed money. If he could sketch donkeys and pigeons, surely he could design a bridge. "I have to take an English placement test tomorrow afternoon." He stumbled to his feet and raised the blinds, no longer able to stand talking to a featureless face. Sunlight shone on Ahmad's deep-set, hooded eyes. They darted around the room as if danger lurked in every corner. His skin, bronzed and scaly from working in the sun, stretched over high cheekbones. Ahmad's brow descended low; his eyebrows arched high, exposing only a small patch of forehead lined beyond his years. His nose was nearly nonexistent: two round nostrils on either side of a slight ridge of puckered skin. Hossein wanted to ask Ahmad if he had broken his nose but thought better of it. His father had once pointed out a boy in Tehran with a nose similar to Ahmad's. "That boy has a sinful disease his own father caught from foreign women and passed to him." These women occupied a section of the city where Hossein's father forbade him to go.

"The English exam isn't hard. You get the answers ahead of time." Ahmad slithered down on his mat and stretched.

"How do you find someone who has them?" Ahmad kept shifting his eyes, assessing him, it seemed, just as Hossein was evaluating Ahmad.

"I was in the university for a semester last year," Ahmad said. "Stuck in the English Department."

"I didn't realize that." If he had known Ahmad in the village, he could have expected Ahmad's help in getting the test answers.

"You have a stipend to come here, don't you?" Ahmad's eyes circled around Hossein's mat and *tar* and bed covers, then rested for a minute on Hossein's face.

"Enough for books and food. My uncle's paying for the room. I pick up the first payment of my stipend today." Taking money from this despicable government shamed him.

"I know about your family's troubles."

Ahmad stuck his tongue out and put a sliver of apple on it. In an instant, tongue and apple disappeared into his narrow mouth. "I'd like to help you, Hossein-*jan*," Ahmad said, his mouth full of apple.

"Did you like the university?" Hossein asked. He was uncertain if he wanted help from Ahmad, although he had no one in Esfahan he could trust. But then, it was always that way. He never had friends.

"I hated it. I hated foreign teachers. You get them in the English Department."

"My family—they expect me to graduate. Get a job."

"At the university, students who do well on the English placement exam go to advanced courses. The teachers they get are supposed to be the best."

"But aren't advanced classes harder?" Hossein had learned most of what little English he knew as a boy in Tehran. "In Khafr, we didn't have a very good English teacher."

"Why would you have?" Ahmad heaved an exaggerated sigh, and a tremor slid down his body.

"People in Khafr hardly ever see a foreigner." Hossein swallowed the last bite of his cucumber. "Except for a Peace Corps teacher. He left before we moved back. I didn't know him. Did you?"

"The Peace Corps teacher?" Ahmad jerked his chin up and clicked his tongue. "Peace Corps? Useless—American propaganda."

Hossein retrieved his *tar* from where it stood in the corner. He tuned its three strings with a mixture of relief and wariness now that he had sounded out Ahmad. The music would tell him where it needed to go, just as Ahmad's answer had told him what he needed to know. Ahmad's and his similar political views, though, entitled him to neither trust nor friendship. Ahmad was not family.

Hossein plucked the *tar*'s strings. Notes meditated in hushed quarter tones while he figured out how to eat less so he could afford the answers to the English test.

Getting the answers to the English placement exam was the most foolish thing he had ever done. The advanced class was too hard. How could he pass? In the village, everyone passed, and the teacher expected students to feed answers to test questions to each other. You were bound by duty to your friend if he asked you for help. But the foreign university teachers expected students to do their own work. He had already heard rumors that they failed students. Who would help him? Ahmad lacked the proficiency in English. Ahmad must have failed his university courses. Why else would he take such a low-class job as gardening? Hossein chewed on his thumbnail. He had to pass this course. But how?

He leafed through the pages of "The Fly in the Ointment," the short story for Tuesday. It was anything but short. He recognized few words. He fumbled in his book bag for a Persian-English dictionary and pulled a knife from his pocket. As he shaved an unsharpened pencil, the knife's monotonous scraping and the wood's faint scent relaxed him, eased his fears. Wood shavings sprinkled on the floor beside his mat. When the lead formed a point, he wiped the knife's blade on his pant leg. Uneasiness drifted over him again. He would get no help from other students. He had little to say to them. The girls' frivolous ways offended him. The male students engaged in acts of posturing: they adopted attitudes of self-confidence; they vied for positions of superiority. Some showed off their family's social status through the popular music they liked, the Persian vocabulary they used, and the shiny shoes and flashy watches they wore. Hossein knew these games well from his time in Tehran. He would hold himself aloof to prevent other students from talking down to him. It was his only option.

Mrs. Weston—a mystery. But the girl named Mitra was right: Mrs. Weston was American. American CIA spies had interfered in Iranian affairs in the time of Prime Minister Mossadegh, ousting him from office and bringing the Shah to power. Because of oil. Mossadegh had nationalized Iran's oil, and foreign governments—British, American—had opposed him. Hossein's father had explained all this to him. His father thought Iran would be better off without oil. Iranians saw little money from petroleum sales. The Shah dispensed the proceeds for bribery and corruption, his father said, to ensure loyalty. Yet Hossein's father differentiated between a government and the governed. Although devoted to Islam, he accepted Christians and Jews as people of faith in one God. Hossein had no idea which religion Mrs. Weston followed. Her presence disconcerted him: he was poor; his English was bad; she was a woman. An American woman who wore lipstick and showed off her hair. How could he respect a woman university instructor? Even if she welcomed him to her class and cared enough to ask about his family? What would his father have advised? Such a topic had never arisen in the Rahimi household. Until now, the situation would have been unthinkable.

He had to work this out himself.

A half-hour later, Hossein busied himself with his assignment again, looking up English words and jotting down Persian translations in the text. Mrs. Weston discouraged this practice. She instructed her students to learn the meanings of words without their dictionaries. Something to do with reading the entire paragraph. How could she expect that? Didn't she know that Iranian students memorized the meaning of words like they memorized passages of the Koran? How could he read a paragraph when he did not understand one sentence in it? He paced up and down, repeating aloud each English word and its Persian equivalent until voices and footsteps resounded in the stairwell.

Ahmad and two of his friends burst through the door, destroying Hossein's efforts to study. They pounded him on the back, congratulated him for joining what they called their movement. Stupefied, he searched their faces for clues, hesitant to show his ignorance, especially when the others had brought dinner.

Soleiman, the one with a bulbous nose and bushy mustache, spread a newspaper on the floor. Ahmad dished out servings of rice from a copper pot. Dariush covered the rice with stew.

"My mother made this *khoresht* for us." Dariush had the typical sing-song Esfahani accent. In spite of his mother's cooking, he was skinnier and shorter than the others.

Aromas of lamb and rice and apricots filled the room, and Hossein's stomach sent him an unmistakable demand. Months had passed since he had eaten a feast like this. He accepted a full plate from Dariush and relished each bite. Dariush's mother had used perfect proportions of oil and salt, water, and rice. Each rice kernel lay separate from its neighbors. The combination of meat and fruit created a subtle sweetness. But the meal's price worried Hossein. He already owed Ahmad a favor. Ahmad had declined his offer of a thousand rials for the test answers. Hossein understood what receiving the answers—and this meal—free of charge meant.

Something, sometime, would come due.

Dariush offered Hossein the last serving of rice from the pot. Hossein loved *tahdig*, flat pieces of toasted rice caked on the pot's bottom, but he refused this sought-after delicacy. "I am not an honored guest or a family member." His words prompted Dariush to insist over and over that he help himself to the *tahdig*. Hossein would violate the unwritten law of *ta'arof* unless he accepted. Seconds later, he found himself crunching on a generous piece of *tahdig*, savoring its nutty flavor.

The price was getting higher.

They sucked strong tea through brown sugar lozenges tucked in behind their front teeth. Afterward, drowsiness enveloped Hossein, and he lay sprawled on his mat.

"You have suffered too much from this regime, Hossein-*jan*," Soleiman said. Hossein-*jan*. Hossein, dear one. "We need an ally in the university. Someone who reports to us what is going on there. We know there are university students who are anti-Shah. We want to persuade them to join forces with us. Together, we can rise up against the government." Soleiman pumped an angry fist in the air. Ahmad and Dariush did likewise.

Hossein, not at all surprised at the group's anti-government stance, sat upright and stretched his legs out in front of him, his back against the wall. "I couldn't help you much. I don't know any other students." He hated those who gained favor by reporting others for supposed anti-government activity. The role Soleiman proposed for him seemed much the same. Spying on his fellow students to determine their political stance—whatever it was—went against the social and religious practices his family had ingrained in him.

"It's only the first week, *baba*." Ahmad clapped a heavy hand on Hossein's shoulder. "You made it into the advanced class. That's where we think most anti-Shah students are." Ahmad, with his hand tight over Hossein's collarbone, fixed his eyes on Hossein's face for the first time.

"I see," Hossein said. In this political climate, seeing was not always something to be desired.

"If you argue in a clever way in class," Soleiman said, "students will pick up that you are their ally in the cause. They will come to you."

"And if they don't?" His family would want him to stay clear of these schemes. Involving himself in them would put his loved ones at risk.

"They will." Soleiman threw him a sharp look. "I'm sure you aren't in favor of the Shah," he said, his remark both a question and a threat.

Hossein folded his arms to conceal his trembling fingers. Rumors abounded about SAVAK agents infiltrating every university class. How would he identify who was trustworthy? But Soleiman had asserted himself as this group's leader. He expected compliance to his demands. "I'll do what I can," Hossein said, working hard to steady his voice.

It was a question of honor rather than allies.

Debtors have obligations.

CHAPTER FIVE

Before he accidentally paid six thousand rials for a bed, his level of comfort in this house had grown. It was safe, secluded. Doug liked the design. The house wrapped itself around the garden like a small but modest Shah Abbas Hotel. The garden lived up to the owner's billing. Last week, the gardener had dug shallow trenches to channel water to beds where Angela had him plant rose bushes.

Doug sketched a rough map to situate where he and Angela lived in relation to other places in the city. This house stood in the center of Esfahan at the end of a dead-end *kucheh*, or alley. He pinpointed the location on his map and drew a rectangle. Another rectangle inside it for the garden. His pencil flew over the paper. A bigger rectangle for the Shah Abbas Hotel. A series of domes for the bazaar. Waves for the river. A circle for the *meidan* at the far end of their *kucheh*. At a right angle, two swift strokes: Khiaban-e Chahar Bagh. At the street's far end where the Shah's statue stood near the river he penciled in another circle. He drew a miniature Shah's head inside the circle, making it look like a coin. He pressed hard and marked the SAVAK building: XXX. It took two minutes to walk from their *kucheh* to Chahar Bagh and another twenty to the statue at the street's other end. He wondered if Angela chose this house because the long, busy street separated it from SAVAK headquarters.

The house and its location had turned out better than he

expected, but then, this morning, he had given in to Angela's desire for a traditional Iranian bed, a *takht*, as she called it. Worse yet, he had volunteered to go to the carpenter's shop alone to order it while Angela busied herself arranging their new dishes on the kitchen shelves.

At the entrance to his workshop, the carpenter had wiped sawdust on his baggy black pants and bargained. At last, proud of the sum they settled on, Doug held out six hundred rials. But the merchant kept signaling to Doug to pull more bills from his hip pocket. Twenty minutes later, on the way home with sawdust tickling his nostrils, Doug puzzled over his remaining money. Somehow, he had spent six thousand rials rather than six hundred. Yet, he was certain he knew the Persian word for hundred.

He was still counting his money when four boys delivered the bed. Once inside the compound, they dumped its two sides in the garden, attached the sides with hooked latches, and demanded tips of five hundred rials each. This time, he stuck to his original offer: he gave each porter fifty rials and shooed them out the garden doors.

The next thing he knew, Angela had come up with the absurd idea that they should leave the bed in the garden. That had not been part of the bargain, either. Now, she perched, facing him, on their new blue quilt, her eyes fixed on the sky. Blue above her; blue below her. The satin quilt covered a wooden platform with legs a foot high. A rail around it extended six inches higher than its surface. So this was what Angela called a *takht*.

"I feel like I'm in a playpen." Doug abandoned his pencil and paper and crawled over to pick a pear out of a bowl in the corner. "I can't see the point of a bed in the middle of a garden."

"Old Persian tradition." Angela's face glowed in the autumn sun. "The famous Peacock Throne was a *takht*. Silver encrusted with jewels."

"They cheated even the Shah in those days, I bet." He was still seething over the ordeal of buying the blasted bed. "No wonder the Shah has to have SAVAK for protection."

Angela glared at him. "That is inappropriate." She tore a bite off a large piece of the flat bread baked in adobe ovens. "Would you like a piece of *nan?*"

"The guy cheated me. No way should I have owed him so much." Doug tossed up his pear and snatched it with a vengeance. Why did Angela have to pepper her English with Persian here in their own garden? "He knew what I meant." He peeled his pear, holding it over the side of the *takht.* Pear juice dribbled on the ground. "Six hundred rials, not six hundred tokens or whatever you call them."

"Tomans," Angela said. "One toman equals ten rials. You didn't think you could get this bed for six hundred rials, did you? Ten dollars?"

"I didn't think they talked in money that doesn't exist. There is no such thing as a toman coin."

"They have a ten-rial coin, which equals a toman." Why did she have to enunciate each word as if explaining the world to a child?

"They don't have one hundred-toman bills, or five hundred-toman bills, or any amount of toman bills because tomans don't exist. And look at this bed. Shoddy carpentry." The quilt hid stains on the bed's unfinished surface. The rails were nicked, and the legs uneven. "I think the guy capitalized on his chance to cheat a foreigner and sold me his own bed. Your buddy Mahmud told us it often takes weeks to get a craftsman to complete the simplest order."

"He's not my buddy, Doug."

"Mahmud said *bazaaris* always say '*farda, farda.*' Tomorrow, tomorrow. And every tomorrow you come back, it's the same thing. *Farda.* There's a word I won't forget."

Angela shrugged her shoulders. "Apparently, Iranians don't like to rush."

He stabbed the knife into the goat cheese, crumbling it into bits. Angela always excused the most irritating habits here in

Iran. "Apparently, they do like to sleep in gardens. And so do you, although I want to move the bed inside." Sleeping outside at night made them vulnerable. The neighbors harbored dovecotes on their roof and played with homing pigeons that roosted there. They could see down into this garden. The bed belonged inside. "Tell me you don't expect us to sleep here in winter."

"We'll move the bed inside when it gets cold." She pointed at one of several rooms with French doors opening onto the walled garden. "And when we've painted that bedroom. It was nice of the landlord to let us make cosmetic changes."

"He's getting all these repairs at no cost." Doug had spent much of his free time working on window latches, cleaning out flues, and fixing kitchen drawers.

"You were the one who insisted on a Western toilet." Angela giggled.

"I didn't want you to have to squat." He passed her the bowl of fruit. "So why don't you want to move the bed inside now?"

"I didn't realize you would feel so uncomfortable in the garden. And we have to paint the room. It's easier without the bed in there." Angela rattled on about the colors in Iranian houses, the only detail she seemed to dislike in Iran. He had already painted over bright green and hot pink but had not yet managed to paint the lavender room. Every rental property they had seen had the same lavender room with a bare light bulb hanging from the center of the ceiling.

Doug lay back on a pillow covered with Esfahani cloth, his cheek on Shah Abbas's polo players. "And what will I tell Mahmud?" he asked Angela. Mahmud had talked a real estate agent into showing them this place. No Iranian would want to live here, according to Mahmud. Iranians would opt for a modern apartment. Doug could not imagine Mahmud subscribing to the old practice of sleeping on a *takht* in a garden.

"You're right. He's sure to ask how much you paid for this *takht*," she said.

"Oh. The expensive *takht*." When he tried to pronounce the word correctly, he felt he was going to gag.

"Tell him you got it for four hundred tomans if it makes you feel better."

"He'll say he could get it cheaper."

Angela picked cheese crumbs off the plate with her fingertip. She spread them on a piece of bread and folded it the way Iranians did before she passed it to Doug. He stuffed extra bread in his mouth to take away the sour taste of the goat cheese she liked so much.

In the far corner of the garden, crows squawked and pecked at ripe pomegranates. "I'm going to pick pomegranates later. The man at the fruit stand said to eat the seeds with salt." Angela wiped the cheese off her fingers.

Doug turned up his nose at the thought of ingesting salted pomegranate seeds.

Angela stretched out next to him. The September sun bore down, releasing the heady perfume of Persian roses, warming his exposed cheek. Scents of late summer fertility lingered over the garden—mimosa, mulberry, quince. Somewhere a bee buzzed. Red and blue medallions reflecting off the house's stained glass windows danced on the garden wall. Angela's chest rose and fell in deep breaths. Dozing in the golden light, she looked as comfortable in her skin as the desert lizard sunning itself on the garden wall. He himself was far from at ease with the food, the language, the currency, the bargaining— the *takht*. People here sometimes slept on their roofs on warm nights. And then, there were the pigeons. What if a late-night pigeon dropped his load?

Winter was weeks away. He would paint the bedroom tomorrow. The following evening, he would move the bed inside.

No one was going to spy on his private life.

*　*　*　*　*　*

The song was about love.

Its quarter tones made her squirm. She imagined them alive, amorphous as amoebas, sliding into gaps between piano keys. Doug worked his jaw as if the music put pressure on his ear drums. If it did not stop soon, Angela feared, he would leave Vicky's party before she introduced him to her colleagues. Doug needed friends here—people to keep him from evenings spent drinking alone.

Angela slipped off her sandals and waited while Doug untied his shoes and left them in the row of discarded footwear. On the far side of the room, Iranian professors clustered around a buffet table loaded with chafing dishes full of lamb and chicken kabobs, pilafs, and *khoreshts*. The food scented the room with hints of coriander, cinnamon, and saffron.

A break in the music. "Hi, y'all." The Louisiana accent floated over the din of voices speaking Persian. Cecil Chauncey, decked out in Purple People Eater socks, slid across the marble-tiled floor and hugged her. "Good to see ya, sugah."

She unwrapped his arms and pushed herself away from his paunch. Cecil's sandy hair curled across his forehead in bangs. Along with his Roman nose, the hair gave him an imperial air that his purple-striped Western shirt with mother-of-pearl snaps utterly destroyed. Cecil marked student papers with purple pens, additional evidence of his purple fetish.

Now, seemingly for Doug's benefit, Cecil tapped a knife against a glass and announced a routine called "Two Iranians at Any Entrance." Angela had seen it before. A cross between mime and slapstick, it reminded her of an ill-advised Beckett play, but Cecil's sense of humor made him popular among both faculty and students. He could get away with satirizing ex-pats and Iranians alike.

Cecil's announcement drew an audience and, with it, silence. He explained that his one-man show had two characters.

He mimed a doorway. Character One pretended to turn the knob to enter.

Cecil switched to Character Two and approached the door.

Character One held out his hand to Character Two and gestured for him to go through the door first. "*Befarmayid, agha. Befarmayid.*"

Back to Character Two. Same gesture, same words.

The two characters volleyed back and forth, each trying to convince the other to go first through the imaginary door. At last, one pushed the other through and fell, sprawling on the floor, after him.

Cecil bowed twice, once for each character. The audience greeted his performance with guffaws and applause, most of the laughter coming from the Iranian guests. The *ta'arof* ordeal had ended.

After Cecil's foolishness, the guests talked louder, laughed harder, and mixed more. Cecil nabbed the Westons and pummeled Doug with questions about his background. As the two men talked, Doug's expression became more animated, his gestures more expansive. Cecil had won him over.

Someone turned up the music, and Cecil clapped one hand on Angela's shoulder and the other on the elbow of the slender man next to him as if itching for Angela to meet his American date. Cecil had made it no secret that he came to the Middle East because "the pickin's are good heah for gay guys." He had been disappointed in his quest. Iranian males had to marry to have sexual relations with women. Any interest they had in foreign men was often due to this requirement rather than a natural inclination, Cecil claimed. The fun, he said, "was nevah reciprocal, so damn it, darlin', I'll have to find my tricks elsewhere."

Angela introduced herself to Cecil's guest, a Southerner like him but quiet and self-effacing. He told Angela he worked for Bell Helicopter, and she caught Doug's amused expression. Doug must be thinking what she was: Guy would likely be appalled to see a fellow pilot out with Cecil.

Angela searched the crowd for Vicky but found no sign of their hostess. Kamran, though, had sauntered up and was following the conversation from the group's periphery. Angela introduced him to Doug. She helped herself to a drink at a side table where she could observe the men's interactions, pleased Doug had met Kamran before the overbearing Vicky. Kamran was, as always, well-dressed. He had the high cheekbones and slightly frizzy hair of the Qashqai, once one of the most powerful tribes in Iran. Angela had read that, years ago, the government had forced the Qashqai to cease summer migrations to mountains north of Shiraz. The Shah wanted the military to keep them under closer surveillance. Most settled in the heat of the high plateau, where many died from illnesses to which they had no immunity. *Khans* who posed a threat to the regime lived in exile in Switzerland.

Angela got herself another drink and rejoined the men. "Mosquitoes," Cecil said, referring to the thin-bodied Cobra helicopters recently arrived from the States. "They look like pesky mosquitoes. They sound like pesky mosquitoes."

The topic bored her, although she thought it odd that Doug flinched the moment he heard that Iran now possessed Cobras. Kamran withdrew from the discussion of fighter whirlybirds, as Cecil's date called them.

Angela turned toward Kamran and asked about his father's health. Kamran took care of his father, who suffered from emphysema. Too much strong tobacco, she suspected.

"So-so. He's old and tired. How is your Persian coming?"

"I listen to the radio, and we bought a little TV." She abhorred the propaganda referred to as the nightly newscast. "But we usually watch the English station so Doug can understand." She herself preferred avoiding the TV programs in English—reruns of American shows she would never have watched in the States and old John Wayne or karate films. "I can understand Persian pretty well now, but I need help with grammar and reading." Kamran appeared distracted. His eyes worked the crowd, and he stood on tiptoe to survey a group of Iranians that had just entered. Perhaps he was waiting for someone. A woman who had caught his attention? Kamran was single.

He dropped back to his normal height and suggested one of his fourth-year students as a tutor for Angela. "Mahtab's an older woman with a family. Very Westernized. You'd enjoy getting to know each other."

"Westernized?"

"Well, modern. And interested in making foreign friends."

Angela thanked Kamran for his help. Then, curious about his family history, she asked, "Does your father miss the Shiraz area? There aren't many other Qashqai in this part of the country, are there?" Although the Qashqai came from Fars province, the tribe spoke a Turkic tongue. Kamran's father might not get along well in Persian.

"He is very old," Kamran said. "He will stay inside the house wherever he is."

"The sedentary life must be difficult for someone who migrated so many years." Kamran's father had been a *khan* responsible for safeguarding his people as they searched for pasture and water, their black tents on the backs of horses or donkeys or camels.

"Qashqai clothes would look good on you," Kamran said. "Women wear as many brightly colored skirts and gold bracelets as the family can afford."

"My eye color would betray me." She fingered her gold bracelets. Kamran seemed out of place in Esfahan with his immaculate Western clothes and proficient English. She found the silver hair at his temples attractive.

Someone tapped her shoulder. Vicky.

"I just graded mid-terms." Vicky rolled her eyes. "Pathetic." She brushed aside her platinum-blond bangs with the back of a chubby hand. Vicky's breath smelled of alcohol, although her husband, Reza, was drinking a Coke. Angela had already endured an outburst from Vicky about how Reza had neglected to tell her that his family lived in a village. When he brought Vicky to Iran after their marriage in the States, the couple moved into the family's mud house with Vicky's *chadori* mother-in-law and an outside, hole-in-the-ground toilet buzzing with flies. Vicky did not bother to learn a word of Persian. After a sweltering summer, she insisted Reza find a proper house for them in Esfahan.

His parents had since moved to Natanz, but the mother-in-law spent much of her time here in her son's house, a source of unending irritation for Vicky in spite of the care Reza's mother gave to the couple's three boys.

"My students are much more proficient in English than I expected," Angela said.

"They're a handful. You'll find out. You can't believe how clever they are at cheating. If only they spent half as much effort on their homework."

"So far, I've had no problems." Kamran and Reza were within range of Vicky's disparaging remarks. How could she be so insensitive?

"Let me tell you something. The students hate that you're an American. And they hate that you're a woman."

Angela's discomfort grew. Vicky never knew when to stop.

"These kebabs are great." Doug held up a skewer of lamb. He and the Couple Cecil had made a fruitful trip to the buffet table. Angela smiled. Doug was getting the full experience of Vicky.

Cecil snapped his heels and saluted. "Hail, Lee Hub." His southern accent massacred the Persian words for very good.

"You must make it clear from the beginning who is boss in the classroom. Expect to be tested." Vicky flipped a strand of hair out of her eyes. "Too bad you know Persian. You'll have to hear the nasty things they say about you."

"They don't question my authority." Angela finished her drink. Doug, engrossed in his kebab, said nothing to ease the tension. "They act happy to have the chance to improve their English. They interpret symbolism better than most American students."

"This new class is the best yet," Kamran said, still eyeing the group at the buffet table—all male from what Angela could see. "I have the lower half in a remedial reading class. They have the same aptitude as my advanced class last year."

His comments embarrassed her. He had every right to resent her. She had been assigned this year's advanced group because she was a native speaker and thus replaced Kamran, who had more experience teaching advanced students. "How are students placed in the advanced section?" She had never asked about the process used to split the incoming students into two groups. Clearly, Mr. Rahimi did not belong in her class.

"We gave them an English placement test before the semester started," Kamran said.

"That's another joke." Vicky lashed out as if intent on exerting her authority over Kamran. "It's the same exam year after year. They get the answers in advance from sophomores. You just need to know someone willing to help you cheat. Or you . . ." She rubbed her thumb and middle finger together dramatically.

Angela failed to imagine Mr. Rahimi knowing anyone who would help him cheat. In her classroom, he sat at the back, away from the others. He always studied apart from the students who congregated under the mimosa trees in front of the building or on the benches at the university gates. Loners were uncharacteristic of students here. Even the shyest girls compared observations on readings in the hall before class. Mr. Rahimi had no friends at all.

"So why do you keep teaching, Vicky?" Angela could no longer restrain herself. Doug's sharp glance told her she had breached the boundaries of pleasant party chit-chat.

Vicky pointed a finger at Reza, who lowered his eyes. "I wouldn't if he worked harder."

"You've put on a great party." Doug put his arm around Angela's waist, their agreed-upon signal that one of them was ready to leave, if not the gathering itself, at least the present company. They skirted a couch where a French professor was lecturing on the Iranian film industry to a dazed Cecil. Cecil flagged them down.

"All hope is not lost," he whispered in Angela's ear and motioned toward an Iranian server stacking clean plates on the buffet table. Slender build. Delicate fingers. Graceful movements.

"Hush, Cecil. You've got a date." The Bell Helicopter escort had disappeared for the moment. Despite the French teacher's efforts to discuss *film noir*, Cecil kept his attention fixed on his new find.

Angela nestled into the sofa, wishing she could forget Mr. Rahimi. Although she hated to admit it, Vicky was right. Mr. Rahimi must have cheated on the placement exam. His disdain for studying English seemed to be increasing. Recently, he had objected to the readings on medieval world history in the prescribed curriculum.

"You want us to be Christian." He brandished the text's illustration labeling architectural elements of Gothic cathedrals. She suggested he bring a picture showing the parts of a mosque. He never did.

The potent drinks had gone to her head, and Doug offered to bring her something to eat. Cecil leaned his head close to her waist and asked if she felt sick as he peered up at her, pop-eyed. He was too much.

The French teacher excused himself and joined Doug at the buffet table. Alone on the couch with Cecil, Angela complimented him on his routine. "You put everyone at ease. You're good at not offending anyone, even when you satirize Iranian *ta'arof*." She tried to enunciate each word so she would not appear tipsy.

"People like to laugh at themselves sometimes," he said. "Jokes like that can be easier to take from a foreigner."

"Only from one whose goodwill is beyond question. I hope Iranians know *I'm* not what they might expect of some Americans," she said. For weeks before she and Doug arrived in Esfahan, she steeped herself in Iranian history, read translations of the poetry of Hafez and Sa'adi, studied the country's noted tilework and miniatures, researched Islam, and learned about tribes—Kurds, Turkomans, Baluchis. "I can transcend my cultural background." She poked Cecil in the chest between two pearly buttons.

"Whoa, transcend." Cecil whistled. "That's heavy." He pulled his legs to a lotus position on the sofa and intoned a resonant "OMMMM."

"You're impossible." She should have kept her mouth shut. Not the subject to bring up at a party. Not when she was feeling her liquor. She had overdone it.

Doug returned, juggling two plates. *Fesenjan.* Her favorite dish, this one made with chicken. "Good time?" she asked, to no avail. Cecil had already pulled Doug aside, babbling again about the cute server.

Steam rose from the plate in Angela's hand. From somewhere far off in the foyer, Vicky preached in shrill tones. Her words faded in the fogginess of Angela's mind, surpassed by the aroma of cinnamon and walnuts and pomegranates.

CHAPTER SIX

Ahmad had never invited him anywhere before.

Hossein plunged his hand into the back corner of the chest's top drawer and drew out a few coins. Could he afford a movie? He would manage if he ate only a little for the three days remaining in this month. He would take advantage of this chance for friendship.

The best was yet to come: Soleiman would meet them in front of the cinema. "He especially wanted you to come." Ahmad winked at Hossein, whose excitement swelled like a pomegranate in late summer.

The movie, a kung fu extravaganza, attracted a full house. Inside, the air reeked of male sweat and breath soured by yogurt. The film's unabashed violence, however disciplined, stunned Hossein. With a series of movements faster than the blink of an eyelid, Jackie Chan defeated his opponents one after another. Each time, Ahmad and Soleiman, who sat on either side of Hossein, cheered and clapped and slapped him on the back. At long last, they had accepted him.

The film ended. Soleiman leaned behind Hossein and whispered something to Ahmad. They stood and lifted Hossein from his seat by his elbows. His enthusiasm shriveled. He knew what was coming. He should have realized it sooner.

Outside, Soleiman slipped into cadence with Hossein's

steps. They strode down Khiaban-e Chahar Bagh in the fading light, Soleiman clutching Hossein's hand, Ahmad trailing behind. The three distanced themselves from the movie crowd, and Soleiman steered Hossein down an unfamiliar side street. "What progress have you made for us at the university?" Soleiman asked. "Who can we count on from your side?"

The questions Hossein had expected.

He had made no progress.

The students at the Foreign Language Faculty, like Ahmad and his friends, avoided him on the worst days, barely tolerated him on the best. Soleiman asked him again for names of students who would ally themselves with the movement.

He had no names.

They passed under a streetlamp where, for an instant, Soleiman's nose caught the light and bulged bigger than ever over his full mustache.

"I don't want to disappoint you, *baba*." Hossein searched for something to say and came up with only the truth. His father would have commended him for his honesty. Soleiman would condemn him. "I need more time to know someone's heart." Hossein's own heart pounded in his fingertips under Soleiman's tight grip.

"Our group is starting slowly and small." Soleiman stepped back and folded his arms across his chest. "But our ranks will diminish if we suspect anyone of not doing his part."

Soleiman's words weighed as heavy as the wooden clubs men wielded in a *zurkhaneh*, a house of strength. He turned his back on Hossein and retraced his steps toward the main street, his heels beating a rapid staccato against the sidewalk.

Hossein hurried to catch up. "There is one perhaps. Mohammad. I'm not yet sure." It seemed a safe bet. There were three Mohammads in Mrs. Weston's class.

Soleiman's lips curled under his mustache. "Make sure," he said.

Hossein looked back. Ahmad followed close behind them,

his eyes darting back and forth. They reached the shops bordering Chahar Bagh. Ahmad advanced and, tugging at Hossein's cuff, pulled him across the street. "Don't expect me home tonight." He shook Hossein's hand.

Hossein continued down Chahar Bagh until the next cross street. He looked over his shoulder. Ahmad leaned against the grill of a carpet shop where Hossein had left him.

Across the street, Soleiman watched in the shadow of a plane tree.

Hossein kept up a rapid pace along the river and across the Si-yo-Se Pol, the Bridge of Thirty-Three Arches. At the far side of the bridge, he broke out in a cold sweat and collapsed on a ledge under an arch, trembling. The blind man slept under the arch opposite him. Hossein scanned the length of the bridge. Neither Ahmad nor Soleiman had followed him. Ahmad was staying out all night. Where? Why? Surely Ahmad was not SAVAK. His uncle knew Ahmad. His uncle would not have let him rent an apartment with a suspected undercover agent. But what if his uncle did not know?

Hossein mopped his forehead with one of his father's old handkerchiefs. How foolish he had acted. He should have known before going to the movie that Ahmad and Soleiman wanted something from him. Why else would they have invited him? And, he had compounded his foolishness by not offering to help the movement in some other way. He could have volunteered to carry messages or . . . Or what? What could he do? He had no money. He had no influence. His family was under suspicion. That was why Ahmad and Soleiman had trusted him in the first place. If they did trust him. They were bound to keep secrets from him.

He had to protect himself. Not assume Ahmad and Soleiman were revolutionaries as they claimed. But if they were? If they simply wanted to make sure he was what they thought he was? He was. He was against the Shah. And if he passed their tests, they would accept him, wouldn't they? He would prove himself to them in some way. Soon.

He pocketed his handkerchief and sank back into the bridge's niche. The stone felt cool through his thin shirt and jacket and pants. Across the bridge, the blind man had curled into a fetal position, his head on a pile of rags. A few incoherent sounds issued from his throat. Hossein fumbled in his pocket. Did the blind man know he was here? Hossein tiptoed across the bridge and laid a five-rial coin on the stone stoop next to the old man, placing it there without a sound. The blind man did not stir. Hossein picked up the coin and tiptoed back to his niche. He dropped the coin on the ledge next to him. It produced a metallic ping as it hit the stone. On the opposite side, the blind man reached out and clawed in vain at the stone surface.

Hossein smiled into the darkness. The blind man had an acute sense of hearing. If he, Hossein, could trick this blind man, he could find out what Soleiman wanted to know. He had to do what he had just done. Make noise on one side—the Shah's side—to find out who stirred on the other side. Shield himself from SAVAK by pretending he supported the Shah. Make himself secure by clinging to the currency he needed to live. He could do it. Resolved, he bounded across the bridge and tossed the coin into the blind man's bowl. He could do it.

And Mrs. Weston had given the perfect assignment to help him succeed.

*　*　*　*　*　*

The skirmish erupted in her class two weeks after the midterm. The battleground: a discussion of the H.G. Wells story, "In the Country of the Blind."

Mitra, Shireen, Nazi, and one of the Mohammads, Farhad, and Hassan had all written profuse marginal notations on the story's pages. Mr. Rahimi appeared unarmed with notes or underscored passages. However, his hand flew up like a misfired flare as soon as Angela opened the discussion. In the front row, Shireen looked at Mitra and raised her eyebrows. During the entire semester, Mr. Rahimi had seldom participated, and Angela was unsure how much he understood. She called on him, pleased with his eagerness. Sometimes, after months of struggling, a student relaxed, and the spoken language that had formerly trickled like Esfahan's Zayandeh Rood spurted out, a spring from an underground river.

"Wells is saying the ruling class is blind." Mr. Rahimi's words rushed out with assertiveness. Usually, Iranian students spoke at the same time. Today, after Mr. Rahimi's comment, the only sound was the flapping of helicopter rotors as Army pilots flew over the city. Mr. Rahimi eyed Angela. "I am right. Yes, Mrs. Weston?" he asked. Little by little, the majority of the students nodded in assent.

"That is a valid interpretation. You're close to the story's theme." The night before, she had prepared notes for the class and wondered why the prescribed curriculum included such an inflammatory story in a country ruled by a despot.

A smile flickered across Mr. Rahimi's lips. "The government would not like this story. You agree, Mrs. Weston?" he asked. Mohammad muttered something in Persian to Mitra.

Hossein was right, and he was baiting her. She had to think fast. "What do you think of the story's end, Mr. Rahimi? The only sighted person dies, does he not? Makes a futile attempt to escape?"

"Ah, but the blind think he is dangerous to the country. What do you think of countries that cause dangerous people to die?"

Angela's heart raced faster than her mind. The students believed a SAVAK agent was planted in every class. Whoever their operative was, he would be obliged, indeed elated, to report inflammatory comments made by a foreigner. Mr. Rahimi was depending on that.

"*Kafi-ye, agha.* That's enough." Mohammad and Hassan fired explosive phrases of Persian at Mr. Rahimi, condemning his tactics against a guest in their country.

Mr. Rahimi laid his right hand over his heart, inclined his head and upper body in acquiescence toward Hassan, and extended his palm toward Mohammad, sneering. "*Befarmayid, agha. Inglisi harf bezanim.* Let's speak English." Hassan's eyes glittered, but he retreated.

The lull in the discussion had allowed Angela enough time to recalibrate her strategy. "Thank you, Mr. Rahimi," she said. "The discussion you've initiated raises a question. Why do we read literature?" A broader, safer topic. It worked. The students voiced their opinions all at once, apparently relieved to change the subject. She had to quiet them to field individual responses to her question. Mr. Rahimi looked disarmed by her maneuver. By the end of class, when she returned the compositions she had graded, Mr. Rahimi had yet to comment. Instead, he busied himself making entries with a green pen in a pocket notebook adorned with a picture of Esfahan's blue-domed mosque.

But a truce was out of the question.

The bell announced the end of class. Mr. Rahimi charged her podium, brandishing his marked-up composition. He stabbed the red F at the top of the paper with his forefinger. Saliva drooled out of the corner of his mouth. His hand and the paper in it shook. His eyes targeted Angela. She fought for composure, her attention on his trembling fingers, his contorted face. Such anger could precipitate an act of violence. Or was he on the verge of some sort of seizure?

"You gave me this grade because Americans hate Islam," he said.

"Your grade is based solely on your writing, not the content." She spoke with determination, substantiating her authority by her upright stance, even tone, and unwavering gaze. She refused to allow him to intimidate her. Ranting about Islamic doctrine had cluttered his papers even though the topics she assigned had nothing whatsoever to do with religion.

"You are a *kafar*," he said, more agitated than ever.

She resented his allegation that she was an unclean non-believer. One minute, he acted like a baiting SAVAK agent, and the next, like a rabid Islamist. She snatched the composition from his hands, ripping the corner. "Look at this, Mr. Rahimi." She waved the paper smeared with red ink in front of his face. "You leave out ninety percent of the vowels. There are no topic sentences. You repeat everything you say, like the names of Allah on your prayer beads. That's why your papers come back bleeding."

"*Kafars* hate the Prophet, hate Islamic law, hate Muslims."

"Mr. Rahimi, I may technically be an unclean non-Muslim, but I do not hate Muslims. Nor do I hate the Islamic religion." All three of the Mohammads and several other students had gathered to listen to the conversation instead of going to their next class. She handed the paper back to Mr. Rahimi. As he raised his hand to take it, he looked as if he might slap her arm. She stood her ground. "The Prophet Mohammad said all Muslims are bound to be forever grateful to anyone who teaches them a single thing." She felt like a *mullah* preaching in a mosque.

Silence. Heavy, confining silence. For one long moment, it reduced the antagonistic history between the Middle East and the West to this one insignificant speck on the earth's surface. Hassan spoke first, in Persian. He chastised Mr. Rahimi for his behavior. Mohammad accused Mr. Rahimi of adhering to a medieval interpretation of Islam. Farhad demanded Mr. Rahimi apologize. None of the students called Mr. Rahimi by his first name.

Angela swooped up her teaching materials. She need not intervene in the confrontation. As she withdrew to the hallway, Mr. Rahimi's classmates were still taking shots at him.

No one stood in his defense.

*　*　*　*　*　*

"Damn. Damn," Doug shouted, alone in his office that afternoon.

He ripped off the corner of yesterday's page in his day

planner and looked over today's to-do list. It never changed. He moved too many tasks forward to the next day because he spent too much time troubleshooting. The critical path diagram taped to the wall told the truth: the project was already two weeks behind schedule. He had not found a way to motivate these people to work faster. Now they would have to work longer. They had to meet deadlines.

He unrolled blueprints for the administration building on a folding table two meters long.

The edges of the top blueprint flapped in the breeze from the overhead fan. "Damn," he shouted again. If only this place had air conditioning. Above his head, the fan's blades slapped the air. Flashes of light and shadow spun over the plans. Unnerving. He searched for weights to pin down the blueprints' corners. A saucer. His house key. The book on Islamic design he read whenever he got a free minute—traveling from Esfahan to the site, nibbling on leftovers for lunch, waiting for Mahmud to show up. One corner of the blueprints still curled up. Outside the tin shack he and Mahmud shared for an office, Doug found a rock in the area where more classrooms would stand.

Someday.

In the distance, Mahmud and the tea boy were ambling along a dusty supply path. Doug waited until they caught up with him at the office door.

"*Befarmayid*," Mahmud said several times, extending his arm toward the door. Mahmud always insisted that Doug, his senior on the project, enter first. Such exaggerated politeness before a low doorway in a desert—another waste of time.

Inside, Doug plopped the rock on the blueprint's fluttering corner. The fan again. He slid the table to the opposite side of the room, away from the rotating blades and flickering light. There, he and Mahmud went over the details Mahmud would emphasize to the building crew. "By now, we should have had the foundations laid for three buildings," he told Mahmud. "We haven't finished pouring concrete for one."

"Don't sweat it, boss."

Doug swallowed back an irate reaction to Mahmud's off-hand manner. Mahmud must have picked up the expression from reruns of some American cop show.

"When I fly to Tehran, what real progress can I report, Mahmud? We're two weeks behind. We've been working for two months. That's only a seventy-five percent completion record right out of the gate." Mahmud loved to talk in percentages.

"Seventy-five percent." Mahmud smacked his lips as if he were savoring a date. "Not so bad. Two weeks off schedule." He raised his hands in a gesture of helplessness. "It doesn't matter."

"It matters to me." Doug glanced out one of the shack's dust-streaked windows, struggling to appear calm. Mahmud had warned him Iranians would treat an angry person with disdain. As usual, three or four men loitered outside, smoking and talking. "Look out there. That's not acceptable. I don't mind if they take breaks and have cigarettes and tea mid-morning and mid-afternoon. But this goes on all day. We'll never finish at this rate. I can't say '*farda, farda*' to the firm that hired me." He crossed his arms and took a stance directly in front of Mahmud. Cigarette smoke mingled with scents of jasmine, recalling Tian and his betrayal yet again. "Starting now, everyone works a half-day on the weekends until we catch up."

"They will not work on the weekend, boss."

"And why not?"

"When they get off for the weekend, they catch the bus to their villages. Most of them don't arrive until the next morning. They have only two days to spend with their families. They take the night bus back here to start the work week."

"They can leave Saturday afternoon after they work Saturday morning."

Mahmud knit his brows, effacing his scar. "Saturday, boss?"

Doug smacked his hand against the table, and the rock hopped. "I forgot again. Thursday. They can leave Thursday afternoon." He would never get used to a Thursday-Friday weekend. Mahmud still looked puzzled. "Your holy day is Friday. Ours is Sunday. Your Thursday is equivalent to our Saturday." Mahmud's eyes locked in a blank stare. Doug sighed. Mahmud surely knew which days constituted the weekend in the Western world. He had studied in Switzerland.

"Boss, they'll have to take the bus Thursday night and again Friday night to get back." Mahmud smiled. "They will be tired—very tired. And very sad because they saw their families for only one day. No work will get done."

Mahmud's smile struck Doug as misplaced. No doubt Mahmud wanted the two days with his own family in Tehran. Besides, Doug had tutored Mahmud on the project plan and blueprints. Mahmud would profit from sabotaging the project and getting Doug dismissed.

"We would pay them more. Extra for five hours of overtime—seven o'clock to noon." Doug sank into his chair, his stomach queasy. His head ached. He had polished off too many vodka limes at the Iran Tour Hotel yesterday after work. He braced himself for more bargaining from Mahmud.

"They don't care, boss. They would rather spend time in their villages. Extra pay—it doesn't matter to them."

"No. I don't suppose it does matter, and stop calling me boss." Angela knew four different ways to say in Persian that something was not important. She said she heard each of them every day. "But finishing the project on time does matter. They will work Thursday mornings until we catch up." Another dark smile stole across Mahmud's face as insidiously as oil leaking from a tanker in the Persian Gulf.

On his way out of the office, Mahmud winked at Doug. "Yes, boss," he said. "It's your decision, boss."

Prickly heat spread down Doug's chest to the tips of his fingers and balls of his feet. Sometimes, he felt that he might as well speak Swahili to Mahmud. Now, he wanted to run after Mahmud, grab him by his outrageously chic silk tie, and scream obscenities at him. But he had to keep himself in check. After he had returned from Vietnam, he had railed against another junior architect in the firm. Then, the senior architect in charge of his project, a Korean War veteran, stepped up for him and smoothed over the incident. Now, he was alone.

The only native English speaker on site.

The only American.

His hands shook as he documented the exchange in Mahmud's personnel folder. No way would he tolerate this guy pushing him out before his contract expired.

Later, Mahmud translated the new directive to the workers. Doug detected little outward reaction to the news. The men seemed resigned, lethargic in the desert heat. As they dispersed, Mahmud added several more sentences in Persian. Doug opted not to ask Mahmud what he had said. Mahmud would lie to him anyway.

As Doug headed back to his office, footsteps crunched the gravel behind him.

"Hey, mister," someone called, much like boys in the bazaar who wanted to practice their English. The worker hurried to catch up, panting.

Doug recognized the scrawny, dark-skinned man as one of the habitual loiterers. Instinctively, he scanned the man's body and clothing for unexplained bulges. The worker did not appear to carry anything that could be used as a weapon. Doug looked for Mahmud. It figured. Mahmud was out of sight.

"Hey, mister. I am very sad." The man had a thick accent. He brushed the back of his hand across his eyes as if to wipe away tears. "Very sad, mister. I have two son. I want see son two day." He held up two fingers. "No one day." Doug was unaware that any of the men spoke English, however rudimentary.

Thirty or so other workers encircled Doug and the protestor, their faces coated with dust. Doug wiped his forehead with his handkerchief. Where was Mahmud?

"I understand, Mr. . . . What is your name?"

"Ahmad. My name Ahmad. I come from Natanz. Two son in Natanz."

"You must work faster, Mr. Ahmad."

"Ahmad my name. No mister."

"Okay. Ahmad. Work faster. Then you get more holidays."

"How many son you have?"

"I don't have children, Ahmad." Doug's cheeks grew hotter than they already were in the sun. Early on, the tea boy had asked him the same question, as had another man who drove a supply truck. Yesterday, another worker posed the question via Mahmud's translation. Now someone—Mahmud—had put this man up to taunting him, to suggesting he lacked virility.

"No child? No boy?" Ahmad addressed the group hovering around him and Doug in Persian. A murmur rose from the men. A man with tobacco-brown teeth stepped forward and spouted off a paragraph or two in Persian. "He say you very sad man," Ahmad translated. "You have no son. You not want we see our son."

At last, Mahmud appeared from behind a stalled truck, followed by a gesticulating worker whose voice grew louder as they approached. When the two saw the group surrounding Doug, they stopped and fell silent. Doug motioned to Mahmud to join him. "What you say is not right," he said to Ahmad. "Not right at all."

A scornful smile broke out on Ahmad's face as if he had got what he had bargained for.

CHAPTER SEVEN

Doug's frustration had peaked by the time he reached the refrigerator, anger having boiled inside him for the long bus ride home.

He called Angela. They would talk it out together. "Do we have any of that limeade left?" he said when she came into the kitchen.

"I wish you wouldn't," Angela said. She had been getting on him about drinking recently, but she handed him a pitcher of limeade.

He plunked a few ice cubes in a glass and poured a shot of vodka before adding the limeade. "At least city water is safe to drink. This stuff would taste terrible without ice," he said, tired of the tastelessness of vodka and the acidity of the limes. Vodka was the only cheap alcohol in Iran. Limes were plentiful.

Angela trailed behind him into the garden to a wooden table and chairs she had painted forest green. There, he unloaded his day's misery on her. How could this character Ahmad think he had the right to question his decision about work hours? How could Mahmud justify making him look bad in front of the workers and then absent himself when he was most needed? And the workers' attitude on the site—the I-don't-give-a-damn mentality along with the expectation that he should act and think exactly like them. They questioned his manhood because he had no children. They showed no interest in finding out how to work faster and better. Their damned complacency got to him. They kept the same ways of living, thinking, and working—if you could call it work—that had existed for centuries. The cradle of civilization had remained precisely that—infantile.

He stopped ranting and downed his drink.

Angela sniffed a pink rose. "Roses are more fragrant this time of evening." She bent the cane toward Doug.

He sneezed and rubbed his nose. Why had Angela changed the subject to roses when she knew damn well he needed sympathy? "If Mahmud tells me one more time that something crucial to our success doesn't matter, I'll slug him, Angela."

"When you feel that way, think of the bonus. How you'll use it to start your own firm." It was Angela's pat answer since they had come to Iran.

"There won't be any bonus at the rate we're making progress. These guys aren't only slow. They're stopped. No, they move in reverse. Backwards." He knew he was exaggerating. "And, then, there's Mahmud. 'It doesn't matter, boss. It doesn't matter.'" He mocked Mahmud's words again, topping them off with a fake, Cheshire-cat grin. "They're always smiling. They must smile at their father's funeral."

"Kamran says Iranians smile to make light of serious situations so you'll feel better."

"To hell with Kamran." Doug held his tumbler up to the light to see how much liquid remained. The tinted glass and impending twilight coated the world a blurry blue. "You're good at dealing with people. Any suggestions?"

"What if you try to understand Iranian reactions from their perspective? Try to erase your own nationality?"

"That's stupid." He set his glass down hard on the table. "I'm American. That's what I was born. That's what you are. Neither of us needs to pretend otherwise."

"I'm not pretending. But I don't flaunt it like some people I know."

"Oh. I'm flaunting it, you think?"

"I was referring to Vicky."

"Maybe Vicky accepts what she is." He should have expected this from Angela. She was always zealous, forever overdoing everything when she took on a new project or, as now, adopted some arbitrary position. Before, he had taken pride in that quality of hers, but here . . . He rose and stalked toward the house. Inside, he put ice cubes in a bowl and got the unopened bottle of vodka he had hidden behind a sack of rice. Back at the green table, he poured himself a double shot. "Maybe Vicky isn't trying to escape her past."

"I'm not sure what you are implying."

"You can't forget the past."

"What past? Nobody forgets the past." Angela's eyes had widened, and her lips trembled as if she were frightened.

"You can't forget that your mother pitched a fit when you left home to go to Ohio State. You still resent that she got your father to make you pay for your education." Despite a substantial scholarship, Angela had taken odd jobs on campus to support herself—tutoring freshman English students, shelving books in the library, serving alumni banquets. They were still paying off her student loans. A delicate flush colored Angela's neck and cheeks. Roses again. He softened his tone. "You're still rebelling against your mother. That's why you were so keen on coming here. That's why you try so hard to adjust to Iran. But you are American." He became more agitated. "Everyone here knows it. They can tell by the way you look. The color of your eyes. The shape of your nose. The way you dress. They can tell by the way you talk. The way you walk. The way you think." His last word resounded in the garden quiet. "By the way you think, Angela. And by the way that you think they *can't* tell by the way you think. You can't escape it."

Angela looked beautiful, frozen and statuesque in her shock, one leg slightly forward, one arm draped over the back of her chair. "And by the way that you don't have children. They can tell by that, too, Angela. By the way you don't have children."

"You're not questioning your masculinity, are you? Iranians ask everyone how many kids they have." Angela leaned over the table, her forehead resting in her hands.

The concern in Angela's voice sent a wash of self-pity and sorrow over him, followed by a revelation. What bothered him most when someone doubted his manhood was that it augmented the intense feeling of impotency he had harbored ever since Tian's betrayal. He, too, could not escape his past.

Why had he been so harsh? He had blamed Angela for his frustration with the workers, the project backlog, and Mahmud. Indeed, he had been as unfair as life itself.

And all he had wanted was an evening alone with her.

*　*　*　*　*　*

She could tell Doug was still upset by the way he paced back and forth in the living room after dinner. Yet, she had waited until they both were calmer to confide in him about Mr. Rahimi. She downplayed Mr. Rahimi's baiting during the discussion of the Wells story, focusing instead on the encounter after class.

"You need to go to the dean, Angela. This guy is a troublemaker. You can't be expected to listen to that rubbish. You didn't bring up politics. You didn't comment on religion. He's out to get you."

"He was upset about his grade. He comes from a poor village. He's in over his head." She took off her slippers and propped her feet on the coffee table. "I was the obvious one to blame. Besides, I think he may have a neurological disorder."

"Go to the dean. Tell him that if you want, but let him deal with this Rahimi." Doug turned on the shortwave radio. Static. Choppy spoken syllables. More static. The chimes of Big Ben.

"This is the BBC in London." A male voice, the epitome of professional stoicism. "And now the evening news read by Colin Marshall."

"Are you working again tonight?" Nearly every evening, Doug carried a pitcher of limeade and a bottle of vodka to the spare room on the garden's east side. He claimed he was building a portfolio to attract clients to the firm he planned to open in the States. She wondered.

"After the news." Doug kissed the top of her head. "You try too hard sometimes."

She wished there were someplace they could go for an evening out. They had gone out only once—to Vicky's party. There were no English movies or plays. No concerts. Forget dancing. She would welcome a disco's throbbing bass and choking smoke, flashing strobes, and gyrating bodies. Anything to dispel her preoccupation with Mr. Rahimi. On her own, she mulled nonstop over the possible consequences of their conflict. What if the dean heard of her failure to maintain order in the classroom? What if he fired her? What if someone reported her to SAVAK, however trumped-up the allegations? As abhorrent as she considered politics in general and Iranian politics in particular, she needed to take the political climate into account. The English Department head, an Iranian, had chosen the Wells story. What were his motives for having the students read a story bound to be controversial here?

But almost anything the students read could incite contention.

Still, she felt sorry for Mr. Rahimi, now more than ever. Today, the other students had chastised him in public.

Unless they had attacked him only in her presence and only for her benefit.

Maybe they were on his side. How was she to know what they thought? In this country, where the shadow of SAVAK obscured everyone's vision, how was she to know who they were?

Going to the dean would escalate the tension. Mahtab, the woman Kamran had found to tutor her, had offered to help with any delicate cross-cultural situations that might arise. It would be a good idea to ask Mahtab's advice, Angela concluded.

Doug flipped off the radio, the news over. She had missed every word of it, but she often chose to ignore it. News was always entwined with politics, and here, she tangled with political issues every day. Mr. Rahimi was turning into a frequent problem at the university. And at home, she had to deal with Doug's drinking and paranoia. Was Doug hiding something that contributed to his unhappiness here? She would be a hypocrite if she blamed Doug for keeping something from her. She had her secret to bear, yet another burden weighing her down.

On his way to the spare room, Doug stopped and looked down at her. An acidic scent of lime came from the pitcher he held. "This character Rahimi's an obstinate, crazy Iranian," he said. "God knows I work with them every day."

And he left her there.

He crossed the garden, shadowless in the moonless night. He sometimes made situations so simple, reduced people to so few words. Obstinate. Crazy. What words would he use to describe her? Idealistic or practical? Conscientious or reckless? Unpredictable perhaps? How little she knew him. She used to believe people gained insight from exposure to the foreign, the unknown. Instead, it seemed their darkest quirks bubbled to the surface, side effects of isolation and the unfamiliar.

Later, she sat outside in the dark under the walnut tree. Cold. Alone.

*　*　*　*　*　*

He needed something to ease his frustration at his failure and give him relief. During the afternoon, his rage had dissipated, but a foreign female teacher shaming him in front of the class and then his classmates criticizing his behavior had made him lonelier than ever.

On his way home from the university that evening, Hossein passed a kiosk that displayed newspapers, including the *Kayhan* and the *Tehran Journal* in English, magazines, paperback books, and pirated tapes of Western music. None of these items would bring him solace. A few steps farther away, someone called his name: Ahmad.

"Look what I just bought." Ahmad flashed open his jacket to reveal what appeared to be a magazine wrapped in brown paper. "The latest *Playboy*. The guy at the kiosk saved it for me under the counter."

"Play boy?" Hossein had no idea what Ahmad meant.

Ahmad laughed at his confusion and rushed him to their room. There, Ahmad ripped the paper from the package to expose a half-nude, blond woman. Despite the model's seductive demeanor, Hossein stewed over the day's events. His plan to pretend to be pro-Shah had flopped. He should have known the students would not outwardly split into factions. They feared public exposure of their political leanings. No matter which side they supported. And that F on his paper. Why had he directed his rage against Mrs. Weston and blamed her for his deficiency in English? He had to pass her course. And he had to get names of anti-Shah students for Soleiman. Now that Mrs. Weston had defended herself with a saying attributed to the Prophet, no one would confide in him. No pro-government loyalist would whisper the name of a suspected rebellious student in his ear. He had failed on two counts. Three, if he added the F.

He dropped onto his mat. Ahmad sat next to him and leafed through the glossy pages of nearly nude, amply endowed women, then spread the magazine's centerfold on the floor next to the mat. Ahmad fixed his gaze on a redhead's breasts and traced her nipples with his forefinger. "What do you think of this one, Hossein-*jan*?"

Hossein grunted, disgusted with the way the afternoon had turned out. His father would certainly have disapproved of his looking at such photos. Besides, his thoughts kept turning back to his composition with the bright red F on the first page. He had chosen to write about the Crusades because he thought that topic allowed him to express his opinion on foreign intervention in Muslim countries. Soleiman would consider the F that he received as a signal of defeat at the hands of the infidel. Hossein grumbled that he was tired. He lay down and shut his eyes, but he could not sleep. He detested his life at the university, accompanied as it was by the pressure of his family's expectations, the requirement to learn English, his lack of friends and family, and his discomfort with foreign instructors—especially Mrs. Weston now that she had humiliated him.

Ahmad lay on his own mat, still glued to the photos of beautiful women. He must have experienced difficulties at the university, too. Hossein tapped Ahmad's shoulder, complaining about a female foreign teacher. To Hossein's surprise, Ahmad appeared curious and got up to light the cylindrical gas heater. After adding water and a few spoonfuls of loose tea to the kettle, he set it on the Aladdin's warm top. While they waited for the tea to brew, Hossein told Ahmad about his encounter with Mrs. Weston. The last time someone near his age had listened to him and commiserated with him was years ago—before his family left Tehran. Hossein blurted out that Mrs. Weston had intended to shame him in front of his classmates. He elaborated on the disdain she held for Islam. He was exaggerating, but Ahmad kept nodding his head, smiling, sympathizing with him. Encouraged, Hossein embellished the story: his American teacher embodied moral corruption. She often sang strange chants in the hall between classes. Once, she had touched Mr. Chauncey's arm on the staircase.

"What did you say her name was, *baba*?" asked Ahmad when Hossein gave him a chance to comment.

"Weston." Hossein spit out the word as if it were pork. "Missus Weston." He wiped his mouth with the tea-stained towel he had wrapped around the kettle's handle.

"She is married?"

"Yes, but what man would want her?"

"Mister Weston." Ahmad grinned, his eyes bright. "The only American who works on the technical university is named Mister Weston. He is the boss. He wants to make us work on Thursdays." Ahmad recounted his conversation with the American about overtime. "We've already figured out what to do to make him see we need more holidays. The more he wants us to work, the slower we'll work. He'll get angry. His face turns scarlet as a watermelon, and he sweats like swine when he is angry." Ahmad poured himself a glass of tea. "I've made contacts." He swallowed a sip of hot tea and sucked air in and out of his cheeks with a whistling noise. "There are four of us now." As usual, Ahmad's beady eyes wandered around the room as if walls or mats would report their conversation to the authorities. He listed the names of the collaborating workers, counting them off on his fingers.

"I'll never find anyone now that I've been disgraced by that woman," Hossein said. "I know there have to be students who want to change the government even if they aren't Islamists."

Ahmad settled his gaze on Hossein's *tar* in the corner. "Who cares?" he said. "We can deal with the students later."

"Soleiman wants names."

"Relax, *baba*. So what if we have only construction workers in our group? That gives us a start. Soleiman always says we need to start small. I can find enough supporters to get a strike going on the site. If we strike, the students will follow like sheep." He snickered. "Baa-baa-baa."

"I want Soleiman and Dariush to trust me," Hossein said, puzzled. Surely, Ahmad had noticed how irritated Soleiman had been at having no contacts at the university.

"Think of something else to do. I hear the *bazaaris* are copying tapes from Ayatollah Khomeini to distribute to the people."

Hossein mulled over what his something else would be until the time for the evening call to prayer. On his prayer rug, he laid a clay stone that represented the earth where the Shi'ite martyr Hussain was assassinated. The call floated on the evening air, no longer from a *moazzin* who had climbed winding stairs inside a minaret but from a tape the neighborhood mosque broadcast over speakers. Hossein prayed, resting his forehead on the stone each time he bowed in submission to Allah.

Ahmad sipped his second glass of tea.

Later that night, Hossein had trouble falling asleep. His mind swirled like a desert whirlwind around ways to gain full inclusion in Soleiman's group. If only he had the power to influence the entire bazaar to strike. Would the electrical workers join in? Or the oilfield workers who provided the country's lifeline? They were the key, but did they have the raw courage to defy the Shah's Army? How could the anti-Shah movement touch the armed forces, make them more vulnerable and less likely to fire on protesters or harass workers on strike?

Hossein pressed his head against his mat. He tried to remember something he had heard about foreigners. Something significant. The effort of recalling it made him dizzy, and he grew frustrated again. He had to extract this thing that lay hidden beyond the threshold of his memory. Finally, it came to him: Dariush had speculated about foreigners the night they ate *khoresht*. If foreigners left, the Army and other branches of the service would no longer work with American flight instructors or U.S. military advisors. Iranian military personnel would likely side with Iranian civilians.

How to get rid of Americans on military bases? Start small, Soleiman had advised. Ahmad had agreed. But where to start? Hossein sank into that heavy drowsiness in the No Man's Land between wakefulness and sleep before he hit upon the answer. Mrs. Weston was an unimportant English teacher, but she was an American. The only American he knew. Start small. Make Mrs. Weston so uncomfortable she and her husband would leave. Others would follow. Hossein's mind revolved around the how of this as he descended deeper into unconsciousness.

He hoped he would remember tomorrow what he had discovered tonight.

* * * * * *

It had turned into a chaotic scene in an old-time *caravanserai*, or so she imagined. A scene complete with charlatans—bartering thieves, walking cripples, stealing merchants, lusting holy men. Angela saw herself as a servant, hot and dusty, maneuvering her way through brazen intimidation, false alliances, and bogus sincerity. Mr. Rahimi alternated through all the roles, but she identified him most as the *caravanserai*'s keeper, taking advantage of everyone's thirst and exhaustion, charging more than they could or would pay, even though the student travelers sometimes tried reason, sometimes spurned negotiation.

All this in her classroom in the week since she had last seen Mahtab.

At home now, Angela closed her copy of Firdausi's *Shahnameh*, her lesson over.

"*The Book of Kings* is beautiful, isn't it? Such vibrant colors." Mahtab touched the book's cover. It portrayed a miniature from an extant manuscript of the fourteenth-century epic.

"The tiny faces hidden in rocks remind me of my students." Angela pointed to one of the grotesque faces. "Not that I think of my students as *jinn*. But they peer at me like that. They watch to see what will happen every time Mr. Rahimi comes up with another absurdity. My wits are always on trial."

"I wondered if something had happened," Mahtab said. "You seemed nervous today. Look at your thumb."

Angela made a fist to conceal hangnails on either side of her thumb. "I haven't bitten my nails since I was a child." She expounded in detail on everything from Mr. Rahimi's calling her Satan to the most recent incident, started by a reading lesson on Alexander's conquest of Persepolis. According to the author, awkwardness had plagued Alexander at the Persian court. A warrior by profession, Alexander had declined at first to adhere to the court's rigid formality. Courtiers had to school him in the Persian practice of prostrating themselves at the monarch's feet.

"The writer is laughing at Persian kings," Mr. Rahimi said. "Persian kings made the people obey them in all matters."

"If anything, the author shows how crude and barbarian Alexander and his men were," Angela said. "He tells you Greeks and Macedonians were an unrefined bunch. They sacked and burned Persepolis. They destroyed the riches of the Persian Empire." The students squelched any other remarks from Mr. Rahimi during that class period. But she believed his disruptions would never stop.

Mahtab seemed hesitant to comment and lowered her eyes—dark eyes fringed with heavy lashes. She had a mature but svelte figure. A small nose for an Iranian. Full lips slightly puckered at the corners. All the qualities prized in a classic Persian beauty, save one: her eyebrows did not extend over her nose in one continuous line. Despite her separated eyebrows, Mahtab would make a fine model for a modern-day miniaturist.

"I don't think you'll ever win him over," Mahtab said at last. "You scorned him in front of everyone. Losing face is devastating in Iran. Especially for men."

"How did I scorn him?"

"You let the others hear about his grammar mistakes, for one thing. And it sounds like you showed anger, which means he now has no respect for you."

Angela chewed her thumbnail. There was no valid rebuttal.

"But worse," Mahtab said, "when you brought up the Prophet's attitude toward teachers, you used Mr. Rahimi's religion to shame him. The other students would appear disrespectful of the Prophet if they sided with Mr. Rahimi."

"Oh, God. I was trying to say something relevant to his experience. Something that would help him understand that I respect the Prophet." Angela tore off a hangnail, and blood welled up on her thumb. "Now I've singled him out and made things worse for him. He was already alienated from the other students." From her school days, she knew well how it felt to be a despised minority of one.

Mahtab patted Angela's hand. "But, you see, it backfired a bit."

"More than just a bit."

Angela accompanied Mahtab through the garden on her way out. When she opened one of the wooden doors at the entrance, the oblong knocker rattled against the iron disk on the door's outer surface. "Oops, wrong door," Angela said. Tradition dictated that each side of the double doors have a specific knocker, one for men and one for women.

"People don't pay much attention to that anymore," Mahtab said. She knocked with the rounded piece of metal on the door's other side. "The women's knocker sounds more musical."

Angela tested the male knocker. Its sharp metallic sound clanged in contrast with the mellow tones produced by the female knocker. She and Mahtab played with the knockers, beating out a make-believe conversation. A short time later, Mahtab kissed Angela on each cheek.

"What can I do with Mr. Rahimi?" Angela said. "He's intent on harassing me." She resisted going to the dean and abandoning Mr. Rahimi to either the rigor or the whims of university administration. She owed him something better, especially now that she herself had isolated him more than ever from the other students.

Mahtab pursed her lips and let out a long breath from which issued no answer.

CHAPTER EIGHT

Going to the dean was the only solution. She had to protect herself and her professional reputation. In addition to Mr. Rahimi's threats and disruptive behavior, he was on a course to failure. If the dean put pressure on him, perhaps he would try harder or consent to a tutor.

In the front office occupied by the dean's secretary, Angela rifled through papers until she found Mr. Rahimi's quiz on James Joyce's *Araby*. How could he have failed so miserably? She had framed each question to present two options for the answer: *Was James Joyce Irish, or was he English?* Mr. Rahimi's answer: *NO!!!* Guessing, a student should score ten out of twenty, fifty percent. Mr. Rahimi answered each either-or question with yes or no, the no's in emphatic abundance. *NO!!! Yes. NO!!! NO!!! NO!!!* At the bottom of the page, his signature closing: the Arabic inscription for "In the name of God, the Compassionate, the Merciful." An ornate design in multi-colored inks enclosed the words. Mr. Rahimi had obviously spent more time on calligraphy than on the quiz itself. Was he daring her to fail him?

The door to Dr. Aminipour's office fanned open. Inside, several male Iranian faculty members seated against the far wall twirled amber prayer beads around two or three fingers. Cecil had briefed her on Iranian appointments: they were never private. She would be obliged to discuss her issues in front of these French or German instructors, most of whom understood English even if they did not speak it fluently. And, in case some did not understand, Cecil said, someone would come to the rescue with a running translation. In addition, the attendant faculty members would deem it appropriate to comment and give opinions in Persian.

The secretary ushered Angela into the dean's office. Dr. Aminipour greeted her and requested his secretary to bring tea and *gaz*. His reddish hair was atypical of Iranians, as were his gray eyes. Probably, he came from the north—the Azerbaijan region or the shores of the Caspian. From the city of Rasht? Her students told jokes about Rashtis—their big noses, their foolishness. Whether the stereotype held true, she did not know. Dr. Aminipour's nose did not overwhelm his face. His astuteness commanded respect.

She took a piece of *gaz*. If she refused, Dr. Aminipour might consider her rude. She and the dean sipped tea, letting the honeyed nougat dissolve in the hot liquid. This variety did not taste of rosewater.

"They use a gummy substance to make *gaz*," Dr. Aminipour said. She suspected he was trying to put her at ease. "It's produced when a worm chews the leaves of a desert plant. I don't remember the plant's name."

She envisioned a worm chewing an ingredient of what was now in her mouth. She chewed slower, reconsidered if she wanted to chew at all. Did the plant and its worm exist elsewhere in the Middle East? Manna in the desert?

"Please, Mrs. Weston, *befarmayid*." Dr. Aminipour's invitation for her to speak quieted the men's chatter for the moment.

Sunlight shone through the blinds at the dean's side. Light reflected off his glasses, making his eyes look white and blank, as if he had cataracts. Angela fought off an uneasy feeling. "I came to discuss the advanced first-year reading class." She shifted to one side to reduce the glare, and the dean's eyes appeared gray and healthy behind his specs. This man had hired her based on her experience with inner-city students. He told her he wanted someone with the skills required to enable less-educated villagers to succeed. Her professional pride demanded she not disappoint him. She folded her hands in her lap. Out of her mouth tumbled an avalanche of praise for her students, their attentiveness and conscientiousness, their progress and openness to the texts they read. "They've taught me more than I imagined possible, not just about what they expect from a teacher, but also about Iranian customs and Persian expressions."

"It's always good to hear our students are improving," the dean said. From the spectators behind her came mutters of assent and an outburst of clicking. The men had set their prayer beads—worry beads, Vicky called them—in motion. "It sometimes takes a while for first-year students to settle in. Freshmen, you know." Dr. Aminipour tapped his fingers on his desk. Time for her to go.

Before leaving, she congratulated him on his end-of-term appointment as guest lecturer at Oxford, his *alma mater.* "When will you be leaving us?" she asked.

"In ten days' time," he said, adding that his Canadian wife was excited about spending the holidays in England.

Back in her office, Angela cranked open the window. A thin, white line stretched across the summit of the mountain to the south. Rock striation. It snowed on the mountaintops in the winter, but rarely in Esfahan, she had heard. Only now, in late October, was the air turning cooler. Pedestrians, who in summer had taken pains to stay in the shade, now chose the sunny side of the street.

On her desk, Mr. Rahimi's failed quiz with its elegant inscription stared up at her. She had ten more days to confide in Dr. Aminipour if she wanted a resolution before the end of the fall semester. Why had she backed out of talking to the dean about Mr. Rahimi? The discomfort of an audience during a meeting with a dean? No, those instructors stayed in there discussing students for half the afternoon. She had changed her mind because she wanted to deal with Mr. Rahimi herself. She had to prove herself here, not only because she was a foreigner.

She had deeper reasons for wanting to handle professional issues herself. For years, her mother had drilled into her that she would conform to her parents' traditional Catholic way of life. Angela need not go to college. Money spent on higher education for girls was money wasted. Angela should expect to marry, have as many children as possible, and stay close to the nest her entire life. She would learn to cook and clean and take care of sick infants. Women's lib was anathema. If Angela ever so much as thought of chaining herself to the Statue of Liberty or burning her bra, she, Sofia, would denounce her own daughter. And forget any demonstrations against the Vietnam War. The Communists and the Black Panthers instigated that sort of rebellion. Freedom meant practicing the religion of your choice and voting for the public officials you wanted to serve.

There was more. She realized that if her mother had known that she had been molested, Sofia would have laid the blame squarely on her. Sofia would have believed that she had ditched Robby, who always walked with her on the way home from school. Instead, that day, Robby had insisted on staying behind to play softball on the school playground.

No wonder shame and guilt still overwhelmed her, Angela thought.

No wonder she always felt the need to prove herself.

The inscription on Mr. Rahimi's quiz blurred as she looked down at it and searched for a solution. He might have eked by in her class had he not made a zero on this quiz. She could drop each student's lowest quiz score at the end of the semester. She had thought of doing it before. She would inform the students of this policy tomorrow. It was a common practice in the States.

Outside, the sun's rays hit the mountain from a different angle. The color of the slope had deepened to a darker blue, close to indigo.

Earlier, she must have imagined that thin, white line on the mountain's craggy summit.

Angela cracked the joints between the chicken's legs and thighs and cleaved them in two with two blows. The day had not gone well. She had made a proposal to Mr. Rahimi during his midterm conference: she would find a tutor who would not charge him. No other students need know.

"I do not want your help." He tossed the back of his hand toward his shoulder and drew himself up straight in his chair, his usual defiant pose.

"You want to pass the course, don't you?"

"I will pass without you." He clenched his jaw and stared at her without budging.

"I would find a tutor for any student who is struggling. I want you all to do well."

After a few moments, the belligerence in his face faded. His lips and cheeks relaxed. His eyes softened. She had gotten through to him. But then his lips worked their way into his usual sneer. He snatched up his book bag and swaggered out the door without looking back.

Angela cracked the chicken's backbone. The garden door banged shut. Doug loped into the kitchen, waving two blue aerograms.

"Bill sounds fed up with his job." Bill, Doug's college roommate, worked as a lab supervisor at Doctor's Hospital on Staten Island. "He's going to apply to med school." Angela pictured Bill in a doctor's white coat with ink-stained pockets, his wire-rims too far down on his nose, his stethoscope dangling lopsided across his chest.

Doug laid Bill's letter on the table for Angela to read later and offered her one from her mother. She busied herself browning the chicken.

"I'll open it after dinner." Her mother always said something offensive or irritating. Better to read the letter in private. Especially after the day's events.

"Can I read it if you're too busy?" Doug tore open the aerogram without waiting for her reply.

She pressed her lips together, bracing herself. Doug would feel compelled to discuss Sofia's news. She would have no chance to mull it over alone.

Doug scanned the aerogram. "You better read this." He flopped it in front of her face, forcing her to dry her hands and take it. Angela ran her eyes down the page. Sofia had attempted to interfere in her life yet again. Angela tossed the letter on the counter without a comment, retrieved a head of lettuce from the refrigerator, and ripped up the leaves for a salad. Water from the lettuce smeared some of her mother's words.

"You've Rocaled that lettuce?" Doug asked.

"I always do." She hated cleansing fruit and vegetables with chemicals like other foreigners did, but Doug claimed farmers threw animal waste directly on produce to fertilize it.

Doug moved the letter to the table, out of the water. "This could be serious. You should go home for a while when the semester ends. Personally, I'd love to, but I can't."

"I wouldn't leave you here alone." She buried her fingers in his hair and brushed it away from his forehead. She would trim it for him tonight. "And I couldn't bear to stay at my parents' house for long without you." Doug enjoyed the good-natured bickering and constant uproar in her parents' household more than she did. Yet, he had always supported her struggle to liberate herself from the limits her family imposed on her. But Doug had not been with her the day she broke the news about his new job in Iran to her mother.

"You're going where?" Sofia's voice rose and hit the high notes of a soprano singing "*Addio del passato*." "You're going where?" Sofia's hands flew up, palms turned toward her face. "*Cielo*, what did I do to deserve this daughter? Tony, did you hear that? She's going to live with the A-rabs." Angela's father sank farther into the couch and held his newspaper higher over his face.

"They're not Arabs, Mamma. They're Aryans."

"*Dio Mio.* Tony, they're going to live with Nazis."

"We have Nazis in the States, Sofie. It's a free country," her father said, his voice matter-of-fact behind the *Evening Star.*

"We should never have let you go to college. Then you go to Detroit to teach. The only thing they have in Detroit except slums and race riots is the Ford Motor Company."

"You forgot the Detroit Tigers." Tony folded the newspaper in his lap.

"Mamma. Not Detroit again," Angela said.

"You had to go live in Detroit. And drive a Toyota. Why can't you settle down? Here in Cleveland. Down the block. The Coltanos have put their little ranch up for sale. Have a coupla kids before you're too old."

"Mamma, for God's sake, I'm only twenty-eight. We're going to Iran for Doug's job." Angela flopped on the free end of the couch and hit her forehead with flattened palms. No imploring the heavens for her. "I *want* to go to Iran." If Doug had been there, he would have slowed the tempo and chimed in with a reasoned explanation, a less strident tone.

"What American would want to live with foreigners who don't speak English? They don't even write American. How you gonna read the signs? Tell me, how you gonna communicate? How you gonna survive, Angela? How you gonna survive?" Sofia shook her hands in front of Angela's nose. Angela jumped up and headed for the door, scents of garlic and oregano lingering in her nostrils.

"What you want me to do, Mamma?" Her voice echoed Sofia's *fortissimo.* "Settle down in Iran? Have a hundred babies there? Never come back?" She flung open the screen door and shouted over her shoulder. "Not even to live in Detroit?"

Before Angela got out of the house, Tony leapt to his feet and put his arms around the sobbing Sofia. "Have a good time, honey," he said to Angela, freeing a hand from Sofia's back long enough to wave. "Have a good life." And, "Sofie, Sofie, it's time for dinner."

Angela had taken Doug with her to say goodbye the day before they left. Thankfully, Sofia had kept her dramatic outbursts to a minimum. She had merely wiped her eyes the entire two hours they were there and reminded them that, by the time they returned, she would be in her grave. Doug had assured her she would not.

Doug's eyes were still fixed on Sofia's aerogram. Angela squeezed his arm and turned back to the stove. "My mother's not that sick. She enjoys guilt-tripping me. You know that. It's not the first time." It had started before she left for college. Then, Sofia had tried similar tactics, supposedly having been diagnosed with heart failure and ovarian cancer one year, a blocked bowel the next, and melanoma during Angela's senior year. Now, her mother reported a mysterious kidney disease that doctors could not quite figure out. Angela lifted the top of the frying pan and checked the chicken. "It isn't enough to read between the lines. You have to break the code." She raised her voice over pops and crackles from the frying pan. "She wants us to come home, obviously. But check out that last paragraph."

While Angela mixed a salad dressing, Doug read Sofia's words out loud. "'If you can't come back soon, my hope can reside only in somehow seeing you again. At least for now, my condition seems stable, but who knows when things may suddenly turn for the worse? The way I feel that may well be the case before too many weeks pass.'" He blew on the wet letter. "And?"

"And, she wants us to send her a ticket to come visit." No need for a second reading to decipher the intent.

"That's not such a bad idea. She can see for herself we don't live in a smelly tent in the desert and ride camels among a tribe of A-rabs, as she calls them. Maybe she'd feel better about our being here."

Angela plunked the salad bowl down on the table. A piece

of onion popped up and fell to the table's surface. Doug had not yet figured out Sofia's code. "My mother always takes the direst view of any situation. If she came here, she would drive me crazy. She would think Rocale would give us cancer. No, she would say we already have cancer, but no doctor here could diagnose it. She would say breathing in stench from *jubs* pollutes our lungs. She would say all Iranians are anti-American and we'll end up in an Iranian jail. Never mind that thousands of Americans live and work here. She would stay awake at night because our house would definitely cave in during an earthquake, which would definitely occur while she's here. And God knows the mission in life of every *bazaari* would be to cheat her out of her money."

"She might have a point." Doug looked as if he were trying hard to suppress a smile.

Angela pulled out her chair, and its legs screeched against the tiled floor. She must seem ungrateful in Doug's eyes. "I'm warning you. My sanity will be in question if Sofia comes." Doug's mother had died when he was only five. Another dose of guilt.

Doug chewed his first bite as nonchalantly as a grazing sheep. She had lost her appetite. She got up from the table, her legs wobbly, her stomach churning.

"You need to learn not to let your mother get to you so much," Doug said. "If I try my best to mitigate your stress, would you agree to my buying her an airline ticket?"

"Mitigate my stress? You make it sound like I'm a crossbeam." She shook her head. "You'll be at work. I'll be at the university. What would she do here alone? She'd be afraid. I know she would."

"But what if she is sick this time? You're her only daughter."

"I have a father and four brothers there." As if her mother had not already caused her enough trouble, now Sofia had precipitated this disagreement with Doug.

"Call your mother, Angela. Find out if she is sick."

Angela opened her mouth but shut it before she spoke,

quelling any angry reply. It was not Doug's place to interfere in her relationships with her family. Still, he was her husband. She would compromise. "I'll call Robby on Saturday when he's not at work. He's the most level-headed. Dad can't talk with Sofia always hovering over him." Robby was Doug's favorite person in her family. If, by some unlikely turn of fate, her mother were ill, Robby would know what she should do. A lump rose in her throat, and she fought back tears. What if her mother were in a hospital undergoing CTs and MRIs with a chalky, pink drink in her stomach and dye in her veins? Perhaps they had catheterized her. Or put her on dialysis. Or hooked her up to IVs with bed and vomit pans handy and monitors beeping away and neon green lines jumping up and down in the dark.

Between them, her mother's soggy aerogram lay on the table. Angela picked it up. Blurry streaks of ink ran down and across the page like the wild imaginings of a diseased mind. She needed to stop frightening herself and concentrate on the actual problem at hand—Mr. Rahimi. He seemed to think she was some foreign monster intent on giving him the evil eye.

She had to figure out a way to make him believe she was his ally.

* * * * * *

He had dreaded this dinner—Iranian food in a typical Iranian restaurant with an Iranian couple—but he had promised himself to make the best of it for Angela's sake. She needed a night out. She had fretted about that unruly student and her mother's letter all week. "Mahtab. That's a pretty name," Doug said after Angela introduced him to Mahtab and her husband, Hamid. "Does it have a special meaning?"

"It means moonlight, a fitting tribute to my wife." Hamid gazed at Mahtab, who wore a silk blouse of shimmering silver. "To me, moonlight shines with an iridescent glow. It blurs edges and dissolves the sharpness of shadows." Hamid looked at the table-cloth and rolled the handle of his fork between his palms, seemingly embarrassed after making such a disclosure to strangers.

Mahtab blushed. "I always tell Hamid he should write poetry. Instead, he immerses himself in architecture."

"Poetry couldn't pay any less." Hamid directed his comment toward Doug.

"But you like the work?" Doug asked, wondering if Hamid hailed from a city on the Persian Gulf. Ahwaz or perhaps Abadan. Hamid had kinky hair.

"Unfortunately, I took a job with a rich *bazaari* who wanted what he called a splendid home," Hamid said. "In other words, an opportunity to flaunt his wealth. We had argument after argument until, finally, I gave in to most of his demands. What we designed was ugly. Nasty as a two-humped Bactrian camel. Working on that disaster prevented me from applying for the technical university project. The idiot with the grandiose house won't recommend me to his friends. Not that I'd want another project like his." Hamid shook his head. His hands fell on the table. "Now I'm out of a job with not much on the horizon."

"I'm here to help implement the university's design," Doug said. "Not my specialty, but the experience couldn't hurt."

"I'd take it at your salary."

Doug squirmed in his chair. He had become less and less sure of his survival on the job. The workers protested about everything—their hours, heavy lifting, too few tea breaks. Did Hamid expect a job offer? Obviously, he was jealous, resentful of an American taking a position he had wanted. The conversation tapered off into an uneasy silence interrupted only when the waiter returned with plates of rice sprinkled with turmeric and topped with lamb kabobs. He presented a raw egg yolk nestled in a half-shell to Doug and dumped the yolk on his rice with a flourish.

"You're supposed to stir the yolk in the rice. It's hot enough to cook the egg," Mahtab said. "Some people add butter."

Doug mixed a slab of butter into his rice, grateful for the distraction. Angela had described Mahtab's diplomatic ability, saying she could smooth over prickly situations. Moonlight.

A group of Iranian diners passed the table on their way out, leaving only the four of them in that section of the restaurant. Hamid broached the subject that splashed on front pages and headlined BBC broadcasts. A fire had destroyed the Cinema Rex in Abadan on a Friday, the day families attended. Trapped inside were over four hundred men, women, and children, most burned beyond recognition. "They say someone locked the exits. On purpose," Hamid said.

"My sister's husband is from Abadan." Mahtab's eyes were moist with emotion. "He had family who died. My sister heard more than eight hundred may have been killed."

"I've heard conflicting rumors about what happened." Hamid stopped stirring his rice. "I think it was—you know, the big S. So do most people. Naturally, the government claims the Islamic movement is responsible."

Doug glanced at the busboy clearing the recently vacated table. Hamid had just referenced SAVAK. Did the busboy understand English? "The government's explanation seems more plausible." Doug kept his voice down. "Why would the big S want to get involved? Why would they kill their own people? Innocent people. It doesn't make sense."

Hamid dropped his spoon, and it clanged against his plate. "Of course, it makes sense. Here are the scenarios: One, S did it to put the fear of the devil in anyone thinking of revolution—and rumors about revolution abound right now." He counted the possibilities on manicured fingers. "Two, the Islamic movement did it to blame S and the government and thus glean support for their cause. Three, S did it so the government can blame the Islamic movement, and four, a third party—say the Marxists—did it so some people will blame the government and others will blame the Islamists, and when people are sufficiently divided against each other, this third group will prevail."

Doug pretended to wipe his lips with his napkin, hoping to disguise his disbelief. On the wall between panels of mosaic mirrors, murals displayed Scheherazade with scenes from her thousand and one tales. Not one of those tales could have been as fabulous as the contorted reasoning Hamid had just put forth.

The others seemed absorbed in their dinner. In the restaurant's center, water splashed in a turquoise-tiled fountain. Canaries twittered in cages hanging above the Scheherazade frescoes. Echoes of Middle Eastern luxury designed to soothe the spirit, Doug assumed. But tranquility escaped him. More than ever, he considered himself a straightforward, simple, honest American. How could Iranians live with such Byzantine speculations, perverse behaviors, and destructive games? In this country, truth would never out. One thing seemed evident: events like the fire that augmented distrust and division would strengthen the existing power. Temporarily, at least. Despots hungry for wealth and power loved fomenting chaos.

The two women resumed chatting. Small talk. Neither man joined in. On the wall in front of him, the mosaic mirrors shattered Doug's reflection into a myriad of tiny faces. He, too, had heard worrisome rumbles about subversive activity. Were workers like Ahmad and his cohorts involved? Ahmad barraged him with questions daily—mostly irrelevant ones—to waste his time and try his patience.

From across the table, Hamid was studying his face much the way Ahmad did. Was Hamid waiting for him to break? To say something that would get him booted out of the country? It would be to Hamid's advantage if he were fired. What if Hamid were conspiring with Ahmad? Or with Mahmud? If Hamid's thoughts were as twisted as his explanation of the fire, Hamid could conjure up any scheme to get the position he wanted on the site.

Mahtab and Angela were bent over a photo of Mahtab's children, which she had produced from the depths of her purse. Doug expected Hamid to ask why he had no children, but Hamid remained sullen and quiet. Arguing with him might jeopardize Angela's friendship with Mahtab.

Doug caught Hamid's eye. "About the fire—whatever you say," he said, convinced whatever Hamid said was suspect and threatening.

Later, the two couples said goodbye in front of the restaurant. Above, the moon brushed a few passing clouds in the eastern sky with silver. Angela pointed upward. "Moonlight does give the world a magical aura."

"It'll take more than magic to keep this country from self-destruction," Hamid said, no longer poetic. His somber mood had not lightened after the talk of the fire.

As Doug and Angela strolled down Chahar Bagh toward home, moonlight threw shadows of plane trees across the sidewalk. The two of them drifted along, separated by silence, like political factions entrenched in secret strategies to shield their vulnerabilities. Doug slid his hands in his pockets, out of the chilly air. How long would he survive in his job if the country grew more unstable? How could he placate workers who considered the American presence an extension of the Shah's corruption? He had little faith in the diplomatic channels manipulated by the Carter Administration.

Angela wrapped her scarf around her neck. "Do you think revolutionaries started that fire in Abadan?"

"I don't think there is any way to know the truth here." His own voice seemed as hollow as if he were speaking in a vacuum, solitary, unheard. How could he answer? What should the government do? And which government? The Iranian regime? Its American ally? The revolution would come—when, he could not predict. Regardless of political unrest, he intended to hold out until he earned his bonus—even if that meant sending Angela home alone.

A stench invaded his nostrils, dispelling the freshness of

the silvery atmosphere. *Jubs* and their contents were like governments. Moonlight could no more subjugate the inevitable than could the harsher light of logic.

CHAPTER NINE

She had waited all afternoon in the post office for a phone connection to the States. Finally, the attendant yelled, "*Amrika*," and pointed to booth four. Angela hurried across the vestibule and slammed the booth's door shut behind her. "Hello. Robby. Robby," she said into the grimy receiver.

Robby's voice drawled sleepily on the other end. "It's five o'clock in the morning, Angela." A pause. "Nothing's wrong, is it?" He shouted as if he were trying to bridge the ten-thousand-mile distance between them.

His familiar voice affected her more than she had anticipated. If only Robby were here. He had always supported her attempts to break away from the family trademarks. When she had burned her scapula on the eve of her first Holy Communion, Robby had buried the ashes. She was only seven. The scapula was only a silk string. It could not protect her against evil. Besides, the paper pictures of the Blessed Virgin and St. Teresa of the Little Flowers hanging from the scapula over her breastbone and between her shoulder blades made her itch under the stiff organza of her communion dress. Years later, Robby had covered for her when she came in after curfew; later still, he had sided with her when she wanted to go to the university. Robby was the first in the family to accept Doug with his Swedish heritage. Yet, Robby himself was no rebel. He relished his status as first-born son. He still lived in his parents' basement.

The heat inside the phone booth was sweltering, and she cracked the door open. To reassure Robby, she outlined daily life in Esfahan—Doug's work, her classes, their home and garden. How easy it would be to fall back into the patterns from her childhood and confide in Robby about her struggles with Mr. Rahimi. "Robby, there is one thing wrong."

"Shoot, Bitty Bird," Robby said.

Her mouth fell open like the gaping beak of the bird he had just invoked. It had been years since he had called her the ridiculous pet name.

"What is it? What's wrong?"

"Nothing." His use of her childhood nickname was no more absurd than her obsession with a testy student. She needed to solve her own problems. "Can you hear me? Nothing at all. You must have misunderstood something I said. There's a lot of static."

"Weird. I hear you perfectly well."

Angela fanned herself with an envelope someone had left on the ledge under the phone. She asked Robby about their mother's health.

"Mamma's not sick, Angela. Nothing wrong with the kidneys. A little anemic, the doctor said. So now she feeds us liver three times a week. She misses you. She heard something on the news about a fire in a movie theater."

"And expected a call any minute from the Red Cross saying we had burned to death. Abadan is hundreds of miles from here."

"That's what we told her. You know how she is. She needs to see for herself."

Angela bumped the receiver against the wall a few times. How exasperating. Robby, too, supported the idea of Sofia coming for a visit. "Hear that, Robby? I'm running out of money." Mission accomplished. She could hang up now.

On the sidewalk outside of the post office, Angela brushed past a row of makeshift desks where scribes wrote letters for the illiterate. She wove homeward through crowded evening streets, fighting guilt about making an excuse to hang up on Robby. His assessment of Sofia's health did bring down the curtain on Doug's idea of her returning to the States at semester break. A more satisfying trip waited in the wings: Kamran had invited her and Doug to visit Persepolis with him during the holiday for the Shah's birthday.

Cecil approved Kamran's invitation. Going to Tehran for the three-day weekend as she and Doug had proposed would frustrate them, Cecil said. People from the countryside would pack the streets, bused by the government into the city to attend a birthday celebration in the stadium. The previous year, employees of government-controlled industries had mounted shows of support for the monarchy. According to Cecil, Peykan, the Iranian automobile manufacturer, stole the show. Its employees assembled a car on the stadium's field in minutes and drove it away to thunderous applause. Ever cynical, Cecil speculated on how short a distance outside of the gates the Peykan had traveled before it disintegrated into a heap of scrap metal.

"I bet Peykans are as flimsy as children's plastic Model Ts stuck together with glue," Cecil said, playing to his audience of two—Kamran and Angela.

Sometimes, even Cecil flaunted expatriate arrogance.

*   *   *   *   *   *

His sense of time must be distorted. Doug had arrived home an hour ago, but it seemed he had already waited three for Angela. He downed his third vodka lime. Where was she anyway? Did she get delayed by Kamran? Impossible to know the secret places in Esfahan to which Kamran might lure Angela. Kamran, though, would know of a hidden room behind some cousin's sweet shop, above a friend's jewelry store, or adjacent to a fellow SAVAK agent's garden. Doug poured himself two shots of vodka to drink straight and opted for the sweet shop. Kamran had a penchant for those awful cookies made with lamb fat.

Someone unlatched the garden door. Finally. It was Angela, and she was alone.

"Robby sends his greetings." She tossed her book bag on a garden chair. "Sofia's fine. Busy stinking up the neighborhood with liver and onions. Regardless of the outside temperature, she always insists on opening the windows when she cooks liver."

Doug raised his eyebrows. "A little respect for your mamma."

"You look tired." She curled up on one of the wicker chairs.

"The sign of a defeated man." He was tired. He had paced the floor every night this week while the two of them brainstormed how he could motivate the construction workers. "Every time I make an announcement to the workers, Mahmud twists the truth. He took credit for my reinstatement of the Thursday holiday—or so I hear from my friend, Ahmad."

"Ahmad? I thought he was the trouble-maker."

"He is. As usual, I'm not sure what the truth is. Ahmad is probably right, though. I know Mahmud."

"But you aren't sure."

"Hell no, I'm not sure. When can anyone be sure of anything here? Everything's painted in ten shades of gray, each one depending on ten different ways light shines on it. Like Scheherazade—a different story every night."

"You need to get away." She took his hand. "We should reconsider our weekend in Tehran. A lot of people will go there for the birthday-do. Crowds. Traffic. Pollution." Angela sniffed his vodka and turned up her nose, then told him of Kamran's proposal for a trip to Persepolis.

"I can't go." Angela and Kamran were plotting behind his back again.

"You have the Shah's birthday off. We could go for one day."

"Not feasible."

"Not feasssssible?" The word hissed from her lips, a cat's claim for territory.

"You heard me—although I didn't pronounssssse it like

that. I want to work on my portfolio." He stood and started toward the living room, where he had left the vodka bottle.

She followed him. "You said more than once that you want to visit the Achaemenid ruins. You said you wanted to sketch columns and pedestals and griffins. To get ideas for the very portfolio you're using as an excuse for not going."

Doug removed his shoes to avoid tracking dirt over the new carpet before entering the living room. The expensive Esfahani carpet that Kamran had helped them purchase for Angela's birthday. It was Angela's idea to meet Kamran in the bazaar that day. Kamran was used to bargaining, she said. The whole scene in the bazaar nauseated Doug, starting with his allergic reaction to the dusty rugs the carpet dealer plopped on the floor for Angela to see. The bouquet of roses Kamran brought for Angela's birthday infuriated him. While Kamran and Angela examined the backs of the carpets to figure out the number of knots per square inch, Doug ended up holding the roses. While Kamran and Angela passed their hands over the carpets' pile, the roses exacerbated Doug's hay fever. Their thorns pricked his fingers.

"I don't want Kamran intruding on our exploration of Persepolis." Doug finished his drink.

"He's being hospitable."

"He's following us around."

Angela bent and traced the silk outlining a blue flower on the carpet. Since they had bought the carpet, Angela had made that same gesture each time she entered the room. "I love this carpet," she said.

"It is beautiful, but I'm angry that Kamran spoiled the surprise." When Angela could not choose between the Esfahani and a tribal carpet, Doug had taken Kamran aside and asked him to bargain for the Esfahani. He himself would distract Angela in the bazaar. When Kamran caught up with them later, panting under the weight of a carpet wrapped in brown paper, he had wasted no time before exposing which carpet was in the package. "I knew you preferred this carpet but were afraid it would be too expensive. I wanted to surprise you. I told Kamran not to let you know which carpet he bought."

"I doubt that he meant to spoil the surprise. Besides, he got a good price for the carpet. Better than you could have."

Heat spread over Doug's cheeks and forehead. He clenched his teeth, and the muscle at the juncture of his jaw bones pulsated. He could not speak, fearful that incriminating words would escape into the charged space between them. His own wife doubted him. It probably did not stop at that.

Angela's face turned red. "Doug, I only meant that, naturally, an Iranian can get a better price than we can. They're born bargaining. I didn't mean what I said the way you took it."

"You don't know how I took it." His words thundered off the opposite wall. "How did I take it, Angela?"

"You seem upset. You are upset."

"How did I take it?" His voice exploded.

"I don't know." Her voice wavered. "Let's drop it. I'm sorry I upset you."

"How did I take it? How? How?" He kept repeating the word like a warped record, forever flawed. He shot toward her, bumping the side table with his leg. An antique wood block, once used to stamp images of polo players on Esfahani cloth, crashed onto the floor, startling her and quieting him. He stooped to pick it up. "I don't want to spend my day off in Kamran's tow—Persepolis or not. We can stay home." He topped off his glass with vodka and headed toward his workroom. "I'm tired of competing with Kamran."

*　*　*　*　*　*

She had never felt afraid of Doug before. When he had rushed toward her in the enclosed space, memories of the gang of boys closing in on her reared up before her. Her heart pounded so hard she thought it would burst. Her limbs shook. Angela collapsed onto the *takht* in the bedroom. She needed to calm herself before Doug returned from his workroom in search of dinner.

That Doug felt jealous of Kamran was absurd. But Doug did not know about her inexperience with men. She did not go out with boys during high school, thanks to the blond boys in the empty lot. In college, she realized that the thought of being alone with a male terrified her, and she went to therapy for two years before she tried dating. Later, Doug's gentleness gained her trust. He was the only man who ever accomplished that feat. What had happened to him? His drinking and crying out in his sleep, his jealousy of Kamran and hostility toward Mahmud, his suspicion of Hamid—all inexplicable. Telling him what had happened to her should alleviate his jealousy, but only when he was sober. And what about the rest? Some of Doug's behavior must reflect culture shock—the stress of isolation in a strange environment. He knew no American males here except Cecil, whom he rarely saw. She could ask Cecil to go to Persepolis. Make it a foursome. Doug would not be jealous or resentful of Cecil. He liked Cecil.

Less shaky now, she went to the kitchen to prepare dinner. A bottle of vermouth sat on the counter. Half empty. Doug must have had the equivalent of four martinis before she came home. Expensive martinis, too. Unlike domestic vodka produced near the Caspian Sea, foreign vodka went for a hefty price due to Iranian import taxes on liquor. Doug preferred Russian vodka for martinis. Italian vermouth was the sole choice here.

Angela was still contemplating the bottle when she heard Doug open the living room door. She looked in and caught him staggering across the carpet. He stumbled and nearly fell over the coffee table on his way to the couch, in worse shape than she had seen him since their arrival in Iran. In the States, only on special occasions—her twenty-first birthday, his nephew's christening—had he indulged to the point of showing his liquor, but not much.

"I've had it with everyone challenging my manhood." He slurred over the L's.

"No one is doing that, honey." She scooted close to him on

the couch. He needed reassurance, a little coddling, she thought. She needed to get him sobered up.

"They do ev'ry day." Doug slopped his drink on the coffee table, and she jumped up to get a dish towel.

By the time she returned from the kitchen, he had slumped into the paisley pillows strewn on their drab couch, his glass empty. Angela wiped up the spilled liquid.

She stroked his shoulder and cheek. "You feel feverish," she said. "I'll get the thermometer."

Doug's red-rimmed eyes rolled in their sockets. He grabbed her forearm, preventing her from rising. "I am not sick. I am a healthy American male." His breath stank of alcohol. She drew back. "Why are you avoiding me?" he asked.

"I'm not, Doug. I'll bring you some soup if you feel like eating."

"I don't need soup. I'm strong. A healthy American male." He picked up his glass and extended it toward her as if he expected her to tend bar for him.

Angela took the glass with no intention of filling it. What had caused him to question his virility this way?

"Let's make a baby," he said and pulled her closer, pawing at her skirt.

She pushed him away. "Remember, we agreed to wait. Besides, we know nothing about the quality of gynecological care here." She needed more time, too. Three of her college friends had started families. They spoke of constant squabbles with their mothers about child-rearing. If Angela were to have a child, Sofia would insist on coming to Iran. She would rattle off a plethora of maternal must-dos: Bottle-feed from birth. Start cereal at six weeks. Potty-train by fourteen months. Not what new parents would need on top of adjusting to a new culture.

Angela touched Doug's forehead. "No, you don't feel that hot. My hand must have been cold earlier."

Bleary-eyed, Doug rambled on about his strength and

vigor, his desire to father a child. He boasted he would show "them" how robust he was. He caught her arm again, his grip an ever-tightening vise.

"You are strong," she said. "You're hurting my arm. Let me go brew some tea."

"No tea. They drink tea all day at the site. All day, they stand around drinking tea." He did relax his grip, and she managed to escape across the room. Doug rose and supported himself, wobbling, on the arm of the couch. "They hate us," he said. "All of them. They hate us *harams* or whatever the word is."

"*Harams*? You mean *kharejis*. Foreigners."

"You didn't think I knew that word, did you? They say it all the time."

"You always point out we're foreigners. So what if they do, too?"

"Your friend, Kamran. He hates us. He wants to get rid of us."

"Why would you think such a thing?" Mr. Rahimi had demanded that she leave, but he was a confused university freshman trying to make his way in a class in which he did not belong.

"I bet Kamran is the one ..." Doug let go of the couch and teetered toward her. He veered to the left and ran into a side table. Angela lunged forward to steady the lamp. "Kamran," Doug said again. "He is re'pon'ble, I bet."

"Responsible for what, Doug?" She steadied him as he lowered himself to the couch.

"Against us *haramis*. Like the rest of them."

"Kamran and whoever the rest of them are do not plot against us. That's absurd." She refused to give in to Doug's paranoia.

Doug stretched out on the couch with his eyes closed, and she left the room. In the kitchen, she scrambled eggs and piled unleavened bread on a plate, hoping the combination would absorb some of the alcohol in Doug's system. He scoffed down the food like a man who had wandered in the desert for weeks.

Surely, with food in his stomach, he would cease spouting off delusional allegations and bigoted slurs.

"The room is spinning." He pushed away the glass of water she offered him.

Angela rushed to the kitchen and found a plastic bowl. She thrust it under Doug's chin. He waved it away and crouched over, his head in his hands. She set the bowl next to his feet and backed away.

After a few minutes, Doug raised his head. "Better," he said with a half-smile. "I'll sit here a while and then go to bed."

"Do you want me to turn on the TV? Some music?" She shuffled through the classical tapes they had brought from the States. "Brandenburg Concertos?"

"Forget Bach. My head is way too heavy."

She searched the tapes for something lighter, more lyrical. She was opening a cassette of Rubenstein playing Chopin's nocturnes when Doug lumbered up behind her, his breath hot on her neck. Startled, she dropped the tape and whipped around.

"Kamran is the one," Doug said. His eyes sparkled with unrevealed accusations. "Kamran is egging them all on."

Angela backed away from him until her head hit the wall behind her. Anything she said would spur Doug on and give him an excuse to build some perverse case against Kamran.

"Kamran is behind Rahimi's revenge. I'm sure of it," Doug said. Oddly, he seemed sober now and in control of his faculties, if not his absurdities.

"If anything, Kamran would be embarrassed a student would behave like Mr. Rahimi." She had never disclosed Mr. Rahimi's provocations to Kamran.

"Kamran is playing both sides. Don't you see? It's as Byzantine as Hamid's speculations about the Abadan fire. If we've got to live here, we have to think and act like Iranians. They don't trust anyone. We can't trust anyone."

Doug looked as earnest as a choir boy—as innocent. She should have seen this coming. The past few nights, he had screamed out in his sleep and mumbled about betrayal and revenge and hidden enemies. Last night, he rained blow after blow on his pillow, his fingers closed in a hard fist, his T-shirt drenched in sweat. She flipped on the light and called his name and listened as he muttered unintelligible phrases. Something about tea, she thought. And next, "He's not here."

"I'm here, Doug," she told him. She ran her fingers through his hair and across his flushed cheeks until he fell asleep. Could he have had mild sunstroke at this time of year?

Now, though, he was paler than usual.

"Don't trust Kamran, Angela," he said. "Don't believe a thing he says. Promise me you won't. I have to protect you. You can't protect yourself against him. Kamran is a traitor."

"I'm not a child. I can protect myself. I do have some discretion." His desire to protect her from imagined traitors wore thin on her nerves. "I understand Persian. I hear things you don't. I can appreciate the way the language informs the culture."

"You're right. There are informants. Everywhere. Informants. All they do is rat on each other. Kamran may be a SAVAK agent." Doug pointed at her and waved his finger as if scolding her. "Kamran and Rahimi. Plot together. A perfect duo. Black and white make gray." Doug stammered more jumbled words, disjointed phrases. His eyelids closed, opened, closed again. A giant, overwrought toddler, he battled against the bedtime hour, repeating fantasies to himself.

Angela got him back to the couch, and he lay down. When his breathing became heavy and regular, she tiptoed toward the bedroom and opened the door. A wail, desperate and infantile, echoed through the house.

"Wait," Doug yelled and started in again about Kamran.

"I'm not listening to this anymore, Doug." She interrupted him, aware of how much she sounded like Sofia. "Not one more word. I've heard more than enough about Kamran. I'm going to Persepolis for one day with him even if you don't." She was the one who had to get away if Doug continued to act like this.

Doug rose, mouth open, arm extended toward her.

Angela rushed into the bedroom and locked the door behind her.

From the adjoining room came a solitary question: "When are you going to talk to the dean about Rahimi?"

Angela pretended she did not hear.

PART II

I am Dariush, the great King, the King of Kings,
The King of many countries and many peoples
The King of this expansive land, the son of Wishtasp Acamenes
Persian, the son of a Persian, Aryan, from the Aryan race

- Epitaph engraved on the rock façade where Dariush's tomb
is cut into a cliff at Naghsh-e Rostam -

CHAPTER TEN

The bus rounded a corner, and its taillights disappeared, leaving Doug in a dark mood as dusk swallowed the evening sky. By the time he reached the Meidan-e Shah, shadows had hidden its splendors. A solitary light shone from Bahram's workshop near the vague mass of the Sheikh Lotfallah Mosque on the square's east side. He had not met Bahram, had only heard of the man's miniatures from Angela, but the lone light lured him into its embrace. Inside the shop's open doorway, an elderly man crouched over a worktable, his straggly, white beard brushing against his chest. According to rumors, Bahram, a known opium addict, was losing his eyesight.

"Agha-ye Bahram?" Doug felt awkward about disturbing the artist, but he could not bring himself to return to his empty house.

The man raised his head and beckoned him to enter.

Doug flipped his billfold open to a photograph of Angela. "*Khanoum,*" he said and pointed to himself.

Bahram drew the photo under his worktable lamp and studied it. "Ah, *khanoum-e shoma,*" he said. "Missus Weston. Mister Weston?" he asked, and Doug nodded.

While Bahram prepared tea in the back room, Doug browsed through the shop. A scent of paint, as delicate as silk draped over a woman's body, floated in the air. Bahram's work was exquisite, not at all like the crude—and cheap—miniatures of polo players or court scenes on display in the main bazaar. After tea, Bahram disappeared again, this time returning with a miniature bigger than most, about six inches tall by three inches wide. Blue velvet matting surrounded it; an inlaid frame encased it.

"Like, Mister, yes? Today, you take home."

Doug stepped closer to see the painting in better light. Anything to avoid going home, to enjoy Bahram's hospitality a while longer despite his efforts to make a sale. In the miniature, a woman gazed into an oval hand mirror. Her nipples appeared through sheer fabric covering her breasts. Just below her waist, her belly protruded slightly as if she were three or four months pregnant.

Soft purring came from the corner of the shop where Bahram was stroking a tabby cat. He ran his fingers along the cat's mustache, pretended to clip a hair, and mimed painting. Doug tilted his head in acknowledgment. Bahram must use cats' whiskers to craft miniature details on ivory.

Doug examined the miniature again, this time with Bahram's magnifying glass, lingering over every strand of hair, every eyelash, the pucker at the corners of the voluptuous lips, the embroidery in the folds of the robe. The work's perfection exceeded anything imaginable. It was an act of sacrilege to look at it or to breathe in the presence of its creator. He laid the magnifying glass on the worktable and backed away, his eyes glued to the three-quarter profile reflected in the woman's mirror.

"It is so beautiful it must be forbidden," he said, hoping Bahram could understand his emotional response, if not his English. "Does the power of your own creations ever amaze you?" Bahram took his hand and, holding it, lowered his eyes.

"How much is it?" Doug could not believe he had asked.

When Bahram pronounced the sum of five thousand tomans, Doug sighed. The asking price amounted to roughly eight hundred dollars.

"How much you want pay?" Bahram said, initiating the

insane bargaining that ended in his wrapping the miniature in brown paper, tying string around it, and placing it in both of Doug's hands with both of his.

Doug left the shop, numb. The miniature had cost as much as the savings he put away each month, but he had to have it.

It looked so much like Angela.

*   *   *   *   *   *

Zoroastrians venerated the sun. On this high, sun-soaked plateau, Dariush and Xerxes paid homage to their god, Ahura Mazda, over two millennia ago. Angela shaded her eyes. The bright morning cast gold over a mammoth stone horse head lying broken in the dust, its nostrils wedged in the earth. A short distance away, Kamran gazed at desert hawks soaring across an endless sky, his skin the same hue as the surrounding stone, his face timeless and noble, and his bearing as iconic as a statue that had survived for centuries while Persian dynasties had come and gone.

When he stirred and looked back at her, the spell dissipated like afternoon shadows at dusk. "The Achaemenids believed in the divine nature of fire." He described practices formerly observed by the Persian Empire on the solar New Year. "We still celebrate Nawruz on March twentieth at the exact hour and minute of the first day of our year." Angela tried to concentrate on his explanation. If only he would stop speaking and would become still and statuesque again.

She busied herself snapping photos of curly-bearded tribute-bearers carved on the side of the razed palace's staircase. She coaxed Kamran to pose for a picture on a pedestal that had once supported a pillar. Her camera would never capture Kamran as she had seen him earlier. Such glimpses of eternity are granted with sparing generosity—and never repeated.

He leapt off the pedestal and took her camera.

She climbed up and struck a silly pose, flinging one arm toward the sky and the other toward the earth, her fingers splayed outward. "I'm a dancing girl," she called out to Kamran.

He took two shots and held out his hand to help her down. "Be careful. The ground is uneven below. You could turn your ankle."

"I wish Doug could have come," she said, full of remorse at leaving him home alone. Since she had met Doug, she had not been alone with another man. Nor did she feel comfortable doing so, although a few tourists roamed around the site. Cecil had accepted her invitation to come but backed out at the last minute—a better offer, no doubt. Even then, she could not persuade Doug to change his mind.

She and Kamran proceeded to various vantage points. He indicated where archeologists believed specific buildings had stood before Alexander's men pillaged and destroyed the city, ironically by the fire so revered by the Achaemenids.

"Surely most Iranians don't have this much knowledge about this site," she said.

"Fars province is my birthplace. And the place where the Persian Empire and the Persian language were born." Beads of sweat shone on his forehead. "But the sun beats down without mercy here. The driver will take us to the tombs at Naghsh-e Rostam."

"I thought Rostam was a fictional character in the *Shahnameh*." Angela fanned herself with her hat.

"He's a myth as far as we know. Peasants living around here may have imagined the place as Rostam's tomb. It would have taken a strongman like him to carve out royal burial sites so high on the cliff wall. The kings thought the location would prevent their graves from being vandalized. They were wrong."

"And now the country worries about its oil fields being vandalized." She regretted her words. Politics was never a safe topic.

Ahead, a pillar towered some five hundred feet toward the sky. A double-headed griffin crowned it, having miraculously escaped the fate of the dismantled horse head. The pillar had once supported a wooden roof, Kamran told her. What a shame Doug had missed such an architectural wonder.

Circular, blue-and-white tents dotted the bleak plain not far from the taxi they had hired. "Those tents were put up for the two-thousand-five-hundreth anniversary of the Persian Empire," Kamran said. "The Shahanshah hosted a party catered by Maxim's of Paris."

Angela lifted her eyebrows, more at hearing the Shah's official title, King of Kings, than at Kamran's reference to Maxim's. Perhaps her comment about oil rig vandals had won Kamran's trust.

"Men dressed like leaders of lands that once paid tribute here paraded in costumes designed from the carvings on the grand staircase. Modern heads of state stayed in these tents. Each guest received a silk carpet that was a portrait of the guest himself." He laughed. "Including your President Nixon."

She made no comment. Hard to visualize Nixon's face woven in silk. Harder to account for Kamran's tale of the Shah's flaunting of wealth in an oil-rich country with a low per capita income, high illiteracy rate, and short average lifespan. Maybe paranoia had not spawned Doug's suspicion that Kamran was a SAVAK agent.

During the walk to the car, Kamran outlined the rest of their day back in Shiraz. The sun beat down now from high in the sky. A wind kicked up dust. The day itself had soured with doubt. Was Kamran other than what he seemed? Later, strolling with him through the coolness of Shiraz's main bazaar, Angela's pessimism declined. By the time they boarded the bus to Esfahan, she had discounted Doug's suspicions—and her own.

As he had the previous night, Kamran found her a seat next to an elderly woman. The woman's smile revealed only a few teeth as she positioned a bundle wrapped in a frayed *chador* at her feet. From his seat across the aisle, Kamran offered Angela and the woman cold Cokes he had bought at a shop near the bus station.

"Isn't that Ali Habibi?" Angela whispered to Kamran when a young man with a thin mustache mounted the bus. "I didn't know he was from Shiraz." Kamran taught Ali first-year reading; Angela had him in her conversation class.

"Looks like him." Kamran buried his nose in the Persian edition of *Kayhan*.

Ali Habibi sauntered down the aisle without greeting either of them, but as he swept past Angela, his eyes gleamed with recognition before they darted away. She found it disconcerting that Ali and Kamran ignored each other, that Ali ignored her. She would speak to Ali when the bus reached Esfahan the next morning if she survived the grueling ride home. Two villagers settled in the seat behind hers and unwrapped their evening meal. Smells of sweat and onions reached her nostrils. Onions with a dash of cumin. After the night-long journey, she would welcome the comfort of her own cool garden, the fragrance of its roses, the minty scent of Doug's skin after his morning shower.

She should have stayed home with Doug.

She pawed through her purse for the book containing the assignment she had given for Sunday. But how could she concentrate on Poe's horror story after the grandeur of Persepolis? Little by little, Poe's prose and the Iran Tour bus blurred along with the people in it—the gap-toothed woman mumbling to herself, Kamran sipping his Coke behind his newspaper, a man two rows away jiggling a swaddled baby. Angela fought to keep her eyes open for a last glimpse of the ancient ruins. When the bus sped past Persepolis, her book slipped from her hands into her lap. She fell into daydreams: Dariush dined on golden vessels in the great hall; Alexander's men threw flaming torches onto silken draperies; Alexander himself perched stiffly on a cushioned throne before prostrated Persian courtiers.

But as sleep overtook her, these past marvels dissipated, and in their place was Kamran's figure in profile, framed by golden pillars against a backdrop of purple mountains.

*　*　*　*　*　*

"I can't find him. Where is he? Where?"

Doug bolted upright on the *takht*, his T-shirt wringing wet, his mouth dry. His body shook so much that the quilt slid onto the floor. Darkness. A red glow. He took cover, fell flat on his stomach, and sheltered his head with his arms. After an eternity, he lifted his head and shoulders and squinted through the smoky dimness to detect what deadly weapon was perched near his head. The bland face of the bedside clock read 3:16 a.m. Light from the adjacent house's rooftop shone through the stained glass in the bedroom window, casting a red target onto the opposite wall.

Doug climbed over the *takht's* railing and put on his slippers. In the living room, he padded over the carpet's flowers to the cabinet where he kept the liquor. He would indulge in a shot of Johnny Walker on the rocks, although he had intended to save the exorbitantly priced Scotch for a special occasion. He put ice cubes in a tumbler in the kitchen and added alcohol up to the height of his hand. If Angela were here, she would chastise him, but he had to drink to gain any relief from the anxiety and the increase in dreams about Vietnam that this place set off in him. So much about Iran reminded him of Vietnam—the environment of lies and deceit set in motion by a despot, the incomprehensible language and indigenous habits, the men's dark faces—all menacing to him and his way of life, all threatening betrayal, all suggesting the guilt and shame he felt at his inability to protect and save his best buddy.

In the living room, he slumped on the couch in the dark. The Scotch—cold and astringent, yet therapeutic—dribbled down his throat. Now, his dream infiltrated the moment, this new, deviant dream, more harrowing than the simpler ones he knew so well.

He is on reconnaissance, hunting for a downed pilot in the Vietnam jungle, searching where Tian told him to look. Tian, his South Vietnamese counterpart, whom he trusts with his life. Only this time, Tian's choppy accent on the radio fades, and Mahmud appears. "Go ahead. Over there. He's over there,"

Mahmud says, smiling to make him feel better, smiling in spite of the false birdsong and monkey chatter of the North Vietnamese, themselves invisible among the jungle's vines. Or were they hidden in underground tunnels connecting desert *qanats*? As in the nightmare's true-to-life variation, he discovers no downed helicopter burning in the vicinity, no wounded pilot radioing for emergency assistance, only Viet Cong. Human forms shift through the mist, closing in on him. He looks for Mahmud, but Mahmud has disappeared. A voice calls from the upper branches of a eucalyptus tree. "Mister Weston, Mister Weston. Up here." At the top of the tree, a smile grows and glows. The teeth separate, flash, sparkle, and rain through the heavy air. He is in the midst of a firefight. He hits the ground and waits for the shot that will kill him. Next to him is a member of his platoon, his buddy Kevin Skyler. Kevin's brains are oozing onto the ground, yet he can talk. "Get him. He's over there," Kevin says. "Over there." Is Kevin referring to the downed pilot? Or to Mahmud? Or to the traitor, Tian? Doug touches Kevin's brains, but their slick surface slips through his fingers. Frantic, he rifles through dense foliage in search of the top of Kevin's skull. He finds it covered with slime and undergrowth like a rotting melon rind. Doug grasps it, and it, too, squishes through his fingers. He cannot use it to contain the brains, now dripping over Kevin's face, down his body, slithering away into the jungle like steaming snakes. "It's all right," Kevin says. "They don't hurt anymore." Doug has to turn away. His vomit tastes like rancid lamb fat. It falls on a blood-red-and-puke-green carpet Mahmud has laid on the jungle floor. Mahmud offers him a glass of tea and clicks his tongue, and Doug half expects the carpet to sprout a Cobra's main rotor and take off in flight. Instead, Ahmad storms into his office with the other workers and demands more holidays and higher pay. They say Tian has told them where Angela lives. They will kidnap Angela if Doug doesn't give them what they want. Tian himself appears, and Doug hits him, but Tian is not hurt. "You get a holiday," Tian says, "a long holiday in the Hanoi

Hilton." Tian's face grows longer, his eyes rounder, and he sheds his military garb for a dusty pair of floppy black pants and an Iranian villager's loose shirt and brown-felt knob of a hat. "We have your son now," says the newly evolved Ahmad. "You cannot have another one. You have no children at all." Ahmad and the construction workers puff away on a three-foot-tall turquoise *ghalian* in a tea house. They are too tired to work, they say.

"I can't find him. Where is he? Where?" Doug shouts, beside himself when he realizes he was searching for his son all along.

He poured more Scotch. The last drops slid down the inside of the glass and coated slivers of ice on the verge of liquefying. Military doctors had told him his Vietnam experience would always remain part of him as much as being a man or an American, an architect or a husband. He must live with it; he would live with it alone. Angela could never understand what he had been through. You had to have been there to understand.

He swigged down the rest of the Scotch and went back to bed, but at 4:47 a.m., he threw the quilt on the floor in disgust. He had not slept at all since the nightmare. He might as well get up, although Angela's bus would not arrive for two more hours. In the bathroom, he conducted his morning routine, taking longer in the shower, where warm water washed fatigue from his limbs. He rushed through a cup of coffee and a bowl of cornflakes. How ridiculous that he was eating cornflakes in Iran. He never ate them in the States. Last night, after his visit with Bahram, he had bought them in the Indian super on a whim. There, he had run into Guy and Maryanne—a chance meeting, the first since the night he and Angela had eaten in the hotel garden. This time, Guy had spotted him at the end of an aisle cluttered with canned vegetables.

"Where's your wife?" Guy's voice had boomed. "Back in the States already?"

"She had the holiday off. Went to Shiraz." Guy had caught him off-guard.

Guy had taken him by the elbow and drawn him aside.

"Without you? Sorry, pal. Iran is hard on marriages." He had thumped Doug on the back, pulled a scrap of paper and a pen from his shirt pocket, and jotted down some numbers. "If you need someone to talk to." He had handed the paper to Doug. "Anytime. Day or night."

Maryanne had tossed a second package of spaghetti into her cart and then pointed to her watch. "Honey, the van is waiting."

Doug imagined how he must have looked as Maryanne had hurried Guy toward the check-out counter and he, Doug, had remained confused in front of the cereal with Guy's useless phone number in his hand. Thus, the cornflakes. Now, the comedy of the scene burst through to him, even though he sat alone eating breakfast in the empty house. Guy would never have guessed that Doug and Angela had no phone in this old house. Angela had not deserted him. She had begged him to go to Shiraz again when Cecil opted out. This brief separation from Angela had given him time to examine what had been going on between them and to realize how jaded his views toward Iran and Iranians were. Angela was naïve and idealistic about Iranian culture, but she had always been loyal to him. His negativity was a source of contention between them, and his jealousy would push Angela toward Kamran if he did not curb it. He could see that now. He needed to curb his drinking as well. He could do that now. His marriage depended on it.

He grabbed a light jacket and flung open the garden door. Maybe the 6:30 bus from Shiraz would come early. No, not in Iran. He loped through the *kucheh*, up Chahar Bagh, and onto the street leading to the Meidan-e Shah. The brisk October air invigorated him. A queue had already formed at the bread shop three stores down from the square. When Doug's turn came, the shopkeeper used his paddle to flip bread away from the sides of his clay oven. He delivered it, wrapped in paper while warm, to Doug. Outside the shop, Doug inhaled scents of charred bread as wafts of steam floated toward his nostrils. He tore off a piece and stuffed it into his mouth, eradicating the cardboard taste of cornflakes.

At the far end of the square, the mosque's blue dome rose toward the sky. It dominated the Meidan-e Shah, preceded in size only by Beijing's Tiananmen Square. The previous times that he had admired the mosque, Doug had focused on the tile work and calligraphic inscriptions, the stalactites on both sides of the open entrance, and the designs on the inside of the dome. Today, from his position on the opposite side of the *meidan*, he realized he had missed the most telling element of the architect's brilliance. Usually, a mosque's entrance led straight into the courtyard and faced the *mihrab*, the niche designating the direction of Mecca. But worshippers at this mosque entered at an angle and made a sharp turn in order to face Mecca as they prayed. For the first time, Doug believed he had figured out the architect's dilemma and his creative solution. This unknown genius had designed the entrance at an angle to the *mihrab*. In doing so, he ensured the visibility of the mosque's blue dome and four minarets throughout the *meidan*.

Doug entered the bazaar, excited about his conjectures. He had to know if his hypothesis was right. Behind the grillwork of a slipper shop, the shopkeeper had just finished rolling up his prayer rug at the conclusion of his morning prayers. Doug rattled the grate, and the man lifted it. "Mecca?" Doug said and pointed to each of the four directions in turn. The man gestured in the direction Doug expected. Elated, he picked out two pairs of embroidered slippers and gave the *bazaari* more money than his asking price.

At the bazaar's entrance, Doug gazed again towards the mosque, calculating the position of the inner courtyard. He repeated his calculations at the square's opposite corner. He had no doubt: the architect had situated the mosque at its unique angle to display the perfection of its form from any perspective.

How had he failed to observe the overriding principle of the mosque's design? Like all the discoveries he had made during Angela's thirty-six-hour absence, its simplicity had initially escaped him. What harmony the architect had achieved through his elegant use of space.

Doug had lingered longer in the square than he intended. He would barely have time to make it to meet Angela by 6:30. With bread under one arm and slippers under the other, he raced toward the bus station.

Iranians did not exaggerate about this city: Esfahan was indeed half the world.

CHAPTER ELEVEN

She was on a mission, although she disapproved of missionary tactics—coercion, flattery, dissimulation. Regardless, she was on a mission. A mission to regain control of her class and, to that end, a mission to encourage Mr. Rahimi to accept Mahtab as his tutor. Angela vowed to catch him alone today instead of asking him in class to see her in her office, which would cause him to lose face with his classmates again. He seemed to play into her hands as he sorted papers at his desk after the other students swarmed out of the classroom. When she requested that he talk with her, he replied agreeably, much to her surprise.

She pulled his paper from the bottom of her pile of marked multiple-choice quizzes from the previous day and had him read the questions and possible answers aloud to her. When she encouraged him to decipher the precise meaning of each answer before selecting one, only five of twenty correct answers eluded him. If he had answered yesterday the way he just did, she told him, he would have scored seventy-five percent. "Not the best grade, but better than a zero. However, I'm giving you a second chance." She handed him a blank copy and instructed him to retake the quiz.

When he brought the paper to her podium, the usual multi-colored inscription adorned the bottom of the page, and she complimented him on his calligraphy. "You have artistic talent."

"I do it with the help of Allah."

"Many artists—writers, too—say their creative gifts come from a Higher Source." She studied his face for a reaction, hoping she had not offended him.

"There is only one God." He pronounced his edict with finality.

"I didn't indicate otherwise, Mr. Rahimi." She clenched her teeth. Her response was overly defensive.

The din of helicopter rotor blades drowned out his reply, and she had to ask him to repeat. He looked at the ceiling in disgust. "The Army. They will use helicopters against the people."

"Let's hope not," Angela said, realizing at once that Mr. Rahimi could construe her comment as anti-government. Without a word, he returned to his desk and engaged in his usual ritual of stuffing books and papers into his canvas bag.

"Mr. Rahimi, I've thought a lot about your work," she said, nervous he would leave before she could bring up the subject at hand. "I'm sure your first year here isn't easy. I know someone who could tutor you." She strolled toward his desk, blocking the path to the doorway.

"Tutor?" He drew his arms across his chest.

"A tutor would help you with the readings—make sure you understand. Help you learn to read carefully."

His eyebrows joined to knit a sharp V above his nose. "I told you. I do not like tutor."

"But you have not tried her. I have. She tutors me to improve my Persian. She is very good. Patient with my mistakes. And I make plenty of them." Her laugh faded in a second as if the sound had died upon reaching his ears.

He glared at her, his arms still folded.

"You need to pass this course. Your grade is quite low as it stands."

"I cannot pay tutor."

"She would do it for practice. You wouldn't have to pay." This was the offer Mahtab had proposed.

His cheeks puffed out, and he made a hissing sound between his teeth. "They always want something. Always more." He hissed again, and a drop of spittle issued from the corner of his mouth. "And more."

Angela stepped backward in dismay. His cheeks had become mottled, his lips purple. What would she do if he fell to the floor, arms and legs thrashing, tongue and eyes rolling back? She shuddered involuntarily as if she were a victim of seizures. "You would give her exactly what she wants," she said. "She needs your help. She needs practice teaching English. She expects to start teaching next year."

He relaxed his arms and shifted his posture. No response came from him, but his skin had assumed its natural color, and she sensed a lessening of his wariness.

"I very much want you to pass. You bring a different perspective, a special point of view, to the discussions we have in class."

Still no response.

Time to follow the loaves with the fishes. "The tutor is a devout Muslim, of course. An older woman with children. A fourth-year student."

Mr. Rahimi tilted his head and glanced askew at her. "Who is this tutor?"

Angela wrote Mahtab's name on a slip of paper. "Come to my office tomorrow afternoon at three o'clock. I'll introduce you to her."

"I will come." As he leaned over to shoulder his book bag, a photo slipped out of his shirt pocket. It landed face-up on the floor. Angela picked it up.

"Is this you?" She pointed to one of the three men in the photo. "You play the *tar*?"

"Yes."

"So, you're a musician as well as an artist. What kind of music do you play?"

"Classical Persian music." He indicated a *santur* player with bushy, white eyebrows. "He is my uncle," he told her. "I play with my uncle and his friend." The friend posed delicate fingers on a *donbak*.

"I like Persian music very much," Angela said. She lied. Her ear was far from accustomed to quarter tones. Should she ask if Mr. Rahimi's group would give the class a private concert? Such a request might demand too much of him and still fail to gain him acceptance from his peers. Undecided, she handed him the photo.

He put it into his pocket, but instead of leaving the classroom, he hesitated as if debating whether to tell her more.

His silence added to her discomfort in his presence, and she returned to the front of the room to erase the blackboard.

"Mrs. Weston," Mr. Rahimi said, now at the classroom door. "We play Thursday night. At the new tea house for tourists. It's on Chahar Bagh. Come with your husband."

His invitation astonished her. "I've seen that new place. It's not far from where we live." She and Doug would come, she promised.

She waited until Mr. Rahimi had time to make his way down the hall before she left the classroom. On the way up the stairs to her office, she met Cecil.

"Angela Weston, do tell! Your smile has swallowed half of your face." Cecil's boisterous greeting echoed in the stairwell.

Later, she felt the smile vanish from her lips. She had succeeded in her mission. Mr. Rahimi would have Mahtab as a tutor. Mahtab could help him but, with Mr. Rahimi's alarming instability, at what cost?

And how could she herself own up to her new career as a missionary?

On her way home from the university that afternoon, Angela found herself reenergized. Today, her conversation with Mr. Rahimi had gleaned positive results. Yesterday, she had received a letter from her mother that bordered on normality.

Sofia's Catholic-school-learned script ran up one margin of the aerogram, dribbled down the other, and spilled onto the back. She reported tidbits of family and neighborhood gossip. She posed questions about Doug's work, Angela's students, sights the couple had seen, and places they had visited. Angela concluded that Sofia must have finally read the books on Iran she had left behind for her mother. Sofia asked if Iranians still fabricated blue tiles, if Doug and Angela preferred tribal *gilims* or city carpets, and if they would send her a tape of traditional *santur* music. *And is it true,* she wrote, *that some Iranians pin amulets on babies' clothing to ward off the evil eye?*

"Amulets to protect against the evil eye," Angela had said to Doug after reading the letter out loud. "Water to cleanse the soul. Not much difference, is there?" She tossed Sofia's letter up. It fluttered to the floor, a bluebird heralding a new season. "No words like exile or dysentery. No reference to the unspeakable filth we supposedly encounter daily. Not one word of complaining or guilt-tripping." Finally, her mother had accepted that she and Doug lived in Iran. And, most important, Doug, too, had adapted, it seemed. Recently, he had expressed regret about not having more time to study Persian. Since her return from Persepolis, he had labored two hours each night on his portfolio without resorting to alcohol. She respected his disciplined coping mechanism, although she wished he would spend more time with her during the long evenings.

Later, after Doug had closeted himself in his improvised studio, Angela picked up her mother's letter and reread it. An unsettling fear came over her. Her mother always mentioned some detail about her health that, according to her, would develop into something grievous in due time, some innocuous complaint that would signal something serious—headaches that were early signs of a brain tumor, difficulty seeing that indicated glaucoma, stomach pains that presaged bleeding ulcers. What if, this time, Sofia did not mention her symptoms to prevent her, Angela, from worrying? She visualized her mother at the Queen Mary desk Sofia had bought for next to nothing at an auction, a blue aerogram spread over the cherry surface, writing as fast as her pen could move across the page. Her mother, Sofia, leaning her throbbing head on her free hand, slouching over to soothe the pain in her stomach, squinting to make out the words written dutifully to her daughter. Her mother might have decided not to tell her of a fatal diagnosis because she thought Angela would not believe her anyway. Or maybe the dying Sofia pledged herself and the rest of the family to silence in a final act of practiced martyrdom before eternal silence descended on her.

"No," Angela said out loud to no one. Why succumb to guilt when she did not know if she had a reason to feel guilty? In contrast to Sofia, Angela had always refused to react to the unsubstantiated. Had her objectivity deteriorated because of semi-isolation in Iran for a mere three months? Or did she habitually allow her imagination to prevail over her judgment without realizing it?

She was Sofia's daughter, after all.

*　*　*　*　*　*

What had possessed him to invite the Westons to hear him play the *tar*? A sullen mood had fallen over Hossein on his way home from the university. He had gone far enough by letting Mrs. Weston talk him into a tutor, but a tutor could work to his advantage. He had to pass this semester to avoid disgracing his family. His spoken English and listening skills had improved, he knew, but reading and writing, even in Persian, exasperated him. How could he overcome this problem alone?

In front of a fruit shop, he kicked a runaway orange, sending it splattering into the *jub*. Why did he let Mrs. Weston trap him into feeling sympathetic toward her? What was he thinking when he reacted to her concern for him? No matter if she cared about him. No matter that she tried to lessen his struggles at the university. Why did he forget his primary goal to force Americans out and stop them from ravaging his country? Keep them from corrupting his fellow countrymen with their Western ways? What would Ahmad say? Ahmad was coming to hear him play Thursday night. What would he think when he saw the Westons there?

Hossein slapped his cheeks as if to hasten his return to consciousness after an accident. The side of his mouth twitched. Saliva rolled down his jaw. He brushed by a woman standing agape at the sight of his self-punishment. A small girl pulled at her mother's *chador*, pointing at him until the mother snatched her child and rushed away. By the time he entered the *kucheh* where he lived, three other people had skirted around him, staring.

In his room, he relaxed enough to stop abusing himself. He removed his coat and took the photo that had initiated his disgraceful invitation to Mrs. Weston out of his shirt pocket. For a moment, he pursed his lips, ready to eject a stream of spit toward the picture. Instead, he whistled and ran his forefinger over the face of the *donbak* player, Aziz. During the previous night's rehearsal, Aziz's drumbeats had tantalized him, provoked him, and dared him to respond in kind with his *tar*. Clearly, Aziz was proposing more than a musical response to the foreplay evoked by the rhythm of his hands. Aziz had a penchant for men, but Hossein had never considered himself a likely object of Aziz's advances. Hossein's uncle would disapprove—more than disapprove. He would condemn such actions as vile and against Islam.

Hossein stuck the photo into his canvas bag. His hopes of marrying Nasturan, the cousin with whom he had played as a child, had long since vanished. Nasturan was engaged to a banker from Tehran, a prospect much more advantageous than a village English teacher. Hossein knew no other women. Even those living in poverty in his native village shunned him. Perhaps he should fulfill his yearnings with a man. Aziz was twenty years older. He might be seeking someone young now, someone at the peak of virility.

Ahmad entered the room and greeted Hossein, disrupting

his thoughts, then lit the Aladdin and warmed his hands over it. Hossein stretched out his own hands. The warmth seemed to activate resourcefulness in him. He knew what to do now. "Do you think the name Weston is common in America?" he asked Ahmad.

Ahmad shrugged. "Could be. Why?"

"What if your Mr. Weston is not my Mrs. Weston's husband?"

"So what if he isn't? What difference would that make? They're both Americans. They both need to go."

"Just curious." Hossein feigned nonchalance. After a few minutes, he added, "I invited Mrs. Weston and her husband to hear me play Thursday."

Ahmad screwed up his face around the flat ridge of his nose. "Whatever for? You like the lady now?"

"We rehearsed at the teahouse last night. They use candles under light diffusers on the tables. If you got there early and sat in a corner, no one could recognize you."

A slow smile spread across Ahmad's face. He fixed his eyes on the opposite wall, nodding. "I get it," he said. "I get it." Ahmad punched his fist into the air multiple times as if cheering for his favorite team in a soccer match. "I could identify Mr. Weston," Ahmad said, triumphant. "If we knew for sure your Mrs. Weston is married to my Mr. Weston, well . . ." Ahmad narrowed his eyes and tapped his fingers on the low table next to his mat.

On edge, Hossein waited for clarification. Why had he mentioned the invitation? He wanted only to suggest an excuse for his blunder in case Soleiman found out about it from Ahmad. Why this much excitement? What dreadful fate was Ahmad concocting for the Westons? Mrs. Weston seemed harmless. She hardly fit his image of a CIA operative, although he could not know for sure. Her sincerity about helping him seemed authentic, touching even.

Ahmad thumped Hossein on the back with his fist. "*Mobarak,*

Hossein-*jan, mobarak.*" Accepting the congratulations, Hossein shook Ahmad's hand and guffawed. He would rejoice in this moment. He had never received such praise, such appreciation. Never known camaraderie like this. And Ahmad was sure to report his strategic invitation to Soleiman. The back-pounding from Ahmad and his own earlier cheek-slapping had proved worth it.

Never had he received so much absolution from so little bodily mortification.

Never.

Not even on Ashoura, the holy day during the month of Moharram when the Shiite pious march in the streets, flagellating their bare backs with chains, mourning the martyrdom of Hussain on the plains of Karbala fourteen centuries ago.

* * * * * *

She sealed the deal with Mahtab without delay. As Angela expected, Mahtab refused to let her pay for Mr. Rahimi's English lessons. Mahtab did agree to stay for tea.

"I'm grateful, Mahtab. Mr. Rahimi needs help to pass my course. I need help getting him to pass." Angela set a tray with some lemon cookies on the coffee table.

"*Inshallah.* God willing," Mahtab said.

Angela poured tea into blue pottery cups and passed Mahtab the sugar bowl. Mahtab had given her the perfect opening to broach a troubling topic: whether Iranians used the expression *inshallah* simply as a habit of speech or whether they truly believed God foreordained every incident, no matter how insignificant.

Afternoon sun filtered through the windows in the French doors, highlighting the auburn tints in Mahtab's hair. "We do say *inshallah* without thinking." Mahtab's forehead puckered into a frown. "And we do believe God has determined everything that will happen."

"So God's will is paramount? We humans have no power over our own actions?" Angela studied her friend's face. Had she overstepped her boundaries?

Mahtab stirred a cube of sugar into her tea. "Islam says we must submit to God's will, to everything He has designed for us."

The way Mahtab skirted her own personal beliefs disappointed Angela. "Do you yourself—you, Mahtab—believe we cannot do anything to influence our own fate?" Could someone as ostensibly "Westernized" as Mahtab espouse such fatalistic thinking in the twentieth century? "If that is true, it makes no sense for us to go to the doctor when we are sick because whether we perish or get better depends only on God's will."

Mahtab bit her lip, pensive. "It's not that simple. If God's will is that we go to the doctor, regardless of the outcome, then we go to the doctor."

"But how do you know what God expects you to do?" It was the old question of predetermination or free will, of Calvinism or some other, more liberal viewpoint.

"Being devout in Islam is the start. The five pillars. You know them?"

"Yes." Angela ran down the list in her mind: alms-giving, the *haj* to Mecca at least once in one's life, prayer, fasting during the month of Ramadan, and the belief in one God and Mohammad as His prophet. "All I have to do is observe these five pillars?" The Koran itself was much more prescriptive.

"You are thinking of becoming a Muslim?"

"Sorry. But no." Angela popped another lemon cookie in her mouth to stave off further questions. She passed the plate to Mahtab, who had already eaten two and now held up her hand in refusal, protesting that she would eat them all if she kept on.

"All I can tell you, Angela, is I do believe in the tenets of Islam. I submit myself to God's will as He sees fit. Don't you believe in God's will?"

"I have to confess," Angela said, amused suddenly at her choice of the word confess in the face of a religion that relied on little, if any, built-in guilt, "that the idea of total submission to God's will seems too fatalistic to me." She related Guy's account of Iranian student pilots who, when warned they were on the verge of crashing, would panic, say "*Inshallah*," and release the controls. "They survived only through the intervention of their American instructors."

Mahtab twisted a lock of hair around her finger without commenting, then asked point-blank, "What do *you* think, Angela? Do you believe you can make choices God has not willed?"

She had dreaded this question. If only she were as adept as Mahtab at avoiding the crux of an issue. "No, I ... I don't think there is a Supreme Being at all." Her honesty had won out, but the fear of losing Mahtab's companionship loomed over her. This once, she had made a real confession, one she would not make to family members. Only Doug knew of her lack of faith, and his religious convictions were, at best, lukewarm.

"You don't believe in God at all?" Mahtab's voice registered shock. Her face fell and grew pale. She drew back into her chair, away from Angela. If an earthquake had just leveled the roof, Mahtab would have looked less alarmed.

"I'm sorry, Mahtab," Angela said. There was no turning back. "I consider religion a social phenomenon designed to keep individuals under tabs. It gives them something to hope for in times of crisis." Mahtab's shocked expression remained unchanged. Angela wondered if she was seeing her friend for the last time. "It satisfies a human need for rituals and myths—all fabricated to endow life with meaning. That's something, I suppose—a comfort—but that's all."

In the heavy silence, she heard Mahtab swallow. Angela exhaled, drawing out her breath. She had allowed herself to go beyond the pale by expecting someone in this half of the world to debate issues fundamental to her own way of life, her own manner of thinking. How could two people like Mahtab and her ever come to understand each other? Even if they spoke the same language. Language was often a cover for a person's thoughts, for what that person kept close to the bone. Doug maintained that humans were products of their cultural upbringing—nothing more, nothing less. She had always embraced individualism; he forever clung to determinism. Yet he would argue that her belief reflected American culture with its guarantees of individual rights. For once, her attitude was more American than Doug's.

Mahtab reached out and touched her arm. "I can't doubt God," Mahtab said, "but I can accept your doubt. I can enjoy our friendship without believing what you believe or expecting you to believe what I do. I try hard not to render judgment on others on that account."

Angela nodded. Mahtab had hit upon the right word—judgment. Judgment, the curse that prevented a human being from accepting those different from him or herself.

Mahtab rose to go. "You do know I accept you the way you are, don't you?" Her eyes took on their characteristic twinkle. "I know you are not a *sheitan*."

"Thank God for that." Angela's lips twisted into a wry smile.

CHAPTER TWELVE

"To our hosts for a fantastic Thanksgiving dinner." Vicky hiccupped and raised her glass of champagne.

"Aye, aye." Cecil clicked his glass against Vicky's.

"You mean hear, hear, silly," Vicky said.

"Tell Reza we missed him," Doug said. Reza was visiting a sick relative. "And here's to the chef." He toasted Angela.

Cecil burst into a chorus of "She's a jolly good fellow," and Angela's cheeks, already rosy from the drink, turned crimson.

Doug snuggled close to Angela. Her vivaciousness had reappeared after her trip to Persepolis. The morning of her return, he had admitted that her infatuation with Iranian culture left him feeling abandoned at times and apologized for his negativity and preoccupation with drinking. They declared an end to their arguments and the pettiness that provoked them. His workplace had gained a modicum of order as well, the troublemakers having yielded to his expectations. Weeks had passed with no one questioning his virility or challenging his authority. Yesterday afternoon, his old nemesis, Ahmad, had wished him a happy American holiday. Recalling Ahmad's misconceptions, Doug laughed aloud.

"What's so funny?" Angela asked.

"Let me guess," said Cecil. "You've had a sudden inspiration. You think we all should climb the highest minaret in

Esfahan when the *moazzin* calls *azan*."

Doug shook his head. Leave it to Cecil to come up with something outrageous. "Apparently, Mahmud explained Thanksgiving to the workers. But one guy was a little confused," Doug said. His three listeners had turned eager, flushed faces toward him, and he relished his moment in the limelight. "He thought the early Americans tried to travel to Mecca—pilgrims, you know—and missed the mark. Ended up somehow in North America eating corn with Indians. He asked me why people from India were already in America."

"He had to be putting you on," Vicky said.

"My students say that our Thanksgiving is like the Iranian *Eid-e Ghorban*, the day they feast and give thanks at the end of Ramadan," Angela said.

"When is Ramadan this year?" Cecil asked. "We've got to get all our partying in before it starts. Last year, a couple students objected that we foreign teachers were eating apples in our offices. Those students had prowled around looking for something to complain about because they were fasting in misery. Ramadan is not a barrel of laughs." Cecil popped open the last bottle of Dom Perignon he had brought.

Doug pulled Angela's earlobe, wishing that the others would leave. "I'm glad we splurged for that turkey. The dried apricots in the stuffing added a Middle Eastern touch." Esfahani apricots were juicy, with the taste of floral honey. He had never had any like them.

Vicky confirmed that Ramadan would fall during the Christmas holiday this year, and they all groaned. Cecil jumped up and rifled through the cassettes. "In that case, we'll do our celebrating now." He put on a tape of modern Iranian music, a singer whom Angela's students had recommended. A violin's shrill quarter tones came screeching through the speakers. Doug held his hands over his ears.

"Cecil," Vicky shouted. "Turn it down. Better yet—turn it off."

But Cecil was already gyrating his paunch. He lifted his

hands and curved his wrists in an evocative, Middle Eastern fashion, separating his fingers and rotating them through figure-eights. Resigned to the whining tonalities, Doug leapt to his feet and pulled Angela to hers. He held his arms above his head, twisting his wrists and fingers. "Let's make this a half-Persian, half-American holiday," he said, but his fingers felt stiff. He could not twist any of his body parts with Cecil's fluidity.

Giggling, Vicky joined them. "Yeah, we've already had the American half."

Cecil turned the volume knob to full blast and swung open the French doors to the garden. As alluring as Ali Baba, he danced out onto the pillared porch and down the steps where the others followed him, stealing inspiration from his evocative twisting. Above, a cold moon cast silver over the rose bushes, now devoid of new blooms. In spite of the late November chill, Cecil stripped off his shirt and jerked his hips backward and forward. Doug could not decide if Cecil was imitating Elvis or a belly dancer. He opted for the belly dancer when Cecil cupped his hands under his fleshy breasts and shook them. His dark nipples quivered in the moonlight.

Vicky caught Cecil's hand and led him to the reflecting pool. "Look at yourself. Aren't you ashamed?" she scolded before her laughter betrayed her.

Doug followed Angela as she skirted around a rose bed, her gyrations graceful and beguiling. It had been ages since they had danced together. Mesmerized, he could not take his eyes off her; she kept hers on him. Her fingertips, bathed in moonlight, extended toward him, beckoning as she swayed backward in time to the music. Doug reached his hands toward hers. They danced as if a silken thread, airy and all but invisible, bound them one to the other, weaving their steps into a shimmering fabric of silver. The Angela of the past, shy and fearful, had become an enchantress—all provocation and seduction. She enticed him under the mimosa tree where neither Vicky nor Cecil could see them. Low-hanging branches forged a lattice of light and dark across Angela's forehead and cheeks. She danced forward a few quick steps and, placing her hands on his shoulders, drew him to the leaf-strewn ground. A willing partner, he embraced her, his lips on her lips, his hands on her breasts.

Only when the doors to their compound creaked shut did they realize the moonlit Persian garden belonged solely to them.

Listening to Persian music all evening would torture him, but conducting reconnaissance on this character Rahimi would be worth it. Doug needed to judge for himself what kind of rabble-rouser Rahimi was, how much of a threat he was to Angela. He could not rely on Angela's assessment. She stewed over Rahimi's abrasive comments, worried about Rahimi's academic failures, and agonized over Rahimi's social situation—in short, Angela was inexplicably obsessed with Rahimi.

In the tea house, Doug sank onto cushions in front of a low table after having been instructed by Angela that *ghalian* was the correct word for hubble-bubble in Persian. Another word whose initial sound made him gag when he tried to pronounce it. A waiter brought a turquoise *ghalian* supported by a glass jar filled with water. He stuffed tobacco in the metal cup at the *ghalian*'s top, attached red tubes with wooden mouthpieces to the stem, and lit the tobacco. Once the smoke flowed freely through the water and entered the pipes, the waiter disappeared behind a sequined curtain.

Doug eyed the pipe. "We're not going to smoke this stuff, are we?"

"Try a puff or two to be polite." Angela handed him one of the mouthpieces.

The strength of the smidgen of smoke he inhaled sent his lungs into a spasm. Coughing, he wiped tears from his eyes. At another installation of cushions and low tables, a group of well-dressed Iranians laughed. Doug joined in, feebly, and head-nodding accompanied by *salams* followed.

"They've got a decent crowd," Angela said.

Doug twisted around and glanced over his shoulder. He and Angela occupied the table closest to a makeshift stage. He felt conspicuous. Through the room's smoke and stippled candlelight, he counted thirty people, mostly Iranian men. Wax must have extinguished the candle on the table in the far corner. Darkness prevented him from detecting the gender or nationality of the person seated there. "I think we're the only tourists here."

"We aren't tourists. We live here," Angela said.

Doug refrained from voicing his irritation. Complaining about Angela's obliviousness to their foreign looks and temporary status would mar the evening's festivities. She had been on a high recently, excited about accepting their first invitation from a student—all the more so since it came from Rahimi.

Three men filed to the wooden platform in the front of the room. The *donbak* and *tar* players took their places on straight-back, wooden chairs; the *santur* player stood with his instrument on a table in front of him. A tea-house employee with a towel draped over his shoulder adjusted spotlights on the musicians' instruments. Only the *tar* player was young enough to be a university student. His demeanor was distasteful. The guy had twisted his upper lip into a sneer. Without a doubt, this Rahimi character was staring at them through his thick, tinted glasses.

"I think he sees us." Angela smiled as if the *tar* player had a salubrious effect on her.

After sounding a few tuning notes, the *santur* player bent his white mustache over his instrument and hit his mallets on the strings, playing the first number alone. The mallets flew with fury, incessant motion transforming them and the *santur* player's hands into the blurry images of an accelerated movie reel. When the music stopped, the hum from the strings' overtones lingered in Doug's ears. "Amazing," he said out loud.

"He's Mr. Rahimi's uncle," Angela said.

Apparently the glare bothered Rahimi, and he removed his glasses before he began to play the *tar* in a meditative fashion, his eyes as darkly vacant as *qanats* on the desert floor. He focused on some point in the space above Doug's head, his regard inhospitable, as empty and devoid of humanity as the desert. Angela worried that Rahimi had a neurological condition. To Doug, this trance appeared self-induced, befitting the sinuous, hypnotic nature of classical Persian music. As Rahimi's fingers plucked the *tar's* strings, the music, too, worked itself into a trance, its notes twisting and turning in agonizing quarter-tone cadences, always returning to the same hollow tone.

Angela leaned forward, elbows on the table, eyes fixed on Rahimi. Others in the tea house also seemed enthralled with the music. Was he the only one who had not fallen under the *tar* player's spell? The only one who had not succumbed to a trance that precluded objective observation?

The *donbak* took up an accompanying rhythm, its masculine drumbeats overlapping with the *tar's* more feminine notes. The *donbak* player gazed at Rahimi as if challenging a response from the *tar* or calculating whether the notes would rise in a flurried crescendo or settle into clusters around the mother tone. Rahimi paid no visible attention to the *donbak* player. Instead, he played as though dazed, his eyes never wavering. Music emptied the mind momentarily, Doug thought, but in the absence of conscious cognition, the soul never ceased churning.

Doug concentrated on the music, aware of a new tension impossible to shake off. Traditional Persian music was improvised, Angela had told him, but this improvisation lacked the fluidity and looseness, the extravagant expressiveness of American jazz. These notes remained under tight control, taut, rigid, recursive, and incapable of breaking out in a riff. This music demanded a constant recall of the stabilizing tone, affording listeners no emotional release. It was as refined and constrained as uncorked champagne, its bubbles imprisoned until one day, something happened—the wire holding the cork in place snapped, a tiny leak of air entered the bottle's neck—and an explosion shot the precious liquid high into the atmosphere until it descended as foam, delight forever wasted.

The concert continued after the *tar* piece ended. Perspiration trickled down Doug's sides, as when he had sensed the presence of the enemy in Vietnamese jungles. When the musicians stopped playing, his limbs were unsteady, his shirt soaked, and his back and chest chilled.

The Iranians next to them rose to leave and chatted in Persian with Angela for a few minutes. Doug helped her with her jacket as she said, "I want to congratulate Mr. Rahimi, but I don't see him anywhere." Angela scanned the milling crowd, now eager to disperse.

"Guess we missed him." Doug handed Angela her purse and hurried her into the thick of the crowd pressing toward the exit. He had already spotted Rahimi skirting the room in a quick retreat to the corner table with no light. Once outside, relief soothed Doug's apprehension. His evening's repertoire did not include chin-wagging with Rahimi in a dark corner.

Angela pointed upward through the December night. "A shooting star."

He wondered how the star could have shot across the sky so fast he had missed it.

He learned too late that Angela had invited Rahimi to Christmas dinner two weeks after the tea house ordeal.

A Ramadan dinner, to be exact.

A Ramadan dinner set for thirty minutes after sundown since Rahimi would spend the day fasting.

Angela had refused to retract the invitation. Doug's only recourse would be to maintain a protective presence, and he would have to conceal his animosity toward Rahimi lest Rahimi take it out on Angela later at the university. Neither alcohol nor pork sausage stuffing would grace the Yuletide table, nor would other guests. Cecil had chosen to spend Christmas in Kashan where, it was said, because of a star, three Magi began a journey to Bethlehem. Reza, with a white beard and an overloaded bag of toys, would celebrate at home with Vicky and the three boys.

Christmas morning, Doug told Angela to close her eyes. He fussed with the clasp and fastened a turquoise pendant around her neck. Looking in the mirror, she fingered the stone set in gold, then fumbled to take the necklace off.

"I love it," she said. "But I can't leave it on tonight. Mr. Rahimi would think we lived in opulence like other foreigners."

"Compared to him, I'm sure we do," Doug said, but he slid the gold safety catch and let the necklace slither off into her open hand as if he had practice in releasing pieces of exquisite jewelry from exquisite necks.

It was his turn. He ripped the silver wrapping from her gift to him and discovered a backgammon set. Angela hurried back to the kitchen, leaving him running his fingers over ivory and mother-of-pearl inlays. The gift placated him a bit about Christmas with Rahimi—only a bit. He tossed the dice. They clattered across the board's surface. Snake's eyes. At least he had rolled a double.

"Think your Mr. Rahimi plays backgammon?" he called out to Angela. He dubbed Rahimi "Mr." on purpose, believing it would add a note of acceptance and cover up his misery. He ambled into the kitchen and stood by the stove, taking care to keep out of Angela's way. She was fretting over stuffing, mixing it with her hands, up to her elbows in almonds and onions, sultanas and currants, rice stained yellow with saffron.

"I unearthed a Persian recipe in a cookbook in the English bookstore on Abbas Abad." Angela rinsed off her hands and wiped them on her apron. "A huge turkey would have been overly extravagant for the three of us, don't you think? I'm sure American-style stuffing, even without pork, would not be to Mr. Rahimi's liking."

No scent of sausage or pumpkin or bourbon-laced eggnog. Nothing traditional. Nothing that would remind him of Christmas at home. Doug peeked in the refrigerator. The prospects looked grim, and Angela, chatting merrily as she boiled raisins, confirmed his suspicions. She would complement the anemic-looking chicken with Persian greens, goat cheese and onions, unleavened bread, and yogurt. And for dessert, nothing other than a plate of *gaz* and roasted pumpkin seeds. What a Christmas feast!

As Angela set the table for three, Doug sought refuge in the living room. He plugged in the lights on a scrawny pine tree for which they had paid an extravagant price at the Indian super. He brushed past the tree on his way to the cassette rack. A handful of needles fell on the floor. He would have to find music that would please their guest, he supposed, although he himself felt anything but pleased about that guest. Perhaps a Peter, Paul, and Mary tape would fit the bill. The words might be easy enough for Rahimi to understand. Folk music would set Rahimi at ease more than a Beethoven Sonata or a Mahler Symphony or Dave Brubeck or Stan Getz. As a standby, an Ella Fitzgerald tape, one of his own favorites. Rahimi might relate to Ella's style. Or would her scats send him straight into a trance? Somehow, though, that tape had gone missing.

As the time for their guest's arrival approached, Doug's disgust grew. Their Christmas had become their "opportunity to reciprocate for Mr. Rahimi's invitation to the tea house," as Angela termed it. Doug had suggested inviting other students. Angela would have nothing of it. If they had four or five in their home, she maintained, it would smack of favoritism for a certain clique. Mr. Rahimi was the only student who had offered them the only hospitality he had available here in Esfahan. Besides, Angela reasoned, he tended to avoid other students. How could she identify four or five students with whom he would be compatible? She wanted to keep it simple, she said, arguing that Mr. Rahimi was making progress under Mahtab's tutelage. He would pass her reading course this semester with at least a low C. Even so, he needed special attention. Getting to know him better would give them more insight into real Iranians who did not live in cities.

"And people who live in Esfahan, or Shiraz, or Tehran aren't real?" Doug had argued. "You've gone overboard wanting this particular student to like you, Angela." Why was Angela so obsessed with this guy? It defied logic.

"Not at all," she said. "But if he accepts us for who we are rather than labeling us as corrupt or, at best, weird Americans, wouldn't that be a coup?"

"You're a teacher, not a State Department diplomat."

Doug rummaged through the collection of folk music. How could Angela, with her aversion to being labeled American, want to assume a role as an unsung ambassador for her native country? Another of her many inconsistencies—like the way she had fought for vocational programs to train the mentally challenged in the States, yet when the administration lacked resources to support such programs, Angela had refused to lower standards or make any concessions whatsoever for the few mentally challenged students enrolled in her classes. She was a black-and-white thinker. And she accused him of the same. Yet he loved her in spite of her quirky contradictions.

"It's getting late," Doug yelled from the living room to Angela in the kitchen. "You're sure he understood the directions?"

"I drew him a map," Angela yelled back. "He'll get here. Actually, it's common here for people to be an hour or two late."

"You should have told him to come an hour or two ago then."

"Couldn't. Ramadan. It would be rude to expect him to come when the sun is still aloft in the sky."

Outside the French doors, darkness settled over the garden. Doug's watch read seven thirty. The sun had not been "aloft in the sky" for a good hour now. Surely, Rahimi would show up by nine o'clock. Doug pressed the play button on the tape recorder.

"I'm a leavin' on a jet . . ." resounded through the house.

Angela rushed out of the kitchen, her fingertips saffron-yellow. "Music? We can't have music. It's Ramadan." She jabbed at the tape recorder's stop button and pulled the plug on the single strand of lights decorating the pitiful little Christmas tree on the coffee table. "No lights. Too festive." Angela tilted her head in Doug's direction and gave him a wan smile. "Ramadan."

"I thought music and lights were forbidden during Moharram, not Ramadan." A blank look fell over Angela's face. She had confused the two holidays. For once, he had more knowledge of Shiite practices than she.

"We'd better play it safe," she said after a pause. "They could be *haram* now, too. It's Ramadan."

"It's Christmas, Angela, for God's sake. To hell with Ramadan." Doug pushed the start button on the tape recorder. "Don't know when I'll be back again" drifted over the darkened tree while he and Angela stared each other down in the middle of the room. "He's not here yet." He barred her access to the recorder. Throwing up her arms, she turned and exited the room. "And we don't know when the hell he'll get here. Is that because it's Ramadan?" Doug shouted after her, more exasperated than ever. But he resolved to turn off the music if and when Rahimi's shadow fell across the threshold.

Two hours later, the chicken cold and shriveled on the platter, the golden rice glazed with hardened bits of formerly melted butter, the fresh coriander, parsley, and dill as wilted as their Christmas cheer, Doug sat across the table from his wife. "He betrayed you, Angela. He purposefully spoiled your Christmas. Our Christmas."

"Nonsense. Something must have come up." She leaned over the table, her cheek resting on her hand, a strand of hair falling over one eye, so overcome by fatigue that he felt sorry for her. Tired himself of springing to the garden door at every sound resembling a knock, he closed his lips to avoid saying the provocative "I told you so" or the mundane, and somewhat untrue, "It's not your fault." To be fair, Angela appeared more miserable and let down than he had seen since their arrival. Did a spoiled Christmas chicken merit an argument over the danger of a reckless and volatile student? No, he would delay talking to her until New Year's Eve. Then, they could make resolutions, some to help them survive in Iran. Better said—survive Iran. He would again urge Angela to report Rahimi to the dean, would emphasize how essential removing him from her class had become.

He popped a few pumpkin seeds in his mouth. They tasted bitter. Tomorrow he would buy an expensive, imported can of pumpkin at the Indian grocer's and make a belated Christmas pie.

CHAPTER THIRTEEN

She was thrilled that Bill had accepted her offer of a plane ticket to Esfahan. As he crossed the tarmac, Angela waved at him from the terminal window. Beside her, Doug clasped his hands and shook them above his head in triumph. Bill picked up his lanky gait and pointed in their direction. She could count on Bill. He possessed what Doug, at times, lacked: unflappable enthusiasm for foreign travel, unshakable trust in humankind, and unwavering optimism about life in general. No need for her to play missionary during Bill's stay. All she had to do was play tour guide.

"You came at the perfect time even if the airports are jammed," Angela said to Bill in the taxi on the way home. "Iranians travel during the Nawruz holiday, mostly to visit their families or sites in Iran. Or, if they can afford it, they go to France or England."

"The whole country shuts down for two weeks except shops and tourist venues," Doug said.

The taxi lurched through heavy traffic. Bill stared out the window, his knuckles white as he clutched the back of the seat in front of him. She had braced herself in the same way months ago when their taxi screeched onto the Si-yo-Se Pol. Today, the March breeze was soft with long-awaited moisture—unlike that sizzling August day when she and Doug had landed in Esfahan. And today, the blind man was absent from his niche on the bridge. If vendors took off for Nawruz, they risked losing a good source of revenue. Nawruz was a time of cleansing and renewal, and that included lavish spending—on furniture, carpets, cars, whatever one could afford—and gifts of crisp bills fresh from the mint.

"So, how *are* you getting along here?" Bill asked as if they had failed to tell him the whole truth via airmail.

"Great," Angela said without hesitation. This semester, no disconcerting incidents had erupted in the classroom. Mr. Rahimi had assumed an air of cautious solicitude toward her ever since missing Christmas dinner. Unforeseen family circumstances required his attention that evening, he had said. She wanted to invite him again, but Doug objected. "Rahimi is making excuses. I won't have him hurting your feelings again like that."

She countered, saying Mr. Rahimi had no way to let them know he could not attend the dinner. Neither he nor they had a telephone.

"I won't have it," Doug stated firmly. No amount of pleading persuaded him to change his mind, and she backed off. Doug had been doing well. She would do nothing to jeopardize his new-found comfort here. Not only had Doug shown signs of settling in, but he had also recently mentioned the possibility of staying an extra year.

"Adjusting to the food?" Bill's voice boomed out next to her. His hair was longer than when she had last seen him. Otherwise, he looked much the same. She could have sworn he had on the same beige pullover, faded jeans, and shabby sneakers he had worn to see them off seven months ago. "I brought you some taco shells and seasoning. They were staples when we were roommates," Bill told Angela.

"Better than Iranian stew any day." Doug gestured toward a construction site on their left. There, shirtless men with pajama-like pants hitched up around their calves stomped barefoot on mud and straw. A man with a back as dark as cured leather hoisted a bucket of the mixture with a rope and pulley up four levels, where a boy plastered the outer walls with bare hands.

Bill whistled. "Handmade, or rather foot-made, adobe."

"Medieval." Doug spoke louder than necessary. "This, my friend, is the great Persian civilization."

"Doug, please." Angela inclined her head toward the taxi driver. Doug's comment was out of line, especially to someone who had just arrived. Bill deserved to gather his own impressions, form his own opinions.

Already, Doug had painted the conversation black with ex-pat sarcasm.

The following day, she dragged Doug and Bill, still drowsy with jet lag, to the bazaar. Afterward, they would stop at Bahram's workshop. The three of them browsed through winding alleyways, and Angela encouraged Bill to wait before he purchased anything. "It takes a few trips to develop an eye," she said.

Under the arched roof, *bazaaris* peddled their goods to shoppers. Rich scents of cumin and coriander, saffron and cinnamon wafted through the air. Angela showed Bill wool dyed pomegranate-orange and left to dry on rounded rooftops. She demonstrated how to bargain for apricots and almonds and when to accept carpet merchants' offerings of tea and nougat. She narrated anecdotes of their experiences in Iran.

"You're a modern-day Scheherazade," Bill told her.

She laughed and shook her head, gratified at his appreciation for such a minimal effort on her part. "I think not. Scheherazade told tales woven as tight as Esfahani carpets." They passed a jewelry store. Angela drew Bill's attention to the display. "Scheherazade's stories were as elegant as gold filigree set with emeralds." She would enjoy guiding Bill around the city, under blue-tiled domes, through palace arches, beside reflecting pools, and over stone bridges. Perhaps Doug would appreciate these sites through Bill's untainted eyes rather than contesting what he called her flowery impressions.

They emerged from the bazaar and paused to let Bill admire the blue-domed mosque at the other end of the Meidan-e Shah. Someone called out Angela's name. Kamran. He often materialized unexpectedly when they were sauntering around this part of the city. Doug crossed the street and shook Kamran's hand. Would Bill's presence discourage Doug from questioning Kamran's intentions? These days, Doug accused Kamran of operating as a SAVAK agent charged with spying on them more than of having an interest in her. Each time they met Kamran, she would remind Doug that Kamran and his ailing father lived near the places she and Doug frequented, that Kamran shopped for food deep in the maze of the main bazaar. But Doug's suspicion of Kamran remained second only to his disdain for Mr. Rahimi.

Kamran approached, carrying a shopping bag in which nestled a cucumber, two apples, and greens wrapped in newspaper. He inspected Bill with what seemed undue curiosity, his questions accompanied by artisans hammering brass and copper in the distance: Where in the States did Bill live? How did he know the Westons? Where did he work? How long would he stay in Iran? Which other Iranian cities would he visit? They reached Bahram's door, and Kamran's questions faded away as the intermittent tapping grew fainter. At least Kamran had not asked Bill, who had just broken up with a live-in girlfriend, why he was not yet married.

But Kamran had, she noticed with growing discomfort, scrutinized Bill's left hand as if he were reading Bill's palm or memorizing his fingerprints.

She was one of a handful of foreign women in the Iran Tour Hotel two days later. A mixed crowd lined the bar, some spilling out onto tables arranged around an empty swimming pool.

Doug greeted a few regulars: an American helicopter pilot, a Dutch journalist, a couple of British nationals who taught English. Well-dressed Iranian men bantered with Scandinavian tourists at a nearby table.

After polishing off a beer, Bill busied himself shelling pistachios while they waited for another round. Doug shook his knee up and down under the table; Bill played with the empty shells. Both remained unusually quiet until Bill turned toward her. "I have to tell you something, Angela," he said.

His nervousness gave her the impression that he had fretted all day over what, or how much, to say.

Bill cupped several tiny half-shells together. "Your mother called before I left."

"My mother?" Bill had met Sofia once—at the wedding where he had served as Doug's best man. Twice, if she counted the rehearsal dinner.

"She wanted me to spy on you two during my stay, tell her how you're doing. I'm supposed to sound you out about how soon you'll come back to the States. Use my influence in that regard." Bill studied the tower of shells he had built on the table. "Not that I have any."

"I'm mortified." Angela clamped her hands over her face and let flow a stream of apologies.

"You don't have to feel embarrassed. She's your mother— doing what mothers do, I guess."

She cringed. Bill had lost his mother in childhood around the same time as Doug.

"What do I tell her?" Bill grinned miserably. "Make it good if I'm supposed to lie."

"Tell her we love it here." Angela's words spewed out like red-hot lava. "Tell her we love it so much we're staying an extra year—two years—if it works out with Doug's job."

Bill raised his eyebrows. "Thanks for making me the messenger."

Doug, now deep into his cups, erupted. "Why tell her that,

Angela? I've been reconsidering." He downed a double shot of vodka. "To be honest, I can't bear to look at Iranians at work anymore. They're lazy liars. Whiners. Hypocrites." He jabbed his forefinger on the table at each new accusation, then pointed at her. "You love the tiles, the frescoes, the brass and miniature shops. That's what Iran is to you, a quaint country of poetry and palaces where refined Persians stroll along riverbanks memorizing verses from Sa'adi with their noses buried in roses. You forget the lame beggars. You forget the lice-infested urchins. You ignore the filth and falsehood, the daily deception. I work with these people, Angela. Not with those trying to get an education. With those who have none. I know what they're like. I've told you before they pull everything imaginable to sabotage the project."

Flabbergasted, she traced a circular pattern in the condensation coating her glass. She had not witnessed an outburst like this in recent weeks. Did Doug's frustrations come out now because he could vent to an old friend whom he trusted? And, if so, did he no longer trust her?

Doug grabbed her glass and set it out of her reach, toppling Bill's pistachio-shell tower. "The other day, one of them told me we should leave the country. Why? He thinks you're Jewish. Forget Jews have lived here since Cyrus the Great. When I said you were of Italian descent, he insisted I was lying. Me. Ly-ing." He stabbed his forefinger into his chest, punctuating each syllable. "The quaintness of this place is just another veil. Hell, you might as well be wearing a veil, too. They don't see us, and we aren't allowed to see them. Anyone who doesn't agree is living under an illusion."

She hated stereotyping. "Please don't generalize. You know that all Iranians are not alike." She reeled off names of Iranians who had extended them hospitality, Kamran's name topping the list. But her efforts fueled his ire.

"It's a veil, Angela. A façade like the east side of the square. You think more shops are behind those facing the square. That's the case in the bazaar on the north side, but on the east side, it's only an illusion. It's not real. This whole country reeks of falsehood from the Shah on down."

Heads jerked around, and Bill summoned the waiter. Angela had warned Bill that using the Shah's name in public could lead to reports to SAVAK and suspicions of conspiracy against the regime. He pressed a wad of paper money into the waiter's hand. "Let's talk at home over that duty-free bottle of St. Emilion I bought in Paris," he told Doug.

The waiter must have heard Doug's raised voice. He nodded toward a door behind a beaded curtain. There, an exit led to a maze of alleyways hidden behind buildings on the main street.

At home, Doug fell into bed without resuming the conversation or mentioning the wine. Bill uncorked the St. Emilion and poured Angela a glass.

"He doesn't want to stay. What will you do, Angela?"

"For a while, I was afraid Doug was losing control, but since Thanksgiving, he's been back to his old self. Until tonight. I was blindsided. You've known him longer than I have. Any suggestions?"

Bill picked up the Bahram miniature from its place of honor on a shelf near the French doors. "This woman does look like you," he said.

"Hardly." She would not allow Bill to tease a smile from her. "In Persian art and poetry, the woman represents the Divine. Union with the Divine is the ideal for the artist."

"So why is she looking in the mirror?"

His question unnerved her. How could she think of contemplating Divinity in any guise when she could not fathom her own husband's complexity? She shuddered, caught unawares by sudden fear. What consequences might arise from Doug's public outburst about the Shah? The waiter who had guided them out the back way could now be informing on them. In that case, the best outcome would be immediate deportation; the worst . . . But she had forgotten Bill.

"Why the mirror? Because the sky is high." Bill looked askance at her, but she only said, "It's an old Persian saying."

She racked her brain and finally came up with Yazd.

Not far from Esfahan, Yazd was the last habitable outpost on the western side of the Dasht-e Lut, the Great Desert that extended across the country's interior toward the Afghani border. Weeks ago, Doug had mentioned that he wanted to see the Tower of Silence there. Angela had no desire to go. Doug's interest in the tower smacked of morbidity. In former times, Zoroastrians had laid the dead there for vultures and wild animals to devour the flesh. Yet, if going to Yazd could improve Doug's outlook, she would go along.

Before Bill left for the States, Angela meant to press him again for possible causes of, and solutions to, Doug's unhappiness. Doug had kept his disdain for Iran under cover since the debacle at the Iran Tour. Her fear about SAVAK had subsided somewhat since no one had pounded on the door to arrest them in the middle of the night. Even so, she had lived looking over her shoulder for the past few days, wondering if someone was following them. Another public incident could undo them. She abhorred censoring their words to comply with a police state's dictates. She especially detested worrying about the outcome resulting from a breach of any required behavior. It gave her a sense of helplessness akin only to the feeling she had experienced during that dark incident in the vacant lot. She tried to will the feeling gone, vowing to adopt neither a victim's attitude nor a victim's fear. Her success was partial, at best.

The following morning, Doug borrowed Mahmud's car, and the three of them set off. Few vehicles chugged along the road to Yazd, only an occasional brightly painted truck with garlands of pompoms strung across the windshield or a beat-up minivan serving as a local bus, sacks of casaba melons or wilting coriander bouncing on its roof. A few kilometers outside of

Yazd, the terrain changed from the brown, pebble-strewn dirt prevalent around Esfahan to amber sand dunes.

This was real desert.

Streets in Yazd teemed with turbaned men in white robes. Hole-in-the-wall tea houses reeked of tobacco laced with hashish. That evening, they gulped down underdone *shishlik* and sour yogurt at their hotel's rooftop restaurant.

"I never believed Persian blue was a real color," Angela said. Here, the night sky was the same color of Persian blue as the crayon in her grade-school box of sixty-four.

Stars shining with an intensity she had never seen sequined the heavens, their light reflecting in the blue haze of Doug's eyes as he gazed at her over one of his many beers.

The next morning, the tower loomed ahead on a flat hilltop a few kilometers from Yazd, neither narrow nor particularly high. It did not look like a real tower. Angela's stomach turned queasy when she imagined bodies decaying under the scorching sun. The stench must have been overwhelming even if vultures raced to devour the pickings.

Doug parked the car on a patch of gravel at the foot of the Tower of Silence, and she stepped out into stifling heat. Vultures soared above the tower. "If no bodies are up there now, why are there vultures?" she asked.

"They probably get leftovers from tourists," Doug said.

"Maybe the leftovers they get are tourists," Bill said, and the three of them tittered nervously.

They struggled up a steep path, picnic supplies in tow, trying not to slip on pebbles. The sun knew no mercy.

There were no other tourists.

Forty minutes later, at the top, they dropped their loads and fell to the ground. Doug swigged something out of a hip flask Angela had not realized he had brought. She wondered again if Bill's presence had paradoxically prompted Doug to relapse into excessive drinking. Dehydration from the combination of intense sun and alcohol concerned her. She passed out bottles of water Bill had carried in his backpack, sweat dripping into the corners of her eyes. Doug wiped his forehead with his shirt tail; Bill fanned himself with his cap. She touched the top of her head. Her hair burned hot without the straw hat she had left in the car.

After they ate cold lamb kebabs wrapped in bread, Angela ambled around the flat, circular area where the dead were to have been deposited. "There's nothing here," she said, disappointed at their wasted effort. A few thistles crackled in the dry breeze as if about to ignite spontaneously.

Doug trotted back from the opposite rim, holding something slender and white. "This might be part of an arm or leg."

"It's disrespectful to move it from where it was left," she said.

"You think evil spirits inhabit it? After all these years?" Doug circled back and deposited his discovery where he had found it.

While Doug and Bill scoured the area for evidence of Zoroastrian rites, Angela returned to the path's terminus, where they had left the remains of their picnic. Still sweltering from the climb, she perched on a ridge high above the surrounding desert. If she moved a little or blinked her eyes, she had the sensation someone below was sending a coded signal with a mirror, but it was the sun glaring off the car. Flat land extended as far as she could see, parched and desolate. Heat rising from the earth's surface dissolved the distance into a watery mirage. Vultures circled above. The only sound was her own breathing, amplified by emptiness. The tower rose above the endless expanse, buoyed by invisible waves. She felt herself floating in vast, absolute blue.

Still drifting in the rarefied atmosphere, she became aware that she was alone on the hilltop. Bill and Doug had already gone halfway down. Doug held something above Bill's head. Bill latched his hand onto Doug's forearm. Their voices rose, the words garbled. They gestured and sidled closer to one another as if on the verge of blows. What had precipitated the disagreement? A remark of Doug's? An effort by Bill to stop Doug from drinking before he drove them back to Yazd?

She gathered up the picnic trash and started down, but the going was slow. The two men reached the hill's base long before she did.

In the car, little was said in the strained atmosphere. Neither man's demeanor harbored clues about what had happened on the way down. Doug shifted gears, and the tires spun on gravel before he pulled back onto the pavement and sped towards Yazd.

She shut her eyes, but the disembodied, floating sensation she had experienced earlier had abandoned her.

Human consciousness, it seemed, shifted as randomly as sand dunes in the wind.

Doug insisted on going to a *chelo-kebabi* once back in Yazd, and she humored him. Bill returned to his hotel room for a nap. The one-room establishment she and Doug stumbled into was the only choice now in mid-afternoon when Iranians had already eaten lunch. She selected a table in the back, away from the other customers, all male. At least they did not serve alcohol here.

Near the door, two locals in loose, desert garb and turbans bent faces as shriveled as tea leaves over a game of backgammon. A knife's ornate handle protruded from one man's cummerbund. The other's heavy mustache drooped down to his chin. Other men smoked and talked, their accents flatter than the sing-song Esfahani accent she had acquired, their speech peppered with the word for foreigner, "*khareji*," accompanied by a barrage of guttural exclamations that escaped her.

"D'ya t'ink these men are Zo'astrians?" Doug asked.

"I don't think many are left here. A lot migrated to India—the Parsis." Disgusted at Doug's drunkenness, she focused on her current mission: to get him to feed his alcohol and return sober to the hotel. She motioned to the waiter to bring tea.

After they ordered, Doug groped in his back pocket.

Instead of the flask she anticipated, he produced a domed disk, its slightly convex surface porous and bleached by the desert sun. "A skull fragment," he said. Angela gasped. This must be what caused the argument between Doug and Bill. Doug's behavior repulsed her. Why would he steal from a sacred site?

The waiter set a plate of steaming rice and ground lamb in front of Doug. Doug grabbed his sleeve. "Tell him where we got this, Angela. Ask him if he thinks it's a skull."

"No, I will not." She would not participate in Doug's act of vandalism.

Doug released his hold on the waiter's sleeve. The man peered with curiosity at the skull. "*In chi e?*" He ran his fingers across the skull's surface.

"It's a skull." Absurdly, Doug answered the waiter's question in English. "From the Tower of Silence."

The waiter frowned and shook his head, his eyes blank. Doug pulled a pen from his shirt pocket and sketched the tower on his napkin. He pointed to his head and back to the object the waiter turned over in his hands.

"Yes, yes," the waiter said. "*Amrikai hastid?*" Are you American?

Doug nodded, smiling as though his life depended on it. "Born and bred." He continued to ignore the waiter's lack of comprehension.

The waiter stepped over to the other occupied tables and showed off the booty. The men passed the skull around in silence until the oldest among them rose from his metal folding chair. He wore a green turban, designating him a descendant of the Prophet Mohammad. With the aid of a cane, the white-bearded man hobbled to the center of the room. The other men stared at Doug, now shoveling rice into his mouth with a soup spoon.

"You Americans desecrated a venerated site." The old man spoke in Persian. "You stole from it today. You steal from us every day. You violate what is sacred. You violate *Iran zamin*, our fatherland." He waved the skull fragment above his turban, nearly losing his balance with the gesture's ferocity. His voice split the silence with a lightning-like crackle as he declared his verdict: "*Jihad.* The ayatollahs should issue a *fatwa* calling a *jihad* against you all." At the moment the elder pronounced the word "*jihad,*" the backgammon player fingered the hilt of his knife.

The room erupted with a chorus of angry assent. Angela threw the tomans she had on the table and pulled Doug's arm with all her strength. Doug could not have understood a word, but he had to know the old man's oration had aroused the others. Her violent gesture, augmented by her urging him to leave at once, got him to his feet. She pushed him into the street and broke into a run, pulling him after her, looking back toward the *chelo-kebabi.* If only the men settled back down to their tea and backgammon, the skull in contention in their possession, she would have time to get Bill. He could drive, albeit illegally here. They could return to Esfahan that evening.

"What the hell, Angela?" Doug's voice reverberated through the town's main street. A runny-nosed boy cracking stones on a cracked sidewalk jumped out of their way as they rushed past.

"Quiet. Be quiet. Trust me," she said in a half-whisper.

At the hotel, she fumbled with the key to their room, her hands shaking as she unlocked the door. Doug collapsed on the bed and muttered a few nonsensical protests about losing the skull. He needed to put it back on and cover the brain, he claimed. The alcohol still overpowered the little food he had managed to eat. Sighing, he gave up and descended into a drunken sleep. She left him snoring on the bed and hurried through the hall to Bill's door.

Angela condensed the incident to its bare bones. Bill's face registered shock. "A *jihad*, Bill," she said. "A *jihad.*" The word's sharp edges stung the silence. "My God, we've created an international incident." She shook Bill's arm to urge him to action.

Without a word, Bill threw his clothing and toiletry items into his duffel bag and zipped it shut. "We may have trouble getting him to the car."

"He'll probably be half-asleep."

But Doug was so hard to wake that she had to ask for help from the hotel staff to get him to the car. "He's taken ill," she told them. "Possibly sunstroke. He needs medicine we have at home in Esfahan."

The car rolled down Yazd's main thoroughfare, Doug passed out in the back seat, Bill behind the wheel, Angela riding shotgun in search of would-be *jihadis*.

Once on the open road, Bill accelerated. "Doug doesn't want to face up to finding another job in the States. Since his military days, he's been more remote, contrary at times, with me at least." Gravel from a passing truck hit the windshield like a spray of bullets and ricocheted across the roadway. A shiver shot up Angela's spine. "Working for a big company can be drudgery. I imagine it's the same in an architectural firm," Bill said once the car had picked up speed after slowing in the wake of the gravel. "Some people make you do everything according to the book. Your job becomes boring and routine and bureaucratic. Doug needs to work for himself. Being here has its advantages. Anything he implements will be an improvement over straw and mud squishing through someone's toes. It looks like he's learning what he needs to know to produce executable designs. He has time to work on his own. And he can innovate. He doesn't have to fit in here. Yet, he acts out, drinks too much, makes outrageous remarks. It doesn't make sense. Maybe he's using culture shock as a cover for his insecurities about his career after Iran."

"I don't understand the skull thing," Angela said. "How can he take grave robbing so lightly?" Death equalizes, she thought, even across continents. But Doug would be buried in a clean American cemetery, and grass would blanket his grave, and some cemetery gardener would clip it and electric sprinklers would come on and water it, and she would lay yellow roses—one thing Doug liked about Iran were Persian roses—under the stone inscribed with something inane like *Doug Weston Husband and* (perhaps) *Father He will be missed.* No vultures would soar overhead. No one would disturb Doug's remains. No one would steal a part of his skull.

The trip to Yazd had compounded instead of assuaging Doug's condition. Bill's observations seemed valid, but how could she manage a grown man's behavior? She would have to confront Doug and reassess their plans even though she wanted to stay. Staying would not be an option if Doug's lack of self-control kept putting them in jeopardy. Unless . . . unless she stayed without him. The idea of it shocked her, and she tried it out again, staying here without Doug, living here on her own. This relapse into drinking and the behavior it induced meant she could no longer trust her own husband. In essence, she was alone here. She had no choice but to make decisions for both of them.

On the edge of sleep, she remembered something she had read in her world religion class at the university: once vultures had devoured the flesh on Zoroastrian corpses, officials would gather and burn the bones to prevent their decay from contaminating the natural world. The piece of skull Doug had coveted was not from a human skull at all. But he believed it was, as did the men in the restaurant. Maybe the skull fragment granted him something his life of exile had not bestowed on him. Maybe Doug wanted to possess something eternally human, something vultures and the desert sun could not destroy. Or maybe he simply wanted to hold a shell that once protected another mind, another life.

A few minutes later, she opened her eyes. Doug slept without stirring in the back seat. Bill's cheeks and nose had reddened from the morning's hike. The road meandered through sand dunes. Bill suddenly slowed the car and, leaning toward the dashboard, pointed in the distance where the last light of evening spread over the horizon. Against a backdrop of soft azure, two camels straddled by two men in white glided parallel to the road. From the faded blue cummerbund of one man, a dagger's brass handle caught a dying ray of sunlight. The other man effaced his drooping mustache when he wrapped the end of his turban over his nose, mouth, and chin as protection against wind and sand. The camels' strides were slow, undulating as the sand, and as silent. The riders and their camels angled away from the road toward the horizon, their silhouettes dark against the fading light. They swayed from side to side as they sank behind the dunes, vanishing bit by bit into a wasteland of shifting sand.

This was no mirage.

CHAPTER FOURTEEN

Angela flipped through the pages of her worn copy of *The Scarlet Letter*. Why, on her latest reading of the novel, did she identify with Hester Prynne? She, Angela, had not committed adultery. She wore no bright red A pinned to her blouse. She had not sinned. Unless considering a separation from Doug qualified as a transgression. Again, she questioned the English Department head's choice of assignments. How could a novel that covered the sin of adultery be deemed appropriate for a non-Muslim to teach to a mixed-gender class in Iran? And a foreign female teacher to boot? Hawthorne's dreary book was the last text in the spring semester.

The students tromped into Angela's class, laughing and chatting, their faces vibrant, their speech animated. Their holiday must have been restorative; hers had been a drain on her energy.

The evening before Bill's departure, she had joined forces with Bill to suggest to Doug that he approach living in Iran with equanimity. Doug interpreted their efforts as an act of betrayal and charged them with ganging up on him when they encouraged him to lay off alcohol. There were benefits, they had told him: he would feel less threatened in a hostile environment; he would cease committing rash acts or speaking indiscreetly; he would react in a more effective way when confronted by workers at the construction site.

The list went on.

The attempt backfired.

After Bill had left, Doug had accused her of everything from inducing him to come to Esfahan, which she had not done, to putting him in an inferior position by her command of Persian, which she would not do. She dreaded Doug's coming home that evening. After his first day back on the job, she expected he would be as bitter and paranoid as he had been in the fall. Last night, he had warned her again of "getting in over her head." She tried too hard, he said, to placate troublemakers like Rahimi. His unprovoked ranting disturbed her. Bill had spoken of a change in Doug post-Vietnam, but she had met Doug after his tour of duty. Had Vietnam contributed to his current instability? Her sin, if any, she concluded, was one of omission. When she was busy packing for the move to Iran, Doug had gone alone to his battalion's reunion. If she had accompanied him, she might have met military wives and learned of their husbands' post-war difficulties. Doug never spoke of Vietnam. He would never return to the States without her. But then what? It did feel good to be back in the classroom where the red letter of sin, imagined or real, was invisible.

She surveyed the students to see how many had read the holiday assignment. The nearly unanimous show of hands surprised her. Most had read the entire *Scarlet Letter* during those two weeks. Some indicated they had only a few pages left, showing her where they had stopped. As usual, they had penciled Persian translations in the margins.

"Remember, I will test you with unfamiliar readings." Her gaze fell on Mr. Rahimi, one of the biggest offenders. His Persian notations enclosed in multi-colored geometric designs likely had nothing to do with the lesson. "You have to learn to guess the meanings of words from context," she said, her eyes still on Mr. Rahimi. He had a failing grade so far this semester in spite of Mahtab's continued efforts. But Doug's contempt of him had reinforced her mission: she must instill hope for future employment in Mr. Rahimi and his family, beleaguered though they might be.

The students took to Hawthorne better than expected. Shireen proposed hypocrisy as one of Hawthorne's themes. Before Angela could comment, a book slammed against a desk in the back of the room.

"Wrong!" Mr. Rahimi waved a crimson copy of *The Scarlet Letter* in the air. His bony, veined hand clinging to the book trembled like a dried leaf on the verge of being engulfed in flames. "This book supports sin and prostitution. Hester is like all of you American women." His lips, purple, spit out the insult. "Hester ... Hester is sin." Hassan, who usually disputed with Mr. Rahimi, blanched.

"If the book supports sin, Mr. Rahimi, why does Dimmesdale accept his own guilt?" Angela folded her arms across her chest and twisted the end of the red scarf tied around her neck.

Mr. Rahimi shot to his feet, snatches of English exploding from his lips like machine-gun fire. "It dispenses sin. Like nothing. Because of their illegitimate child. Pearl. Sin made Pearl, but Pearl is good. It dispenses sin. Like nothing."

She frowned and leaned forward, still clutching the swatch of red silk at her neck. "Dispenses sin? Dispenses?" She repeated the awkward phrase until she understood. "You mean it dispenses *with* sin. Dismisses it as if it were nothing. And you think that is because of Pearl?"

"Yes, yes, because of Pearl. Pearl is good. Hawthorne means sin makes something good."

"Absolutely not." In the front row, Shireen jotted down a flurry of words on a scrap of paper and passed it to Mitra. Angela's mind raced through possibilities for dealing with Mr. Rahimi's remarks. How could she gloss over his erroneous interpretation and profit from it to make a teaching point? She cleared her throat. "Hawthorne is using Pearl as a symbol of innocence and purity *in spite of* her parents' sin." She paused. The students fixed their attention on her. "Not *because of* it."

Mr. Rahimi rapped his fist on his desktop. "You want to trick us. You want us to think what you make us read is not against Islam."

Several students nodded their heads in agreement. Angela stepped away from the podium and closed the door. This was outrageous. The book had nothing whatsoever to do with Islam. She had to stop Mr. Rahimi from inciting the class to rebel against her. Incredible. Mr. Rahimi, and perhaps some of the others, accusing her of what must be to Muslims a teacher's worst transgression? Unbelievable. Accusing her of using class assignments to denounce Islam? She had had enough. She marched to the back of the classroom and halted in front of Mr. Rahimi.

"Remember the words of your Prophet." Her warning rushed into air heavy with righteousness.

Next to Mr. Rahimi, Mohammad clutched his fists. Angela's stomach rallied against her and rose to the roof of her mouth. A tremor raced through her body as she recognized the vacant stare invading Mr. Rahimi's eyes. Never had she paraded so foolishly into enemy territory. Again, she identified with Hester Prynne, imagining herself wearing a red A. A for anger. A for arrogance.

Months before, she had shamed Mr. Rahimi in front of the class by referring to the Prophet's admonition to respect teachers. That first time, she had engaged in a venial error of ignorance.

This time, she had committed a mortal sin in total awareness.

*　*　*　*　*　*

It mustered force like a desert sandstorm—his rage at Mrs. Weston, the Shah, Ahmad and Soleiman and Dariush, his uncle, the world as he defined it.

Hossein rushed out of the university gates north toward the city center. He reached the end of Chahar Bagh before his rage coupled with shame: he had shot himself in the foot—not from cowardice. From awkwardness. He had botched his attempt to intimidate Mrs. Weston, butchered his status among his class-mates, and betrayed his religion by treating a teacher with disrespect. Not just any teacher. Mrs. Weston. The teacher who, with his tutor, sympathized with his battle with the English language. And, he had committed these atrocities for an ephemeral booty—to please Soleiman and save face.

Soleiman had dished out disdain to him the night before. "What have you done for the cause, Rahimi? Still no names. Still no foreign teacher packing to leave."

Ahmad insulted him more. "You are failing your English class. So why are you there? To protect Mrs. Weston? Are you against us?"

And then Soleiman issued a decree. He would oust Hossein from the group if he did not show some small contribution in ten days' time. Only Dariush kept silent, eyes downcast as if he were mapping the warps in the wooden table.

By the time Hossein turned into the street leading to the Meidan-e Shah, he was shaking. Warm streams of spittle spewed from the corner of his mouth. He wiped the drool with his coat sleeve. His muscles were on alert; his body was ready to attack. He shoved aside an old woman standing outside the baker's shop near the square. Shouts from the bread queue burst out behind him, women accusing him of disgraceful behavior. He picked up his pace and kicked aside the edge of a prayer carpet on his way, glaring at the shopkeeper who had unrolled it for a customer. Hossein swiped at a stack of copper vessels in front of a metal worker's shop, sending them clanging down the side-walk, flashing in the warm spring sun.

He headed straight for his habitual refuge, the blue-domed mosque, where he went—not to pray and submit to the will of Allah. For that, he joined the faithful at the older Friday Mosque farther away. He went to the blue-domed mosque to calm himself, to stop rage and despair from mastering his actions, to prevent any more wanton fits of violence. Breathless, he halted before the mosque's grand portal, taking in the shades of blue and the Arabic script. Hossein crossed the threshold. He made his way, with mincing steps, to the central court where water and sun, earth and sky merged in silent space. Except for the ablution pool, the central court was empty now. It was the space he liked most, as immaculate as if the sun purified every speck of hatred, every grain of brutality in the hearts of those who came here. He would stay until the light dimmed and the turquoises and indigos and sapphires deepened and dissolved into the darkness and the wind whispered as it swept away clouds tinged with streaks of sunlight and ushered in glimmering stars.

Only here was he at peace.

*　*　*　*　*　*

Doug had never liked Ahmad.

He hated the way Ahmad's eyes looked hard and round and dark like gunshot.

He hated the way Ahmad's tongue slithered out of his mouth like a rattlesnake's.

When Ahmad asked about his weekend, Doug considered it an ambush. Ahmad had no doubt fortified his arsenal with political comments and was scouting the territory before launching his attack. Hoping to ward off any full-scale engagement with the surly worker, Doug replied that he and his wife had finally made it to Persepolis.

"Just the two of you?" Ahmad asked, letting the first barb fly.

Camouflaging his annoyance, Doug extolled the setting of the ancient city and the magnificence of its architecture before Alexander's men had destroyed it. Ahmad ignored his enthusiasm and delivered an unexpected blow. Ahmad, whose English was minimal, signaled for Mahmud to translate for him. When in Persepolis, Ahmad pointed out, Alexander the Great had to be schooled in the Persian practice of courtiers prostrating themselves in front of royalty. Ahmad did not understand that Alexander's discomfort with such formalities was because they were unheard of in the Macedonian court. Instead, Ahmad's interpretation centered on Alexander's so-called belief that Persian kings held too much power, too much prestige, too many rights over the lives of their subjects. Surely Doug agreed?

"I am an architect, not a historian." Doug maneuvered his way out of a counterattack.

The smirk on Ahmad's lips and the hard glare in his eyes testified to Ahmad's disdain.

Doug shaded his eyes and strolled toward the second building under construction. He had heard this line of reasoning before. Now, he remembered that the Persians had not required prostration before the Achaemenid kings. His college history professor believed that Herodotus had likely made up this myth. But, who else had baited him this way? Who else among his Iranian acquaintances had put him in such an awkward position?

No name came to mind.

"I tried to be noncommittal," he told Angela at home that evening. She squinted up at him, her face contorted with alarm. She had been especially jumpy since returning to the university after Nawruz. "Didn't you have the same discussion with *your* Mr. Rahimi?" he said. He studied her expression. Angela's face took on a green tinge in the low light from the blue lampshade. She always grew irate when he referred to *her* Mr. Rahimi.

"Mr. Rahimi tried to manipulate me into declaring whether I am for or against the current regime. He did bring up Alexander's lack of knowledge of the Persian courtiers' practice of prostrating themselves before the king," she said. "As if it had anything to do with the present regime." Her head was bowed, her voice low and halting, her hands folded in her lap. Her lower lip trembled. "You don't think my Mr. Rahimi and your Ahmad know each other, do you?" He could detect no irony in her question.

"I don't know. But I'm going to find out. Where did you say Rahimi is from? What village?"

"Khafr."

"And Khafr is close to Natanz, you say?" He repeated the village's name several times. "How's Rahimi doing this semester?"

"So-so. When he comes."

"You shouldn't take it personally. The country is in turmoil these days. People don't know what to think or who to believe. They're saying the Shah is sick every time his picture isn't on the front page of the papers. And his neighbors, too, are in dire straits." If Angela would listen to the BBC and gain a broader perspective, she could come to grips with some of the inexplicable behavior of a student like Rahimi. "Look at what happened to Daoud in Afghanistan. Bhutto's still on death row in Pakistan."

"I don't think he himself is dangerous. Or violent." Angela picked up a pen and a pile of papers to grade.

"Who? Bhutto?"

"You know who I mean. Mr. Rahimi." She pulled the cap off her pen and made a few red marks on the first paper.

"Anyone can resort to violence. People snap, especially if they perceive their way of life or their families are threatened. Did I ever tell you about a Vietnamese friend I had? He turned out . . ." His voice trailed off. Thinking about Tian sharpened the pain and caused his fear of betrayal to resurface.

Angela looked up. "He turned out how?"

He had piqued her interest. He waved her question off, shaking his head.

"How? Why don't you ever tell me about Vietnam?" she asked. "Maybe I'd understand better those times you wake up shouting 'Where? Over here?' Maybe I could help you when you sit on the side of the bed and I can feel the sheets on your side soaking with sweat." Her voice was soft and full of concern. "It's been much worse since we've been in Iran."

"I didn't realize I disturbed you. I thought you were

asleep." He always checked her after one of his dreams. Her eyes were always shut, and she never stirred except to roll over and put her arm across his chest when he lay back down. "It's not going to benefit anyone to talk about it."

She pleaded with him. She wanted to help, she said, to relieve the anxiety he must feel. She would do anything—get him warm milk, turn on lights, walk around the garden with him—anything.

"You can't help me, Angela," he said. "It's not your ordeal to overcome." He pulled her close to him and kissed both her eyelids. But her sudden concern alerted him. She had been withdrawn lately. What was she hiding? She returned home from the university well before he arrived home from work.

He should—he would—check the house every night for signs of someone else's presence.

*   *   *   *   *   *

She owed them a favor.

Thus, Angela was not surprised when Hassan and Mohammad showed up in her office for the second time. The first time, they had appeared at her office door at 4:30 on the afternoon of the discussion of *The Scarlet Letter*. Mohammad had stayed back, lingering in the doorway. At intervals, he had peeked out the door as if expecting someone to show up in the hall. Hassan had approached Angela's desk with furtive steps. She had awaited him, nervous, expecting repercussions from the morning's discussion. If only Vicky, her office mate, had not left early to pick up her youngest son from school.

Hassan had stood close to her, too close in American terms of comfortable distance. "We need to tell you something." He had spoken in a hoarse whisper and then hesitated. She had nodded permission. "There are rumors. They say Mr. Rahimi is part of a group."

"What kind of group, Hassan?"

"His group says it is for the revolution." She had waited for him to continue, not willing to repeat such an inflammatory word, not wanting to involve herself in politics. "They are not making revolution the right way. They believe in violence. Not in peaceful protests or strikes. Not in passive resistance. Not like Gandhi in India." Hassan was quite fluent in revolutionary vocabulary. "They are—how do you say in English?—tugs."

"They are what?"

"Tugs." Hassan's tongue had hit against his palate rather than protruding past the bottom of his front teeth.

"Thugs. You must pronounce the 'th' even though it is hard for Persian speakers. Otherwise, it means a kind of boat."

"Sorry." Hassan had grinned and tried to make the dreaded "th" sound, but it had come out somewhere between a D and a Z. He had taken another step closer to Angela. "You must be careful, Mrs. Weston. Mr. Rahimi's group thinks foreigners all work with the government."

"You mean they consider us collaborators."

"Collaborators." Hassan had seemed pleased to add another politically charged word to his English lexicon. "Be careful."

She had opened her mouth but closed it again over a thousand questions, relieved despite Hassan's accusations against Mr. Rahimi. Rather than renouncing her for shaming Mr. Rahimi, these two stellar students had warned her against more such indiscretions. She had muttered her thanks and put on her jacket, ready to go home. Hassan and Mohammad had trailed her at a distance until she reached the university gates, where they loitered, scanning the crowded sidewalk, until the door of a taxi slammed shut after her.

Now, they again waited until she was alone. Again, Mohammad guarded the door, casually intercepting other students and informing them that the queue for a conference with Mrs. Weston formed behind him. Again, Hassan did the talking, edging closer to her and asking for her help. From what she understood, Iranian social mores required her to repay them without questions, to comply blindly with whatever they requested. Both Hassan and Mohammad—Moe Number One, she called him privately—were A students. They would have no reason to want her to change a grade. Nor would they expect her to overstep the boundaries of a teacher-student relationship.

Hassan removed a sheet of paper from his notebook and slid it under the dictionary on the corner of her desk. She scooted the dictionary in front of her and opened it. From underneath the book, she retrieved a copy of a typewritten flyer and laid it on the dictionary's right-hand page. Hassan lowered himself into the chair reserved for students at the side of her desk and leaned on his elbow with a pen in his hand as if the two of them were going over an essay. Angela studied the paper, trying to decipher the Persian. Once she realized what Hassan had given her, her hands grew clammy. The flyer, full of revolutionary jargon, some of which she could not make out, called for a general, peaceful strike against the Shah's government. No wonder Hassan knew the appropriate vocabulary when he accused Mr. Rahimi of being a thug a few days before. He must have translated some of these words into English before he spoke with her the last time. But what did he want from her? She was a foreigner employed by a state-run institution. Condoning acts of civil disobedience or engaging in any political activity would compromise her position and put her at risk of charges of conspiracy. She folded the flyer lengthwise as if it were a student paper and returned it to Hassan, who secreted it between the pages of his notebook. The door creaked. Mohammad had pushed it nearly shut and taken up his sentinel duty outside in the hall.

Hassan chewed the end of his pen. Surely he knew the U.S. government supported the monarchy. Had these two students somehow intuited her private political stance? How could they know she favored overthrowing the Shah and establishing a democracy in Iran? She hardly admitted her political views to herself. Did she let something slip that gave her away?

She pivoted her chair toward Hassan, who, clearly, had no

intention of speaking first. "And?"

"We have heard they . . ." Hassan turned the corners of his lips into an upside-down smile, causing his neck bones to stick out. Were the subject not so serious, his expression would be comical. "That they can match words on paper with the typewriter that produced them."

"Perhaps," she said. They must be SAVAK.

"One day in class, you said you have a big garden. No one would ever find a typewriter there. No one would ever think of you or look in your house." Hassan kept his eyes on the door, his chest rising and falling with heavy breathing accompanied by a slight wheeze.

"I see." If Hassan and Moe Number One had produced the original flyer, they possessed the typewriter. Their scheme was preposterous and pathetic at the same time, but they asked for little on her part. And they had tried to protect her, although Mr. Rahimi had missed class since his last outburst. "Where can I find the typewriter?" she asked. Hassan's paranoia seemed far-fetched, but she had heard of the imprisonment of former students. The slightest chance two of her favorites would be lost forever to their families required her to help them.

"I will leave it outside your garden door at midnight," Hassan said. "Unless someone follows me."

"You know where I live?" Hassan nodded and got to his feet, his expression blank. The conference was over. How he had obtained her address would forever remain a mystery.

Mohammad swung the door open and entered. "Your work is excellent, Hassan," Angela said in a voice loud enough to be heard in the hallway. "Keep it up."

After Hassan left, she continued the charade, the door wide open as she chatted with Mohammad about his last assignment, which he had conveniently remembered to bring with him.

She would need help burying a typewriter under the mimosa tree.

When she confided in Doug at dinner that night, his mouth fell open so wide she had to laugh. "I know. It's cloak-and-dagger, but these kids are afraid of being caught. It's sad to have to go to such extremes because you live in a country without freedom of speech."

Doug was quiet, seemingly mulling over the situation, until his fork clanged onto his plate with a bite of chicken still on it. He sprang from the ladder-back chair, shoving it back so hard it overturned and clattered on the floor, and pushed his plate toward the center of the table. "I can't believe this." His hands flat on the table's surface, he leaned toward her, crouching down to her eye level. "You like it here. And now you're putting us in jeopardy."

"You're telling me *I'm* the one who has jeopardized us? I trust Mohammad and Hassan. They recently warned me about an anti-American gang of thugs clamoring to rid the country of foreign influence." Better not to let Doug know Mr. Rahimi was supposedly in that gang. Better to emphasize that the flyer preached passive resistance.

"They warned you? The same two who want to give you a . . . a guilty typewriter?"

"I didn't know a typewriter could be guilty." Doug was so angry he could not think of the right phrase. Her attempt to lighten up the conversation failed.

Doug banged his hands on the table. "They're setting you up, Angela. They warned you of someone else to make you trust them. They'll give you something—the typewriter—that will incriminate us, and after they report us, we'll be interrogated by SAVAK and, at best, deported. They'll distribute the flyers and proceed with their little revolution."

"You said you wanted to leave this summer anyway." In the past week, they had discussed returning to the States at the end of their first year. She was standing now, her hands on the tabletop, leaning towards him. The set of his jaw hardened, and he held his position.

"I changed my mind. The bonus, Angela. The bonus. I need that two-year bonus." He was shouting, his face flushed. Who was this man she had married? Had he stopped at the Iran Tour Hotel for drinks after work?

She took a seat and began eating, hoping the simple, everyday act would quiet her anger at his unjust accusations and unexpected contradictions. He picked up his chair and sat down.

"Forget it," she said. "I'll tell them to find another place to get rid of the typewriter. Wipe their fingerprints off it. Dump it in the desert or something." Neither of the two students likely had transportation to get to the desert. She pictured them boarding a minibus, typewriter in tow, hidden in a knapsack. Somewhere near Yazd, they would dig deep into a dune to bury the typewriter and count on shifting sand to obliterate their footprints.

"I can't believe you considered such a thing," Doug said.

His face looked unfamiliar and distant, although it had resumed its normal color.

At midnight, with Doug sound asleep, Angela tiptoed through the garden in her bathrobe. She pressed her ear against the compound door and held her breath. In the *kucheh*, a cat in heat howled. At 12:15 by her watch, she released the metal lever locked into place on the door's frame. The door creaked as she edged it open. She peeked out into the *kucheh*, darker than usual in the absence of moonlight. As far as she could tell, no one was there. If someone had trailed Hassan and Mohammad and was now hiding in the *kucheh*, turning on a flashlight or lighting a kerosene lamp could put her in danger. She stepped over the door jamb into the dark and stubbed her toe against something on the ground. Her hands groped an object with metal casing. Angela slipped her fingers under the frame, scraping her knuckles on the gravel, and lifted the typewriter over the threshold. After latching the door, she stowed Hassan's typewriter under the garden table and fetched a tablecloth from the house. Its white folds billowed in the dark as she shook it out, a floating phantom that vanished when the tablecloth settled over the table, all four sides puddling on the ground, screening the telltale typewriter. In the morning, Doug would rush, still sleepy, to catch his bus to work and never notice that a white tablecloth had materialized overnight on their garden table.

She climbed onto the *takht* beside Doug, but as the moon had abandoned the night sky, slumber had deserted her. She knew Hassan and Mohammed, had seen them interact with Mr. Rahimi for almost two semesters now. She would not go back on her word to them. But she detested having to make decisions alone without Doug. This was the first time she had ever done anything to deceive or trick him.

How long would it take her the next afternoon to dig deep enough to bury a typewriter?

She had no shovel, only a rusty trowel.

CHAPTER FIFTEEN

Monotony. Sheer monotony.

Flat, barren land rolled by as the minibus cranked its way forward on the gravel road. Khafr should be close now. Angela fretted that the driver would forget to let her out nearby. She took a swig from her water bottle, her mouth dry, not only from desert air but also from anxiety. Meeting Mr. Rahimi's parents was a last-ditch effort. In Detroit, she had often been successful in engaging parental involvement in their off-spring's education. Here, too, she thought it might work. For centuries, people in Iran had trusted members of their own tribe. Family bonds became inviolate in Iranian society. Fathers especially received homage from their sons. Mahtab had told her all these things. Kamran had also told her. Her students had told her.

Much had happened in a few days—none of it encouraging. Two days ago, Dr. Aminipour stopped her in the hall and engaged her in small talk: summer session hours, fall semester textbooks. Once the hallway had cleared of students, he brought up the reason for his sudden interest in her.

"You have Mr. Hossein Rahimi in your advanced reading class, don't you?" Dr. Aminipour frowned and pushed up his specs. "His family is not well off—poor villagers. We want students with his background to succeed at the university." The dean drew his heavy eyebrows over the bridge of his nose and squeezed his lips together. Goosebumps erupted on Angela's arms. "We don't want someone like Mr. Rahimi to fail. Especially not now." He stared at her pointedly. "We are experiencing a little unrest in the country. Poor students must hope for a better future." He turned on his heel and dashed away without waiting for her response.

His words added to her despair over what she thought of as her Rahimi calling. Mr. Rahimi had started attending class again in the last ten days. Had he complained about her to the dean? Or had someone informed the dean about Mr. Rahimi's revolutionary leanings? Maybe Mr. Rahimi had threatened Dr. Aminipour. In any case, Dr. Aminipour was threatening her. The prospect of losing her job and her access to learning more about Iranian society sickened her. She had worked hard to gain her students' acceptance. She would not survive here if she had to sit all day alone in her garden, her social contacts limited to Americans like Guy and Maryanne. She might as well be Stateside in suburbia. She groaned at the thought. Her knees had turned to jelly, and she found an empty classroom where she sank into a student desk.

And there was the revelation earlier this morning. Another blow. She had spent the previous night with Vicky's in-laws in Natanz. Vicky and Reza were staying another day, but she had told them she needed to get back to Esfahan and Doug. Vicky had made a point of volunteering to deposit her at the Natanz bus station. "I wanted you to come alone for a day, not only to meet Reza's parents," Vicky told her before she boarded the bus, making Angela uneasy as she waited for Vicky's explanation. Vicky could not know that she planned to stop in Khafr. She had told no one.

"I heard a rumor," Vicky said. "Thought you should know."

Angela edged toward the bus. Vicky reveled in her role as a gossip monger.

"Hossein Rahimi is spreading rumors about you." Vicky paused. "You and Kamran. It seems the students think the two of you are . . ." She held up two fingers and crossed them.

"Who told you that?"

"Have to protect my source." A smug smile. "But it's not only the possibility of an affair."

"Which you know is not the case." Angela interrupted Vicky, seething. "I hope you made that clear to your protected source." All this had to have originated with Ali Habibi. He had seen her with Kamran on the bus the day they returned from Persepolis. But that was months ago. Why had this surfaced now?

"They think you and Kamran are collaborating." Vicky cast a paranoid look around. "Working for the Shah," she said in a low voice.

"You're kidding."

Vicky grabbed her arm. "Kamran works for SAVAK, according to Rahimi." She was warming up to the subject, saving the best for the last, no doubt. "You are a CIA agent."

"Preposterous." Angela shook her head. It was all so ridiculous it hardly merited comment. Doug also kept making allegations of Kamran's ties to SAVAK. Was she the only sane one here? "I hope you set the story straight." She was sure Vicky had not vouched for either her or Kamran. Vicky reveled in egging on the students who had high gossip potential.

Now Angela fretted that Dr. Aminipour had heard these rumors. If so, they would serve as more justification to get rid of her. The situation embarrassed her. She would have to sidestep Kamran whenever possible for both their sakes, but she would not curtail their friendship because of a student's stupid speculations.

A short distance later, the bus rumbled to a halt, throwing her to the edge of her seat. "*Unja, khanoum.*" The driver motioned to her. He swung the door open and pointed to some mud huts in the distance. "*Dota kilometr-e digeh.*" She thanked him and bounded down the steps, eager to get off the shaky bus. The driver gunned the engine, and the bus kicked up a spray of dust as it spurted down the road. Angela hoisted her backpack in place and hiked the remaining two kilometers, her eyes watering from the dust.

On the way, she rehearsed what she would convey to Mr. Rahimi senior. His son had neglected to hand in an essay. He failed a test on Wednesday. She could pass him if he submitted extra assignments. With the final exam four weeks away, he had to improve soon. She had to contrive a diplomatic way to persuade the father to put pressure on the son. There were risks: she must succeed in convincing the parents of her goodwill and sincerity; Mr. Rahimi's father might resent a foreigner bearing such grim news; he might see her concern as interference by a woman and an infidel and reject her outright. His status as a villager would likely prove an obstacle to his understanding of what university studies entailed. And this latest rumor. Had Mr. Rahimi stated his opinions about her and Kamran at home? But everything else she had done had failed. The father was her last resort.

By the time she dragged herself into Khafr, grains of dust had seeped into her tennis shoes. Her lips tasted of dirt. She was thirsty. Her eyes stung. Sweat trickled down her back and off her forehead. The path ascended a slope lined with abandoned mud buildings with rusted door handles. The only vegetation, a plum tree orchard, struggled to survive behind a crumbling mud wall. Ahead, a donkey overloaded with bags of flour straggled after a villager armed with a switch. Flies swarmed over animal dung in the alleyways. Angela breathed through her mouth to avoid the stench and watched where she stepped.

Relief came when she spotted a bread shop. A boy squatted next to the adobe oven, slurping yogurt from a clay bowl. Angela bought a piece of bread and buried her nose in it. The smell of charred dough mitigated the odor coming from the piles of dung. She picked a few rials out of her coin purse and asked the baker where she could find the Rahimis' house. The boy, lips rimmed in white, jumped up and pulled her hand. Three other barefoot boys with shaven heads paraded with them around the corner. The troop stopped before a door with peeling blue paint. The boys pounded on the door with their fists and screamed, "*Khanoum-e Rahimi, Khanoum-e Rahimi.*" Women with *chadors* wrapped over their hair and under their breasts stuck their heads out of doors on both sides of the *kucheh.* The Rahimis' door cracked open. A short woman in a threadbare, black *chador* peered out, her eyes squinting in the bright light. They widened when she caught sight of Angela.

"*Befarmayid,*" the woman said and flung open the door.

"I am Mr. Hossein Rahimi's university teacher. Is he your son?" Angela said in Persian. It was obvious that Mrs. Rahimi knew no English.

"*Baleh, Baleh, khanoum, befarmayid.*" The woman's smile revealed teeth black with decay. "I am honored to have you as a guest."

Angela stepped across the threshold, fighting a sudden desire to turn around and run. It was too late now. She would have to live with the decision she had made.

She knew as soon as she entered the courtyard that Mr. Rahimi was right in his assessment of his family. They would understand nothing about the university and how it operated. The courtyard offered no respite from the heat. Two scrawny chickens and a rooster pecked in the dirt. A goat chomped on the leaves of a stunted pomegranate tree.

Mrs. Rahimi flapped back a faded, red curtain and led Angela into a living area. The room had no ventilation and little light. Mrs. Rahimi directed her to sit on a frayed pillow, one of three surrounding a garish, tea-stained carpet that covered part of the dirt floor. She dipped some water from an earthen jug into a teapot and added a few tea leaves from a dinted tin. A low voice grunted from the back wall, startling

Angela. Someone else was in the room.

A girl in baggy pants and an oversized shirt grunted again and jabbered nonsense syllables. Angela guessed she was three or four years younger than Mr. Rahimi. The girl bore him a faint resemblance. Her arms and legs were short and stubby. Her eyes registered little acknowledgment either of Angela's presence or of Mrs. Rahimi's movements. The girl's hair, heavy and matted, fell over her brow, one wisp plastered to her cheek by dried snot. Her nose ran. Drool trickled from her thick, parted lips.

Angela struggled for words. The scene of squalor and poverty, worse than anything she had expected, distressed her. She felt she was living in a Dickins novel transplanted to Iran. She presumed the girl was Mr. Rahimi's sister. As repulsive as her appearance was, it filled Angela with pity. If only she could wash the girl's face and hair and soothe her agitation.

Before Angela could object, Mrs. Rahimi offered her a dish of rice topped with a thin stew of greens. *Ghormeh sabzi* minus red beans and lamb. A poor man's version without protein. It looked and smelled foul, but Angela took a few bites of the concoction, holding her breath to avoid the odor of rancid oil. The stew tasted of strongly acidic lemons. Not what she needed for her stomach. Little food remained in the pot for the family's evening meal. Perhaps later, when they were alone, the mother would offer the daughter what Angela would leave on the plate. Angela presented the bread she had bought earlier to Mrs. Rahimi, and the girl stumbled forward, her hand extended to grab it. Mrs. Rahimi slapped the girl's hand away. Only after Angela persuaded the mother that the bread was a gift for her daughter did Mrs. Rahimi allow the girl to have some. The child stuffed a piece into her mouth. Slobber and wads of barely chewed bread dribbled down her chin and formed a puddle on the worn carpet.

Outside, the courtyard door clicked shut.

"*Jan-e man*," Mrs. Rahimi called out. "We have a guest."

Angela rose to greet Mr. Rahimi, the father. She had forgotten to bring a headscarf. In Esfahan, it would not matter much;

in Khafr, it might matter a lot. A man ducked under the red curtain draped over the door jamb. His plastic sandals flew across the threshold before he stepped barefoot onto the carpet. She made out his face, and her carefully planned words slipped away from her like a desert mirage vanishing in the changing light.

"Mr. Rahimi." Shocked, she stammered a few perfunctory words. Mr. Rahimi, who had dropped on the nearest cushion, recognized her and clambered to his bare feet. His pupils, although behind thick lenses in dim light, struck her as disproportionately small. "I didn't know you would be here for the weekend," she said.

He placed his hand over his heart, inclined his head, and mumbled a greeting, calling her "Esteemed Teacher, Honored Guest."

"I'm honored to meet your mother and sister." She had put him in an awkward position. He was treating her with deference because *ta'arof* required him to offer hospitality whenever asked, even to a mortal enemy. She prattled on about anything she could think of: how special for her to see where he grew up; how pleasant for his family to live in this lovely village; how nice for his mother to have him home this weekend. She went on and on, trying to ease his distress at her visit, but without easing her own.

Mr. Rahimi refilled her tea glass, insisting she stick a hard, brown lozenge of sugar behind her teeth as she sipped the hot tea. With a flash of pride, Mrs. Rahimi showed Angela the only picture of her son that the family owned. A black-and-white photo with a photographer's backdrop of a mountain brook rushing through a meadow bordered by pine trees. Nothing like the landscape around Khafr. A six-year-old. Surly. Skinny. Shaven head. White shirt. Miniature dark suit much like the one he always wore. It looked as if that same suit had somehow grown along with the boy in it. In the picture, as well, the pants were too short.

"A handsome child." She handed the picture back to a

beaming Mrs. Rahimi. At his mother's request, Mr. Rahimi cleaned up slime and breadcrumbs from the carpet and cleared away dirty dishes. He snatched a tissue from the box used for napkins and wiped his sister's face, pulled a comb from his pocket, and arranged her hair out of her eyes. The girl gurgled in delight. She grasped her brother's hand and kissed it.

"He is good with your daughter," Angela said. She would never have guessed this of the Mr. Rahimi she knew at the university. Mrs. Rahimi praised her son, referring to him again as "*jan-e man*," my life.

The family fell silent and looked at her as if they expected her to take the initiative in the conversation. She groped for words. "I would be honored if I could meet Mr. Rahimi's father." Mrs. Rahimi shot her a look of alarm coupled with anguish. Angela froze, afraid to speak, overcome by unanticipated foreboding. Was it forbidden for a woman to ask to meet an older man in Iranian culture?

"He is dead," Mrs. Rahimi said, her pronouncement blunt in its stark reality. She wiped a tear from her eye with the end of her *chador*.

"I didn't know. I'm sorry."

Mr. Rahimi picked up his mother's hand and held it. "My father died ten months ago." His voice rang with the usual defiance, missing today until now. "He was *killed*."

"Killed?" Angela asked. Mr. Rahimi glared at her as though his father's death, accident or murder, were somehow her fault. A chill worked its way up her spine in spite of the close, warm air in the tiny room. How should she respond? What prescribed phrases of sympathy should she offer? Should she have visited a home during the first year after a death in the family? The silence bore down on her like the desert sun. "I wish you would have told me," she said at last in English to her student.

Mr. Rahimi clenched his jaw, and she could hear him grind his teeth. He settled his mother's hand back into her lap. "It doesn't matter." He flung the back of his own hand away from his body. That familiar, fly-swatting movement spoke with disdain: nothing in this world mattered except Allah's will. Not the mother's grief. Not the sister's disability. Not the family's poverty. Angela stifled the urge to empty her wallet and give what few tomans she carried to Mr. Rahimi's mother. Right there. In front of him. But that would never do.

Instead, she changed the subject. Had the Rahimis always lived here? The three of them chatted about the family's days in Tehran, Mrs. Rahimi's delicious *khoresht*, and Mr. Rahimi's progress in speaking English.

Angela prepared to leave, explaining that she did not want to miss the last bus to Esfahan.

She had tried to match Mrs. Rahimi's kindness with compliments and gratitude, but to her mind, anything she said was meaningless in the face of this family's desperation.

Her afternoon visit had compounded her morning's misery.

Angela tromped down the only road in the middle of a plateau devoid of visible human life. How could she expect Mr. Rahimi to concentrate on English with his family in such dire straits? Had his father run afoul of the government? She supposed SAVAK informers ratted on real or presumed offenders in villages, too. Or, had the "accident" happened in Tehran? No matter how Mr. Rahimi acted in class, she admired his obedience to his mother and his tenderness with his sister.

A desert wind whipped up and snaked through her hair. The sun, smirking low on the horizon, gave out no warmth, and even now, in late April, the evening wind chilled every part of her body—muscles, bones, tendons—and frayed her nerves. Dr. Aminipour's words blew over her like swirling dust devils over arid land. She had to pass Mr. Rahimi. She deplored cheating, but she would enter a passing grade in her grade book for this last exam. Not a good grade, but one high enough to give him a strong D or low C before the final. As for the missing essay, she would throw out the lowest essay grade in addition to the lowest test grade for each student.

But passing Mr. Rahimi was trivial. His sister could hardly get enough food, much less therapy or special education. Did the government provide no services to alleviate such suffering? Angela pulled her collar over her mouth to keep out the dirt.

In the distance, a brown cloud barreled toward her—the minibus, the sole object in motion in the 360 degrees around her. It could be true that desert harshness scattered thought, encouraged visions. Moses and the burning bush. Jesus tempted by Satan. The Prophet on Mount Arafat. But religious apparitions evaded her. She felt empty, dried up, meaningless. What she taught had little consequence in this repressive society. And Doug's efforts—meaningless, too—his work on the site, his nights crafting designs or reading textbooks, his money stashed away for his own business in the States.

The bus pulled to a stop.

She climbed the steps. "Esfahan," she said to the driver and handed him a 200-rial bill.

"*Na.*" He refused the bill, shaking his outstretched palm at her. He must not have change. She dug in her pockets. The coins tinkled as her fingers raked through her purse to find exact change. Contemptuous—that sound of money. Contemptuous—all that money, too much money, the money Doug hid at home where he thought it safer than in Iranian banks. It would take so little to make so much difference to the Rahimis. She spent her salary on household expenses. Little, if any, remained at the end of the month.

But Doug. He set aside his entire salary, although the bonus at the end of his contract would also go towards setting up his business. And she would have a salary in the States upon their return.

She settled back in her seat and thought of Doug as she had known him in the States: his clear reasoning, his responsible nature, his desire to protect friends and family. There,

Doug had approved of charity. They had allocated eight per-cent of their combined salaries to their favorite non-profit organizations. Doug would not miss a little money. She could skim off a wee bit for Mr. Rahimi's family. It was not the most honest act—dipping into her husband's savings. But she would pay him back someday.

She had to wait a while before letting Doug know about her new commitment. He still railed about Mr. Rahimi's trance during the tea house performance. Doug still deplored the fact that she had considered hiding Hassan's typewriter.

Now, Doug planted his feet over that typewriter every time they ate dinner under the mimosa tree.

After she returned from Khafr, she had crammed an envelope stuffed with money into her purse.

It was still there.

Where could it have gone in the three days since she had pilfered thirty thousand tomans from Doug's cache? Angela zipped her purse shut. If she were fatalistic, she would have no reason to feel guilty about her actions. She would con-sider them in compliance with the grand scheme of things and believe that she herself was not ultimately responsible for what she did, hence not guilty in the least.

But she was not fatalistic.

The first rays of the sun coated the mountain's eastern side with molten gold. Angela yawned. She usually arrived at the university an hour later, but today, Daylight Savings Time began in Iran for the first time. And she had summoned Mr. Rahimi to her office before class. If only the tea boy would come. He must have overslept today. How many of her stu-dents would miss their first class this morning?

Yesterday, she had told Mahtab about the elder in Yazd, how he had waved what he believed to be a piece of a Zoroastrian skull above his green turban and called for a *jihad*.

"*Jihads* do not have to be acts of violence. Or real wars feeding on death and destruction," Mahtab said.

A peaceful *jihad*? It seemed a contradiction in terms, but if there were such a thing, she had engaged in one. A *jihad* to help Mr. Rahimi and his family have a better life. A *jihad* to prove she was a person of goodwill who believed in the potential of the human species. It sounded self-righteous. She had a broader purpose, a *jihad* to attain greater understanding among humans. If so, she should start by telling Doug about the money in her purse. Fatalism had its advantages. How much simpler to rely on fate, kismet, God's will, universal design, destiny, luck, providence, fortune, one's lot in life, chance, divine intervention—none of which she believed in any more than she believed in a pacific holy war. History had not played out that way.

She did the math. Thirty thousand tomans, three hundred thousand rials, five thousand or so dollars. Two and a half VW Bugs. A down payment on a house in the suburbs. Two normal pregnancies with uncomplicated deliveries. All this paled against a family's minimal requirements for food and clothing. The Rahimis would survive for a year with thirty thousand tomans. One transgression against one person versus one year for three people. No balance there. The side of the scales holding the transgression tilted much higher, weighed much less than three person-years of life. Otherwise put, she could take much more money from the coffers before the wrongdoing balanced out the good. The math bore out. Why did she feel so guilty? If only she could have had enough confidence in Doug to consult him.

An hour later, the tea boy still had not shown up, but Mr. Rahimi did. Late.

"Are you going to have class on God's time or the government's?" he asked by way of announcing his presence.

"God's time?" He was up to his old tricks again, referring to the sun, which signaled the times for the five calls to prayer. "I must hold class on the university's time." She glanced at the wall clock. A slight smile played on Mr. Rahimi's lips as if he appreciated her adroit answer. "However, if you wish, you may step into the hall to pray during the time the university has designated as class time. I'd appreciate your letting the other students know as well."

She snapped open her purse. "I'd like you to give this to your mother." She held out a plain, sealed envelope. "You needn't tell her it came from me."

He stared at the envelope, seemingly taken aback.

Angela rose and strode across the office and pushed it toward him, forcing him to take it. She brushed past him. "Today, the university says our class will start in five minutes," she said and started toward the stairs.

The envelope lay, unopened, in Mr. Rahimi's hands.

CHAPTER SIXTEEN

The *bazaari* stretched out a grimy hand, his fingers twitching with greed.

Hossein Rahimi trickled a few tomans into it, reiterating that he was going mountain climbing in the Alborz range north of Tehran. He coiled the rope over his shoulder and hugged the metal spikes under his jacket against his ribcage. His shoulder sagged under the rope's weight as he searched for a back way out of the bazaar. Finally, he emerged on an unknown street where he tried, and failed, to pick up speed. Instead, he lumbered along in the opposite direction of the room he shared with Ahmad. Ahmad and Soleiman were in Qom for the weekend. There, they would present the *mullahs* with 25,000 tomans, Hossein's gift to the revolutionary cause. Soleiman had banned him from the revolutionary group in spite of Hossein's other schemes—his challenges to Mrs. Weston, the rumors he started about her. But the money redeemed him in Soleiman's eyes after all these weeks. Soleiman's fingers had grasped for the money with a *bazaari's* greed, but unlike the *bazaari*, Soleiman would invest it in the revolutionary cause. Or would he?

"This money will help defray expenses of producing and distributing tapes," Soleiman had said, referencing the fiery speeches the Ayatollah Khomeini recorded in exile on the outskirts of Paris. "We need bribe money for government officials, police, military men. They must turn their backs when the time comes for rioting in the streets." Soleiman had grabbed Hossein's shoulders with both hands and looked into his eyes. "Well done, Hossein-*jan*."

Hossein congratulated himself. He had played the game well. When Soleiman had asked where he had gotten the money, he had replied, "Allah provides." Refusing to say more gave him a certain power over Soleiman. Soleiman would retain him in the group at least for a short time if he believed there was the slightest chance of procuring more funds.

Hossein shifted the rope to his other shoulder and suppressed a smile. The amount of money Mrs. Weston's envelope contained had flabbergasted him so much that he nearly succumbed to his first reaction—to shred it and send cash confetti floating over the street. How dare Mrs. Weston imply that his mother needed filthy money gleaned by foreign infidels from the country's coffers? But something stopped him: the hand of Allah. Allah kept him from squandering what rightfully belonged to the struggle for Islamic rule. Allah's fingers were not twisted with greed.

Ahmad helped. Ahmad's cousin, Khosrow, studied in Qom at the *madresseh*. Khosrow would find contacts to put the money to good use, Ahmad had said, and he had separated out five thousand tomans for Hossein's mother.

"Tell your mother to hide the money," Ahmad had said over Hossein's protests, "in case someone in our group needs to escape from the authorities." Money, he had elaborated, was essential in times of crisis. They needed to protect each other, especially now. Rumblings about SAVAK infiltration into the underground revolutionary movement increased daily. Extra tomans close at hand would provide a safety net.

Hossein entered a *chelo-kebabi* and ordered *shishlik*. He chewed each bite with deliberation, measuring the time before midnight. By then, activity on the city streets would come to a halt. The night promised no moon. Even so, he must take care. By midnight, many people would have fallen into their first, light sleep. An unaccustomed noise would easily awaken them, an unusual presence easily alarm them.

At eleven o'clock, he paid for his meal and shuffled out of the restaurant. Behind him, the grill clanged as the drowsy restaurant owner lowered it over the *chelo-kebabi*'s façade. Already the other small businesses were as dark as death, with no living soul in sight. Hossein meandered along the sidewalk. He had an hour to kill.

Under a streetlamp, he studied the map Mrs. Weston had drawn for him at Christmas. Other Iranians might enjoy a happy holiday—Shiite feast days were often sad—a holiday with gifts and bright lights and huge meals of foreign food, perhaps *haram*. Other Iranians might use Christmas as an excuse, if they needed one—not often the case—to drink alcohol. The idea of foreign food and drink sickened him. He had made the right decision to avoid Mrs. Weston's Christmas dinner. He stuffed the scrap of paper into his pocket and readjusted the rope and spikes. Crossing Esfahan on foot would take nearly an hour.

At his destination, he located the Westons' compound, the last on the north side of the *kucheh*. A dead-end—silent, dark, deserted. He slouched against the outer walls to rest. He still had time to abandon his project. But, no, he would surprise Soleiman with a new success in case Soleiman still distrusted him. He would pay back Mrs. Weston for her betrayal in class yesterday. During a discussion about artistic mentality, she had asked if he found himself in a separate reality when he played the *tar*. Until then, his classmates had known neither of his passion for traditional music nor of his invitation to Mrs. Weston and her husband. She had exposed his secret. He was proud of his playing, but many of the other students considered the traditional arts old-fashioned. They preferred Iranian pop singers or modern Western music, which they played at high volumes on imported boom boxes. His embarrassment and anger peaked when Firouz attacked him.

"You are a hypocrite if you play music," Firouz said. "Islam forbids it, and you pretend you are religious."

An argument broke out. Hossein asked Firouz what he knew of religious *ghazels*, spiritual poetry, often set to music, in which God is referred to as the unattainable Beloved. The only answer was the bell ringing at the end of class.

A *jub* dog trotted down the *kucheh*, sniffing for garbage, its yellow eyes gleaming in the dark. The dog loped off, but not before sending tremors over Hossein's sore shoulders. Its eerie eyes reminded him of Mrs. Weston's separate reality. What did she mean? The trance-like states he had known since childhood for which his uncle offered music as a remedy? The pleasure he experienced when smoking opium, which he did only in Khafr with Agha-ye Farhadnejad, a documented addict with legal access to it? But he had recently sworn off opium. The day of Mrs. Weston's visit was the last time he had stuck the brown substance on his pipe's hot, porcelain bulb and sucked smoke through the bulb's tiny hole into his lungs. That day, when he ducked under the curtain and saw a woman there through an opiate dream, her bloodshot eyes resembled those of a hag who would turn an evil eye on them all. Her hair frizzed around her face like the tentacles of a monster from hell come to sweep up his family, drag them to a cave, devour their flesh, and crunch their bones into desert sand. His state of opiate euphoria kept him from terror, and he experienced a profound curiosity when he saw Fatimeh's hair crawling with vipers. He combed his sister's hair, freeing the vipers, not caring which way they went once they slithered to the earthen floor. After he cleaned the carpet and removed the dishes, the opium wore off, and the dream dissipated until, eventually, the evil intruder assumed Mrs. Weston's familiar aspect; its voice, formerly a gust of unintelligible words, her voice, speaking Persian with an American accent; its hair, her hair, unruly from the dry wind; its eyes, her eyes, mattered with dust. That day, he divined an evil Mrs. Weston, a gift of the opiate cloud. And then, this gift of money?

Perhaps he had misjudged her. But there would be no more money to pacify Soleiman. Staying in the group depended on the ultimate triumph—making Americans leave Iran.

Convinced, Hossein anchored a spike as high on the garden wall as he could reach and, using another as a hammer, tapped it in. Once assured of its stability, he lassoed the spike with the rope and tightened it around the metal. With a second spike clenched between his teeth, he walked his hands up the rope, his feet up the wall. Perching on the top, he released the rope from the spike and, with his shoe, hammered the second spike to the wall's inside surface, secured the rope on the spike, and lowered himself into the garden.

No light came from the Westons' windows. Crouching low to the ground, Hossein worked his way among the bushes toward the rooms on the wall's west side until he ran into a tree that smelled sweet. Mimosa. His hand groped a piece of furniture underneath the tree: a table with a cloth draped over it. Foreigners had strange dining habits. He peeked above the tabletop. Still dark. Rising, he reached above his head and grasped one of the tree's smaller branches. He snapped it off and squatted again, hidden by the covered table, listening for some sound in reply to the branch's crack. Nothing. He skirted the east edge of the house until he got to the northwest corner, where he flattened himself on the ground under the windows. A fruity scent perfumed the air. He rose to the window's level, and the scent grew stronger. He pressed his face against the windowpane. A few round objects rested on the ledge. Apricots. This must be the kitchen. The next room in the middle held no clues to its purpose. He could neither smell nor see a thing.

Outside the last room, he froze. A cough. A faint clearing of the throat, the kind someone might make in sleep. Barely daring to breathe, he knelt near the room's French doors. Another sound. Perhaps a rustle of bedclothes or someone turning over on a mat. He brought himself up to his full height, the broken branch clutched in his hand, and touched the door's outer knob. Both doors stood slightly ajar, probably to temper the heat with a breeze. This was going to be easier than he had imagined. His back against the wall, he used the branch as a lever to open the door opposite him, then tiptoed to the mullioned windows of the door closest to him. From inside came breathing. A man. A man on the verge of snoring. Another softer sound. A woman. A woman dreaming perhaps. If only he had cats' eyes and could watch them sleeping there in the shadows. What would it feel like to lay there with a woman's soft body? How would it be possible to sleep? Would she wake up if he touched her arm, her leg, her breast? Or would she sleep on like the dead and disregard him like most of the living? He broke off his reverie. He must act with swiftness and accuracy. Behind him, the mimosa spread its branches above the table. He listened again and heard again male and female breaths. Now. Now.

In one motion, he slammed the far side of the door shut and thrust the branch through one of its windows. Glass shattered. A man shouted. A woman screamed. Hossein rushed toward the mimosa and scurried under the tablecloth. His hands passed over soft dirt. Someone had shoveled here. Under the table. Strange. Nothing would grow here without sunlight. From inside the house, frantic voices. Footsteps. Louder, closer. A light close enough to be visible through the veil of cloth flashed from side to side like a police searchlight. He forced himself to stay still, to stop his thighs from trembling. They already hurt from crouching and squatting. His hands burned from the rope. Climbing out of the garden would irritate them again. Suddenly, something hard beat on the tabletop. He jerked but managed to steady himself on his haunches, swallowing a cry before it could fill the night air.

"Damn," said a man. "Damn. Damn. He must have gotten away." The man's voice sounded angry rather than frightened.

Footsteps again. They grew fainter until they faded into silence somewhere near the house. A woman said something, followed by what sounded like glass being swept across the floor.

Hossein waited under the table long after the voices and glow of lights disappeared in the compound. He shifted to a sitting position, his knees bent to keep his feet beneath the tablecloth, and tried to lean more weight on his hands and buttocks to relieve his aching thighs. He bent his neck to keep his head from hitting the tabletop. When he estimated two hours had passed, he crawled out on all fours, moving away from the house. He shook off his curiosity about shoveled soil under long tablecloths in a garden. He would never understand the strange ways of foreigners.

At the garden wall, he fixed the spike and rope back in place for his ascent. A hoopoe warbled its first notes to the approaching dawn. Hossein glanced back at the garden. Few of these old houses and gardens were left in the cities these days. Like so much of traditional culture, they were on the decline. A decline furthered by the regime's dependency on foreign intervention. Yet these foreigners showed more interest in the old culture than his contemporaries. Odd. He hoisted himself over the garden wall and, a few blocks away, ditched his rope and spikes in front of a hardware shop's lowered grill.

The *moazzin* began the call for morning prayer. On the Si-yo-Se Pol, the blind man muttered in his sleep. Below, a crane on a sand bank lifted one foot and tested the river water. Hossein felt in his pocket for his colored pens. He would go home and sketch that crane with its claw poised over the water, that bridge, that sleeping old blind man, those first rays of light painting the tips of the rushes golden before his eyes.

He trudged along, tired and hungry. Exhilaration about his night's work evaporated with the morning dew, replaced by remorse.

* * * * * *

She had just finished grading the spring semester's final exams when someone tapped on her office door. Kamran opened the door and crossed the room. His open collar exposed a tuft of dark hair at his throat. He could play Cyrus the Great in a movie, Angela thought. She swiveled her chair around to face him and slid it back until it hit the windowsill. No need to feed the gossip about her and Kamran that Vicky had delighted in reporting. Anxiety that Kamran had come to talk over the rumors took away her satisfaction at teaching the last class of the semester.

"How did your students do on their exams?" he asked.

"Some quite well. Others less so." She shifted Mr. Rahimi's exam to the bottom of the pile, out of Kamran's sight. After she had given Mr. Rahimi money for his mother, he showed up more and disputed less. But his final proved that he had little knowledge of the works discussed in class. His answers to essay questions rambled through vagaries. In the section with a passage followed by comprehension questions, Mr. Rahimi missed all fifteen. Mahtab confirmed that he had skipped the last three weeks of his tutoring sessions.

"I hear you're teaching the first month this summer," Kamran said.

"I volunteered to teach both sessions. We aren't going anywhere. It keeps me busy." After Doug's latest eruption, he had not mentioned returning to the States early. He could not afford to be away from the site at all this summer, he said. She was ecstatic. Mr. Rahimi would need her help to get through the summer course. How humiliating it would be if he failed after all her efforts. She would turn into a laughingstock, the brunt of student jokes, the scorn of those close to her—Mahtab, Doug.

"I'm going to be here all summer, too," Kamran said. "We could team-teach the courses. That way, we could each take long weekends now and then."

"No time off? Surely you need some." She scooted her chair farther back toward the corner.

"I must take care of my father. I might as well earn some extra money."

"I'd be happy to look after your father for a few weeks. You could profit from a month or two off," Angela said. As far as she knew, no one at the university had ever met Kamran's father.

"He'd never consent to that. He's . . . feisty. Is that the right word? He doesn't like change. He holds on to all the old ways."

She drummed her fingertips on the desk. "Would you explain Iranian mourning customs to me?" she asked. Kamran responded, but in lieu of listening, she contemplated how to refuse his offer to share a class without offending him. Cecil planned to teach this summer, claiming to be too poverty-stricken to travel, but he avoided Kamran these days. Cecil had probably made advances that Kamran had rejected.

"We drink coffee in the mosque on special days of mourning," Kamran was saying. "Unsweetened coffee. Strong. It symbolizes the bitter cup Allah has given us, a cup we must accept and savor."

"I'm not quite in mourning, Kamran, but I'm sorry I can't team-teach this summer." She sighed. "I've never done it."

"I can help. Last summer, Vicky and I shared a class."

"I don't think I'd be any good. Like your father, I'm set in my ways. And I don't believe it would be ideal for my class at this point. They've learned what I expect. I hope to capitalize on that this summer and have them build on skills they've developed over the past two semesters." Kamran appeared crestfallen. She hated letting him down. "I trust your abilities. My own are in question." She doubted her capacity to deal with more pressure at this point. Organizing the material would take hours of working together outside of class. Doug would be suspicious. And there were already rumors.

"Persian newspapers are emphasizing the threat of Islamic Marxism these days," Kamran said, adopting a nonchalant attitude.

"English-language newspapers as well."

"Be careful. Some of these people campaign against the presence of foreigners in Iran." His voice had thrown off its customary musicality, his now stark monotone either a cover-up for hurt feelings or an expression of conviction. "You haven't experienced any incidents, have you? Anything that would seem directed at you because you are a foreigner?"

"Of course not." Could Kamran know about the attempted break-in? She and Doug had told no one. The episode was merely a failed robbery. Nothing worth reporting. Best not bring attention to themselves, she told Doug, remembering the buried typewriter. She suggested moving Doug's money to a safer place, a corner of the kitchen counter behind her copper canisters. Not necessary to count it, she pointed out. The thief had fled after he broke the window.

"Don't think most of us want you to leave. We don't. Not at all." Kamran closed the office door behind him.

Alone again, she shuffled the papers on her desk, incensed and saddened. Why did she have to offend Kamran? She had told him the truth. She did have misgivings about her ability to take the pressure that teaching with Kamran would exert on her although she knew others had faith in her. Doug questioned her need to prove herself in every situation, but he did not doubt her abilities. Sofia did not often agree with the choices she made, but she bragged about Angela to anyone who would listen.

Yet, she had blamed Sofia for not preventing those boys from molesting her. Why? Intellectually, it made no sense. Sofia would have given her own life to protect her daughter. Emotionally, it made as much sense as anything in this world. At age twelve, she had wanted to assert her independence from her mother, but she had still needed Sofia's guidance. Yet, through no fault of her own, Sofia had not been there when Angela needed her most. How complicated human relationships were.

* * * * * *

Grinding. Stone against stone. The sound coming from the kitchen grated on his ears. From his lounge chair under the mimosa tree, Doug squinted over the top of an architecture book. Angela was making circular motions with a pestle, its head buried in a marble mortar.

Mahtab's profile came into view at the open kitchen window. "Grind the walnuts finer." She took the mortar from Angela and rubbed the pestle against its surface. "They will thicken to a paste when cooked with pomegranate juice."

Angela groaned. "I'm getting tennis elbow." She shook her right arm. The two women moved farther into the room, out of his sight.

Doug laid the book face down on his lap. The lemon-colored roses, his favorites, were at the height of their beauty now in late summer. According to Mahmud, Iranians considered the color yellow undesirable. Cecil called it a halfway color, neither as flashy as orange and red nor as tranquil as blue and purple. Cecil preferred a deep crimson, the color of the roses near the north wall. Their petals overlapped to form showy blooms four inches in diameter. Doug picked up his book, but it failed to divert his attention from the crimson roses. They reminded him of blood-soaked wounds, the rosettes decorating bodies in Vietnam. They had blossomed over Kevin's brain when Tian betrayed them—red roses springing up among the gray canals, flooding them with crimson faster than the Red River flowed in springtime through Hanoi to the Gulf of Tonkin.

Someone beat both knockers on the outer doors, and Doug opened them to find the mailman with two aerograms, one from Doug's sister in Chicago and the other for Angela. Hers had unfamiliar writing on it with her parents' return address. It must have come from her father. If so, it would be the first Sofia had not penned.

As he crossed the garden, the two women emerged from the kitchen. "Simmer it two hours," Mahtab said. She adjusted her sunglasses and smiled at him. "Angela is practicing *fesenjan* for the picnic next week."

He flared his nostrils. The syrupy scent of pomegranates and walnuts laced with cinnamon drifted out the kitchen door, veiling the roses' perfume, less now at midday. An aroma both exotic and erotic because of the pomegranates, which Iranians considered to be an aphrodisiac.

After seeing Mahtab out, Angela read her aerogram. "My father says my mother is sick again. He never writes. This time, it could be something serious."

Doug took the letter from her. It was in the hand of someone unused to the fine motor skills of writing. Unlike Sofia's letters, Tony's contained no glitz, no turns of the screw, no guilt-inducing innuendos. Tony wrote simple, straightforward sentences. His personality filled the page as if he were present, talking to them here in the garden. In a matter-of-fact voice, Tony said Sofia had lost interest in almost everything. She lacked vitality and her usual curiosity. She had little or no energy, not enough to telephone her cousin Lydia on Sundays or make ravioli for a church supper. Sofia felt nauseated at times and had trouble sleeping, growing clammy at night. She experienced migraines every two or three days. The letter listed a barrage of tests Dr. Fontini had ordered, some of which had benign results, others whose outcomes were not yet available, and still others yet to be run. Tony suggested that Angela call at the end of the month when Dr. Fontini would have made a diagnosis.

"He sounds worried," Angela said. "I think it sounds like menopause." She calculated her mother's age at her upcoming birthday. "If she hasn't already gone through it."

Doug swatted away a fly. Should he encourage Angela to go back to the States for two or three weeks before the fall term began? Mahmud had given him a grapevine report on the political situation: something was in the works, something supposed to happen in September, probably in Tehran, a report like so many others—idle gossip in a country where information, much of it faulty, spread through word of mouth. Still, a turning point had to occur soon. There was too much repudiation of Islamists by the government-censored press. There were too many wild rumors flying about, even among people like Reza and Hamid and Mahtab and Mahmud, recalling the old proverb about smoke and fire.

"My father does not cry wolf." Angela was reading the letter again. Doug nodded. Another Western saying. Wasn't this one from a Grimm tale? Grim, indeed. If Angela left now, without him, political events might separate them for months. What would he do if the airport were closed? Foreigners detained? Americans, God forbid, jailed? He chided himself for his selfishness. If any of those things happened, it would be better if Angela was in the States. He could look out for himself.

Angela studied her father's words. "My grandfather died unexpectedly when Dad was away during World War II," she said. "That's what he meant there at the end." She read out loud. "*Please don't let this upset you. I wanted only to give you a little warning. It's never easy to deal with bad news all at once when you aren't expecting it and you're far away.*"

She folded the letter and stuffed it into her pocket instead of throwing it in the waste basket as she usually did. An uneasiness settled over Doug like oppressive summer heat over the dust-dry garden. He had other disturbing news. *His* Ahmad had an uncle and a brother in Khafr, *her* Mr. Rahimi's village. No need to tell Angela about the connection now in the wake of the bad news about her mother. The information came from his having Mahmud complete the absurd task of gathering each employee's address of origin along with other family data for the company files. Employee records here were sketchier than in the States. Here, it was simple. You work. You get paid. You don't work much. You get paid. You don't work any. You get paid.

At least in the case of a few, like Ahmad.

CHAPTER SEVENTEEN

Alone.

Angela made her way alone toward the Si-yo-Se Pol.

Doug had seemed troubled before he left for Tehran to report on the project, although it was back on schedule. He apologized more than once for having to miss the picnic. "Don't let anyone know I'm out of town," he told her. So how would she explain why he had not accepted her students' invitation?

She weaved through stalled traffic on the street leading to the bridge. The mid-August breeze hinted at the cooler weather typical in the Iranian month of *Shahrivar*. She crossed in front of a taxi as circulation picked up, and a driver honked and cursed at her, gesticulating with one hand out of the window, beating on the dashboard with the other. She rushed to reach the bridge. Mahtab and the students awaited her on the opposite bank. In the week prior to the picnic, Mahtab had taken charge, saying the event represented an occasion for students to express gratitude to Angela.

"We'll spread a red Bakhtiari carpet over the grass as a place of honor for you," Mahtab said.

"It's a celebration after a year of hard work." Angela did not want to be the guest of honor. "I want the students to relax before they begin again in September."

Mahtab would hear none of her objections. "I've told the

students to come at six. You shouldn't arrive before seven." Mahtab explained that, while Angela would arrive on time, her students would likely trickle in as slowly as the Zayandeh Rood meandered through the reeds. "All of the students have promised to attend."

"Even Mr. Rahimi?" Angela raised her eyebrows. Once more, she had finagled a passing grade for him at the end of the term.

"Even Agha-ye Rahimi. I know you were going to make *fesenjan*," Mahtab said. "Please don't bring anything at all. You're a guest."

"Why not? Couldn't I come as a teacher and still contribute?" Her *fesenjan* was probably inferior, but Mahtab's insistence on honoring her perplexed her.

"There's a lot of tension now. If you're the class's guest in a public place, everyone will treat you with the proper *ta'arof*." Mahtab kissed her on both cheeks and rushed off to give assignments for food and drinks to students gathered on the faculty steps. Mahtab had answered her question: the plan required Mr. Rahimi to show Angela the respect he had exhibited toward her during her visit to his mother's home. Mr. Rahimi would behave himself. He had accepted the steady stream of tomans she gave him for his mother. He would want to avoid alienating his source of income.

At the midway point of the bridge, Angela slipped under one of the arches and observed the students gathering on the bank. A male student busied himself pouring ice into a plastic container while another loaded it with bottles of lemonade and *dough*, the milky-white yogurt drink prized in Iran. Strains of the husky Egyptian voice of Omm Kulthum drifted through the air from a tape deck. Hassan squatted beside three braziers, fanning charcoal. Moe Number One spread blankets on the grass. The descending sun colored the western face of the bridge's stone arches amber against a backdrop of deepening blue in the eastern sky. Mahtab was climbing the bank's slope in the distance, coming to extend hospitality. Angela paused to give her time to reach the bridge. Mahtab would no doubt escort her to the Bakhtiari carpet as if it were the walled garden of her home.

In an arch near the bridge's end, an immobile figure squatted—the blind vendor. On the ledge next to him, he had spread out his coat. On it rested his food, some bread and greens, along with an open pack of cigarettes that he would try to sell one at a time. There, Mahtab paused to dig out a few tomans from her bag for alms. The setting sun's last rays pierced the arch across from the man, settling upon his hooked nose and wrinkled face, bronzed from decades in the sun, striking also his folded, skeletal limbs. Angela shaded her eyes. The blind vendor resembled a gargoyle carved in the bridge's stone. But Western, not Islamic, architecture incorporated grotesque images to ward off evil. Islam forbade human representations, including those of saintly features. Angela reframed her comparison. The boiled-egg blankness in the man's eye sockets was reminiscent of portrayals of Islamic holy men, in which white spaces replaced the forbidden faces.

"In the name of Allah, the Compassionate and Merciful." Mahtab's coins jangled in the blind man's bowl. The old man trembled. The coins must have aroused him, although he remained in a darkness known only to those without sight. Perhaps the absence of vision sometimes made him register terror when confronted by signs of a world outside of himself.

A third of the way from the bridge's south end, Angela waved to Mahtab, who returned her salutation. Behind Mahtab, a moped sputtered. Mr. Rahimi was riding lazy circles, showing off, Angela assumed, in front of his classmates. She was a few arches away from Mahtab when Mr. Rahimi gunned his moped. Backfires tainted the air with fumes. Perhaps he was trying to work up enough courage to greet her himself. She slowed her pace to let him provide the official motorcade.

In clear view not far from Mahtab, Mr. Rahimi crouched over the handlebars and revved the motor. The moped burst forward, gaining speed, racing straight at Mahtab. She jumped under an arch for protection. Angela gasped, her knees shaking. Mr. Rahimi must have planned some violent disruption after all. Supported by the pedals, he reared up to his full height, arched his back, stuck his chest forward. The back of his head rested for a moment on his shoulders, his neck exposed, as if he were drawing on a primal force festering inside him. He jerked his head back upright. Man and moped spurted in a burst of speed toward Angela.

At first, she could not tell what glittered through the evening's last breath of sun-filled air. She could detect only a shiny, spherical mass like a chaotic moon spinning out of its orbit. Mr. Rahimi sped past her. By the time he reached the opposite end of the bridge, a dark splotch had spread over her blouse, and she covered it with her hands. Paralyzed, she looked for Mahtab, still immobile in the niche, staring at her. Liquid pearls dripped from Angela's hair, flowed down her right cheek. Mr. Rahimi's timing had been perfect. Harboring a mouthful of *dough*, he had raced towards her and spewed it out, a mass of liquid hate.

But what could she say to Mahtab, frozen there on the bridge, staring at her? Mr. Rahimi, had, no doubt, used Mahtab as bait, intending to implicate her as his accomplice. Anger at his scheme overcame Angela's initial shock. She must assure Mahtab of her trust. Yet, at this moment, she felt filthy beyond any other time in her life save for the assault during her childhood. She could not face Mahtab now. She could not face her students in this shape. If she did, their humiliation would be as great as hers.

No one but she and Mahtab had witnessed Mr. Rahimi's act in the deepening dusk, the moon heavy in the eastern sky, the sun long gone in the west. At the end of the bridge, the blind man stretched out on the stone slab and pulled his jacket over his head. His bony hand extended from under his coat and clawed at the rim of his bowl, pulling it closer.

Before Mahtab roused herself from her stupor, Angela gathered what little dignity she had left and dashed back toward the far bank all the way to her secluded Persian garden.

*   *   *   *   *   *

Alone.

Hossein had never felt more alone.

He had severed ties with the university, with his fellow classmates, with his one source of income.

Hossein wheeled Soleiman's moped onto the sidewalk and engaged the kickstand. Above, in his living quarters, light seeped out of minute cracks in the blinds. Ahmad, Dariush, and Soleiman were waiting for him. He had to convince them he had succeeded in his most recent assignment. Soleiman always wanted more from him. Soleiman still wanted him to prove himself in spite of all the money he had contributed.

Hossein bounded up the stairs and threw open the apartment door. Three expectant faces turned towards him; three pairs of questioning eyes fixed on his. A racing heartbeat thumped in his ears.

"Done." He managed to spit out the single syllable. The others jumped to their feet and pummeled him on the back and chest and upper arms.

"How? With what weapon?" Soleiman's voice rose above the clamor.

Hossein grinned and pointed to his own head. "A make-shift grenade," he said. He had avoided a lie.

"Did you kill her?" Dariush said.

"I didn't stay there to see."

"How do we know if your mission was a success?" Soleiman again, skeptical.

"You told me to scare her, to wound her. You didn't say anything about killing anybody," Hossein said.

"Did she bleed a lot, *baba*?"

"Wait until tomorrow's *Kayhan* gets wind of this!"

"Did anyone see you?"

"What if the police follow you here?"

Ahmad opened a crack in the blind and peered out into the dark street.

"The only one to worry about is the blind guy on the bridge," he told them, and they all howled.

"I can hardly wait to go to work—that's an all-time first. I'll check out her husband if he's there." Ahmad's eyes darted around the room, already on the lookout. "I'll make him angry." Ahmad's tongue slid around his lips, already forming venomous words.

Hossein threw his jacket in the corner and collapsed on the mat next to Soleiman. "So, I'm still in?"

"In? You're the hero of the day. Our Rostam. They'll leave now—all of them. Americans won't stay here unless they feel safe. Once they go, Old Man Mohammad Reza Pahlavi won't be far behind. We'll talk tomorrow about what to do next. I want to get my moped off the streets in case someone recognizes it."

Ahmad closed the door behind Soleiman and Dariush and grabbed Hossein's arm. "I never thought you had it in you, Hossein-*jan*." He twisted the light bulb hanging from the middle of the ceiling until darkness flooded the room and flopped on his mat, yawning.

Hossein slipped off his dusty shirt and pants and lay prone on his mat. Impossible to sleep. Riding a moped made him jittery after what had happened to his father. Figuring out a way to wound Mrs. Weston without hurting her had added to his anxiety. He had pulled it off this evening with Soleiman and the others. The newspapers would never report that someone had spit on a foreign teacher as she walked across a bridge to a picnic with her students. Still, Soleiman called him a hero, Rostam. Soleiman had more than his share of pride. He would never take back his own words. Soleiman would never boot him out now, even if his spitting incident, his makeshift grenade—about which Soleiman would never know the truth anyway—had no results.

Hossein rolled on his side and pulled a light blanket over his legs. Nausea came over him as he speculated on Soleiman's next move. He knew Soleiman too well. Mrs. Weston and her husband stayed in Esfahan after he broke their bedroom window. Thankfully, Soleiman knew nothing of that escapade. But what if, again, he had failed to frighten Mrs. Weston enough to force the Westons to leave the country? Soleiman would insist, next time, that Hossein actually injure or maim or kill Mrs. Weston. Hossein pulled the blanket under his chin. Mrs. Weston was not his enemy. She had shown kindness toward him and his family. Why did she have to be an American? Why couldn't she become a Muslim? No way to convert her now. He could not go back to the university. When he reared up and sent his spit flying toward her, he sealed his contract with Soleiman forever. Why did he have to choose between Soleiman's brand of religion and the decency his father had taught him was part of Islam? If only his father were alive to give him advice.

Ahmad's wheezing snores annoyed him. Hossein tossed on his mat, and his blanket twisted around his legs. Wrestling with his blanket in the dark brought back his despair and confusion during the black days following his father's disappearance.

He could never accept a regime that left boys orphans and women widows.

*   *   *   *   *   *

She felt violated.

Visions of the boys in the back lot materialized before her. That day, she saw them ahead of her, not knowing, in her innocence, that they had identified her as their prey and were waiting to pounce. The same scenario repeated itself today. She had proceeded toward Mr. Rahimi, without apprehension, unaware of his carefully designed plan to degrade her.

Angela ripped off her clothes and dumped them in the washer on hot with extra soap and two rinses before jumping into the shower. In a flash, shampoo streamed down her cheeks, mixing with her tears. She scrubbed herself until her skin was red.

Doug had booked the last flight back from Tehran. It was unlike him. He usually spent the night and returned at noon the following day.

Before he left early that morning, he had awakened her. "I'll be back around midnight." He kissed her cheek with lips warm from coffee and picked up his briefcase. At the bedroom door, he hesitated. "If anyone knocks after dark, don't answer the door or go out into the garden."

She had attributed Doug's caution to his concerns about Mr. Rahimi or to plain paranoia, and then, there had been that attempted burglary, the broken bedroom window. Her shower had washed her fear and anger away, but now she was more ashamed than ever. She had disregarded Doug's warnings. Doug was right about Mr. Rahimi, his trances, his ability to do something harmful, perhaps far more harmful than spitting.

She flipped the cassette player on without caring which cassette was already inserted. Diana Ross wailed blue notes. Angela pushed the eject button. She tried to read, to watch a John Wayne movie on the English channel, and to listen to an interview with Yasser Arafat on the BBC. In the States, she would have had a telephone, a friend at the other end of the line. Here she was isolated. Besides Mahtab, Cecil was the only one to whom she had expressed anything at all personal. How would Cecil react if she told him about the spitting incident?

She had always put spitting in the same category as pinching—something not to be taken seriously. Now she knew how degrading and insulting it was. Did she have to experience something firsthand to imagine how others might feel? She had shown little sympathy for Doug's difficulty adjusting or for her mother's distress at their move to Iran. Did she possess no empathy whatsoever? Angela checked her watch. It was only 10:30. She wanted Doug here now to lessen her distress like a child wanting a parent to kiss a scuffed knee. How hypocritical! What right did she have to expect Doug to ease her pain? Had she stolen Doug's money to gain Mr. Rahimi's approval rather than to help his mother? If so, she had done it because of her ludicrous notion that her self-worth depended on convincing every person who came from this vastly different culture to accept her.

When Doug arrived at last, Angela was curled in a fetal position, her hair in disarray from neglecting to dry it before she wallowed on the sofa's cushions.

He slipped down beside her and listened to her description of the encounter with Mr. Rahimi. Doug let out a stream of obscenities and threw his briefcase across the room with such force that a shower of papers and pens rained down on the carpet. An hour later, in the midst of kissing her face and hair inch by inch where the spit had defiled her, he asked, "Did everyone there see what happened?"

"Just Mahtab." She would speak with Mahtab on Saturday, she told him. "Friday is their day with their families."

"You're not going to fold up in fright because some nutcase is picking on you, are you?" Doug's arms encircled her body. Drawing back, he said, "You didn't ask about the meeting." He hurried to tell her, the discussion of spit and disgrace now closed. "They're pleased things have picked up. Emory Watkins flew in yesterday for the meeting." Emory was Doug's Stateside boss, a senior partner in the consulting firm. "He'll add thirty percent to the bonus if we finish early. Thirty percent." He stood, hoisting her up with him.

In the bedroom, Angela lay on the *takht* as Doug undressed. He opened the closet to hang up the gray suit he reserved for meetings. Newspapers and tattered paperbacks cluttered the closet floor where he had previously hidden his savings, now relocated behind her copper canisters.

She had to tell him soon how little money remained in his stash.

* * * * * *

They had never visited on a Friday.

They had never come so early in the morning.

Doug rushed to throw on a pair of jeans and a denim shirt and get to the door. Angela hurried out of the house in wrinkled clothing. Both Mahtab and Hamid showered her with apologies for Rahimi's behavior. Their expressions of regret distressed Doug. They acted as if they had somehow been responsible because they shared Rahimi's nationality.

"Nonsense," he said, leading the way to the kitchen. "You can't help it if the guy is a pest. He's nothing more than a neurotic grasshopper spitting tobacco on a leaf of grass. Grass that nourishes him no less." His attempt at humor brought about a distant smile from Hamid.

Doug cracked open eggs to make omelets while the other three gathered around the kitchen table.

"I had to tell the students the truth, Angela," Mahtab said. "They knew I had gone to meet you on the bridge, and some of them saw Agha-ye Rahimi take off on the moped."

Doug added milk and whipped it into the eggs with a fork. He had not yet figured out where someone as poverty-stricken as Rahimi had come by a moped.

Mahtab threw up her hands and let them fall in a helpless gesture into her lap. "They wanted to go after you, but you must have made haste." Doug smiled. Mahtab must have learned that expression from a book. "By the time they reached the bridge, you were gone."

"I couldn't let them see me like that," Angela said. "My blouse and hair on one side of my face were soaked." A lone piece of butter sizzled in the skillet while Doug waited for his wife's inevitable apology. "I'm sorry I left you to make excuses. The students must think I was terribly rude to turn back like that."

Doug inserted a spatula under the omelet and flipped half of it over.

Mahtab planted her elbows on the table and clasped Angela's hands in hers. "They're embarrassed he treated you that way."

The first omelet slid out of the pan, puffed up and wholesome. On the plate, its golden face shone in ceramic blue. Doug served the omelet to Mahtab, her brow clouded with a frown.

"At first, I worried I was wrong to organize the picnic and invite someone like Agha-ye Rahimi. And . . ." She lowered her eyes, exposing puffy, red eyelids. "I was afraid you would think I had something to do with what happened."

"He set you up, Mahtab," Doug said.

"That's what angered me most." Angela's protests rang through the room.

The second omelet hissed on the stovetop. A speck of hot butter splattered on Doug's arm. He rushed to the sink and ran cold water on the burn.

"Mahtab didn't sleep all night," Hamid said.

Again, Doug examined Mahtab's face. Her eyes now brimmed with tears. Her cheeks were sallow. Her shoulders drooped.

"I made the students agree not to take out their anger on Agha-ye Rahimi. Mohammad especially—the Mohammad who is Hassan's friend—he—they actually, as well as some of the others, wanted to go after him. Farhad knew where Agha-ye Rahimi lives. I did my best to dissuade them." Mahtab's voice broke. "Angela, I refuse to tutor him again. Theoretically, Agha-ye Rahimi's supposed to meet me tomorrow for a session. He won't show up, but I wouldn't be there if he did. I'm finished with him."

"I don't want Mahtab around him." Hamid stabbed a bite of omelet but left it on his fork, which he waved in widening circles. "He's crazy. Crazy."

"If Rahimi is not pathologically insane, he's at least a fanatic. The more the political tension increases, the more fanatics get by with destructive behavior," Doug said, his hand on Angela's shoulder. Hamid knew better than they how to deal with Angela's renegade student.

Doug flipped the last omelet, his, onto a plate and covered it with pepper.

"I guess you haven't had the TV on today," Hamid said. "Esfahan is under a curfew starting tonight for an undetermined period of time."

"But why Esfahan?" Angela asked. "Nothing has happened here."

Hamid shrugged. "There's a major military base here. Lots of Americans work on that base."

"What time does the curfew start?" Doug asked. Perhaps the Shah actually was training Army helicopter pilots to squelch any forthcoming rebellions.

"The time of the evening call to prayer. A half-hour before sundown."

Doug pushed away his plate, his omelet half-eaten. In this instance, the Shah's time and God's time matched. Ironic, considering the dissension on Daylight Savings Time last spring. "We'll have some long nights if this persists into the winter months," he said. "I've finished that architecture text I told you about. Want to borrow it?" How stupid he had been to distrust Hamid in the early days.

Hamid followed him to his study in search of the volume, and the two men pored over Doug's designs incorporating Persian with Western architecture.

"It's a wonderfully aesthetic fusion." Hamid paid his compliment with enthusiasm, and they mulled over a few alternatives. Doug spread out an earlier version of his design for an open city space surrounded by arched shops. Before long, the two were entertaining the specifics of collaborating on additional designs and arranging times to work together. Female voices intruded through the study's door. Their wives, seated in the garden, were still bemoaning the disastrous picnic.

Hamid glanced nervously at the open door. "We've got to leave Iran before long," he said, his voice lowered. "I've heard of the possibility of violent clashes between revolutionaries and the armed forces. I've also heard military leaders may be ready to turn on the Shah." He mouthed the inflammatory royal title. "If so, that could mean a military government. If not, we may be in for Islamic law like the Saudis. I'm Muslim, but I can't live under that kind of repression." He listed the names of moderates who wanted to install a social democratic regime—Karim Sanjabi, Shahpour Bakhtiar—Western-educated men with backgrounds in political science and economics. "The *mullahs* have a stronger voice, I'm afraid," Hamid said. "I want to get Mahtab and the children out by next Nawruz. But a lot can happen between August and March." He smiled wistfully and traced his finger over the cover design on Doug's architecture book.

That afternoon, alone in his study, Doug had trouble concentrating on arches and domes, sculpted lintels and mullioned windows. He hated that Hamid felt he should leave his own country. As Westerners, he and Angela would have to observe Islamic law if it were imposed by a change in regime. They had to survive another year until his contract terminated unless he could get the project completed earlier. The thirty percent additional bonus made him more invested in motivating the construction crew to speed up. In any case, he would see the project to its end.

In the living room, Angela had switched on the BBC loud enough for him to hear across the garden. In professionally enunciated British English, a voice announced the headline item of the day's worldwide events: the imposition of a curfew on the central Iranian city of Esfahan.

CHAPTER EIGHTEEN

"*Marg bar Shah.*" Death to the Shah.

"*Marg bar Amrika.*" Death to America.

And her day had started with such anticipation. She had looked forward to the first day of the fall semester, had rehearsed how she would greet her students as if the picnic incident never happened. If—when—they brought it up, she would brush it off as an unfortunate occurrence, ensure them she harbored no ill will, and apologize for having to leave before the picnic began.

And now this.

The shouts grew louder, more frenzied.

A hundred meters before the university gates, the cabbie slammed on the brakes. Angela and the four other passengers, all women in black *chadors*, jerked forward. The car slowed to a crawl. Scores of young men filled the street's four lanes. "*Marg bar Shah. Marg bar Amrika.*" The demonstrators punctuated the syllables of their chant with pumped fists. Waves of men and boys emerged from adjacent streets, and the crowd became more disorganized. Demonstrators teemed around the taxi. Shouts reached a higher pitch. Gesticulations grew more emphatic. The car came to a standstill. The driver stared forward, gripping the wheel, and growled like a wounded animal.

Protestors rushed toward them, closing the gap that

remained in the road ahead. They rocked the car. It teetered from right to left and left to right, each time at a wider angle. Angela braced herself. The other women in the car screamed and chattered, fear underpinning their cries. Angela gripped her book bag close to her chest. If the car tipped over and burst into flames, they would be trapped inside.

The crowd rocked the taxi with greater ferocity. Tasseled prayer beads dangling from the rear-view mirror swayed uncontrollably. Infuriated protestors pressed their palms against the windowpane next to Angela. She tried to push down the door lock, but it did not work. Faces of shouting demonstrators crowded toward the windshield, eyes bulging with anger and despair. Angela bit her lip and waited for the sound of shattering glass.

The *chadori* next to her stared at her with moist eyes that seemed to plead with her to do something. Angela grasped the woman's hand, but the *chadori* jerked it away with a horrified expression. The abrupt action made it clear: she, Angela, was the target.

She was the only foreigner.

The only American.

The crowd's actions could be directed only at her.

She would not let these innocent women come to harm because of her presence.

She groped for the door handle. The instant she opened the back door a crack, the protestors rocking the car stepped away and faded into the throng of demonstrators. Surprised at how calm she felt, she got out of the car and heaved her book bag onto her shoulder. She fixed her eyes on the university gates, ignoring the angry faces and raised fists, and started to weave her way forward. The crowd parted before her like the Red Sea before Moses. She had called the protestors' bluff.

Angela had nearly reached the gates when the taxi driver gunned his motor. The car, intact with the four women inside, sped south on the main thoroughfare as if nothing at all had happened. Ahead of her, next to the gates, she spotted Mr.

Rahimi and three other young men, none of whom she recognized. They were watching the path into the university. Watching—and noting—anyone who dared pass. At the gates, she greeted several of her students. They returned her salutation but did not accompany her inside. The surveillance of the hardliners must have intimidated them.

Inside the gates, silence reigned. There was none of the usual chatter and shuffling of feet on the sidewalks. No pale faces of freshmen trying to discover where their classes met. No smug glances of upperclassmen testifying to their prior experience of university life. The mauve fuzz of sweetly scented mimosa drifted from overhead branches. Angela's footsteps crunched on gravel. An occasional professor hurried head down to a class destined never to convene. Willows bowed before the faculty doors. Now and then, the flap of helicopter rotors drowned the usual birdsong.

Angela closed her office door and dropped into her desk chair. She was clothed in sweat despite the coolness of the autumn morning. The calm she had maintained as she plowed through the crowd abandoned her. She had a sudden urge to cry as unacknowledged tension drained from her neck and shoulders. She had escaped this time, but what about the next time—and the next?

Later, she sat, bored, in an empty classroom. How long should she wait for any students brave—or foolish—enough to attend class? In her college days, students had been expected to wait ten minutes for a late instructor, twenty for a professor, and more for a full professor. She opted for fifteen minutes. No need to reread the next day's assignment or work on next week's lesson plans. Tomorrow she would bring a novel.

Strikes.

Shops shut tight. The city shut down except for necessities. The post office closed. Angela could not call home.

"How long will they do this?" she asked Doug, who shook his head. An Iranian—Mahtab or Kamran—would say, "The sky is high." She felt low. She should have called home last weekend. Why had she put it off? Because she did not want to hear bad news? Hardly a justifiable reason for negligence. As usual, her imagination punished her.

This time, her mother wears a blue hospital gown. Tubes drip out of her nose, her arms, her bladder, her side. Blue lights zigzag across the surface of monitors that beep erratically or, worse, fall silent. Under a thin sheet, Sofia's thin chest rises and falls. Hospital smells fill the air: chemicals meant to heal, fading chrysanthemums, and urine and blood, body odors of the sick and dying. She runs her fingers over her mother's hollowed cheek. When she leans over Sofia, her mother's breath barely stirs the hair around her ear. A nurse's cart rattles in the hallway. A fluorescent glow leaks under the closed door.

"Don't obsess about it," Doug had told her more than once. But she did.

She had no idea they would be cut off with no way to communicate with the outside world. They were at the mercy of a political uprising bigger than one student's rebellion or one parent's illness. She had not asked for this. Or had she? Had she believed she could survive in a hostile environment just because she wanted to prove her cultural sensitivity? She should have joined the Peace Corps, should have experienced firsthand the bitter cold in Outer Mongolia or malaria-infested mosquitoes in Zaire. Instead, she wanted to come here where Doug had a salary that allowed them to live better than almost all the indigenous population, where they could afford Persian carpets and turquoise set in twenty-four-karat gold and brass trays with scenes from Persepolis. She wanted to live here where she could luxuriate in a walled garden, enjoy Iranian friends like Mahtab and Kamran with their patient explanations, and American ex-pats like Vicky and Cecil, both so eccentric she doubted if they would fit in Stateside. Yet, she had made others feel awkward. She ticked off her transgressions: her uninvited visit to a student's mother, her uninformed way of shaming that student, her abandonment of Mahtab at the picnic.

And Doug thought she resembled the woman with the long hair and full lips? The woman looking in the mirror in his miniature? She studied him as he listened to the evening news—the faint lines across his brow, his easy gait as he crossed the room and switched off the short-wave radio, his resonant voice asking what she was thinking, his total acceptance when she answered with a shrug, "Nothing. The sky is high."

It had gone on too long. Forever, it seemed. This revolution.

Angela paced the garden's perimeter, plodding past the rose bushes, their leaves brittle and yellowed, along the length of the reflecting pool and the east garden wall, next to the northern terrace and its two wooden pillars, by the mimosa tree to the house's west side, in front of the entrance doors on the south. She retraced her steps past the pool, east wall, north terrace, mimosa, west façade, wooden doors. She was sick of dried rose petals cluttering the flower beds, tired of the pool darkening at sunset, and fed up with scrawny zinnias clinging to life this late in the fall. By the twentieth lap around the garden, she was jogging, panting a little.

She had gone on long enough. The afternoon sun slipped below the western wall; a November chill rose with the shadows.

She blew on her frigid fingers, lit the gas Aladdin in the living room, and shut off the adjoining rooms to keep in the warmth. She was too restless to sit in the leather Tabrizi chair where she had spent so many evenings preparing classes and studying Persian. No point in any of that now. Classes had not reconvened since the students went on strike at the beginning of the fall term. She had not worked on her Persian for weeks.

Expressions and grammatical points that used to fascinate

her no longer piqued her curiosity. Now she found the myriad ways to say "it doesn't matter" irritating and irresponsible. She preferred not to know what was said on the street or in a shop. It was too painful. She was beyond the point of caring whether language ordained a worldview or vice versa. She knew that the two coupled to create a body of arcane knowledge nearly inaccessible to outsiders. Language carried a cultural DNA that made subtle differentiations possible. Those minute linguistic subtleties separated humans of different classes and cultures from one another. The bilingual Iranians she knew faced difficulties with the cultural subtext in English, just as she did when she spoke Persian. One could speak a foreign language perfectly without always understanding the implications the words carried for a native speaker. Another piece of information she had gleaned from observing her students.

She stood on tiptoe under the stained glass in the arch over the French doors. Aloud, in Persian, she counted the blue pieces in the central panel, repeating the first words she had learned, picturing the corresponding written numerals. "*Yek, doh, seh, chahar, panj.*" *Panj* looked like an upside-down heart with one exception. At the top, there was no sharp point. Rather, the right side extended a little and curved slightly. The windows on the French doors had clouded from the warmth of the Aladdin, and she drew a *panj* in the filmy moisture. An upside-down heart. She lived in the heart of this country midway between Greece and India, a midpoint between Europe and the Far East, the crossroads for caravans. A country whose heart had been invaded, ravaged, converted, inverted. *Yek, doh, seh, chahar, panj.* She could repeat those numbers for eternity, but each time she bought food, she still had to translate the monetary calculations into English before she could respond in Persian. This, in spite of thinking the other words she needed directly in Persian, only in Persian: *sabzi, morg, naranj, limou, shekar.* Greens, chicken, oranges, limons, sugar. But numbers. They were among the first words she had learned in English. She could write them at an early age. No upside-down hearts for fives. No dots for zeroes.

A sharp rap on the compound doors. Someone was knocking forty-five minutes before the curfew began, had begun each night for weeks now. Doug must have forgotten his key. She flung the doors open. No one at the threshold. Footsteps running toward the main road a block away. At the far end of the *kucheh*, two men. One with a familiar, dusty, black coat. He turned his head and glanced back at her. Light from the corner streetlamp played across his glasses. She rushed into the alleyway. He was already gone, swallowed by a flock of shoppers on their way home before the curfew.

Angela drew in her breath. Words were scrawled on the outside wall in black. *Westons. Dirty dogs. Leave Iran.* And, in Persian, *Marg bar Amrika.* Pathetic, the crudity of it all. Especially ludicrous, that *dirty dog.* In Persian, it must be an awful insult, the worst Mr. Rahimi could imagine. Dirty dogs. Dogs like *jub* dogs that roamed the countryside in packs, occasionally coming into inhabited areas to feed off garbage. Dogs that wanted something to sustain themselves before they returned to wherever they came from.

She turned to go back into the garden. Something was carved on the compound's far door. A painted heart. A bleeding, red heart. Blood gushing from a wound made by a scimitar whose handle had fluid curls and spirals, intersecting figure eights and arabesques. In the handle's center, a miniature dome and minarets, Esfahan's blue-domed mosque. She drew her fingertip over crimson curlicues and curves, Mr. Rahimi's stab at striking terror into her heart. She considered scraping the paint off but changed her mind. Rather than frightening her, the drawing filled her with sadness for the misapplication of Mr. Rahimi's gifts, for her longtime inability to see him for what he was, a misguided soul needing vindication for his father's death. She felt cleansed of the anger she bore him. Both she and Mr. Rahimi had ventured alone into places they should not have gone, filled with expectations of escape from situations they could not forget.

The two of them were alike in ways she would never have guessed.

PART III

In the country of the blind, the one-eyed man is king.

- From *Adagia*, compiled by Erasmus and later
quoted by H.G. Wells -

CHAPTER NINETEEN

It had taken all the arguments Hossein could conjure up and not a few lies to convince Soleiman he needed more time before killing Angela Weston and her husband.

As usual, what worked best in the end was money—the five hundred tomans he had put back to give his mother. And the empty promise of more to come. Rumor had it that Mrs. Weston sat in her empty classroom day after day without resigning her post. Ahmad said workers checked the construction site intermittently and always found Mr. Weston at his desk, hovering over blueprints, pretending nothing unusual was going on.

After he and Soleiman parted ways in the streets adjacent to the Westons' compound, Hossein ducked into a tea house and washed red paint from his hands and shirt cuffs. When the tea house shut for curfew, he circled through back alleyways, returning to the Westons' dead-end *kucheh*. All was quiet; all was dark; all was well. Earlier, Soleiman had insisted on going with him to splash the Westons' wall and door with black threats and scarlet omens. Soleiman came not because he wanted to intimidate the Westons. He was finished with that strategy. It was obvious. Soleiman came because he suspected him, Hossein, of buying time in the hope the Westons would leave. Soleiman wanted to know where they lived. And he wanted Hossein to know that he knew.

Hossein could not make out the bleeding heart in the darkness. If only Mrs. Weston had stayed inside after Soleiman pounded on the door. She had already seen the heart. Scraping it off now would do no good. At the corner where the *kucheh* met Chahar Bagh, a military truck's brakes screeched, the sole sound from the usually busy street. Hossein flattened himself against the wall and pulled his black coat over his face. The truck passed. He was in violation of the curfew now. It would be dangerous to return home. Ahmad had told him about Soleiman's narrow escapes as he went to and from illicit meetings after sundown. Soleiman would break curfew with no hesitation, especially to harm the Westons. Hossein had to protect the Westons. He toyed with the idea of beating on the door, warning them, and asking them for refuge for the night. But Mrs. Weston had seen him running down her *kucheh*. She would not trust him—even if he could persuade her to forgive him for the spit. And, even if she let him in, would she believe his warnings? What would he do if Soleiman found out? Cold crept up Hossein's back and neck. If the military sighted him, he would say he had nowhere to go and give them a false name. But they would know his name. They had to know his name. They knew his father's name. He would be doomed if he were taken in.

The wall towered over him. He would need equipment to scale it. Tonight, he had no rope, no spikes. Hossein lay crumpled under his coat like a homeless beggar. Allah would protect him. *Inshallah*. In return, he would protect the Westons. He refused to have their innocent blood on his hands. If Soleiman showed up here tonight, he would tell him the truth: the money had come from Mrs. Weston. Soleiman would want to spare her if he thought Hossein could wheedle more money out of her. Hossein would never ask Mrs. Weston for more money. If necessary, he would fight Soleiman.

Hossein nestled into the corner and fell into a restless sleep. When the curfew lifted the next morning, he made his way to the bus station and bought a ticket for Khafr. He would bring his mother and Fatimeh to Esfahan, get Ahmad to move out, and look for work that paid. This way, he could break with Soleiman. He would tell Soleiman that he was burdened with family cares now that he had relinquished his mother's five hundred tomans to the revolutionaries. Soleiman would not argue about family obligations. Strangely, the university was still providing student stipends even though everyone was on strike. His uncle would help until he found a job. He would spend nights guarding the Westons until they left.

Hossein kissed his bus ticket as if a verse from the Koran were inscribed on it. He could hardly wait to see his mother's surprise when he told her she would have indoor plumbing and blinds over the window.

He never did anything right.

Last week, he believed he could provide a better life for his family. This week, they struggled to survive.

Precious grains of rice trickled from the bottom of an improvised newspaper cone, pinging against the stone-tiled stairs like sand blown against a bus window. Hossein stuck the end of the cone in his pocket and rushed up the remaining six steps and into the apartment. He had stood in line all after-noon, waiting to get enough rice for three. Now, his mother, alarmed at the way he burst through the door, had to see his coat pocket overflowing with rice. And she had already com-plained about the filthy room.

While Hossein was out, Ahmad and Soleiman had come to gather Ahmad's belongings. Only Ahmad's carpet was left. Hossein coughed as Ahmad shook it out in the room before rolling it up. Breadcrumbs, apple peels, pomegranate seeds, dead roaches and live ants, cigarette ashes and burnt matches, congealed drops of yogurt, shards of a broken tea glass, and clouds of dust all flew to the ceiling, congesting the air. The debris settled on the floor.

Soleiman, his face a livid purple, shouted accusations at

him. "You're using family as an excuse to abandon the revolution. You could have left your mother and sister in Khafr." A nasty comment with his mother standing there, coughing because of the dust.

"My family has given more than yours," Hossein said to Soleiman, surprising himself with his boldness. "My father was a martyr for the anti-Shah movement." He had never drawn attention to his father's mysterious death, but it was less risky now. Everyone knew—had known for at least two months. The Shah would not survive.

Ahmad took up for him. "Americans are leaving," Ahmad told Soleiman. "That's what we wanted. Now we have to work to make sure the Ayatollah will rule instead of some corrupt guy who went to school in Paris."

Soleiman bared his teeth under his mustache. "What about the Westons?" He glared at Hossein. "The only Americans you were supposed to get rid of. You never proved yourself." His face took on a sinister grin. "But others have. And others will."

Hossein backed against the wall for support. Why hadn't he realized breaking with Soleiman would give Soleiman yet another reason to wreak revenge on Mrs. Weston? Soleiman would want to show him up by committing some violent act against her. If only the Westons would leave.

Soleiman and Ahmad pitched the ragtag carpet out the window to be strapped to the moped parked in the street below. "Your contribution was never anything but money." Soleiman stomped out of the apartment, leaving the mess intact. The mess to which the spilt rice had added.

Hossein's mother, on hands and knees, sifted through the filth on the floor, plucking grains of rice one by one like the hen she had left in Khafr. His sister slept propped up in the corner, her thick mouth open, her cheeks chapped and red with weeping sores. Her hair fell in a sticky mass over her forehead and eyes. Hossein searched the room. Where was the comb?

"They thought the Shah left today," he said. "People in the

streets yelled and honked. But no. It was only a rumor." He took what was left of the paper cone, flattened it, and used it to sweep some of the litter into a pile. "I couldn't find any shops open for a broom. I wish he would leave so they would open again." At least he had enough kerosene for the lamp. According to his mother, the nightly voices chanting from rooftops agitated his sister. Fatimeh would howl and scream well beyond the time the voices stopped. When sleep finally came, she would continue crying out, waking his mother throughout the night. His mother seemed to have aged in the few days since her arrival. Her eyes were bloodshot, and both she and his sister had coughing fits. Tuberculosis was rampant, especially in the countryside. This move had not turned out as he had intended. His father would have done much better.

"*Jan-e man.*" His mother handed him the small bowl of uncooked rice, and he helped her to her feet. "What about the tea house?"

"Still closed." He knew what she was thinking. They had little money left. The tea house always needed dishwashers. Because they knew him there, he had hoped to help out during the day. The few extra tomans he earned for two hours' work at the newspaper kiosk were not enough. He had told his mother the money was for his services sleeping in the kiosk at night in case vandals broke the curfew and tried to damage the vendor's goods. Instead, he slept hunched over in the Westons' *kucheh*, jerking awake at the slightest sound, afraid Soleiman's shadow would fall across the Westons' door.

"When is he going to leave? When?" He had shouted without realizing it, and his sister opened her eyes and let out a shrill cry. His mother rushed to calm her.

Hossein beat his fist against the belly of his *tar*. Discordant tones filled the room. He could do nothing. Nothing at all until something happened in Tehran. Others had the same dilemma—he knew from the grumblings of customers who could not afford a newspaper. They gathered to read the censored headlines of those hanging from the kiosk's awning.

The university would stop paying his stipend someday soon. Certainly, after classes resumed and he did not return. How stupid of him to give all of Mrs. Weston's money to Soleiman. How stupid of him to wage his little *jihad* against Mrs. Weston and cut off the possibility of getting an education. Soleiman was right. What good had he done—either for the revolution or for his own future?

The minute he picked up his *tar*, his sister's wails stopped. The music always had the same dreamy effect on her as it did on him. The notes clustered around the mother tone while his own mother, on tiptoe, prepared the smattering of rice that she had worked so hard to separate from the filth. But the music he played today did not take flight. The notes did not soar and fall and rise again. Nor did he lose himself by riding on their wings. He kept playing; Fatimeh kept quiet. She rocked back and forth, sucking on two fingers. The quality of his music did not matter to her. He resolved to play again after lunch, although he would have liked to take a nap. If only he could play for his sister after dinner when the lights went out and voices chanted in the dark. By soothing his sister, the music comforted his mother.

It neither comforted nor soothed him.

He was not worthy of being his father's son.

*   *   *   *   *   *

They could survive this revolution. Surely they both had pioneers or explorers somewhere among their forebears.

Doug squatted on his haunches and fiddled with the tuner. No matter which way he turned the dial, the radio emitted static. It hardly mattered. It was almost seven o'clock, the time when, each night, electric company employees sabotaged the nation's power, preventing the populace from hearing the propaganda the Iranian news agency broadcast each evening.

He smelled kerosene. Across the room, Angela was lighting the lamp. "Hard to say which is worse—radio interference or smoking wicks," he said. The electricity would come back for the unbiased evening BBC news, and he liked to adjust the dial in advance of the blackout. According to Mahmud, those Iranians who had access to a shortwave radio could not tear themselves away from the monitor. Events in Iran always headlined BBC broadcasts these days.

At last satisfied he had tuned in the radio as well as possible, he took the glass of tea Angela had poured for him. Steam bathed his nose and cheeks, giving him a cozy feeling despite the chilly room. "You're sure this isn't poison?" He tipped the glass to his lips. Angela responded with that look that meant she found his ex-pat humor too glib, too black. He had to find something comic in the situation to keep sane. The neighbors had pounded on the doors the night before and warned them the water supply might have been poisoned. Government supporters, angry over the strikes plaguing all sectors of the workforce, were the culprits, they said. Doug figured the anti-Shah movement had initiated the rumor. Or perhaps government supporters themselves circulated false information to blame striking protestors. Or pro-Shah people started the rumor so the anti-Shahs would blame the pro-Shahs. The pro-Shahs would retaliate by declaring the anti-Shahs had disseminated the lie to frighten people. They, the pro-Shahs, would set things right: there was nothing contaminating the water supply. That, at least, had proved true.

Doug encircled the tea glass with his hands, warming his fingers on the glass's surface. He was getting good at Byzantine thinking. And at appreciating the gamesmanship of it all. He would have to get Hamid's read on his progress.

Despite the strikes, they could buy the essentials. The man across the street saved Romanian eggs under the counter for Angela. The merchant at the corner always had enough yogurt. A block away, a shopkeeper supplied them with sufficient rice, walnuts, honey, and dried fruit. "You have to know when they'll open and for how long," Angela had told him. "My schedule is non-existent anyway." The university remained closed. Dr. Aminipour had instructed foreign teachers to stay home until things improved. Yet, Angela still collected her salary each month, enough to live on.

His own company promised to pay him in arrears. With the stoppage of postal services and money transfers, the company's in-country funds had dwindled. The few other consultants, all based in Tehran, had already left. Mahmud encouraged him to go, too, worried the striking workers would destroy half-completed structures and sabotage the project if an American stayed in charge. Doug and Mahmud took turns guarding the site's stockpile of unused materials.

"It's too risky—especially for you," Mahmud told him again last week, his eyes bloodshot from taking the night shift. But Mahmud and his family were more vulnerable. How shameful that he once thought of Mahmud as a jealous competitor at best, a devious enemy at worst. Mahmud occupied every spare minute plotting how to slip out of the country with his family and the resources his father had accumulated in his halcyon days as one of the Shah's henchmen. Mahmud was probably innocent of any wrongdoing, any corruption or direct collaboration with the current regime. The revolutionaries, though, would insist he had profited from his late father's enviable position. What that had been exactly Mahmud had never explained, and Doug did not want to know. Ignorance could be a safeguard, if not for himself, then for Mahmud. Mahmud had grown thinner and warier as the Shah's departure appeared inevitable. He no longer sported fine clothing. The gold watch that displayed the time on three continents no longer flashed on his wrist.

A few words from the BBC trickled in before the next hour's talk program. Only headlines. A full report would come at the eight o'clock hour. "The airport in Tehran closed today for an undisclosed amount of time amid rumors that the Shah of Iran, Mohammad Reza Pahlavi, may leave the country. There are unconfirmed reports that the Ayatollah Khomeini will arrive in two or three days' time." Periodic airport closings had become standard operating procedure.

"I wonder who else may be leaving," Doug said to Angela. The muscles in her jaw twitched. She seemed troubled tonight. Perhaps she was still mulling over their visit yesterday to Vicky and Reza. Vicky, adamant that all Americans should go back now, had already sent the three boys to her sister in the States. So far, she stayed with Reza, who needed a U.S. visa.

"As your husband, I thought he has a right to one," Doug had said to Vicky. She met his comment with silence, deferring for once to Reza. He was contacting European embassies in Tehran, Reza said, as well as the Canadians. "The U.S. is always hard to get in." Reza glanced at the bookcase. On the second shelf, a blown-up photo showed him and the boys splashing in water. Vicky had taken it, he said, during their vacation at the Caspian Sea the previous summer. All three boys had his dark, curly hair rather than Vicky's blond fluff. "I hope the boys like their new school in the U.S.," he added. Afterward, Angela said Reza used visa difficulty to save face. Vicky, it seemed, wanted a divorce. Doug's sympathy lay with Reza. His life had probably been anything but pleasant since he married Vicky.

The lights flickered and went off. The radio fell silent. They waited in lamplight for the next act in the revolutionary drama. Within seconds, voices from windows and rooftops took up a low chant: "*Allahu akbar.*" God is great. Male voices from unseen bodies floated above the city, circling through the darkness where once streetlamps and traffic and shop lights glittered. The voices seemed prehistoric and the utterances guttural, primal, and yet still human, invoking vague divinities—mysterious, absent, omniscient. Doug put his arm around Angela. The chanting frightened and unsettled her. To him, it lent rich mystery to the night. Past occurrences tempered his view: tropical bird calls, animal cries, reptilian whisperings—all aped by Viet Cong under the cover of steamy foliage. Although the chanting recalled invisible soldiers in a jungle dripping with death, it left him with no wheezing, no gasping or sweating. It seemed paradoxical. As the political situation in Iran deteriorated, he relaxed more, confident in his ability to take appropriate action if necessary to protect Angela and himself. Was it because the desert, dry and devoid of vegetation, stood in stark contrast to Vietnam's humid jungle? Or was he more confident now that he had to ensure Angela's safety and their future together?

He raised his tea glass to Angela. "Cheers." The word hovered over the drone from the protestors on the rooftops, reflecting his make-believe toast the day they landed in Esfahan. He had stopped drinking alcohol since Iranian troops fired on demonstrators in Tehran during the September Massacre. At first, he found it difficult to substitute tea or lemonade or a soft drink for his nightly cocktails. But he wanted his mind and body alert, observant and on edge, in case he needed to act without prior warning.

"What's going to happen to Kamran?" he asked.

"He can't leave," Angela said. "His father is too ill to travel. He's keeping quiet, staying out of the fray."

The praises to Allah waned. In a few minutes, the electricity would come back on. They waited in the silent room. On the street outside, an Army truck shifted gears and rolled past. Familiar sounds now.

"You still want to stay?" Angela said. Lantern light flickered across her face and threw quivering shadows. The shape of her head fluttered on the wall behind her.

"Sure. I'm finally beginning to like it here. Whatever happens, the university will eventually resume classes. Work on the site will be further delayed, but it will carry on before long. They'll need anyone who knows the plans." He elaborated: maybe Rahimi and a couple of workers like Ahmad would cease their complaints if they saw two Americans stayed, willing to live and work in whatever political system won the struggle. He welcomed the challenge.

He welcomed that alert state in which he felt the most alive, the same one he had experienced in Vietnam attending to the wounded in a firefight.

CHAPTER TWENTY

Someone shoved her from behind. The pottery bowl of yogurt she had just bought splattered on the sidewalk, coating a man's shoe and the hem of a woman's *chador* creamy white. Pedestrians shoved and shouted and elbowed each other. Horns honked. Traffic sped down Chahar Bagh. Empty taxis careened through the streets without stopping for fares.

The woman next to her teetered and grabbed onto Angela's arm to keep from slipping in the yogurt. "What's happened?" Angela asked her.

"They say the Shah has left." The woman pursed her faintly mustached lips. "We've heard that before, haven't we?" She gathered her *chador* tightly around her, clasped her shopping bag next to her thigh, and weaseled through the mass of swarming bodies.

Angela elbowed her way through the crowd, anxious to cross the street and get home. As she reached the street corner, traffic cleared, ceding the street to a mass demonstration. The usual placards with anti-government slogans bobbed above the men's heads. "Khomeini, Khomeini." They shouted in unison. "Long live Ayatollah Khomeini." Their faces expressed a mixture of jubilance and defiance, as if unsure of whether the Shah of Iran had abdicated and the Ayatollah could at last return from exile.

Angela scrutinized the demonstrators. Was Mr. Rahimi that one in black close to the front? Or the one there, in the middle, with a placard obscuring his face? Or the laggard who had broken ranks to tie his shoe? She kept looking for Mr. Rahimi until each man in the throng seemed to wear his black-rimmed glasses and coat with frayed sleeves and worn elbows. Each sported outgrown pants and held his shoulders hunched over a thick neck. Each had a stream of drool issuing from the corner of his lips. Each had become Mr. Rahimi, spitting out insults, raising a fist in her face, then glaring at her in a glassy trance. A hundred, maybe two or three hundred Mr. Rahimis, all shouting and marching, all rebellious and insolent.

The press of the crowd trapped her at the edge of the curb. Would Mr. Rahimi step forward and deliver a blow? Rhythmic cries came and went; marching steps tromped past. The backs of the men on the last row moved steadily down the middle of Chahar Bagh, their voices growing fainter. From behind, their bodies looked different—some tall and thin, others hefty and rugged. Some with bushy hair, others with none at all. Some were old, straggling through their last days; others were boys verging on manhood. The crowd lining the street dispersed. Shaken, Angela staggered home past merchants on footstools in their shops, removing the Shah's pictures from places of prominence and replacing them with photos of the white-bearded, sharp-eyed Ayatollah Khomeini.

Once inside, Angela wiped a splotch of yogurt off her pant leg. She sank onto the couch and closed her eyes. It seemed as if she were descending through meter after meter of darkness in a desert *qanat*. The sensation lingered, like the vision of a moving landscape hours after the traveler had stopped for the night. The *qanat* air carried a whiff of water, barely remembered. Animal remains stank in the well's closeness—sheep skeletons, desert rat dung, shreds of snakes' skin. Cracks where underground moisture had once oozed covered the *qanat*'s walls. What did the guidebook say? Impossible to climb out unless someone threw you a rope. Impossible to yell loud enough to rouse someone on a passing moped. Impossible to distinguish your own fingers in the darkness unless the sun penetrated the spot of sky directly overhead. How had she gotten down here? How would she get out?

Angela opened her eyes. Emerging from the darkness and isolation endowed her with a dangerous truth: she had lost her ability to differentiate. She had engraved the traits of one person on dozens of others. She, Angela Weston, native to a Western culture centered on the individual. Why? Old argu-ments resurfaced. Free will versus fate. Individuality versus the masses. In the demonstration she had witnessed, the men resembled Mr. Rahimi in their political leanings only. Each man had made his own choice to engage in the revolution, regardless of his motivation to do so. She had seen them all as the same person. If she were capable of such a delusion, such an aberration of the truth, it was time to leave.

She would have to convince Doug to go with her.

She pulled herself up, turned on the TV, and listened to Persian for the first time in weeks. The Shah's departure was unconfirmed. Footage from Tehran showed shopkeepers and taxi drivers hastening to replace the Ayatollah's pictures with the Shah's.

The Shah, as always—regal, megalomaniacal, handsome in his medal-strewn uniform.

At his side, a sword dangled within reach.

* * * * * *

"It's over. The company is abandoning ship," he said, realizing at once how jarring the cliché was, given that they lived in a desert.

Doug threw down his backpack brimming with notebooks and copies of project plans, ledgers, and construction esti-mates. Most of the material he produced at work over the past year and a half he had left in his desk at the site. The materials he brought home might aid him in the future. The company would pay for their return to the States, he told Angela. "Brian Jefferies, the Middle Eastern Director, drove down from Tehran. I told him we weren't ready to leave. That we're still holding out for the university to reopen. The government has to stabilize in some form or other. You'll get your job back. They've been more than decent to you, paying you through all this."

Angela's frown disturbed him. Surely, she agreed with hanging on to their life here, to this house with its garden and French doors and stained glass windows and tiled window seats where Angela read during the winter months. He needed more time. He had begun to like it here, to feel comfortable with the relative isolation, to trust Mahmud after all these months, to appreciate Hamid's skills and Mahtab's warmth and the construction workers' naïve attempts at humor, Cecil's audacity. But Cecil was gone. He had come to say goodbye last Thursday.

"It's time for me to high tail it out of heah," Cecil said. "Like a jackass chased by a swarm of bees." He launched a few "hee-haws" and grabbed a cloth napkin from the table. Whooping, he whipped it in a circle above his head. "Move 'em out," he yelled. "Get ready, cowpokes. I'm comin' to Texas." He flipped Angela across the back side with the napkin. "That's Tex-ass to you, ma'am."

Although Doug had advised against it, Cecil insisted on taking a bus to Tehran that very night to "get over his onset of stir-crazy." That the airport was likely closed again made no difference to Cecil. He'd take a taxi all the way to Turkey if he had to, he said. "Got to get rid of those rials somehow." Unfortunately, Cecil had bought Mexican pesos with which he expected to open a bed and breakfast not far from Puerto Vallarta and make a living "sucking up to *gringos*." But the peso was devalued, and Cecil's investment had amounted to very little. Since then, he had refused to change any money. Rials were the only currency he had.

Doug worried that Cecil's cache of rials would tempt an Iranian desperate to pay *baksheesh* and leave the country. Cecil was not prudent. Once, he had visited in the late afternoon and stayed after curfew. No amount of reasoning with him, overdosed on alcohol as he was, had induced him to spend the night. He left on foot, weaving his way home in the shadows. Anything could have happened to him; they would have been hard-pressed to find out what.

"You won't have a work permit or a visa allowing you to stay," Angela said.

"They'll give me one," Doug said. "I'm married to you. As long as you have your position at the university, even if it's on strike, we're fine." They had originally gotten residence permits because of his job.

"I have no idea . . . we don't know . . . I'm not sure if I . . ." A blank look stretched across her face. "Your line of reasoning no longer makes sense."

She was right. Who had the authority to grant residence permits now? And would that authoritative body or person, given the volatile situation, want Americans to stay? He leaned forward, his forehead against the wall. He was not ready to give up. Living here—adjusting—had been too difficult, caused him too much anxiety. Everything he had ever experienced—serving in the Army, going to the university, getting married, living in Detroit, working at the firm—all had required such an effort to adjust. It would require a similar struggle wherever they went, no matter if they moved back to the same apartment in Detroit or settled in one of those black, goat-hair tents the Qashqai transported on the backs of donkeys and camels. As soon as you got used to a place, as soon as you figured out how to get around and what you needed and where to get it and when to ask a question and when to keep your mouth shut, as soon as you knew a little of what you were doing in a place, someone or something outside of you changed all that. As soon as you got a few things right. He needed time before going off on his own. Why, except for the desire to be free of authority, did he ever think he was ready?

It was no longer possible to earn the bonus or add to his savings. There were other reasons for staying now. Angela had invested so much energy in making a life here. And then, there was the sheer adventure of witnessing a revolution. He would have the satisfaction of knowing he and Angela had made it here, could make it here. A little longer.

"Let's wait until we know what to do about the residence permit," he said. They had perfected their waiting skills. He would check his passport to see how much time he had left before his permit expired. Maybe, when things returned to normal, an Iranian company would hire him. "We still have all the money I've been saving. When we do decide to leave, it'll be enough to open a store-front firm with one architect." Before Brian drove back to Tehran in the morning, he would stop by and exchange the rials they had on hand into dollars at the usual rate of sixty to one, he told Angela, a safeguard given that Iranian currency was likely to be devalued on the international market. "We've been through too much here to make a hasty decision, don't you think?"

Angela looked odd, as if she did not understand him. She must have been shocked to hear him say that he wanted to stay.

After the chanting that evening, the electric lights flashed on. Big Ben chimed. Angela turned off the radio. Why now? He had been waiting for the BBC. The lamp's flame sputtered as if it knew it had outlived its usefulness. Smoke clouded its chimney and obliterated his view of Angela's lips for a few seconds. Angela muttered something about Brian, tomorrow morning, his money. "You don't have as much money as you thought. I'm afraid what remains won't be enough for your business—after all the work you've done on the portfolio."

She made no sense to him; he did not know how to reply. He waited, waited like he had waited all evening for one thing or another—lights going out, chanting, lights coming on, the BBC.

A gunshot rang out in the distance. They exchanged startled looks, barely breathing, waiting for what might come next, but nothing did until Angela's words, the words he had been waiting to hear, rushed out in torrents as if gushing from an artesian well and burst against his eardrums. Angela had taken money from their savings, his savings, and given it to Rahimi—a lot of money, she confessed, and anger shot through him like a poisoned arrow, and he grabbed her shoulders. Why didn't she stop talking, stop flooding his heart with doubt in the one place that remained safe and inaccessible? He screamed at her, but she had no answers, no rational explanations, no excuses. Nor did he. This was Iran, and the ground here shifted like desert sand. This was Iran, and none of the rules applied. This was Iran, and he must stop yelling at his wife and hold on to her while the earth slipped and slid and crumbled beneath their feet, his heart racing, hot tears flooding his eyes. Through them loomed Angela's pale face, her agitated hands, her trembling lower lip, her voice begging his forgiveness. Her words describing Rahimi's family: the mother's poverty, the sister's disability, the father's death. Giving them his money was Angela being Angela, Angela acting with good intentions, Angela feeling compassion for the poor, the bereaved, and the sick. This was Iran. Here, he must believe what she had done was not important. It did not matter, as they said here. He tried to remember just one of the plethora of Persian expressions. It did not matter. When a hoarse *"mohem nist"* came from deep in his throat, tears fled from Angela's eyes down her cheeks. For a moment, the ground beneath them stood still in the dry, electric atmosphere of the Middle East.

They had survived his anger.

They would survive her betrayal.

With one arm around Angela's shoulders, he extinguished the kerosene lamp. Soot rose, coating the lantern's glass chimney. He would wash it before the next blackout.

CHAPTER TWENTY-ONE

She could not bear to pick up her last unread novel, *The Tin Drum*.

It sat atop the stack of fourteen or so books Angela had bought before the strikes. Six weeks ago, the Foreign Language Faculty had advised teachers to remain home until the spring semester. Since then, all she did was read.

But if she read this last book, she would make the leap from a dwarf sitting on a rooftop, drumming as his country fell under Nazi occupation, to the current situation in Iran. Idiotic. Equating the Iranian rebellion and World War II was an exaggeration. Yet, yesterday, in the street where she bought eggs, an Army officer had slashed a demonstrator's cheek with his bayonet. So far, none of the protestors waved firearms, but more and more military personnel had deserted to avoid pitting themselves against their fellow countrymen. Weapons must have slipped into civilian hands by now, increasing the odds for armed conflict.

Doug napped on the couch. He had taken to staying up until the wee hours of the morning. He needed to sleep a while longer. She needed to talk over the situation with him again. Now, in the light of day. Not later, when *Allahu Akbar* chanted on the rooftops invaded their consciousness and beat down their thoughts, preventing them from making the best decisions.

Grass's novel still lay on top of the stack, its cover displaying an angular, Picasso-like drawing of the drummer in a triangular paper hat. Angela forced herself to open the book, but the stark imagery on the first pages depressed her. Potato fields. Billowing skirts lumpy as half-mashed potatoes. Brown-skinned, potato-eating Polish peasants. Flat, potato-bearing borderland. Exasperated, she slapped the book down on the arm of her chair.

Doug opened his eyes, and blue pierced the brown distance Grass's book had stamped on her imagination. "Bored?" he asked.

She shrugged.

He pulled himself to a sitting position. His body looked smaller, farther away than just a few feet, more vulnerable. He drew his fingers through his hair, pushed it back from his forehead. She sensed they had come to the same conclusion, but neither wanted to be the first to say the fatal words. In the garden, their hammock, suspended between the mimosa and the fig tree, swayed in the breeze. A smile ripped through Doug's face.

"When?" she said, and they both laughed. She never dreamed it would be this easy.

"On the next evacuation plane?" Doug asked, and she agreed. They would never work again in Iran, no matter how the revolution was resolved. Earlier in the week, the State Department had begun evacuating Americans. They had spoken to an American consular officer from the Embassy.

"If you choose to stay," he said to them, "you'll be on your own."

As if they had not been on their own all this time.

But this time, it was only a matter of time, a short time, before the Shah and his family would go away and Iranian shopkeepers would drag out their pictures of the Ayatollah for the last time. Strikes had crippled the economy. When the oil field workers joined the movement, revenue no longer flowed into the country. The rising middle class of *bazaaris* and production workers would soon bring the Shah to his knees.

"Do you think President Carter would grant asylum to the Shah?" she said.

"Surely he wouldn't before all the Americans left?" Doug said, doubt in his voice. Each time Carter proclaimed U.S. support for the Shah, demonstrations with anti-American slogans occurred. Kamran and Mahmud and the shopkeepers she frequented claimed Iranians protested against the American government, not Americans themselves. "This is a people who have long wanted to oust the Shah," Doug had said repeatedly. "If anyone can differentiate between the government and the governed, they can." Still, assassins had struck with success in past months, killing American colonels and employees of Rockwell, a purported cover for the CIA. An armed Army sergeant often stood guard at the entrance to their *kucheh*. Sometimes, she felt as though her skin were crawling with scorpions.

In the next few days, they cleaned out closets and drawers, discarding some things, packing others, and putting some aside for Kamran to take to a mosque for distribution to the poor. They bundled carpets, selected which garments to take if the flight allowed only one suitcase per person, and which pieces of jewelry to wear under clothing, out of sight. Angela had already emptied her bank account, although she could not change the tomans into dollars. She wrote an official letter of resignation to the university. Airport closures became more frequent, longer, and more erratic, but Dr. Aminipour had left quietly, she learned, over a month ago when it was easier to arrange departures.

The Shah remained.

By the second Sunday in January, they had packed and cleared away as much as they could. They were living in limbo, their souls already departed, inhabiting that endless waiting room where countless innocents paid for one mythical misdeed, one bite out of one apple, a piece of fruit that God—or fate or destiny

or kismet—had forbidden man. Angela passed a restless morning with little left to do except envision a last-minute flurry of
shoving a few changes of clothes and some toiletries on top of
the Esfahani carpet folded in her bag.

Doug opted to transport his portfolio plans between two precisely measured pieces of cardboard. He would pad his suitcase
with three Esfahani tablecloths, lay the cardboard sandwich over
them, and cover it with three shirts and his only pair of dress
pants. He would leave his dress shoes and belts behind, he said,
and wear tennis shoes. "In case I need to run on the way out."

Angela's foot tapped the rhythm of the three-syllable
word playing in her head. *In-shal-lah, in-shal-lah, in-shal-lah.*

"It's hard to stay once you've finally made up your mind
to go," she said. Her words echoed—silly, trite—through the
political vacuum.

"I'm going to take pictures of the Masjed-e Shah one more
time." Doug scrounged through his backpack. "Afternoon light
in winter makes it more photogenic than ever." He located his
camera and loaded a roll of thirty-six.

"I wonder what they'll call that mosque after the Shah
leaves," Angela said. Like Doug, she loved the view of the blue-
domed mosque from all angles in the square. She pulled on a
jacket. It would ward off the cold when the sun dipped behind
the mountain. The light would hold off the curfew for an hour
or more, giving them time to get back home.

Few people were out, and the first taxi stopped for them.
When they arrived at the square, Doug gave the driver five times
more than his asking price and told him to return in an hour.
Amusing. Doug used to get perturbed at cabbies' erratic demands
for fares. The driver thanked him with gratitude. He could not
make enough to feed his family, he said. "Too many strikes.
People stay home, even in the daytime. Nobody has money."

"It will get better," Angela told him, wishing she believed
it would.

The driver tossed both hands toward the heavens. "*Inshallah.*"

And she had just gotten rid of the word from her mind.

The square was deserted. Shopkeepers had lowered the grills on the shops that bordered it. The clang of metal on metal sounded intermittently from the open-air brass workers' quarters. At least one brass artisan must have turned to his craft to alleviate his boredom. He probably needed money, too. Angela walked over, but the man refused to sell anything during the strike until she explained she and Doug were leaving. Finally, he allowed her to select a small, round tray, one easy enough to pack. It depicted the familiar motif of courtiers bearing gifts to Dariush at Persepolis.

Their taxi, still empty, had pulled to a halt near the entrance of the bazaar at the square's north end. They would not be able to peek in the bazaar one last time. Carpet dealers and souvenir vendors and miniaturists had closed weeks ago.

Another empty taxi drew up, and the drivers of both cars got out, lit cigarettes, and conversed with three policemen who had rounded the corner on their left.

Doug touched her elbow. "I'm going closer to the mosque."

Angela paused for a moment in the middle of the *meidan*, surrounded by historical buildings. Her existence was insignificant in this place weighty with time, where shahs had come and gone for centuries. As the last shah would go. Tomorrow. Or the next day. Or the next. She had no sympathy for the Shah. But he was a man like any other with a wife and children. She had seen his son once, Crown Prince Reza (or was he already the former crown prince?), a boy of fifteen, here in this very square when he visited Shah Abbas's palace, the Ali Qapu. He had sauntered over to the edge of a top floor as if he were any other tourist and looked out on the blue-domed mosque and the mountain to his right and next, straight ahead, at the beige-and-turquoise dome of the Sheikh Lotfallah Mosque, and only then down to the crowds below. That casual downward glance cued the crowd to shout in unison. "Re-za Pah-la-vi, Re-za Pah-la-vi." The boy, schooled for his part in the orchestrated outburst, smiled and waved. Applause exploded; cheers resounded. Then, the Crown Prince of Iran was whisked off the terrace and into upper rooms where he no longer was exposed to a mob's whimsies.

She positioned herself in the dead center of what once was the hub of the Safavid Dynasty. There, Shah Abbas's courtiers had played polo. Previously unnoticed and subtle differentiations in the two mosques' blues and beiges, turquoises and taupes, leapt out at her. Had she grown more perceptive, more accepting of whatever reality confronted her? Her tolerance for the designs of destiny had not increased. She had had no unexpected religious revelation. Oddly, living here, she had learned to accept what she was and who she was—Angela Weston, American, twenty-eight years old, English instructor, Doug Weston's wife, and Sofia and Tony's daughter. Angela Weston, born in Ohio, raised Catholic, left-leaning Democrat, Italian by ancestry, and sometime feminist by choice. These attributes described her; they did not define her. And there was something else, some unnamable quality she had acquired in Iran, a product of this space in which she now stood and of these dimensions and designs that moved her to tears, beseeching her to remember them all.

Afternoon sunlight played off the Sheikh Lotfallah Mosque and the pigeons on its dome. To the left, the grill on Bahram's storefront was down. She imagined him inside, stooped over his workbench, cat's eyelash in hand, outlining a tassel on the tip of a woman's slipper.

Turning, she took in the bazaar entrance, the men talking, their arms flying out in excitement or exaggeration, the dark blue of police uniforms against the adobe wall. Inside, she remembered, colored streamers had hung from the top of the great latticed dome, swirling in dank air. A sweet shop was on the right. Next, an antique shop where the merchant had sprinkled water from a plastic jug, forming arabesques in the dirt. On the left, a shop with tablecloths— navy and burnished red paisleys with curlicues in lighter blue or scenes of women balancing earthen jugs on their heads. And the slipper seller, sitting cross-legged, stitching red flowers on white canvas. All of it was there, locked away now behind the great doors, concealed, forbidden—the once-tasted apple.

Turning another ninety degrees, she faced the palace with its terraced stories and tried to retrace the murals on its interior walls in the hope of engraving them in her memory. Each time she turned, her mind parted a veil that separated beauty from her. And the veil fell away. Later, she supposed, remnants of her memories were doomed to fade. And in old age, perhaps, her memory would create fantasies, feeding off tatters of bygone realities.

One last turn, one last time to gaze on the blue dome and the bluer mountain, the slender, blue-tinged clouds in a sky the essence of blue. His back turned to her, Doug held his camera to his face, canted his head back, and shot upwards at an angle. Did he want to catch that tiled stalactite in the corner? Or the bricks fanning out to define an arch? Or the interlocking geometry of tiles that married blue and black, black and beige, beige and blue? Doug snapped, wound the film, studied the perspective, raised the camera, aimed, and shot, then wound, aimed, shot, wound. Then he lowered the camera. He must have run out of film.

The mosque's shadow slipped over him. Angela waited for him to turn around to face her for the final time across half the length of the *meidan*.

* * * * * *

He waited. He had waited for what seemed like decades, although he was too young to measure life in ten-year periods.

He waited for the Shah to leave.

He waited to hear that all the foreigners had left Iran.

He waited to make sure Mrs. Weston left before Soleiman got to her.

On the second Sunday of January, he was still waiting,

exhausted from guarding the Westons' door all night and then working that morning in the kiosk. Hossein paced up and down Chahar Bagh opposite the entrance of the Westons' *kucheh* and came to a halt between a closed antique shop and a tailor's lowered grill. There, he mustered up the courage to cross the street, stride down the *kucheh* as if he owned it, ask any neighbors on hand about the Westons' whereabouts, and knock at the door if necessary. Then, if no one answered, he would go back to the old rope-and-spike trick, hoist himself over the wall, and see for himself if they still occupied the house.

As he started across the street, two people came out of the *kucheh*. He ducked behind a kiosk and peered around it in time to see the Westons hail a taxi, Mrs. Weston wearing sunglasses even though it was winter, and Mr. Weston sporting a camera around his neck like any tourist. Surely, they noticed that today, few cars made their way down the busiest street in Esfahan. He bolstered his hopes: the Westons might be going to the airport. No, they would have luggage. Hossein stiffened. Soleiman. On the shady side of the street not far from where the Westons had exited their *kucheh*, Soleiman emerged from the shadows. And hailed the next cab. And followed the Westons' taxi—or so it seemed.

Hossein ran out into the street, stopped the first cab that idled along, and instructed the driver to follow the taxi carrying Soleiman. Hossein's taxi, an older Peykan with a defective muffler, chugged up to the entrance of the Meidan-e Shah. Ahead, the Westons' taxi had parked, and Mr. Weston was paying the driver. The cab with Soleiman had turned into the *kucheh* nearest the square, its taillights flashing as the driver braked. Soleiman got out. Hossein paid his driver and ducked into an open shop with brooms, mops, and water buckets hanging from rafters. Better if Soleiman went into the square ahead of him. How lucky the shopkeeper had opened today. Hossein's mother had complained again this morning that their room in the city was much dirtier than the village house, where flies feasted on goat droppings in the courtyard. Hossein bought a broom, resisting the temptation to take the time to bargain. With the broom, it would look like he was shopping rather than trailing Soleiman. Or the Westons. He should have apologized to the Westons long ago. And warned them about Soleiman. And thanked Mrs. Weston for teaching him and helping his family. His father would have expected it.

Soleiman passed the shop on his way to the *meidan*, and seconds later, broom on his shoulder, Hossein marched into the square. Soleiman was slumping down in the shade on the opposite side, obviously stalking the Westons. If Soleiman had not followed them, Hossein would have approached them. He was embarrassed, he would tell them. The spitting incident had been a fluke—how could he say that in English?—an accident caused by clearing his throat just as the breeze kicked up and Mrs. Weston walked toward him on the bridge. He would swear to her he had planned to greet her with the other students at the picnic. But what about his drawing on her door? He stopped next to the only open brass shop and pondered. The heart and bloodied scimitar would be harder to justify. Then, as he absent-mindedly traced a heart in the dry ground with the broom's handle, an explanation occurred to him, a gift from Allah. The drawing, he would say, showed how terrible he felt about spitting on her, ruining her hair and her blouse, destroying the occasion for everyone. His heart bled. He himself had willingly wounded it a thousand and one times. He would make her believe him. She was innocent. She would excuse him. He was less confident about her husband's gullibility. Mr. Weston was an unknown, except for what Ahmad had told him, and Ahmad's mean comments revealed nothing about the man.

Hossein scratched out the heart with the tip of his shoe. Soleiman still lurked in the shadows opposite him. Mrs. Weston stood alone in the middle of the square. Suddenly, Soleiman began to stride toward her. Hossein kicked the heel of his shoe in the dust. This was his chance to make amends. *Allahu akbar.*

Allahu akbar. Exultant by this second gift from Allah, he tossed the broom up and caught the handle in mid-air.

He ran toward Mrs. Weston. He would make it to her before Soleiman did.

* * * * * *

It was the scene he would forever associate with Esfahan, the structure that would last in his memory as a symbol of the city: the Masjed-e Shah, the great, blue-domed mosque.

Before he aimed his camera, Doug had the mosque framed in his internal viewfinder. It squatted at an angle on the square's south end, minarets raised in praise, the indigo mountain as a backdrop. He had spent hours investigating its architectural details—angles, weight distribution, pillars, capitals, dimensions, space. Mostly space—how the structure delineated the external space, how the internal space circumscribed the infinite nature of divinity. Today, each time he raised his camera to peer through the viewfinder, he discovered something he had not noticed before—the juxtaposition of tiled surfaces, the harmony of color and line—something else to capture and take home with him on film. But his documentation would never convey the whole. The mosque could be appreciated only in its setting, by moving through it and around it, where water in the central pool reflected the surrounding geometry and shadow and sun played on walls and off domes, through latticed tile work, under arches, and over doorways, around corners. His roll of film was finished. He did not reload his camera. Useless to take more photos. Brief glimpses would never suffice to portray the mosque's presence and the Presence it invoked.

He turned back and looked for Angela. She waved from her position in the middle of the square. He started toward her. Far behind her, to her left, a man strolled in her direction. On the other side, a dark-clothed figure rushed toward her. Doug picked up speed and took longer steps. The dark figure angled toward Angela. He held something in his hand. A long stick? A club? Doug sprinted forward. His legs, much longer than the runner's, covered more ground in a shorter time. Someone, someone with a weapon, was behind Angela, rushing to catch her unawares. Doug called her name. He gesticulated and pointed. The man's glasses flashed in the sun. Angela kept staring ahead, oblivious, without moving. Doug shouted her name again. Shouted it a third time. Shouted, "Watch out," while the man closed in on her from behind. Rahimi. A rush of adrenaline propelled Doug's hips, thighs, and legs faster. On the ground in his path, bands of light and dark flickered, making his legs look like images on an old-time movie reel. A throbbing noise flapped in his head. Only one other time had he run as fast as he ran now, taken strides as long as these. Then, as now, when he looked down, his legs, flickering, seemed disembodied. Then, he had reached his destination too late.

* * * * * *

Angela waved. Doug took a long stride. A voice belted out a harsh word. Doug's voice. Doug, shouting. Flinging his camera to the ground. Shouting. Running toward her. Shouting. Her name. Shouting her name. Running at an angle. Still shouting. Her name. Something else. Her name. Something else. Mouth wide open. Eyes wild. Face contorted. Running past her.

How fast he ran. How long his legs were.

* * * * * *

Hossein angled toward the square's east side to cut off Soleiman. Some twenty meters in front of Mrs. Weston to the right, a man shouted garbled words. For some reason, Soleiman stopped. The strange voice yelled again as the man moved in a blur toward Hossein. Fear gripped Hossein, and he felt as if he would choke.

What was happening? A rush of footsteps on gravel. A face thrust forward in fury. A blow to his face. An arm thrashing at his arm. His hand gripping the broom. A man's hand grasping at it. Hossein knocked the man's legs out from under him.

*   *   *   *   *   *

A helicopter flew over the square as Doug passed Angela, and her body melted into a liquid blur. Ahead, the man's face also liquefied and then reappeared. Spectacles no longer framed the eyes, now slanted, or sat on the nose, now flat. Tian. Tian's buck teeth shone through fleshy lips. Tian's voice lied about the enemy's location. Tian's hands pointed an AK-47 at Angela. A helicopter rotor beat the air overhead. Doug sprinted across the space between him and Tian. He had to get to Tian before he killed Angela. He flew forward and landed a blow across Tian's face. But his feet flew too far, too fast. Tian had tripped him with the gun. Doug fell flat on the ground, limbs akimbo.

*   *   *   *   *   *

Doug was calling her name.

Angela understood that much after he ran by her, his strides long and fast. Doug shouted something again. She understood the word watch. "Watch me," perhaps. She laughed at his antics. Sprinting down the Meidan-e Shah, calling for her to watch him show off. An opportune time to try this, their last time here, no one and nothing else in the square but the jubilant beauty of mosques and mountains and of the palace and the reflecting pool. How far would Doug go? What other juvenile stunts would he perform? He might romp through the cold water in the reflecting pool or jog a few laps around the square's perimeter, turn a cartwheel or two at the corners. She turned around. A couple of taxi drivers and three or four policemen smoked near the bazaar's outer doors.

Doug was sprawled on the ground. A victim of his own craziness.

*　*　*　*　*　*

Bands of light and dark alternated across Tian's face hovering above him. Blood dripped from a corner of his mouth. Doug struggled to get up. He must protect Angela. His hands groped for the gun. The traitor jerked the barrel back toward his own chest, out of Doug's reach.

*　*　*　*　*　*

Hossein clutched fast to the broom he had snatched from the man's hands, pulling it to his chest. Pale fingers groped for it again. He jerked it back again. Up. Free of the pale fingers. High above the pale face. Above his own head. And down. And up. And down again. He struck. And struck again. And again. And again, until his blows rained in rhythm with the alternating light and dark cast by the rotating blade of a helicopter hovering overhead. Who was this man who sheltered his bloodied face with his arms and hands? Not Soleiman.

*　*　*　*　*　*

Angela started toward Doug. And suddenly there was Mr. Rahimi. She would recognize his black-rimmed glasses, the V-shaped eyebrows, the surly lips anywhere. He raised a stick and struck a blow at Doug. What could she do? Fear froze her in a stupor, her mind sending futile alarms to which her legs, paralyzed, did not respond. She was no match for Mr. Rahimi with his stocky build. Another blow from what she now recognized as a broomstick fell on Doug's shoulder. Doug propped himself on one elbow and struggled to get back to his feet. He flung out his free arm to catch the broom, but Mr. Rahimi lifted it higher than his own head. He brought it down across Doug's chest and knocked him onto his back. The broom traveled up again in a sweeping half-circle. Rage built inside her. The broomstick pointed to the sky high above Mr. Rahimi's head. He swung it down again, and she let out screams of rage, sharp overtones to the swish of the stick. Frantic, she searched for a tree branch, a rock—some sort of weapon. But there were no trees on the square's perimeters; there were no rocks in the square's gravel.

*   *   *   *   *   *

Doug raised his hand in surrender. Rahimi. No AK-47. No weapon at all save a broomstick. What had he done, hitting a man with a broom? Rahimi whopped him in the chest again with the broomstick and knocked him on his back in the dirt. Blow after blow on his arms, his stomach, and his shoulders. Doug swiped at the broom as it swept through the air before it whacked down on his body. He tried to stagger to his feet. Each time he started up, the broom came down hard again. A sharp blow crashed against the bridge of his nose and over his right cheek and eye. He covered his wet face with his hands. A blow to his temple sent excruciating pain through his head and face. He registered the smell of JP4, the flapping of a main rotor, the whir of a tail rotor. Somewhere a woman screamed. Angela. Angela was safe.

Safe as long as Rahimi was here, beating him with a broomstick.

*   *   *   *   *   *

Angela had the tray tucked under her arm, and she pulled it free. She positioned herself within a few feet of the flailing broomstick and concentrated on timing her blow, sharpening her aim. Mr. Rahimi paused for a moment and stared at her, eyes fixed in an empty trance. He resumed raining down blows harder and faster than before. Blood gushed from Doug's head and face. Angela edged closer. *Throw the tray like a discus. Spin it straight at Rahimi's head. Hit his head between the upward and the downward swings of the broomstick.* The whacks fell into a rhythm. She counted out four beats and heaved with all her strength, letting out a prolonged scream with all her might. The metal disk whirled through the air toward the target.

*　*　*　*　*　*

Hossein struck again, not heeding the shrieks of terror. Scream after scream with no space between.

Screams that swallowed the bands of light.

Screams that vanished in pain and darkness.

*　*　*　*　*　*

Angela screamed until the disk's edge collided with Mr. Rahimi's temple. Then it spun to the ground, taking his glasses with it. He dropped the broomstick and collapsed. Blood spurted from his temple in time with the beats of his heart.

Only when the exhilaration of her success waned did she hear the shouts and footsteps of the policemen behind her. They latched onto her arms and prevented her from rushing to Doug's side. A helicopter dipped and hovered overhead. The movement of the rotor blades created a revolving pattern of light and shadow on the ground. At the center, Doug and Mr. Rahimi lay crumpled in pools of blood. Two taxi drivers rushed up. Breathless, they kneeled next to the men and pressed handkerchiefs to their wounds. A man with a white beard shaded his eyes and squinted down at the casualties—Bahram. He must have heard the commotion from his living quarters in the back of his shop.

Angela shouted Doug's name and tried to run toward him, but a policeman held her from behind, pulling her arms backward. She felt as if her shoulders would snap. When the two policemen ushered her out of the square, she twisted her ankle

255

trying to move her feet fast enough to keep up with them. She could not turn her head far enough around to see what was happening behind her. She wanted to talk to Doug, she told the policemen, but they ignored her.

She would tell Doug that he was right about the human propensity for violence.

If Doug was still alive.

CHAPTER TWENTY-TWO

It hurt to lift his arm when he tried to touch the skin around his eye.

Doug worked his fingers up the right side of his face. Puffy cheek, tape, gauze, tape again, scratches on his forehead. Touching his face made his head throb more. He tried to raise his eyebrows, to force his left eye farther open so he could see out of that one good eye. His head felt as if it would split open at any movement. He envisioned his brains spilling over the pillowcase and sliding to the floor. A nurse came in with three more pills, red ones this time. He leaned forward to take them, groaning. It hurt to breathe. The rest of his body hurt, too. Even the palms of his hands were sore and blistered from attempts to hold onto Rahimi's broomstick.

He asked again about Angela, but the nurse spoke no English and smiled blankly at him as if this were the happiest day of his life. "*Khanoum*," he said. Wife. "*Khanoum-e man koja?*" Where is my wife? His question was useless: the nurse had no way of knowing Angela's whereabouts. She muttered a few words, fluffed his pillow, checked the eye patch, re-taped his nose, and said something he did not catch about the doctor. He pointed to the nurse's watch. "Doctor?" he said, trying to remember the Persian word for when. The nurse flashed a mouth full of teeth and, putting the tip of her finger on the watch's face, moved it around the circle twice. He had to wait at least two more hours for the doctor to make rounds. Perhaps the doctor would know how to contact Angela. Earlier, on the bedside table, he had left a paper citing Doug's injuries in English, but Doug had not been alert then. Sometime during the past few hours, he managed to focus—with one eye—on the list the night nurse held in front of him. According to the doctor, he had a concussion, some broken ribs, and severe damage to the right eye.

The hospital was noisy. It appeared that Iranians stayed with a sick family member day and night. His roommate's family had been there since Doug arrived. The man had a broken leg in traction. When the nurse finished distributing the man's medication, Doug called out to her. He pointed to the man, who was chatting with family members. The nurse pretended to drive with both hands on an imaginary steering wheel and rammed her hands into the wall. She raised three fingers, then pointed to his roommate while raising only one. Next, she showed Doug two fingers, put both hands under the side of her tilted head, and closed her eyes. Apparently, two people had died in the man's car accident. Traffic fatalities were extraordinarily high in Iran.

A woman, four children, and a younger man who resembled the injured patient crowded around the man's bedside with pots of rice and stew, bread, yogurt, and even a teapot and a gas Aladdin to keep the tea warm. The family could barely fit into the room with the other two adults and a small boy, who had all spent the night on a carpet at the foot of the bed. The constant chatter and stream of visitors grated on Doug's nerves, but as the day wore on, he appreciated the attention and leftover food the women offered him. Later, when he awoke from a nap, the mother, with a beige cardigan seeping into view from under her black *chador*, sent a girl to give him a piece of *gaz*. Chewing the nougat would hurt his head and jaw, but he took a piece and put it in his mouth to please the child, hoping it would soften and dissolve. The girl put another piece for him on top of his chest before she skipped back to her mother.

He sucked on the sweet and closed his good eye, ignoring the voices and clang of dishes while he reviewed the sequence of events that led to his awakening here in the hospital. He remembered running to prevent Rahimi from hitting Angela, passing Angela, swinging the first blow, and landing it in Rahimi's face. The next thing he knew, he was on the ground, Rahimi looming over him with the stick. Rahimi pelted him repeatedly until a sharp pain shot through his head and he heard screams—Angela's screams. But what happened after the world went black? Had he kept Rahimi away from Angela?

He did not know.

He could hear her screams again when he awakened.

He lifted his head and lowered it again in pain, then called her name. Where was she? He reached for the hand lying on the wrinkled sheet.

The woman took his hand in hers. "Doug, it's Vicky."

"Vicky. I thought you were Angela." Vicky's hair seemed darker, as if veiled in shadow.

"We're trying to find her, Doug," Vicky said. "The doctor thinks you're better. You can try to get up later today. Walk in the hall if you feel like it." She placed a flower arrangement on the windowsill—white daisies interspersed with an occasional red rose. Above them all, with the light from the window behind it, hovered a bird of paradise, its sharp silhouette reminiscent of a mangled helicopter.

His free hand found the patch on his right eye and brushed over the bandages on the side of his head. "When can I go home? I need to find Angela."

"Tomorrow or the next day, maybe. You can stay with us until you leave Iran."

"*Farda, farda.*" Anger flared through Doug's anguish. Tomorrow—

the first word he learned in Persian. "Sometime-maybe, some-time-maybe." His English version of the word, how he would translate the Persian.

Vicky squeezed his hand, and he drew it back in pain. Rahimi's blows had not spared his fingers. He wiggled his toes under the sheet, grateful that one part of his body was immune to the throbbing and aching that plagued the rest of it.

"As soon as you're out of danger from the concussion," Vicky told him. "I'm going to stay until Reza joins us later this evening. Then, we'll talk to the doctor again."

"Why can't you tell me where Angela is?" he asked. "Tell me if she's dead."

"She's not dead." Vicky emphasized the "not" and told him that the police had taken Angela.

"Angela? Why?" Angela had been an innocent bystander to his struggle with Rahimi.

The nurse entered, smiling again, and greeted Vicky as if she were his wife. Neither of them bothered to set the nurse straight. She adjusted the IV bag and had him take more medicine, this time two pink capsules and a round, white pill. The man with the broken leg moaned, and the nurse hurried over to ply him with medication. "Why did the police take Angela?" Doug asked again.

"We've learned Angela threw something at Mr. Rahimi just as the police arrived." Vicky leaned close to Doug's ear and whispered. "We're trying to find her, but in this power struggle, it's unclear exactly who's in charge."

Doug told her what had happened, as he remembered it. He was getting drowsy, probably from the medication. Vicky's facial features blurred as if she had draped a gauzy *chador* over them.

Before he succumbed to sleep, he grasped her arm. "I hit Rahimi first," he said. His tongue had thickened, and he was unsure if she understood him. "I hit him first."

But what should he tell Angela?

* * * * * *

No one had interrogated her.

She lay on a rope cot, staring at the cell's ceiling and shivering. The first evening of her incarceration, she had heard an uproar in the street outside—honking and shouting and music—followed by a period of relative quiet. Later that night, she had awoken to discover the policemen guarding the hallway had gone missing. In their place, a Revolutionary Guard with a drooping mustache had worked his way down the row of cells, unlocking them, freeing prisoners. All of them. Except her. At the door of her cell, he shifted the assault weapon on his shoulder and regarded her with hostility before passing on to the next cell. Since then, she remained the sole prisoner under the watch of one or two Revolutionary Guards. They rotated shifts and brought her meager amounts of rice and bread on no regular schedule. When she asked why she was still here, they grumbled about waiting for orders. They seemed childlike, confused, eager to assert authority they had never imagined possible.

The night before, a radio newscast had drifted in through the open hallway door. The Shah had left the country, the commentator said, although no mention was made of abdication. The broadcast had ended, accompanied by the Guards' cheers. They presumed it would be a matter of hours, days at the most, before the Ayatollah Khomeini arrived. They spoke with disdain of Prime Minister Hoveyda, the dapper bachelor with an orchid on his lapel, now in jail, awaiting execution. They hotly contested the worthiness of the new prime minister, Shahpour Bakhtiar, appointed by the Shah to serve during his absence. Bakhtiar had refused to cede his post to Mehdi Bazargan, the man whom the Ayatollah supported for the position. The Guards joked about the country having two prime ministers. This morning, the news, now run by revolutionaries, had reported that Bakhtiar had fled the country and Sadat had greeted the Shah in Egypt. The Guards had whooped and hollered. They believed Sadat had signed his own death warrant. Angela had hung onto every syllable of the broadcasts, but they had granted only a momentary respite. She broke out in a cold sweat. What had happened to Doug? Had Mr. Rahimi's beating killed him? Was Doug recuperating in a hospital or rotting in some other Iranian prison? She had no inkling whether the twists and turns of regime change would result in her release or her trial or her execution. What little she had learned from either the Guards or the revolutionary newscasts might well be unreliable. Truth was more schizophrenic than ever during a political upheaval.

Angela paced her cell. The ankle she had sprained caused her minimum discomfort. She counted one hundred seventeen laps around the cell's perimeter. It must be early afternoon. Another lap or two would not hurt, might keep her warmer. Besides, she needed to keep moving. Whenever she closed her eyes, a disk whirled through a twilit void. She had aimed at Mr. Rahimi's temple, the most vulnerable place on his head. That much was true. Killer. Murderess. Assassin. Were those words applicable to her? If only she had saved her husband yet not mortally wounded her student. After Mr. Rahimi dropped the broomstick and slumped to the ground, blood drained from his head. How could either Doug or Mr. Rahimi have survived the blows and the subsequent loss of blood? Isolation must be distorting her mind for her to believe otherwise.

She slouched in the corner against the icy outer wall. What mind games had other prisoners played in this cell? She had to keep herself sane, allow herself some sort of salutary imaginings. Black capital letters marched over the wall in front of her, newspaper headlines: BRASS TRAY KILLS UNIVERSITY STUDENT or TEACHER ASSASSINATES STUDENT. Too bizarre for anyone who knew her to believe. How would a pro-American headline read? AMERICAN GUILE OVERCOMES IRANIAN BRUTALITY. Not fair. Mr. Rahimi did not represent every Iranian, nor did she every American. What if a headline reported the simple fact: ABUSER FELLED?

It was the sole truth she knew.

A key turned in the lock.

Startled, Angela jerked herself up lest her captors see her cowering in the corner. Two Revolutionary Guards came in without any food. She thought of asking them to empty the overflowing slop bucket, but they took hold of her arms and led her out of the cell. A third Guard waited in the corridor and followed them down the hallway, his gun trained on her back. Tremors spread over her arms and shoulders, through her core, down her legs. She shivered so violently that she had to concentrate on putting one foot in front of the other. She faltered, and the Guards on either side lifted her by the elbows without missing a step. If only she could write her last words to Doug and her parents.

Her empty stomach churned. The procession entered a vestibule, and Angela doubled over, gagging. When she managed to lift her head, her eyes watered from the episode of dry heaves. A mirage of a man in civilian clothes appeared in the bright light from a window across the room. Angela blinked and cleared her throat. Kamran. He neither spoke to her nor acknowledged her presence. She fought to hold her head up and her feelings in check. A display of emotion would play into his perfidy. Her life had come to this—Kamran's betrayal.

The Guard with the overgrown mustache opened a desk drawer and removed an envelope. Orders for her transfer to another prison, perhaps in Tehran? A show trial? A summary execution? The Guard took a watch from the envelope and gave it to her. Absurdly, she asked for her wedding and engagement rings. The Guard feigned ignorance.

"That can wait, Angela," Kamran said, his voice and face expressionless.

She understood: her rings were gone.

The Guard gave her a coat, her own brown suede jacket that she had worn to the square that last day with Doug. She held it limply in one hand as she swallowed acid foam rising in her throat. Did they intend to make her death look like an accident? Or were they trying to assuage her somehow during her final hours?

"Put on your coat." Kamran's order was solemn, flat. He had never spoken to her like that. He opened a door, and bright sunlight streamed in, stunning her. She groped in her coat pocket. Her sunglasses were still there. Outside, Kamran and the mustachioed Guard with the rifle waited in silence while she put them on. Kamran shook the Guard's hand and called him by his first name, Soleiman, as if he knew him. She was ushered a few steps down the street, away from the yellow brick building with decorative tiles and the adjacent roundabout, in the middle of which the Shah's statue no longer stood.

Instead of blue-coated policemen, Revolutionary Guards decked out in Army jackets and camouflage pants and armed with automatic weapons prowled the sidewalks. They had gone a short distance when Kamran opened a car door and motioned for her to get in. He slid into the driver's seat. The car pulled away. No Revolutionary Guard was with them. Angela looked out the back window. No other car followed them.

Her limbs trembled more than they had inside the jail. Kamran put his hand on her arm and steadied it, like he had that day in Persepolis when he helped her off the pedestal. He had looked handsome and monumental in Persepolis that day, his profile striking in the sun against stone pillars and carved staircases. Today, in the driver's seat of a beat-up Peykan, he looked pale, ethereal. Imperial that day in October; today in January, godlike. He had not betrayed her.

"Doug?" she whispered.

"He's going to be all right."

Warmth spread through her, and for the first time since her arrest, she let tears run down her cheeks. "How did you get me out?"

Kamran rubbed his thumb and middle fingers together. "You were not cheap. I would have gotten you released yesterday, but one of them kept holding out for more." He smiled and cast her a sideways glance. "Not that you weren't worth it."

"And?" She did not want to embarrass him more by asking directly what her release had cost him.

"*Bakshesh* is more expensive than ever these days." Kamran kept his eyes on the street ahead. "Inflation in times of chaos."

CHAPTER TWENTY-THREE

Three more days of waiting for someone to give him news of Angela.

Doug slumped in the chair in his hospital room, alone. His roommate had returned home. It was quiet now, but he missed the food and the distractions.

During the past three days, he had grown steadier, capable of navigating through the halls. This afternoon, Dr. Khosrow finally agreed to discharge him tomorrow. The good doctor also told him his eye required surgery by a specialist in the States. In Iran, getting out of the hospital entailed bargaining: he had to agree to stay with Vicky and Reza. It made no difference. He would not leave Iran without Angela.

Dimly, he perceived Kamran peering into the room. Doug struggled to his feet, ready to ask about Angela. From his right side, the side with no vision, he sensed someone rushing across the room. He twisted and held the person at arm's length to align his good eye with her face. Angela was a mess—dirty, pale, thin, tear-streaked—but she was here, jumping up to peck him with kisses. Angela was all right.

Angela stopped hopping, her eyes on his face. Her fingers traced deep abrasions likely to leave scars. When he had first looked in the mirror the day before yesterday, he had questioned the doctor's decision not to stitch several of his cuts.

His nose was still tightly taped, and over his right eye, he wore a patch of grayish cotton held in place by tape over a bulge of gauze. Moshe Dayan, he was not. Angela jarred his dislocated shoulder, and he winced. She drew back with a look of dismay. He could bear the discomfort, he told her, and he enfolded her in his arms and kissed the top of her head over and over, burying his nose in her hair.

"Where is Kamran?" Kamran had disappeared as mysteriously as he had materialized a few minutes ago.

"Gone to our house to finish packing our suitcases. Tomorrow, he'll take us to an evacuation center outside of Esfahan. They'll get us to a U.S. State Department plane in Tehran. We'll be allowed only one piece of luggage each."

They barraged each other with questions, piecing together the events in the square as best they could. "I think I killed Mr. Rahimi when I threw the tray at his temple," she said.

"I started it, Angela. I hit Rahimi first." He had mulled over what and how much to tell her since he regained consciousness. He was certain now. "I ran toward Rahimi because I thought he intended to hurt you. I wouldn't hit a man armed with a broomstick, but by the time I closed in on him, the helicopter . . ." And he told her about Tian and the AK47 and Tian's betrayal and Kevin's brains spilling in a pool of blood and how the trauma had affected his attitude toward Iranians and how drinking had helped him forget but his nightmares forced him to remember and how he needed to protect her even if she didn't need protection because he had failed to protect Kevin. He told her that he blamed himself for not telling her before because if she had known, then maybe—

But she pressed her fingers over his lips and thanked him for trusting her enough to tell her now.

"If Rahimi's dead, then it's the work of both of us. If you hadn't thrown that tray when you did, I'm convinced that Rahimi would have killed me."

Angela bowed her head. "I was afraid to ask Kamran about

Mr. Rahimi. Kamran had trouble enough looking for me." Her eyes were wild when she looked up. "Do you think I killed Mr. Rahimi?"

"We'll never know."

"No. I don't suppose we will." Angela told him of her impressions of Rahimi the first day of class. "I identified with him in a way."

"What? How could you?" Angela had always sympathized with an underdog, but identifying with Rahimi surpassed anything he could have imagined.

And then a litany of woes poured out of her, disjointed yet with a logic of its own. She spoke of ridicule and isolation during her schooldays and of her obsession with helping Mr. Rahimi avoid that same fate. She spoke of how he, Doug, had frightened her when he had drunk too much and of how she had ceased to trust his judgment. She spoke of childhood and adolescence. She spoke of desiring independence and rebelling against her upbringing. She spoke of misplaced blame. She spoke of innocence and guilt. She spoke of shame and secrets. She spoke of flashbacks and fear.

She spoke of what had happened to her on a spring day when Robby was playing baseball.

An hour later, the nurse, all smiles, came in with the nighttime medication. Still smiling, she whisked Angela away.

Doug groaned. It would be *farda* before Angela returned.

When Angela did come back, she wore a clean hospital gown. Her hair was wet, and she smelled of soap. She got into the vacant bed, where she stayed until the nurse turned off the light and shut the door. Before they went to sleep, she cuddled next to him.

"I can't believe I stole the money," she said.

Doug trained his good eye on her. "I can't believe I stole a skull."

—

"What will Kamran do with the boxes we packed?" he asked Angela the next afternoon.

"He says he'll store them in his house until the post office opens again." She sat beside him on the bed and held his hand. "He must have paid an astronomical bribe to get me released. He wouldn't tell me how much."

"You did tell him to get the money pouch hidden in the kitchen?" Doug asked, but he was certain she had.

Late in the afternoon, they stuffed themselves in the back seat of Kamran's borrowed car with their two suitcases, Angela's purse, and the portfolio of work Kamran had packed in Doug's carry-on. The car crossed the stone bridge. At its southern end, Doug asked Kamran to pull over. Kamran had stashed the savings that remained in the carry-on, and Doug took a bill out of the pouch. "Do you have change for five hundred rials?" he asked Kamran. Kamran dug in his pockets but came up short. Doug took the bill, crossed the street to a bank that had reopened since the Shah's departure, and came out with a sack of fifty tomans. At the blind vendor's niche, he stopped and dropped the coins one by one into the man's bowl.

The sound of the coins clanging in the bowl echoed in the arched niche, becoming more muffled as the bowl filled. Doug kept tossing tomans, coin by coin. At least he could give a blind man a little solace. The man ran his fingers over the coins. His profile glowed in the sunlight like the profile of the Shah on commemorative gold coins minted by a now-deposed regime.

"*Shokr-e Khoda, agha.*" The man faced Doug and smiled, shifting his features away from the light. He was not only blind but also toothless.

At the staging ground for the foreign evacuation, they stayed with Kamran until the last evacuees were boarding buses for a night journey to Tehran. Kamran handed them a paper with his Esfahan address written in both Persian and English, along with a London address for Mahtab and Hamid, who had left earlier in the week. Mahtab had been frantic about the Westons' fate, he told them, and he urged Angela to write her soon. He had other news: Vicky had decided not to divorce Reza. They planned to join the boys in the States.

Angela boarded the bus, but Kamran pulled Doug aside and whispered in his ear. Shaken, Doug handed him the pouch with the remainder of their savings. In the end, he had decided to keep the small amount they had left in Iranian currency. "This is for the *bakshesh*. Probably not enough, but it's all I have." Kamran protested, but Doug held firm. "You saved my wife. If you don't want it, give it to a worthy cause. Or keep it to buy a plane ticket later." He clasped Kamran's hand in both of his. "Try to leave if things don't work out here, Kamran." As the bus rolled away in the impending darkness, winter wind swirled around Kamran, veiling his slight form in dust.

It was a sight Doug would never forget: Kamran alone and forlorn there in the desert, holding the pouch close to his chest with his arms crossed over it.

* * * * * *

For the fourth time, Revolutionary Guards boarded the last evacuation plane on the tarmac of Tehran's airport; for the umpteenth time, they examined passengers' passports.

"They're looking for someone trying to escape," Angela said, but Doug was already asleep. She adjusted the blanket that an American flight attendant had given her around Doug's shoulders. Later, she would remove his eye patch and apply the salve and fresh gauze the nurse had given her.

The plane took off, and the pilot's voice came over the intercom. "We aren't yet sure where we will get clearance to land in Europe." He reported how many pounds of fuel the flight was carrying in case it was prevented from leaving Iranian airspace. The number was meaningless to her. Angela opened the window shade. The barren Zagros Mountains stretched out below. No *qanats*. No pigeon towers. No minarets. She settled back, but every fifteen minutes the pilot's voice reported the number of miles remaining before they were out of Iranian airspace. When he announced that the aircraft was over Turkey, the Americans on board cheered. Angela did not join in.

Across the aisle sat an impeccably dressed Iranian woman with two small children leafing through storybooks. The woman's husband was not with her. Perhaps he had been detained by the Guards as a military officer or government official or member of the Shah's family, all of whom were under suspicion now. Perhaps he would soon be put on trial for crimes against the Iranian people, if not executed outright. Throughout all the announcements about leaving Iranian airspace, the woman had assumed an air of quiet composure, a perfect model for her children. Angela felt sorry for her. The woman must wonder when, if ever, she would return to her native country.

An aroma of beef filled the cabin, a smell Angela had rarely experienced in the past year and a half. Trays clattered. Alcohol sloshed over ice cubes in plastic glasses. She would wake Doug when their meals arrived. The previous night on the bus had been grueling. Guards posted along the highway constantly stopped and checked their caravan. Gunfire often broke out as they passed the few towns on the way. At five o'clock in the morning, the caravan pulled to the side of the road and stopped. Due to the curfew, buses could enter Tehran only after sunrise. "We're sitting ducks here," Doug had said, "point-blank targets for anyone who wants to do away with a bunch of Americans."

The meal arrived, steak courtesy of the U.S. State Department, and Angela pulled down Doug's tray. They had not eaten in over twenty-four hours. Earlier, when the Bell Helicopter employee in the seat behind them asked about Doug's eye patch, Doug said he had been thrown through the windshield in a car accident. Now, the man cautioned him to eat slowly and not too much. He had been a medic in the Army, the man said, and Doug thanked him, throwing Angela an amused look.

When the meal was over, the pilot announced that the plane would land in Frankfurt in four hours. A flight attendant relieved them of their trays, and Doug pulled out his carry-on, which was too small to hold his portfolio plans flattened between cardboard. Kamran had rolled and stacked them to prevent them from getting creased. He had wrapped something else in one of Doug's blue shirts.

"Kamran did a good job packing."

"What did he tell you before we got on the bus?"

"It was about Cecil."

"What about Cecil?"

Doug picked up her hand from her lap. "He didn't make it to Texas." His Adam's apple bobbed as he swallowed. "His body was found in a *kucheh* on the outskirts of Esfahan. It had been disfigured by *jub* dogs." He took a deep breath and winced as if it hurt his ribs. "Or humans," he added.

She nestled her face against his shoulder while he stroked her back. She had never felt so exhausted, so empty. "Cecil was too flamboyant for Iran," he said.

"I suppose we all were." She rubbed her wet eyes and cheeks on his shirt sleeve.

Doug unfolded the cloth wrapped around the object he had found in the carry-on to reveal Bahram's woman with the mirror.

Angela studied the miniature. Something familiar yet mysterious was comforting now.

"She does look like you," Doug said.

She had heard those words before in a past that now seemed lost. Bill? She touched the figure below the belt. "She looks about three months pregnant."

"No. It's just the way she's standing."

"When we get to Germany, I'll call my mother. What if she is sick?"

"Actually, the last time I was in Tehran, the embassy agreed to contact your parents, let them know we were okay, and tell them who in the State Department to contact in case of a family emergency. We haven't been out of touch long."

"Why didn't you tell me?"

"You would have said I was interfering, being too protective." He squeezed her against his soggy shirt sleeve. "I know the spiel."

He was right.

She nestled under her airline blanket and adjusted a pillow under her neck. When Doug separated from the consulting company, he had negotiated to retain health insurance for another year. They would need it for the ophthalmologist in Chicago. There, Doug could work for his brother-in-law until he found a job with an architectural firm. "Give me a year," he had told her on the bus. "Maybe two. I'll rethink how to set up my own firm. Hamid and I have already talked about his working for Bob, too. Once Hamid has a green card to live and work in the States, we can continue our collaboration. We'll be ready to go into business together when the time comes."

Angela lowered the shade over the window. The Iranian children across the aisle were sleeping, cuddled against each other, the boy with his closed eyes moving rapidly above long eyelashes and the girl in tranquil slumber, sucking her thumb. Their mother stared at the back of the seat in front of her, an absent look in her dark eyes. She must wonder how she would be able to live outside of a country in which she possibly could never live again. If she, Angela, a foreigner, felt such sorrow at leaving Iran, how wrenching it must be for an Iranian. Angela thought of whispering something to the woman. A word or two of succor. But what words were there? Nothing was adequate. Nothing at all.

Next to her, Doug shut his eye. She touched him on the

side where there were no broken ribs. "Do you still think Kamran worked for SAVAK?" she asked.

Doug half-opened his eye like a drowsy lizard squinting in sunlight. "Angela, the sky is high."

She let her eyes close, lulled by the sound of the plane speeding in the high sky over miles and miles of foreign territory, carrying Doug and her home, carrying the Iranian woman and her children into exile, transporting all of them away from half the world shaped in light and darkness and colored in countless shades of blue.

CHAPTER TWENTY-FOUR

Agha-ye Shahbazi's figure appeared in the open door of Bahram's shop.

Instinctively, Hossein ducked behind the curtain separating the shop from Bahram's living quarters. What if Agha-ye Shahbazi knew he was there? Agha-ye Shahbazi and Mrs. Weston had been friends; they went to Shiraz together. Hossein did not want Bahram to suffer because of his presence. Bahram was his protector. He had paid off the police on the day of the beating and nursed the ugly slash above Hossein's eye, all the while counseling him to keep out of sight. Since that day, Bahram had hidden Hossein in the back room, where he copied the master's miniatures on sheets of plain paper.

Hossein kept close enough to the curtain to hear the two men in the front room greet each other. Bahram called Agha-ye Shahbazi Kamran as if they were old friends. Bahram must know that Agha-ye Shahbazi had taught at the university with Mrs. Weston. Once the boisterous greetings were over, the men lowered their voices, and Hossein could no longer eavesdrop. The cut reaching from the midpoint of his eyebrow to just above his temple itched intolerably whenever he was afraid or nervous. He was afraid now, terrified that Agha-ye Shahbazi would turn him over to the Revolutionary Guards because of the beating he had given Mr. Weston. He had not started that fight. The American had hit him when he was try-ing to protect Mrs. Weston from Soleiman. The policemen had told Bahram that as they hurried across the square to break up the fight, another man with a knife ran into the maze of *kuchehs* leading away from the square. Soleiman had escaped. Hossein had not seen the knife, but he had been right about Soleiman's intentions. He himself was to blame, though, for making Mrs. Weston the object of political vindication—his revenge, in a way, for his father's death. Bahram had helped him understand where he fit in—and where he did not—in this revolution.

Hossein's mouth was dry. He needed water, but getting it would make noise and alert Agha-ye Shahbazi. Reliving that day on the square still made him crazy. His life had become as complicated as the political situation. Demands pushed and pulled him every which way. All he wanted to do now was to return to his village and play his *tar*. Bahram had helped him send word to his mother and sister, telling them to return to Khafr. Bahram would let him know when it was safe for him to join them. He still felt afloat without his music, but when Bahram discovered him drawing with the colored pens he kept in his coat pocket, he began to give him instruction and extra paper. Drawing made the time pass.

The voices moved closer, and Bahram threw open the cur-tain and told him to remove his glasses. Agha-ye Shahbazi held Hossein's chin and tilted his head to the light, looking at the wound. Hossein's knees quaked, and he held on to the back of a chair to steady himself. Agha-ye Shahbazi stud-ied the gash as if he were grading an examination. Hossein clenched his teeth. This would be another test he could not pass. Finally, Agha-ye Shahbazi released his chin, and Hossein put his glasses back on. His scab itched more than ever, but Bahram had forbidden him to scratch it for fear of infection.

"It's healing well," Bahram said. "He lost a lot of blood because it was a head wound. The cut was deep, but it was too high above the temple to do any serious harm."

"You'll have a nice scar there to remind you of your transgressions," Agha-ye Shahbazi said to Hossein.

He did not like the foreboding look in Agha-ye Shahbazi's eyes or the frown that knit his brows together. Hossein tried to recount his version of the incident. "I know what happened," Agha-ye Shahbazi said, raising his hand, and Hossein was afraid to continue. "That's why Bahram has kept you out of sight here." The Westons had left, he said, with Mrs. Weston sick with worry, afraid she might have killed him. "She always tried her best to treat you well."

Bahram pulled Agha-ye Shahbazi toward the front of the shop, and the two men engaged in animated conversation, with Bahram clarifying Hossein's intention to protect Mrs. Weston. Hossein relaxed a little. Bahram could express himself better than he could. And Bahram was Agha-ye Shahbazi's elder. Agha-ye Shahbazi owed Bahram respect. Hossein returned to the table where he had been working earlier and resumed his copying. Bahram had given him a demanding assignment, a scene of the *meidan* with a polo match played in front of the Ali Qapu. Drawing horses in motion pleased him, but sketching the men who mounted them did not. Their turbans and long coats and billowy pajama pants were easy to draw, but he found it hard to portray such tiny faces and bodies. Bahram advised him to study people—their features and figures, their poses and expressions. Hossein had always drawn designs and buildings, an occasional crane or nightingale, sometimes a donkey or camel. He had to work hard to see people inside and out, harder to paint what Bahram called "the human enigma." At this point, Bahram had said, he would not consider letting Hossein draw a figure that symbolized the Divine.

The men in the doorway gestured as if bargaining. Maybe Agha-ye Shahbazi was buying a miniature. Hossein directed his attention back to his work and sketched a polo mallet in the raised hand of one of the riders. He made a good job of it.

The man looked as if he were leveling a tremendous blow to the ball in play.

"Agha-ye Rahimi." Bahram beckoned him to come forward. Hossein placed his pen on the table, where he blocked it with a piece of ivory to prevent it from rolling off. Bahram held a thick stack of bills, more money than Hossein had ever seen. Agha-ye Shahbazi stood, arms crossed. Bahram did the talking: the money was for Bahram to take him, Hossein Rahimi, as an apprentice for the next ten years. Hossein would be his last apprentice, the old man said, someone pledged to carry on this Persian tradition, no matter what form the new government took. Agha-ye Shahbazi also pledged enough money to keep Hossein's mother and sister comfortable. In return, Hossein must make a commitment to write Mrs. Weston a letter of apology and let Bahram mentor him in Islamic art and mysticism. Hossein was overcome with disbelief and amazement. He could pursue something he loved, keep playing the *tar*, not burden his mother, and never have to resume studies in English.

After the inevitable *ta'arof*, Hossein lowered his eyes in deference and gathered the courage to ask Agha-ye Shahbazi what he had wanted to know since the teacher first entered the shop. "How did you know I was here?"

Agha-ye Shahbazi stepped under the grill and onto the sidewalk. He looked back and smiled. "I knew."

Bahram's hand clamped on Hossein's shoulder as Agha-ye Shahbazi receded in the dim light of a winter sun already below the violet mountains. The *moazzin* took up the call to prayer. Its notes resounded through the square where, at different times, in different ages, polo players had ridden, tourists had marveled, and demonstrators had protested. To the south, the outline of the Masjed-e Shah grew fainter with each breath of wind. As Hossein spread the prayer rug Bahram had given him, Kamran Shahbazi's profile slipped into the shadow of the great blue dome. Hossein knelt on the rug, satisfied he had done as Bahram had bidden.

He had memorized that unique human form, that proud way of holding the torso upright, the elegant head, the enigmatic face.

279

END

ACKNOWLEDGMENTS

I would like to thank those at Atmosphere Press who helped make this book a reality, especially Asata Radcliffe, my editor, and Ronaldo Alves, Artistic Director. With fondness and admiration, I extend special thanks to Lawrence Potter and Haideh Sahim for conducting a cultural review of the text and ensuring the accuracy of the transliterations of Persian words to the English alphabet. I am grateful for the generosity with which you contributed your time and expertise. And, to the many readers of the many versions of this novel, I thank you all.

Finally, Dr. Louis Giron deserves an enormous "dose" of gratitude. His support was unwavering and multifaceted, his patience unending, and his encouragement unmatched. Kudos and hugs, Lou, for getting us both through this.

ABOUT ATMOSPHERE PRESS

Founded in 2015, Atmosphere Press was built on the principles of Honesty, Transparency, Professionalism, Kindness, and Making Your Book Awesome. As an ethical and author-friendly hybrid press, we stay true to that founding mission today.

If you're a reader, enter our giveaway for a free book here:

SCAN TO ENTER
BOOK GIVEAWAY

If you're a writer, submit your manuscript for consideration here:

SCAN TO SUBMIT
MANUSCRIPT

And always feel free to visit Atmosphere Press and our authors online at atmospherepress.com. See you there soon!

ABOUT THE AUTHOR

Leissa Shahrak experienced the Iranian Revolution firsthand when she taught English in Iran. Her writing credits include stories published in *Del Sol Review*, the *Bellevue Literary Review*, and a British anthology, *The Final Chapter: Writings on the End of Life.*

A life-long traveler and enthusiast of international literature, she now resides in Asheville, North Carolina, with a chess aficionado, a spoiled Shih-Tzu named Ming, and the occasional black bear.